D1235581

No Long Goodbyes

Books by Pauline Hayton:

A Corporal's War
Naga Queen
Myanmar: In My Father's Footsteps
Grandma Rambo
If You Love Me, Kill Me
Extreme Delight and Other Stories
The Unfriendly Bee
Still Pedaling

Cover created by Lance Buckley,
Contact email: lance@lancebuckley.com

No Long Goodbyes

Pauline Hayton

Enquiries:

Pauline Hayton
3446 13th Ave S.W.
Naples, FL 34117 USA

Library of Congress Control Number: 2019907053

ISBN: 978-0-9835863-9-5

Publisher's Cataloging-In-Publication Data
(Prepared by The Donohue Group, Inc.)

Names: Hayton, Pauline, author.
Title: No long goodbyes / Pauline Hayton.
Description: First edition. | Naples, FL : [PH
    Publishing], [2019]
Identifiers: ISBN 9780983586395 (paperback) | ISBN
    9781732042100 (ebook)
Subjects: LCSH: Women refugees--Burma--History--20th
    century--Fiction. | Remarried people--Burma--
    History--20th century--Fiction. | Burma--History--
    Japanese occupation, 1942-1945--Fiction. | Man-
    woman relationships--Fiction. | LCGFT: Romance
    fiction.
Classification: LCC PS3608.A98 N6 2019 (print) | LCC
    PS3608.A98 (ebook) | DDC 813/.6--dc23

I dedicate this WWII historical fiction to the men and women who fought or worked in appalling conditions, many of whom paid the ultimate price, in CBI (China-Burma-India Theater of War).

Pauline Hayton

Praise for *No Long Goodbyes:*

While classified as a historical romance, the story could just as easily be a women's fiction story . . .

Those looking for a historical fiction story set in a unique part of the globe will greatly enjoy this story. It nicely weaves real life with fiction, and the details in the last half are magnificent, helping readers feel like they are there, battling mud, steep inclines, and rugged pathways while worrying about hunger, violence and disease.—*The Book Review Directory*

Rating 4 out of 5 stars.

ACKNOWLEDGEMENTS

My gratitude knows no bounds to those who contributed to the success of this book:

My valued critiquing group—Linda Butler, Marc Simon, Caryn Hacker-Buechel, Suzanne Haworth, Thomas Small, and Angelina Spencer whose efforts have immeasurably improved my craft.
And Beta reader Carol Glassman with her pertinent suggestions.

Royalties from the sales of my books support remote Mount
Kisha English School, Magulong Village, Manipur, India

FOREWORD

Set in the 1942 WWII Japanese invasion of Burma, *No Long Goodbyes* is a story of people overcoming and surviving horrors brought by an invading force.

Several people mentioned in this novel actually existed and went through the invasion. Events my fictional character Kate Cavanagh/Bellamy experienced during her walk out of Burma were based on the real experiences of refugees.

ACTUAL PERSONS YOU WILL MEET IN
No Long Goodbyes

Australian **Harold Braund**, Steel Brothers employee, who joined Major Mike Calvert's Bush Warfare School.

James Michael Calvert, (1913-1998) Royal Engineer in the British Army involved in special operations in Burma during WWII. In 1941 he was appointed to command the Bush Warfare School in Burma, training officers and non-commissioned officers to lead guerilla bands in China for operations against the Japanese. He frequently led attacks from the front, a practice that earned him the nickname of "Mad Mike" among the men under his command.

Information for characters Jack Bellamy's and Tom Hubbard's walk-out to India via the Chaukkan Pass came from two sources: the diary of railway engineer **John Rowland** who walked out on the most northerly and most dangerous route with a group of men, women and a baby; and **Gyles MacKrell's** diary and video of his elephant rescues.

Gyles Mackrell was a British tea planter working for Octavius Steel & Co. After hearing that refugees were starving and experiencing great difficulty crossing rivers flooded by monsoon rains, he marched a number of elephants to the Dapha River to help the refugees across. He rescued approximately 200 people, mainly British and Indian soldiers, feeding and caring for them until help arrived. He was awarded the George Medal in 1943. I invite you to watch:

https://www.youtube.com/watch?v=XLMj-zG2Vmc

Major William Lindfield Brookes and his family. Major Brookes, an army surgeon who married a Burmese woman and had three children, died in Shingbwiyang of blackwater fever. After his death, Mrs. Brookes and family stayed in Shingbwiyang until the monsoon ended and eventually reached India in November 1942.

Clive North, Administration Officer with the Burma Frontier Force, who oversaw the refugee situation at Shingbwiyang and

Corporal Katz, R.A.M.C., who volunteered to stay at Shingbwiyang to help North.

Both men arrived in India in October 1942.

Reverend Darlington, Missionary. He stayed as long as he could at Maingkwan to hand out government supplies of rice to refugees. Then he re-crossed the Namyung River twenty-seven times on his elephant carrying women and children across a dangerous ford

He and his family arrived in India in June 1942.

Dr. Robertson, an Assam tea planters' doctor, who volunteered to help refugees. He was Medical Officer in charge of Nampong camp.

I would like to mention a man not in my book, A. R. Tainsh, Officer with the Indian Tea Association, who organized the escape route camps (I describe) that provided care for the estimated 20,000 refugees who trekked to India via the Pangsau Pass. He was awarded the MBE.

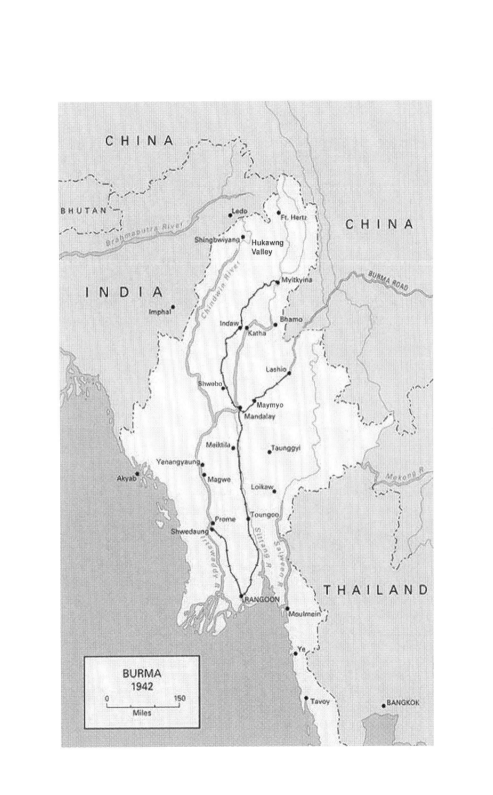

CHINA

BHUTAN

Brahmaputra River

INDIA

Imphal

Ledo

Shingbwiyang

Hukawng Valley

Ft. Hertz

CHINA

Chindwin River

BURMA ROAD

Myitkyina

Indaw

Katha

Bhamo

Lashio

Shwebo

Maymyo

Mandalay

Meiktila

Taunggyi

Yenangyaung

Magwe

Akyab

Loikaw

Mekong R.

Prome

Toungoo

Shwedaung

Salween R.

Sittang R.

Irrawaddy

THAILAND

RANGOON

Moulmein

Ye

BURMA
1942

0   150
Miles

Tavoy

BANGKOK

Prologue

Richmond, England

𝕽𝖎𝖈𝖍𝖒𝖔𝖓𝖉 𝕲𝖆𝖟𝖊𝖙𝖙𝖊

WEDDING ANNOUNCEMENTS 1931

On Saturday, November 28, at Richmond Parish Church, Richmond, Charles Edward Cavanagh, Esquire, only son of the late Charles Alfred Cavanagh, Esquire and the late Edwina Cavanagh of Stonegate Manor, to Miss Catherine Benton, daughter of Mr. James Benton and the late Mabel Benton of Park Mount Cottages.

BIRTHS

Congratulations to Charles and Catherine Cavanagh on the birth of their first child Joseph Edward Cavanagh who arrived September 8th, 1933.

DEATHS

CAVANAGH.— Charles Edward Cavanagh Esquire, aged 57, on March 15, 1939, at Stonegate Manor, Richmond. The funeral service to be held at Richmond Parish Church Wednesday March 29.

CAVANAGH.— Joseph Edward Cavanagh, aged 5, on March 15, 1939, at Stonegate Manor, Richmond. The funeral service to be held at Richmond Parish Church, Wednesday March 29.

CORONER'S COURT

1st May 1939: It is the verdict of the coroner's inquest that Charles Edward Cavanagh, Esquire, of Stonegate Manor, Richmond, Surrey, murdered Joseph Peter Cavanagh then died by his own hand while the balance of his mind was disturbed.

1

In Calcutta, Kate boarded a small steamer to cross the Bay of Bengal to Rangoon. So far, all had gone well during the sea and rail journey she had started one month earlier in England. She felt she was becoming a seasoned traveler. She boarded the steamer, confident of another pleasurable sea voyage, a confidence that soon evaporated. A build-up of clouds, which turned grey then inky black, replaced the clear blue skies. Strong winds lashed the sea into a frenzy. The captain warned passengers the ship was running into the tail end of a cyclone, and they should stay below deck. Kate retired to her cabin. Petrified, Kate clung to her bunk, fear running riot thinking the vessel would be torn apart as it was battered and tossed by a force so ferocious, she could not imagine it. She tried summoning up all her mental strength learned in her jujitsu classes. It was to no avail. She wanted to die; she had never felt so ill. For two days she hid, clinging to her bunk, paralyzed with fear, feeling a dismal failure as a traveler, certain that the other passengers were coping much better than she. Eventually, the sea calmed enough for her to be able to stand without being flung to the floor.

Emerging from her cabin, she was gratified to discover almost everyone else had succumbed to the ferocious storm. Women with pallid complexions sat weakly in the salon chairs, sharing their relief at having come through the tempest alive.

Men with green-tinged faces mingled with blustering bravado, making comments such as:

"I say, old chap, that was a stinker."

"The old tub is tougher than she looks."

Without further incident, the steamer arrived at the Rangoon River estuary, where she took on the pilot and entered the river close to Diamond Point Fort. It ploughed through the murky brown water, passing floating islets of water hyacinths. Even though there was little of interest to see for the first thirty miles, Kate stood at the ship's rail not wanting to miss a thing, not even the muddy riverbanks of the Rangoon River. For five hours, Kate stood at the rail observing the repeated stretches of sand, collections of thatched huts with vegetable gardens and country boats moored beside wooden jetties among patches of palms and mangroves. Kate was happy. Her eyes sparkled with excitement. She was mostly alone on deck for this boring part of the river, her fellow passengers having retired to take a nap or a meal.

Leaving her brother Andy, her sister-in-law Evelyn and her father behind in England had been hard. They had supported and comforted her through the tragedy of losing her son and the scandal caused by her husband's spiteful suicide note. They had also supported her in her quest to start a new life abroad. Her father had counseled, "You can't run from pain. You'll always carry it with you, hoping that, with the passage of time, it will, at least, become bearable."

Images of that wintry March night filled her mind. Was it only five months ago? She had had a premonition that something was horribly wrong. Returning home early to Stonegate Manor, she discovered police cars and ambulances outside her home. Sleet was pelting down, plastering strands of sodden black hair to her forehead, and soaking her slacks and Harris tweed jacket as soon as she left the Jaguar to enter the house.

Chief Inspector Bainbridge had tried to be kind breaking the news that her husband Charles had killed himself after murdering Joey, her five-year-old son.

But Kate had been unable to grasp it, could only feel an unbearable agony. Joey was her joy, the brightness that lifted her spirits as she wallowed in an unhappy marriage. After the police and ambulances left, her housekeeper, Mrs. Mullins, took care of her. It was she who had discovered Charles' body hanging from the bannister. Kate couldn't stop shivering. For a while she was numb with shock. Then when she began to cry, she couldn't stop. She curled up in Joey's bed and wailed all night.

Oh, how she hated Charles.

She had been his father's nurse, residing in Stonegate Manor while she cared for him. He saw something in her that Kate didn't recognize in herself, a greed for the "good life." When he died, he left a will saying that Charles would only inherit if he married Kate and had a child within two years. At first, the will had surprised her. She came from humble beginnings and assumed Charles' father was trying to help her by making her financially secure after the struggles of the Depression. But the truth was he wanted Kate to marry Charles to hide the truth about the son he considered an abomination.

To Kate's dismay, she learned on her wedding night that at fifty years of age Charles had never married because he was homosexual. The marriage was never consummated. She was twenty-eight and condemned to a sexless existence. As Charles could not bring himself to do the deed, he suggested trying to have a child by artificial insemination. He had found an article detailing how to do it with livestock. Unfortunately, it wasn't working and time was running out to be in compliance with the will. Unless they met its conditions, Charles would lose his inheritance and would need to work for the first time in his life, and Kate would lose her comfortable lifestyle.

She met Per Lindquist, handsome, Swedish diplomat, when she was spending a few days alone in London, Christmas shopping and going to the theater. They were two lonely people seeking comfort. Joey was conceived in that one night of passion.

Charles never knew, at least during those first years, but somehow, he found out that Joey was not of his blood. It didn't matter that Kate had saved the day and his inheritance. Vindictiveness must have grown in him like bacteria in a Petri dish. After his death, Kate discovered a blackmail letter to Charles from his dumped homosexual lover, threatening to reveal that Joey was not Charles' son. Kate had no idea how this man had discovered her secret, but he had.

In his new will, written only days before he killed himself, Charles left the estate and his money to Clive and Agnes Ainsworth, his cousins from the Cotswolds. He left Kate £5,000 and the Jaguar. When there was no mention of Joey in the will, all became clear to Kate. She had thought her withdrawn and depressed husband had killed Joey in a fit of paranoia and then had killed himself in a fit of remorse. But it wasn't like that at all. No mention of Joey in the will meant only one thing, Charles deliberately planned to kill Joey, and his suicide note depicting her as an unfaithful harpy was designed to blacken her name so not only would she be unwelcome in his upper-class social circles, owing to her lowly background, but unwelcome because of her terrible morals.

Having left her with only enough to survive on, Charles had completed his *coup d'état*.

To escape the scandal, Kate's brother Andy suggested she speak to his army captain friend Eric Manton. He had an uncle living in Burma, who would be kind enough to take Kate under his wing.

So, Kate decided on Burma as the place to rebuild her life. Now, for better or worse, life would be completely different. She would rise to the challenges her new life presented. Learning a new language and a new culture would occupy her thoughts, distracting her from the past. A smidgen of optimism shone light into the gloom that filled her heart and mind.

She was growing weary on deck, but gradually, the lush green land of Burma appeared. The sight of a golden dome in the distance prompted her to ask the man who had joined her at the rail, "What's that?"

"That, my dear, is the dome of the Shwedagon Pagoda. It's a shrine to Buddha and is covered from top to bottom in pure gold and precious gems . . ."

At that moment, a shaft of bright sunlight poured through a break in the clouds, attracting Kate's attention. It fell on the dome, lighting it as if by magic. A tingle of anticipation ran down her spine. Heart pounding, Kate interpreted it as a good omen.

". . . three hundred feet high, I believe," the man was saying when Kate's attention returned to her fellow passenger.

The ship proceeded upriver. Peaceful paddy fields and riverside villages gave way to sawmills, industrial buildings and refineries and storage tanks. The sight of elephants easing teak logs out of the water thrilled her. She had only ever seen an elephant at the zoo. She was almost jumping up and down with delight.

The man beside her chuckled. "First time in the East?"

"First time anywhere. Is it so obvious?"

"I felt exactly the same on my first arrival here."

He explained how the logs were floated downriver to the sawmills from the teak forests further north, a journey that took several years.

As they neared the port, river traffic increased. Craft of all sizes from sampans to ocean-going liners, dhows and catamarans crowded the waterways. Kate watched with rapt attention as smaller vessels swiftly dodged and darted around the larger ships. The scene was fascinating and different from anything she had ever experienced. The ship edged into the Sule Pagoda wharves. Her stomach fluttered with anticipation.

Norman Manton was waiting dockside. She would have recognized him even without the agreed upon sign, a yellow rose in his lapel. He was an older version of his nephew Eric: tall, with a mustache, a middle-age expanded waistline and blond hair tinged with white. Kate waved to catch his attention.

His eyes lit up at the sight of the beautiful, shapely woman with jet black hair who would be staying with him. "Mrs. Cavanagh?" he called, stepping forward to shake her hand when she descended the gangplank. "Pleased to make your acquaintance. You're to call me Manny, everybody does. May I call you Kate?"

"Of course, you may," Kate said gaily, taking an immediate liking to him. "I hope I won't be too much of an imposition."

"Not at all. I'll enjoy the company, and all the chaps will be as envious as hell that I've such an attractive lady staying with me."

Kate's stomach knotted. Oh, why did he say that? I hope he doesn't make any advances! I don't want any problems to mar my new life.

Manny and Kazi, his Indian driver, organized Kate's luggage into his Humber.

Manny mopped his brow with his handkerchief then helped Kate into the car. "Careful, Kate, the car's been standing in the sun; the leather seats will be hot."

Driving through Rangoon, Kate was surprised to find wide avenues; she had been expecting narrow, mysterious passageways. But the hustle and bustle were all there; Chinese, Burmans, Indians swarmed and jostled along the streets. And the color—the brightly colored silk clothing, worn by both men and women—was startling in the strong, tropical sunlight.

Even though the car windows were open, Kate wilted under the onslaught of the heat and humidity. She fanned her face with her hat. "Gosh, it's hot."

"Always is. It's only five miles to my house. You'll soon cool down once you're indoors away from the sun and under the fans with a gin and tonic in your hands. What do you think of the show so far?"

"Fascinating," Kate said, turning to look out of the window again, thinking she would have to scribble it all down tonight so that when she wrote letters home, she would not forget one detail of her first impressions.

Manny kept quiet, smiling at Kate's various expressions as she stared at her surroundings.

"Manny! What's that man doing? There! On the sidewalk."

Manny peered past Kate to see an Indian, dressed only in a loin cloth. His customer sat on a stool holding up his foot. The Indian worked on the customer's little toe with a long piece of nylon twine.

"Oh, that. He's removing corns and callouses. Sometimes you'll see them using razor blades."

"Surgery, on the street?"

"Oh yes. Dentistry too."

Kate's wide-eyed, stunned expression had Manny patting her hand. "Don't worry. Rangoon is nothing like the real Burma. Rangoon is full of Indians, and so this is more like an Indian city than Burmese."

Kate pointed to some buildings they were passing. "These are so beautiful."

"Built by the British. We'll pass the Secretariat, the main administrative office; the building is very impressive, and also the Victorian style Strand Hotel—I'm sure you'll get to know it well. It's a social hub for plantation managers and others who come here on leave or for business."

Kate turned back to the views outside.

Manny coughed to gain her attention. "Kate, I've spread the word that my widowed niece is coming to stay with me."

Kate's head spun round to look at him, her expression puzzled.

"Had to safeguard your reputation, old girl. Couldn't have those prim fuddy-duddies gossiping about you and trying to blacken your good name?"

Kate nodded, relieved that Manny seemed to have no ulterior motives towards her.

"I hadn't realized people were still so nit-picky about such things over here."

Her heart sank thinking of the class prejudice she had endured at home and her hopes of leaving all that vileness behind her.

"Don't worry. It's a very small, frozen-in-time contingent. You won't have much to do with them. There's a much younger crowd in town, so you'll have a good social life once you recover from your journey."

Manny's reassurance did not lessen Kate's tension. She focused on her surroundings to escape her dismay.

Traffic was thick, a jumble of rickshaws, elegant cars, handcarts, and slow-moving bullock carts. The crammed buses had animals painted on the front—tigers, snakes, deer. Manny explained that instead of route numbers or destination names as on London buses, the animals depicted the areas the buses served. Pedestrians filled the sidewalks; pungent, tangy, fishy, fried food smells filled the air; bicycle bells, bus, car, tuk-tuk and tram engines roared around her, laughter and shrieks from street traders sliced the peace, assaulting and almost overwhelming Kate's senses.

Relief came when they drove to a residential district on the far side of the city and stopped outside a delightful house with a large, screened-in veranda and a multi-hued garden festooned with bougainvillea, laburnum trees, tall blue delphiniums, and poinsettias.

On entering his home, Manny called Sandeep, his Indian male servant, and ordered tea. Another servant retrieved Kate's bags from the car while Manny led the way to Kate's room.

"You should be all right here."

She looked around the cell-like room. Spartan! The complete opposite of her comfortable bedroom in England. No soft oriental rugs to nuzzle her feet, no large luxurious ornate oak bed, and no walls filled with paintings. She hadn't been expecting the same level of affluence, but really! A wrought-iron bed with a mosquito net in the middle of the brown-tiled floor, a ceiling fan, chest of drawers, a mirror and an alcove covered by a curtain where she could hang her clothes—this was it?

Manny shouted something in Burmese. In response, a beautiful young Burmese girl entered the room. She had long black hair fastened into a bun at the nape of her neck, and wore the traditional Burmese sarong, a turquoise-green *longyi*. Her smile was as cheerful as her brightly embroidered, yellow, waist-length shirt.

"This is Mya Sandi. Her name means emerald moon. She is going to look after you."

Kate immediately brightened at having this young woman take care of her. "Hello, Mya Sandi," Kate said with a smile.

Mya Sandi smiled and giggled.

Manny stood behind her and put his hands on her shoulders. His eyes twinkled as he tried not to smile. "Doesn't understand a word of English, Kate."

Kate gasped. "How am I supposed to communicate with her?"

Manny grinned mischievously and winked. "You'll have to learn Burmese."

With still another month to go before the monsoon season would be over at the end of September, the air was heavy and sultry. Every afternoon it poured with rain. The place teemed with insects intent on killing themselves against the bright lights when evening came. Dinner, especially Kate's first in Rangoon, was an ordeal. Insects fell into her hair, crawled on the fish, fluttered against her face, all with little sympathy from Manny for her discomfort.

Dipping his finger into his brandy to pull out a fly, Manny laughed heartily. "You'll soon get used to it."

Stonegate's elegant, dining room flashed into Kate's mind. A pang of homesickness engulfed her. Not for one second did she think she would ever get used to it.

A few days after Kate's arrival, Manny announced, "Did you hear the wireless today? Britain has declared war on Germany. You got out just in time. A few weeks later and you may not have made it."

"Britain is at war? With Germany? My brother will be called up! Oh, I feel terrible. I'm a nurse. I should be there where I can be useful."

"No point in worrying about it now, old girl. Besides, we'll soon have the Hun on the run. It'll be over before you know it."

A large moth flew against Kate's face. "If you'll excuse me, Manny, I'll turn in. I'm extremely tired."

"See you bright and early in the morning for a ride before I go to work," Manny called after her.

Kate noted it was, as usual, not a request but a presumption that she would go. In her room, she quickly undressed and jumped into bed. Mya Sandi hung up Kate's clothes, rolled down the mosquito net and, smiling gently, left the room.

Mya Sandi seems sweet, but if I can't communicate with her, how will I get to know her? Oh, Mrs. Mullins, I wish you were here. I should have stayed in England with the war and all. Manny seems all right. But I'll move out, get my own place as soon as I find my feet. I must write to Andy and Dad in the morning.

Next thing Kate knew Mya Sandi was waking her. It was 5:00 a.m.

Manny, having lived a bachelor's life for fifty-two years, was set in his ways. His early morning ride was established and unchangeable. Kate learned that Manny barely ate breakfast. A few crispbreads or a small bowl of wheat germ cereal imported from England seemed to set him up for the day. Kate, used to a traditional English breakfast of eggs and bacon, had to settle for a rushed meal of Manny's meager rations.

"Come on. Come on. We haven't got all day," Manny said, rushing Kate down the garden to where he had built stables for his four English horses. Kate had soon come to realize that Manny's only two passions were forestry and his horses to the extent that he had their hay and oats shipped over from England, and his garden was devoted to growing tidbits for them, especially carrots.

The stable boy had saddled Raven, a black gelding and Manny's favorite horse. For Kate, he had brought out a white mare named Gypsy.

Manny handed Kate some carrots. "Gypsy's yours while you're here."

Kate stroked Gypsy's face and gave her the carrots. "She's gorgeous. It will be good to be riding again."

"Yes, well, let's be off. Don't have much time."

They rode along a sandy lane behind the house. The foliage was wet, the air heavy with humidity and mosquitoes were a nuisance. Yet the ground was not boggy, even though there had been recent heavy rains. Manny's daily routine when he was in Rangoon, was: morning ride, out to work, home at five. She was free to roam wherever she wished during the day, his driver would take her, but it would be such a pleasure to have her home to greet him on his return from the office.

Over breakfast the following day, Manny announced, "I'm sure you've recovered from your journey by now, so I'm taking you with me tonight when I go out. It's time for you to meet people."

Even though it was a pronouncement rather than a request, Kate's face lit up. She *was* eager to put the ugliness of the past behind her and venture into new pastures.

"Oh, where are we going?"

"You'll see. Lots of young people will be there."

That evening, Manny's driver turned into Halpin Road and stopped outside a large building.

"Here we are," Manny said, climbing from the car.

The driver held Kate's door open for her. They had arrived at a brick and stone building that reminded her of a large private boarding school surrounded by sports fields. The windows were rounded at the top with keystone arches. The red tiled roof covered an open walkway on the second floor, used as á viewing area that overlooked the sports fields. A number of cars were parked on a large area of black top.

"This, dear Kate, is the Gymkhana Club. The membership includes lots of handsome, athletic young men."

Good grief! Manny's match-making already.

Failing to notice Kate's frown, Manny led a vexed Kate under the arched entrance and through a door held open by a uniformed Indian. The large entrance hall with its high ceiling was impressive. Flights of stairs with wrought iron handrails climbed to the next story. Decorative tiles covered the floor. Groupings of rattan chairs and tables, half-hidden behind potted palms of one sort or another, dotted the large space. The hum of voices and laughter spilled into the hall from the social room.

Manny took her arm. "Come on, I'll introduce you to the crowd who will most likely become your companions in the coming months."

"I'm looking forward to making some friends. Apart from family, my life in England was quite isolated socially."

"Don't worry. You'll be fine, a shining star in Rangoon's social whirl."

They entered a room filled with round tables surrounded by rattan and wicker armchairs. As in the entrance hall, potted palms were strategically placed to provide privacy at some tables. The buzz of conversations cheered Kate and lifted her spirits. She was sure she could have an enjoyable time with these people. Manny led her to a large table where several people were seated. He introduced Kate as his niece, newly arrived from England.

"You'll probably see a lot more of these people, Kate. They're part of the thespian crowd." Manny indicated a tall, thin, scholarly-looking man with a thatch of black hair and a bushy mustache. "This is Dudley Davies. Works in local government and is a brilliant director in our amateur dramatics club. Dudley's the man to talk to about an acting career."

Dudley stood and kissed the back of Kate's hand. "Charmed I'm sure. I had no idea you had such an attractive niece, you old devil."

Dudley's charming smile and kiss to the hand dissipated Kate's nervousness. "Pleased to meet you. I've never done any acting, but maybe I could be useful behind the scenes."

Manny next introduced a heavy-set woman in her late twenties, with a pretty, round face. "This young lady is Vera Smythe. Her brother, Michael, is a Steel Brothers district manager and as he is not yet married, Vera kindly left England to act his hostess."

"Pleased to meet you, Vera. This is my first-time outside England. Maybe you can give me some advice on how to adapt to my new life."

Sitting next to Vera was a plain, mousy-haired woman in her mid-twenties.

"Kate, this Daphne Winslow. She has a beautiful voice and is an actress extraordinaire." The two women exchanged nods and smiles.

"And finally," Manny said, "meet Teddy and Grace Winthrop, inspiring teachers at Rangoon High School and stalwart members of all our social clubs."

"Nice to meet you, Kate. Where in England are you from?" Grace asked.

"I lived near Richmond on the outskirts of London. Have you been here long?"

"Sometimes it feels too long," Teddy said.

Manny and Kate, feeling more cordial and relaxed after the introductions, joined the group and ordered drinks.

"Do you sing?" Grace asked Kate.

"Not really. I've never been in a choir or anything like that."

"I thought Manny might have brought you along for the rehearsal."

Kate gave Manny a questioning look.

"Oh, didn't I tell you?" Manny said. "We're having a rehearsal. This year we're singing sea shanties in the annual concert for the Blind School."

Kate's eyebrows shot up. Realizing her mouth was gaping, she quickly closed it with a click of the teeth. Manny rehearsing for a sea shanty concert was completely unexpected. Someone announced it was time to move to the ballroom for the rehearsal. They joined the flow of people to a room where ornate mirrors adorned the walls, reflecting and increasing the light from the magnificent crystal chandeliers. Before joining the choir on stage, Manny made sure Kate was settled on a chair in the front row of lined up chairs on the dance floor in the center of the room, placed there for club members making up the audience. Grace Winthrop took her place at the piano on stage. Vera hurried over to sit next to Kate.

Kate leaned close to Vera. "When Manny suggested he take me for a night out, I never expected this."

"Being in the choir is a popular pastime," Vera said. "My brother loves it. Me? I'm tone-deaf. Can't carry a tune."

Grace played a few chords and the lights in the ballroom dimmed. Never in a million years would Kate have guessed that Manny relished being part of a choir or that he would have a beautiful tenor voice. It was a jaw dropping, delightful moment to realize there were depths to Manny not readily apparent.

When rehearsals were over, Manny and Kate returned to the social room, where he introduced her to the many, single young men in the choir, so many of them, Kate barely remembered anyone's name.

"Don't worry about it," Manny said. "You'll soon know them all. They'll be falling all over themselves to woo you."

In the back seat of the car, during the drive home, Kate and Manny belted out sea shanties. Having been taught popular shanties in school, Kate knew them all. She joined in with gusto, liberated by several Pegu Club cocktails.

What shall we do with a drunken sailor? What shall we do with a drunken sailor? What shall we do with a drunken sailor, early in the morning?

They laughed, guffawed and sang some more. Even driver Kazi joined in. Manny squeezed Kate's hand. "Good evening?"

"Yes."

"Then from now on, I expect you to make the most of Rangoon's social life."

"Do you think I'll fit in?"

"Of course, you will. The time has come for you to have some carefree times in your life, don't you think?"

So began Kate's new life. She didn't know how much Eric had told Manny of the events that had driven her to Burma, but she appreciated that Manny did not pry. She soon learned to fit into his set ways. Conversation with Manny was a one-sided affair: Manny talked; Kate listened. She grew to like him. He was uncomplicated, easy to read. Life was tolerable and she was unruffled by the fact she was not expected to express an opinion.

As she became acquainted with government officials and people working for the teak, oil and trading companies, she discovered how much in demand single women were. She threw herself wholeheartedly into the partying, dancing, sporting events, and cocktail parties. Like opium, the complete social whirl of Rangoon dulled the pain, the loss, and the guilt that would forever be a part of her

Becoming more at ease with her new life, Kate suggested to Manny she might be outstaying her welcome, and perhaps she should move into her own place. Manny immediately shot down that idea.

"No need to think of that so soon, old girl. I'm still enjoying your company."

Kate had been staying with Manny a month when he arrived home from work and announced, "Time for my annual inspection tour. Three weeks and we'll be heading off to the jungle. You want to come, of course, don't you?"

"In three weeks?"

"Yes. Is there a problem?"

"No. I'll simply have to cancel all my dates, that's all."

"*All* your dates! Good Heavens! How many do you have?"

"Lots and lots: there's John Hanson, Tony Sanders, and George Evans. He works for Steel Brothers," Kate said, laughing. "My gentlemen friends will be so disappointed."

"Ah, of course, so, there's no problem. In spite of your hectic social life, you'll be packed and ready in three weeks?"

"Yes. My first jungle adventure—it should be exciting."

"Disappoint all your dates, eh, for a bit of adventure? I said you would be in demand. I take it there's no one serious then." Manny opened his newspaper and disappeared behind its pages, the usual sign that Kate was dismissed. Smiling, she got up to leave. He suddenly lowered the paper.

"You do have the proper clothes for the jungle, don't you?"

"I think so."

"Let me see."

Manny folded his newspaper, put it on the table and called for Mya Sandi. Then he accompanied Kate to her room and examined the clothes she and Mya Sandi pulled from the drawers.

"Yes. Yes. No. Terrible. No. Oh dear. Fine," he commented as they sorted through the items, "We'd better go shopping tomorrow."

Next day, in the store, Manny had Kate dressed in khaki plus fours, long sleeved khaki shirt, a pith helmet, puttees and canvas shoes. She looked at herself in the mirror with dismay.

"Really, Manny! Are you telling me this is what people wear when on tour?" Kate asked. "You wrote and told me to go to Skeetles and Sons to be outfitted. They assured me all my clothing would be perfectly suitable."

Not liking Kate's mocking tone, Manny stuck out his chin. "*I* wear this type of clothing."

"I look like some nineteenth century explorer. I don't want to go into the jungle looking like this," Kate said.

"But you'll be protected from all biting pests in those clothes."

"No, Manny, I'm not going into the jungle wearing these. Let's look at something less clown-like that will still be practical."

Manny puffed himself up. "Let me be the judge of what's most useful and practical."

Sensing an altercation was brewing, the Indian shop assistant stepped back.

Kate looked in the mirror at Manny's reflection behind her and gave him a steely stare.

"I value your expert opinion, Manny," she said in a low, firm voice, "but I will not pay good money to dress in this ridiculous fashion. Now, let's see what else they have that we can agree on."

The assistant hurried back with a pair of long pants and a large brimmed panama hat. Manny folded his arms across his chest, his stance indicating that he would not be swayed.

Seeing Manny's presentation of stubbornness, Kate's lips twitched, and before long, she was laughing heartily. Manny's obstinate expression changed to surprise followed by puzzlement. His mouth turned down at the corners. Then he relaxed, smiled, and nodded, a gracious loser.

2

The household buzzed with preparations for the three-month-long tour. Canned foods, alcohol, soft drinks, books, radio, gramophone, and anything else that would make the tour as comfortable as possible were assembled and packed.

The tour would begin with a day and a night on the train to reach Kyaukpadaung (Chee-ork-padong). Two male servants and the cook, nicknamed 'Casanova,' would accompany them. Despite his physical drawbacks of knock-knees, weedy size, receding chin and protruding teeth, the cook seemed to be a magnet for the ladies.

Manny did not allow female servants to accompany him on his tours. "Too tough for them," he stated.

Manny's words jolted Kate out of her complacency. But all right for me? Manny had implied the tour would require little more exertion than a walk in the park. She was enjoying her good times in Rangoon that, at times, made her feel quite light-hearted. And she didn't mind too much that she was leaving it all behind for an adventure in the jungle. She chuckled, picturing Andy's face when he read her letters from the jungle, painting a totally different picture of her life so far in Burma. Kate's face fell. She was sad that quiet, self-effacing Mya Sandi would not be with her. Mya Sandi's presence brought a soothing peacefulness to Kate's life, for which she was especially grateful during the times her thoughts drifted to the past and to the war situation at home. Kate waited with dread for the next letter to arrive from England. Fortunately, Andy had not yet been called up for military service. So far, not much seemed to have happened since Britain had declared war on Germany. She wondered how long such a situation could continue before the real hostilities began.

On the morning of their departure, with the servants settled in the servants' rail car, and all the supplies stashed in the baggage car, Kate and Manny made themselves comfortable in the train compartment. He opened his newspaper as soon as the train began to move.

Seeing the headlines, Kate asked. "The front-page headlines say the Japanese are invading Hunan province in China. Are we in any danger from them?"

"No, no danger. China's a long way away, except for Burma's northern border. But Hunan province is in central China and it's a big country. The Japs would have to go through Siam and Malaya before reaching Burma and that will never happen. Nasty business this Chinese debacle, but *we're* all right. Don't worry. There's nothing much else about the war in the paper. Poland has fallen to Germany, that's about all."

Kate, worrying about Andy now that Germany had invaded Poland stared out the window at the passing scenes—young boys tending buffaloes or goats, women washing clothes in the streams, villages, jungle, paddy fields, and pagodas.

An hour later, Kate emerged from her anxiety. Worrying would change nothing. She plied Manny with questions about the tour then asked, "Do you have a map of the places we're going to?"

Reaching up to the luggage rack, Manny pulled down his bag and searched a pocket for a map. "There you are, but it won't tell you much about the kind of country we'll be traveling through."

"That's all right, you can tell me. Where are we going?"

"Kyaukpadaung."

"Is it a town?"

Manny chuckled and found it on the map. "No such luck. Only a remote wayside halt in the middle of the jungle."

"Oh! Will we meet many people during the tour?"

"Apart from a few forestry managers and Burmese villagers, you're stuck with me for company, old girl."

Kate studied the map. "So, we're heading north."

"Yes. In Burma all the mountain ranges and rivers run from north to south, or south to north, if you prefer. That makes travel from east to west and west to east very difficult. There are many streams or *chaungs* and two big rivers—the Chindwin and the Irrawaddy." Manny leaned over and pointed out the rivers on the map. "Because there are few roads in Burma, mainly tracks, steamers on the rivers provide the main means of travel apart from the railway line from Rangoon to Myitkyina (Mitch-*ee*-na) and a few branch lines. In the rainy season, the forestry workers set to and float the teak logs downriver towards Rangoon to the port and sawmills."

Kate studied the map further then asked, "What do these dotted lines signify?"

"They're elephant paths cut by the forest department so their officers can travel around to keep an eye on things, decide where to harvest teak next. The single dotted lines are jungle tracks." Manny lit his pipe and watched Kate pour over the map. "You'll devour the print off it."

Kate smiled and folded the map. "I like to know where I'm going, that's all. Besides, geography was one of my favorite subjects in school."

Arriving at Kyaukpadaung, Kate was impressed to find three men with a bullock cart waiting to carry their supplies and baggage. They also had two ponies for her and Manny to ride, underlining the fact that Manny was a person of some authority. They mounted the ponies and left the sunshine of the cleared railway track for the gloom of the forest. The path led through dense bamboo, where the foliage joined overhead to form a tunnel. The canopy of the tall trees shut out the sunlight, making the jungle cool and dark.

To Kate the jungle felt creepy.

"I wasn't expecting it to be so dark, Manny."

"This is dense jungle, lots of creepers and dense undergrowth below the treetops. The natives cleared this path and keep it open, otherwise we'd have to hack our way through with machetes. There are other kinds of vegetation in the jungle. In some higher areas it can be like traveling through an English woodland only without the bluebells."

The ponies plodded along, climbing up one steep hillside and down another. Kate enjoyed the crows flying across their path and the chuck-chuck-chuck of squirrels warning of the humans' passage. Aware the jungle was teeming with wild life, even dangerous tigers, Kate was surprised at how silent it was.

"I thought there'd be a lot more sounds of jungle life, but all I hear are a few squirrels and the bullock carts' squeaky wheels behind us."

"The cart-men never grease the wheels on their carts," said Manny, "so they have their own individual sound. When the cart-man nears his village, his wife will recognize the squeaks and know he is coming."

Kate laughed with delight. "Is that really true?"

Manny chuckled. "Of course, old girl. Would I lie to you?"

Kate was still smiling when the party reached the top of a ridge providing a view of the forested hillsides stretching for miles.

Kate looked down in awe at the green carpet made by the treetops, partly covered by the early morning mist lingering in the valley below. "It's so beautiful."

"Beats a desk job, doesn't it?"

They descended to the valley floor and crossed a dry riverbed. Manny dismounted. "Come and see this."

Kate left her pony and joined him, bending over marks in the soft earth. "What is it?"

"Pug marks. Big tiger. Passed this way a short while ago."

A jolt of fear made Kate's stomach tighten and cringe. She stood up straight and anxiously scanned the area. "How do you know that?"

Manny walked along the riverbed until he reached more marks in the sand.

"These hoof marks have cobwebs over them, so they're not fresh."

Kate joined him, her stomach in knots. "I see."

Manny returned to the tiger's paw print.

"Looks as if he came for a drink. Not finding any water, he wandered further upstream to see if he could find a pool." Manny looked at Kate. "Not frightened, are you? No need to be. Tigers rarely attack a human in the daytime."

"Then where did the stories of man-eating tigers come from?"

"Sometimes, old or wounded animals, who can't hunt for prey, become desperate enough to attack a human, but it's rare."

They remounted and rode another six miles through dense jungle until they reached a clearing where there was a forest rest-house made of teak. It was raised off the ground on posts to avoid flooding during the monsoon season.

"Come and see your accommodation courtesy of the government forest department," Manny said. "We'll be staying here for two nights."

While the servants unloaded the carts and carried boxes of provisions and equipment into their quarters, Kate entered the house and looked around the spacious, sparsely furnished but adequate-for-short-stay accommodation. The bungalow had two bedrooms, a living room, bathroom and veranda. The servants were busy making up the beds and mosquito nets, unpacking gramophone and records, placing books in the bookcase, whisky, gin and glasses in a cupboard for the sahibs' comfort. Cane and wicker chairs, sofa and tables helped fill the living room. She checked the servants' quarters. They were more austere, but no worse than her bedroom at Manny's.

The out-house was on the edge of the clearing, a bamboo cube on stilts with a hole in the floor directly above a hole in the ground beneath it. Kate knew she was going to hate going to the outhouse in the dark. She also knew that when nightfall came, they would be enveloped in darkness for twelve hours, making a nighttime visit to the outhouse unavoidable. Before turning in, she searched for the flashlight.

Manny looked up from his paperwork, reports he was writing to the Burma Government's Forestry Division. "Make sure you shine the flashlight all around to check for spider webs. Nothing worse than walking into one and not knowing where the spider is, and they're big and vile in the jungle. Check for scorpions and snakes too; they seem to like to hang out in the out-house."

"Manny! Is this really true or do you just want to scare me? Because you're doing a good job of it!"

"Sorry, old girl, but it's all true. Yell if you need me."

Kate stomped off muttering, "I'll never get used to jungle life."

She swung her flashlight up and down and all around, heart seemingly at a standstill with apprehension. She moved a spider web with the flashlight and waited, watching intently, ready to run should she see the eight-legged monster that had spun it. Nothing stirred. Gathering her courage, Kate climbed the steps and opened the door. Something scuttled. A quick intake of breath, Kate's heart beating wildly. Then the beam of light found it, a gecko, scrambling along the wall, and in a nest in a corner near the ceiling, a small bird had settled in for the night. Nothing else. The facility was safe to use.

During his tours, Manny passed the evening hours writing forestry reports by lamplight—the number and size of teak trees to the acre, the size of the tree to be cut here, the treatment of an elephant's abscess. As he worked, Kate relaxed in the darkness, watching the stars and the tall trees, tinted silver by the moonlight. Sometimes she read. Other times she laid her book on her lap and listened to the loud choruses of cicadas, the rustling of small animals, and the roars of big cats before turning in. She felt at peace, as if some inner healing was taking place. Sometimes she felt pulled in opposite directions. She wanted the excitement of new experiences in the jungle, but she also wanted to be back in Rangoon where Mya Sandi's attentiveness was balm for her soul, meeting the need for a nurturing touch that had been missing in her life, since her mother's death from cancer when she was ten.

Continual sunshine created hot, wonderful weather during the three months of the winter season. There was no rain. The streams and rivers were almost dry. As they moved from camp to camp, they found welcome shade by traveling along ravine-enclosed streams, where feathery ferns with coppery-pink new growth draped the steep sides, and moss and lichen decorated the rocks. The ponies' hooves clattering on rock and the squeak of cartwheels were the only sounds to disturb the stillness.

Two weeks into their tour, they rounded a bend in the river. Manny stopped dead, put his finger to his lips to warn Kate to be silent, then pointed ahead with his crop to where a fifteen-strong herd of wild elephants was bathing and enjoying the cool water.

Manny whispered, "We're downwind of them. They haven't caught our scent."

Kate thought it the most peaceful scene she had ever seen.

Manny moved close and whispered, "If they turn and charge, run and stand behind the largest tree you can find and *don't* move."

Kate's mouth fell open. Run if they charge! Could they really be that dangerous? After all, the ones she had seen at the circus seemed amenable and tame. However, she stayed silent, regaining her composure as they watched the herd until it wandered away in the opposite direction.

"I can't believe they're dangerous," Kate whispered.

"Oh, but they are. Very. But when they charge and they don't see you, they run right past you if you hide behind something. They rarely turn back but keep on going glad to be away."

The bizarreness of the changes in her life made Kate giggle. She quickly covered her mouth with her hand. In less than a decade she had gone from reading thermometers and emptying bed pans to learning how to stay safe from rampaging elephants. Whoever would have thought it?

One afternoon, during the last week of the tour, soon after they set up their last camp in yet another forestry department's rest house, a man appeared from out of the jungle. He was bare-foot, dressed in a turban, a blue shirt, and the traditional cotton skirt called a *longyi*.

He approached Manny. "*Mingala ba,* I am glad to see you, sir." The man grinned revealing black betel-stained teeth, a shocking sight that made Kate cringe. He nodded to her, acknowledging her presence. Then he jabbered on to Manny in Burmese. Kate understood "good afternoon," but the headman spoke so fast, she could understand nothing further. From his body language and tone of voice, she surmised he was telling Manny a serious tale of woe. By the time the man had finished, Manny's face was a picture of delight. He slapped his thigh and stood up.

"We're in for an exciting time. This is the headman of a nearby village, come to ask for my help. He wants me to kill a tiger that's been killing their buffaloes and terrorizing the village."

"Why would he come to you?"

"Weaponry, old girl. We white men have the best guns for hunting. I'll arrange for a platform to be built above the latest kill. It's a couple of days old, but with luck the tiger may come back tonight to finish his supper."

"By the state of his mouth, I thought he was going to ask you to remove one of his teeth."

"What? Oh, his teeth? He chews betel nut. Gives a boost of energy. Most natives chew it."

The cook made sardine sandwiches and a flask of tea for Kate and Manny to take with them. Late that afternoon, they climbed onto the platform built in the nearest high tree to the kill. It was a tight squeeze and not very comfortable, but worst of all was the stench from the decomposing buffalo carcass.

"Blast," Manny said, tucking into a sandwich, "The kill's probably too rotten to tempt the tiger to return."

He offered a sandwich to Kate who, nauseated by the fetid odor of rotting buffalo, mutely shook her head.

"They prefer fresher meat," he continued, taking another bite of his sandwich.

Kate and Manny sat in silence for two hours. Manny stayed alert the whole time determined to bag the tiger if it came. Kate meandered through the labyrinth in her mind, catching fleeting pictures of her son's joy, hearing his laughter, analyzing her dismal marriage to Charles. Strange, life's twists and turns, bringing me here to this exotic country to perch in a tree with my bottom going numb.

Manny whispered, "It doesn't look as if it will come, but it's safer to wait here until daylight. We'll take it in turns to have some shut-eye." He handed Kate the rifle. "Here, you take the first watch."

Kate gingerly took hold of the weapon. "Manny, I don't know how to use the thing."

"I'm not asking you to shoot anything. Just hold it." There was a thoughtful pause. "Can't use a rifle, eh? When we return to Rangoon, we'll need to do something about this severe lack in your education."

He settled in as best he could, and soon his breathing changed into a gentle snore. Kate sat frozen with fear. In the moonlight, the foliage appeared menacing. She thought she saw movement and eyes shining in the shadows. The platform seemed too low, an easy leap for a tiger. The mosquitoes attacked her hands and face. A ferocious roar rent the air; a buffalo bleated in fear and pain. Sounds of snapping branches, savage snarling and growling and pitiful moaning filled the air. Kate was close to tears picturing another buffalo being ripped to pieces. She could hear the carnage taking place nearby but was powerless to stop it.

Manny woke up and cursed his bad luck at not being able to take a shot. Kate and Manny spent the rest of the night on the platform, listening to what they assumed was the tiger devouring its prey.

Suddenly, silence. With the coming of dawn, the predator appeared to have slunk off. Manny and Kate climbed down from the platform. Kate's face and hands were swollen from insect bites. They went looking for the prey, a buffalo. It was still alive, panting and feebly flicking its ears. Flies were already buzzing and crawling in its bloody wounds.

"Manny, please, shoot it. It's suffered enough."

Manny fired a bullet into its brain. "See how a tiger starts to feed from the tail," Manny said. "Usually, a tiger kills its prey with one blow, but the buffalo's neck was too thick."

Kate looked at the dismembered buffalo and the cavernous hole in its rump. The poor beast.

Manny strode back to camp in high spirits, telling a horrified Kate, "We'll have another platform built over this kill. He's sure to come back tonight. We've got to put an end to him. The village will know no peace until he's dead."

Kate could summon no interest in Manny's plans. She was tired. Her muscles were sore, and her skin aggravated from the insect bites, but at five o' clock that evening, she clambered up to the platform and squatted down beside Manny in silence. As darkness fell, the jungle came alive with sound, led by chirping cicadas. Three hours later, rustling leaves marked the passage of a large animal through the undergrowth then dull, heavy footfalls. A tiger's head poked from the bushes followed by the well-camouflaged body. He looked around before proceeding to the dead buffalo then lay down to tear more flesh from the gaping wound. Startled by the sound of Manny lifting his rifle, the tiger looked up. Manny fired. With a roar the tiger leapt into the air and bounded off into the jungle, a bloody wound in his side.

"Damn and blast!" Manny cursed. "I only wounded him. He'll be a terrible danger to the natives. I'll have to finish him off."

"Let's go," Kate said, moving to climb down.

"No! Not now. It's too dangerous. We'll have to wait for daylight to search for him."

Manny fired twice into the air to signal some villagers to come and escort them back to camp. They rushed into view and, by the light of bamboo torches, scoured the area for the tiger. They were clearly disappointed not to find it. Subdued, they escorted Manny and Kate back to their camp.

The next morning, Kate was relieved to be left behind when parties set out to search for the tiger. The hunt had reawakened bad memories and left her disturbed. She had experienced enough death. On his return, Manny told her the men found the tiger slowly bleeding to death. "I shot and killed it as it lay too weak to do more than snarl."

That night, the villagers celebrated, and Manny could not hide his delight that he had rid the area of a dangerous, jungle animal.

"All in all, a satisfactory conclusion to your first jungle tour, don't you think?"

Some months after their return to Rangoon, there was widespread rioting by the Burmese, not so much against the ruling British but against the many Indian immigrants, who were resented and blamed for taking locals' jobs during Burma's economic depression. Although violence filled the streets, Manny never missed a day's work. Each morning, he put a loaded pistol in his pocket, vowing to shoot the devils if they came after him.

"They're anti-Indian, not anti-British," Kate repeatedly told him, but he was of the ruling class and anyone who caused him trouble must face the consequences. Kate could not help but admire his defiance of danger.

At night, they often heard shots fired in the distance. Looting and burning of homes and property was extensive. Every day, dead or badly beaten Hindus and Buddhists were collected and removed from the streets in all districts.

One day, Manny returned from work with a rifle and a pistol. "These are for you, for when I need to go away on business. While you're living in my house, I feel responsible for your safety. This weekend, I'll give you some shooting lessons. It would be remiss of me not to make sure you can defend yourself. Did you ever do any shooting in England?"

"No, I didn't. That kind of sport never interested me."

"Pity. Well, we'll make a start now, filling in that gap in your education. I'll be happier knowing you can defend yourself, when I'm away."

3

After returning to Rangoon from their tour, Kate resumed her social life, jumping into the Amateur Dramatic Society's activities. Her first role was playing Valentine, a twenty-year-old student in a play called *Land's End,* a thriller. She was really too old for the part, but there was nobody else, and Daphne *had* to have the starring role of being Valentine's mother, unfaithful wife and murderer. Kate was surprised to discover she had a flair for acting, and she soaked up the praise heaped upon her by her friends.

Kate blossomed in the social whirl: a fancy-dress ball where she dressed as Josephine accompanied by Manny as Napoleon; she watched cricket and rugby matches, a fireworks display, and the Caledonian Ball with its energetic Scottish country dancing. She attended with Michael Kingsley, a young man on leave from the oil fields and eager for an English woman's company.

When October rolled around, Manny told Kate he was planning another tour of the teak areas at the end of the month.

Kate was less than thrilled.

"You want me to come with you?"

"Of course. Wouldn't be the same without you. I know you'll miss your social life, but the jungle has as much, if not more, to offer," Manny said, "and besides you enjoy it."

Kate capitulated. Manny was right. She had enjoyed her previous jungle trip. The tiger hunt had given her something exotic and exciting to write about in her letters to England. It would also in some ways be a relief to escape the persistent attentions of certain lonely men wanting to settle down and marry her.

They left Rangoon by train four weeks later. Kate studied Manny's maps during the long journey. After they arrived at the jungle halt, a long pony ride brought them to a pleasant clearing by a stream, where they made camp.

The following day, Kate curled up to read *Wuthering Heights* by Emily Bronte, loaned to her by Vera from the theatrical crowd. She had only read the first five pages when Manny approached carrying fishing rods and tackle.

He held out a fishing rod. "Come on. Let's see if we can catch supper. There should be plenty of mahseer in these waters."

Kate reluctantly put down her book.

"Come on," Manny called, setting off along the bank.

They stopped on a sandy beach half a mile from camp and cast their lines, Manny chattering and laughing heartily at his funny anecdotes. Hearing splashes further up river, they fell silent. Something large was moving through the water. A bull elephant appeared forty yards away from around a bend. He trumpeted and banged his trunk on the water.

Manny took hold of Kate's elbow. "Stay absolutely still."

The elephant flapped his ears and banged his trunk on the water. Then his trunk curled up and his ears flattened against his head.

"He's going to charge! Run!" Manny shouted as the elephant broke into a run. "Up that tree!"

The two ran to a large banyan, the nearest tall tree. Manny shoved Kate up into the fork and scrambled to join her as the elephant reached them.

"Climb further up," yelled Manny, hastily settling himself near her.

"What now?" Kate asked, panting for breath.

"We wait until he gets tired of the chase."

Scared and shaken, Kate looked down at the angry elephant kicking up dust with his foot and straining to reach them with his trunk. "How long will that take?"

"Don't know. Could be a few minutes. Could be a few hours. See the discharge from the glands at the corners of his eyes. That means he's in *musth*. His mating hormones are running rampant and he's highly dangerous and aggressive. We should settle in for a long wait."

The elephant raged and fumed below for an hour and a half. Trapped under the early afternoon sun, their dry mouths felt full of cotton. They mopped sweat from their foreheads with their handkerchiefs.

Manny pointed at the river. "Damned silly thing to do—not grabbing the water bottles."

Eyes looked at the bottles lying on the riverbank, mocking their thirst. Their attention turned to the elephant below as enraged now as he had been when they first clambered up the tree.

Kate moaned. "Will the brute never tire of his sport and leave?"

Two shots rang out. The elephant whirled away, startled. Another shot, and he was off through the brush.

Two men walked into view, a black Labrador at their heels. The dark-haired European, with broad shoulders and athletic build, clad in bush shirt and shorts was accompanied by a shorter Burman. They approached the tree.

Manny leapt down. Kate scrambled down the boughs as far as she could in order to make the jump. The European stepped forward, reached up and put his hands around Kate's waist to help her down.

"Thank you," she said, looking into his hazel eyes and smiling face with its lop-sided grin.

"Some pickle you got yourselves into," he said.

"So pleased you came along. He's been holding us prisoner for almost two hours." Manny held out his hand. "Norman Manton, Deputy Conservator of Forests with the Burma Forest Department. Please call me Manny."

Their rescuer shook Manny's hand. "Jack Bellamy, Forestry Manager with Foucar Brothers." Bellamy turned to Kate. "And this is? Well, I'll be blowed! That *is* a surprise." he said on seeing his dog pushing Kate's hand with its head, asking to be petted. "Bess has always been a one-man dog until now."

Manny introduced Kate. "Kate Cavanagh, a family friend."

Bellamy touched the brim of his hat and grinned knowingly at Kate. "I see."

Kate saw the gleam in his eyes, apparently liking what he was seeing, then appraising the situation, wondering what she was doing in the jungle with a man twenty years her senior. She bristled at the insinuating tone of his voice. You don't see at all, Mr. Jack-jump-to-conclusions-Bellamy.

"We were hoping to make camp in the clearing where you are, but you beat us to it," Bellamy said.

With a flip of his wrist, Manny waved away Jack Bellamy's concerns. "Oh, don't worry, there's plenty of room for you, too. Let's head back. This rescue deserves a drink, don't you think?"

They settled into camp chairs over gin and tonic for Kate and whisky and water for the men. As Sandeep removed Manny's fishing basket and rod to the servant quarters, Manny recounted their adventure with the elephant. Jack was only half-listening. He couldn't take his eyes off Kate.

"Remember, Kate?" Manny said, "You couldn't believe they'd be dangerous when you had your first sighting of an elephant herd."

Kate laughed. "Well, I certainly know now." She turned to the man whose eyes she had been avoiding. "I want to thank you for saving us. We were getting awfully thirsty."

"I'm not in the habit of rescuing damsels in distress. Perhaps I should try it more often."

Manny watched this exchange, put his empty glass on the small table and got to his feet. "Well, this won't catch supper. I'll leave you two to talk. You'll stay for dinner tonight, won't you, Jack?"

"Only if you'll have dinner with me tomorrow."

"Done."

With that, Manny called Sandeep to bring his fishing gear. Manny slipped his fishing creel strap over his head, picked up his rod, and set off to catch some fish.

Jack scratched Bess' ears as he talked. "I was quite taken aback to discover a young white woman in the jungle. I've made many tours working for Foucar Brothers, and this is the first time it's happened. What are you doing here?"

"Manny brought me. He enjoys my company," Kate said, smiling sweetly. *I wonder what you'll make of that, Mr. Jack Bellamy.* She was disappointed to see Jack Bellamy kept his face neutral.

"I'm from the north-east of England, a small coastal town, Whitby. Where are you from?" he asked.

"Richmond, on the outskirts of London."

Jack stayed silent, but Kate did not volunteer more information about herself.

"Been in Burma long?" he asked.

"A little over a year."

"How did you meet Manny?"

At that moment, Jack's camp elephants arrived, and the question was left unanswered.

"I'd better go and tell my men where to set up camp. See you later."

Kate found her book and settled down to read then put it in her lap. Her mind was on their rescuer; *he really was quite attractive, but so annoying. What nerve, assuming I'm Manny's mistress! Well, I won't be correcting his presumptions.*

Two hours later, Manny returned. He proceeded straight to Kate. Sandeep followed behind carrying a nine-pound mahseer. "Sandeep, hold up the fish for the *thakin-ma* to see."

Kate gave her approval.

"Did Jack leave? Pity, I wanted to show off my catch. It will make a fine supper, won't it?"

"It's a prize catch, Manny."

"He put up a good fight." Manny was glowing. His fishing success had put him in good spirits. "Take the fish to the cook," he told Sandeep, "then bring me a whisky and water, will you?"

Over dinner Manny regaled Jack with his repertoire of colorful stories. It worked well. Jack was a good listener and Manny an expansive host. With the meal over, they moved to sit by a log fire. Before Manny could catch his breath to tell his tiger hunt stories, Kate asked Jack, "How long have you been in Burma?"

"About eleven years."

The logs crackled. Flickers of light played over their faces.

"It's a lonely life, isn't it?" Manny said, keeping his attention on the fire. "It takes a special kind of man to deal with the isolation and self-sufficiency required of a forest manager."

"It was lonely at first, but then I met a wonderful woman and made her my wife."

Kate hid her disappointment by poking the fire with a stick. *I shouldn't be surprised that he's married. Some women would consider him attractive.*

"I've known some men who occasionally take their wives with them on tour," Manny said. "Do you ever . . ?"

"I did . . . sometimes. But my wife died eighteen months ago."

"I'm sorry to hear it." Manny stood up. "Well, I'll turn in. Don't let my going drag the pair of you away from the fire."

"I think I'll turn in too. It's been a long day what with one thing and another," Kate said. "Good night, Jack. Good night, Manny."

Both men watched Kate walk to the rest-house.

Over breakfast next morning, Manny said, as casually as he could, "Jack seemed to be showing some interest in you last night. He's a handsome fellow. I was surprised you chose not to stay by the campfire to continue talking with him."

"You wouldn't be trying to pair me off with him, would you? Don't waste your time. This is a passing encounter. We'll probably never see one another again."

Manny went off after breakfast to make a tour of inspection. Kate remained in camp to relax and read. That night, dinner was in Jack's camp. Kate was amazed at the quality of the meal.

A meal on tour with Manny consisted of bland, canned vegetables and soup often served with canned meat. Jack's cook, in the middle of the jungle, had produced a gourmet meal—homemade soup, herb roast guinea fowl and fresh vegetables in a sauce.

A taste of the soup and Kate could not contain herself. "This meal's delicious, Jack! How on earth did your cook manage it?"

Jack grinned. "Tricks of the trade."

At nine o'clock sharp, Manny rose to go to bed. "I'll see you in the morning before you move off, Jack. See you at breakfast, Kate. Good night."

Relaxed and content, Jack and Kate stayed by the fire.

"How did you wind up in Burma?" Jack asked

"Oh, I wanted to make a fresh start, try something new."

"What was wrong with the old?"

Kate stayed silent a long time before she managed to say, "I lost my son . . . and husband . . . unexpectedly."

"I'm sorry, Kate. When did it happen?"

"Eighteen months ago. That's when I decided to leave England. My brother's friend arranged for Manny, his uncle, to take me under his wing for a while. Manny's a confirmed bachelor. I've been feeling it's an imposition to take advantage of his hospitality for so long, but when I suggest I should move into my own accommodation, he says there's no rush, and I should stay a little longer."

Her words triggered a lightness in him, like a canary escaping its cage. He slowly exhaled, put his glass on the table and smiled. She's not his mistress!

4

Next morning, after Manny and Jack had a private talk and hands were shaken all around, Bess licked Kate's hand in affectionate farewell, and the two parties went their separate ways.

Kate gave only a little thought to Jack Bellamy. He had a maturity and depth missing from most of the men she met in Rangoon, but all it had been was a pleasant jungle interlude with no future.

Three days later, she and Manny were walking near a village. The headman came to greet them. Following him down the path at an ungainly gallop was a tawny, probably four-month-old puppy. It stood on its hind legs, front paws reaching up Kate's leg. Kate picked it up. The pup nuzzled her neck, then wriggled, licked her face, and captured her heart. Having seen what a good companion Bess was to Jack Bellamy, Kate thought a dog would help to fill the void in her life.

"Manny, does this pup belong to anyone? I'd love to have him."

"Village dog," the headman said. "Belong no one. Take, if want."

Manny tried to remove the pup from Kate's arms. "Oh no, he won't be an adorable puppy for long. It's a pariah dog. It'll grow up scrawny and ugly and full of diseases."

"Please, Manny, lend me a rupee. He'll be good company for me. Please."

Manny reluctantly pulled a rupee from his pocket and paid the headman, who found a piece of rope to tie around the pup's neck. Kate was delighted and led the dog away.

"I'm pleased as punch, so I'm going to call him Punch."

Manny, uncommonly quiet, merely shook his head and frowned. That evening, as they sat by the campfire, Manny again broached the subject of the dog.

"What do you know about rabies?"

"Only what I read in my textbooks when I was nursing."

"I'm sure you think I'm making a terrible fuss about the pup, but for anyone who lives in the Far East, rabies strikes fear deep into the heart. I've known people who contracted this terrible disease after being bitten by one of these dogs—and there's no cure. I can tell you from personal experience, it's heartbreaking to see a friend who has been vigorous and intelligent suddenly become a slavering lunatic."

"You're scaring me."

"I mean to. You can't take these things too lightly."

Kate stroked the pup's head. "But Punch looks healthy enough. He must be all right."

On the return journey, the pup wormed his way into Manny's affections as well as Kate's with his amusing antics and loving nature.

In Rangoon, Punch settled in, growing into an attractive smooth-haired dog. Manny grew attached to him. Kate adored him. He was friendly and well behaved, but the servants, aware he had been a village dog, kept their distance, scowling in displeasure at Kate's bringing a pariah dog into the house.

One morning, a few weeks later, a diabolical yowl had Kate and Manny rushing onto the veranda in time to see Punch racing through the garden then spinning around in circles as if having a fit.

"Get back in the house and lock the door!" Manny yelled at Kate. "Your dog's gone mad."

As Kate watched in horror from the window, Manny watched from the veranda and looked on as the dog calmed down and returned to normal.

Manny entered the house and went to the telephone. "It might only be a fit, but I'll send for the vet to make sure."

Kate found a blanket and scooped the trembling dog into her arms. Punch was still shaking and panting when the vet arrived.

The vet examined Punch. "I'm sure he'll be all right. I think it was a bout of hysteria. I've given him a sedative, and I'll call back tomorrow."

With the nervous servants refusing to go anywhere near Punch and going about their work muttering darkly about the *youdi quai*, mad dog, Kate tied up Punch in her room to ease their worries and keep him safe. He was sleeping on a blanket in the corner when she left to go to a party that evening. She returned in the early hours to discover all the soft furnishings and her mattress ripped to shreds. In a panic she searched for Punch and found him cowering at the back of her wardrobe. Saliva drooled from his mouth.

"Oh, Punch!" Tears welled up in her eyes.

She took hold of a suitcase and used it to herd the dog into the corner of the room without touching him. She brought another suitcase and a chair to barricade him in. Then she sat, brokenhearted, on her tattered bed. The vet's got it wrong. Punch must have rabies—and she began to sob.

Over breakfast, Kate told Manny about Punch.

Manny looked grim. "The vet will soon be here. I'll check your room, make sure the dog can't escape."

Half an hour later, the vet arrived to examine Punch.

After the examination, Manny took the vet to one side, to keep Kate out of earshot. "I'm not having the dog staying in the house in this state."

"You're right to be concerned, of course," the vet said, "although I'm not yet convinced that he has rabies. Will you be able to take him to the Louis Pasteur Institute for observation?"

"Yes, we'll do that. Thank God we live within driving distance of the only place in the country that can be of help."

"Keep me informed," the vet said.

Once the veterinary had gone, a grim-faced Manny reassured Kate, "I'll send the car back from the office to take you to the Institute. Cheer up. I'm sure he'll be all right. This is merely a precaution."

Kate nodded, too unhappy to speak.

When Manny's driver Kazi returned, Kate bundled Punch into a blanket, and they set off for the Louis Pasteur Institute. On the way, the pup had another fit. He wriggled and squirmed and tried to jump from the car. Kate struggled to hold on to him, wrapping the blanket tightly around the puppy, attempting to make him feel snug and safe. At the Institute, Punch was taken away and placed in a wire cage. He shrank into a rear corner.

"I'll return this evening," Kate told the attendant. "Take good care of him." She hurried away before she started to cry.

That evening, Kate found Punch's condition had deteriorated. She squatted down in front of the cage, talked to him, tried to tempt him to come forward, but the pup cowered in the corner. He did not wag his tail at her voice, neither did he appear to recognize her.

"Oh, Punch. I can't bear to see you suffering like this. I'm so sorry. It's time to put you to sleep. Goodbye, precious."

Dabbing her tears, Kate found the attendant. "My dog is too sick. It's time to end his suffering. Please be gentle when you do it."

"We'll perform a post-mortem and have the results for you tomorrow."

Next morning, Kate and Mya Sandi were sorting through her wardrobe when the Director of the Institute telephoned. Punch had been rabid.

Kate slumped in a chair, stunned. Sorrow at the loss of her pet was replaced by worry that she might be infected. Agitated and unsettled, she paced around the living room all day, unable to read or listen to the wireless. She was relieved to hear Manny's car pull up.

"What was the result of the post-mortem?" he asked as soon as he entered the house.

"Punch was rabid."

Manny reacted to the news with a sharp intake of breath and a sudden ashen complexion.

"Did he lick you? Have you any scratches that the saliva could have got into?"

"No. Really, Manny, I'm fine," Kate reassured him repeatedly throughout the evening, but she kept catching him studying her.

She went to bed and when she undressed, gave herself a thorough examination. She chewed her lip in dismay on discovering just how many small cuts and nicks she had on her legs and arms. Kate spent the early hours rolling in the sheets unable to sleep. She tried to remember what her textbooks had said and recalled Manny's description of the death of a friend from rabies. At three in the morning, filled with terror, she was walking through the house. As she turned into the living room, a shadow fell across her path.

"Manny! I almost jumped out of my skin."

"Couldn't sleep. Neither could you by the looks of it."

"Silly, isn't it?"

"Damned ridiculous."

"Sorry if I disturbed you. I'll go back to bed now. Goodnight," Kate said.

She started to leave the room, thought better of it and turned back to Manny.

Simultaneously, they spoke.

"I think you should have the injections."

"I'd feel happier if I went for the treatment, Manny."

They laughed, relieved.

"Good idea," they said together and laughed again.

"I'll take you in the morning."

Kate touched Manny's arm softly. "Thank you."

Fourteen extremely painful injections into the abdomen, one a day for two weeks, was the treatment. How Kate wished she had listened to Manny's warning about the dog. Feeling sorry for herself, she wiped away her tears. All too painful. The injections. The loss of the servants' friendliness. Loss of playful Punch. Loss of Joey. Too much loss. Too much pain. The treatments left her depressed, but Manny had his own antidote to her misery.

Insisting she ride with him each morning, he would sputter, "Doctors! They'd have you succumb to any minor ailment if they had their way."

"The doctors want me to lead a quiet life for a while," Kate said.

"You mustn't give in," he admonished her. "A morning ride will set you up for the day, keep your spirits up."

Kate complied, wondering if Manny was so wrapped up in his own world, he had little consideration for anybody but himself, or whether he really thought he was doing what was best for her. She only knew this was not the best way to enjoy Christmas, only four days away, and right now, she wanted more than anything to be back in England with her family.

5

Once the ex-pat community had recovered from the hectic Christmas and New Year celebrations, it was full steam ahead for the Amateur Dramatic Society's rehearsals of *Lady Windermere's Fan*. Every week they met in the Gymkhana's hall. Everyone now knew their lines, having worked hard to be ready for opening night in three weeks, when Easter was over.

Dudley clapped his hands to get the players' attention. "Kate, Vera, I'd like you to go over this scene again," he said. "Vera, dear, begin at, 'You have a child, Lady Windermere."

". . . You have a child, Lady Windermere," Vera began. "Go back to that child who even now, in pain or in joy, may be calling to you." Kate, as Lady Windermere, stood up. "God gave you that child," Vera's Mrs. Erlynne continued, passionate and pounding like a prohibitionist. "He will require from you that you make his life fine, that you watch over him. What answer will you make to God if his life is ruined through you? Back to your house, Lady Windermere—your husband loves you! He has never swerved for a moment from the love he bears for you. But even if he had a thousand loves, you must stay with your child. If he was harsh to you, you must stay with your child. If he ill-treated you, you must stay with your child. If he abandoned you, your place is with your child."

Kate in her role as Lady Windermere burst into tears and buried her face in her hands. Vera rushed to Kate. "Lady Windermere!"

Hot tears fell on Kate's cheeks. She didn't need to act this part of the play. The tears were real, for her real child, lost in abominable circumstances almost two years ago. Each time they ran through the scene, Dudley, ignorant of Kate's anguish was effusive in his praise. Tonight was no exception.

"Kate, you were positively wonderful. You have a rare talent. You touch your audiences' hearts. They could all weep with you. Superb acting!"

"Thank you, Dudley," Kate said, dabbing at her wet cheeks with her handkerchief. If only it were acting; it wouldn't tear me apart every time I go through it.

Daphne had wanted the main role, as usual. Dudley had insisted Kate have it, although she didn't care if Daphne got it. However, Daphne did. She had pouted and sulked for some weeks, but after spraining her ankle, she finally accepted that it was not to be.

"Who's for a nightcap at the Yacht Club?" Dudley asked.

"Good idea," Kate said.

Bob caught Kate's eye. "I'm in."

The play's prompter and understudy, Daphne, said, "Count me in."

It was obvious to all that Daphne had been interested in recent-arrival-in-Rangoon Bob Watson for some time, but so far, he had not taken a serious look at her. Kate hoped Bob would soon notice the poor woman and put her out of her misery.

The cast piled into cars for the short drive. Seeing there was no room in the Winthrop's sedan, Daphne joined Kate in Dudley's Austin. Teddy and Grace Winthrop took Vera Smythe and Bob, who, once they were underway, asked, "I haven't seen Kate with a steady boyfriend. Do you know if she's available for dating?"

Vera looked out of the car window. Her lips formed a tight line.

Grace turned around in her seat to face Bob. "Oh, darling, normally, I would warn that you have to be quick, before she's snapped up by some lonely Englishman looking for a wife."

Bob nodded. "I've already discovered there's a shortage of the fair sex in Burma, but with Kate, well, I've watched her. I don't think she's in a hurry to find a husband, is she?"

"Possibly not," Vera said. "She's a widow. Lost her husband and son in a tragic accident. I think she's still grieving. You may want to consider some other young lady."

Teddy looked at Bob through the rearview mirror. "Ask her out. She has to get over it sooner or later—and she's a fine-looking woman."

Vera shook her head and returned to looking out the window. The tight lips formed again.

At the club, Bob joined Kate, Dudley, and Daphne. Vera wandered to another part of the room with the Winthrops. Kate was aware of Bob's growing interest in her. He was a man with no subterfuge, a man unable to hide his emotions. He had a pleasant face with intelligent blue eyes—attractive, with curly hair the color of straw.

Why not go out with him, Kate thought. I'm sure he'll be good company.

Kate raised her glass. "Cheers," she said tapping her glass with Bob's. "How are you adapting to Rangoon?"

"Adapting very well. I've plenty of chaps from Steel Brothers and Company to go to all the cocktail parties, dances and dinners with. I'd appreciate more female companionship, there aren't many English girls around, and I'm not a big drinker. Going out and having a few is becoming old hat. It's why I joined the amateur dramatics."

Daphne touched Bob's sleeve. "It's such fun, isn't it? Nice crowd and everything."

"We're very glad you became involved," said Dudley. "Excuse me, I must go and talk to some other cast members. Coming, Daphne?"

Kate noted Daphne's annoyed frown as Dudley took her arm to propel her across the room. Kate looked down to hide her smile. It would seem Dudley was ensuring she and Bob had some privacy. They watched him steer Daphne across the room then turned to one another again.

"An attractive woman such as yourself must be swamped with dates," Bob said.

"Hardly," Kate said, with a laugh.

Bob's expression was skeptical.

"All right. I can have as many dates as I like—and I do—nothing serious, pleasant evenings spent with good friends."

"Could I be a good friend?"

Kate smiled. "Why not? But I warn you, all I can offer is friendship and flirtation. If you're looking to settle down with someone, you need to date a woman who wants that too."

"You're very blunt, Kate."

"It stops life being complicated."

Bob held up his drink. "Here's to life being uncomplicated. At least, until I can persuade you feel differently."

Kate picked up her glass and smiled. "Here's to life remaining uncomplicated."

Kate and Bob's heads were close. They laughed a lot as they shared childhood stories and experiences in their new country and decided where to go on their first outing together. Then Dudley returned, followed by Daphne.

"Came to offer you a ride home, Kate. Do you need one?" Dudley asked.

Kate looked to Bob. "Do I need one?"

"Afraid so, Kate. I'm without a vehicle tonight. I'll have one for our date tomorrow though."

Kate smiled. "See you at seven."

Kate noticed Daphne had grown sullen. Green with envy, I would say. Kate had no qualms about leaving Daphne alone with Bob. She was not romantically involved with him and was not worried about Daphne trying to land him as a husband. If that's the way it went, so be it.

On the way home, Dudley babbled on about how pleased he was with the play. "Can't believe the only acting you had done was in a school play until *Land's End*. You missed your vocation, Kate."

"I don't think I'd like to be an actress," Kate said. Although I'm the best actress you'll ever know, dear Dudley.

Dudley waited in the car until Kate was safely inside the house then drove away. Before she could turn on the light, a cold nose nuzzled her hand. She gasped in fright, fumbled for the light switch and stared in amazement at the black Labrador heartily wagging its tail. Kate glanced around the room and back to the dog.

"Bess? What are you doing here?" Kate petted Bess, wondering why Jack Bellamy's dog was in the house. She was almost curious enough to wake Manny but thought better of it.

The next morning at breakfast, she asked Manny.

Manny buttered his crispbread. "Oh, the dog."

"Yes. Bess. How did she get here?"

Kate waited impatiently for Manny to finish chewing his crispbread. A thought crossed her mind. Did Jack have to get rid of Bess? Has Manny taken her in to replace Punch?

Finally, Manny swallowed his crispbread. "Jack and I arranged for Bess to come here when we met on our last tour."

"But why?"

"He got the idea when he saw how well Bess responded to you. Jack's gone on leave to Calcutta. He needed someone he trusts to take care of Bess while he's away. "I'm glad I told him it would be all right to leave Bess here. It will help you get over losing Punch. I know you miss him."

"Oh, I see." Kate said, failing to hide her disappointment. "When did he come by?"

"Last night while you were out. He seemed as disappointed as you are now."

Kate tossed her head. "I'm not disappointed!"

Manny smiled. "He'll be back at the end of April to pick her up. Pity you missed him, but I dare say you'll see him when he comes to collect Bess." Manny stood up and dropped his napkin on the table. "Finished your breakfast? Let's go for our ride."

6

Kate enjoyed having Bess around. They went for long walks, played "fetch," and shared companionable silences with Bess lying by Kate's feet as she read a book. A week later, Kate became concerned. Bess did not seem well. She struggled to her feet after lying down. Her breathing was labored, and she couldn't walk far. She was obviously ill.

Kate asked Kazi, to drive them to the vet's office. After examining Bess, the vet shook his head. "She has pneumonia. It's very bad. I doubt she'll pull through. I'll give her an injection. She's going to need intense nursing to have any chance."

Kate's chin trembled, then she squared her shoulders. "I'll see to it."

They returned home. Kate showed the servants where to make a bed for Bess in her bedroom, then Kazi and Sandeep gently brought Bess from the car. She called Mya Sandi. In faltering Burmese, Kate asked to see the medicines in the house. Mya Sandi took her to Sandeep, who led them to a medicine chest in Manny's room. Kate found a eucalyptus chest rub and told the servant to bring some brandy. Then she changed into some old clothes, found a blanket, and settled beside Bess. She rubbed the dog's chest with the eucalyptus mixture and dosed her with a teaspoon of brandy every half hour, determined to keep the dog alive. She had lost Punch, her mother, and her son and Jack had lost his wife. Enough was enough. She would not allow Jack to lose Bess too.

On returning from work, Manny saw Bess' ailing condition and heard about the vet's pessimistic prognosis. He patted Kate's shoulder. "Don't get your hopes up."

"But she's not there yet, and come what may, I'm going to do the best I can to save her. It's time to put my nursing skills to use."

"If you like, I'll watch her later when you go out."

"I'm not letting Bess out of my sight. I've cancelled my date with Bob and all my other appointments until she recovers. No need to look so surprised. They were disappointed but very understanding. I warned Dudley I may drop out of the play, which upset him no end, but my understudy, Daphne, will delighted."

Manny managed to persuade Kate to eat at the dinner table and listen to his opinions about the allies besieged at Tobruk before she excused herself to return to Bess' side. At bedtime, Kate was still ministering to the dog.

Manny stood in the doorway. "You should sleep."

Kate nodded. "I'll go to bed later."

"You should also go on with the play. You're involved in a small community of ex-pats. If you let people down and ruffle their feathers, you'll be ostracized. And that, my dear, is not a pleasant experience. People can be very spiteful when they want to be. A lot of time and energy has been put into that production. If you back out of the play for the sake of nursing a sick dog, you'll pay dearly for it. Your name will be mud. Besides, I heard you were marvelous in the part."

Kate tore her eyes away from Bess and looked up at Manny. "You're right. I shouldn't let the cast down, but I know Daphne will do a good job, so no harm will be done."

"Forget Daphne; I'll take care of the dog. Call Dudley tomorrow and tell him you'll be available for your performances."

Kate laughed in surprise. "You! Look after Bess? Now you've really got me worried."

Manny harrumphed. "All right, I'll get the servants to help me. See you at breakfast."

With Manny gone, Kate turned her full attention to Bess. "Come on, old girl," she encouraged. "My goodness, did you hear that? I'm beginning to sound like Manny. Come on. Don't give up on me. Jack will be back soon."

Throughout the night, Kate continued treating Bess. The few times Kate fell asleep, she woke up with a start, feeling guilty that she had lapsed in her care. She then worked harder on Bess, rubbing her chest, coaxing more brandy down her throat and pleading with tears in her eyes, "Please don't die. I couldn't bear it. I'm counting on you to pull through. Come on, try, Bess, try."

By morning, Bess' breathing seemed less labored, but when Manny urged Kate to change for their morning ride, she refused to leave the dog's side.

"This is too silly. You've done all you can. The dog will either make it or not."

"Manny, I'm not leaving Bess until she's on her feet and wagging her tail. I'd feel terrible if she wasn't here when Jack comes back from leave."

Manny shrugged. "First time I've been stood up for a dog," he muttered, leaving the room.

7

The small steamship carrying Jack, his six-year-old son David and daughter Pamela aged four, along with Upala, the children's *ayah,* sailed toward the Port of Calcutta, ninety miles up the Hooghly River from the Bay of Bengal. Jack was taking his children to visit his friends the Rodwells.

As they neared the wharfs, the children regarded the riverfront activity with interest. Except for departing Rangoon, they had never seen a busy port area in action.

David tugged at his father's trouser leg. "Look, Daddy, like ants," he said, pointing to a long line of coolies carrying heavy sacks on their heads. They were unloading a barge and taking the sacks into a warehouse, known as a go-down. The line going in was passed by a line of men returning to the barge for more sacks.

"Good way to describe them, David. They do look like an ant trail, and they are just as hardworking as ants."

Pamela pointed to a small sailboat. "That boat is full of melons, Daddy."

"So it is. See how they've managed to transport tons more melons in the boat by building a high bamboo framework. Ingenious."

They watched men in dhoti loincloths wade to the boat to fill their baskets with at least a dozen heavy watermelons that they carried ashore on their heads. Some people arrived in canoes to buy the melons straight off the boats. In other areas of the docks, coolies were unloading building bricks. They balanced along wobbly gang-planks, carrying fifteen bricks at a time on their heads to get them ashore.

On disembarking from the steamship, Jack and his family took a taxi to the Grand Hotel on Chowringhee, from where Jack phoned his friends, Bill and Rose Rodwell to tell them he had arrived in Calcutta.

The next day, he asked Upala to take the children to see Walt Disney's Pinocchio at the English-speaking cinema. He hadn't planned to go and watch it with them, but Pamela had other ideas.

She turned on the charm. "Please, Daddy, come and see it with us. I want you to see how his nose grows. Please, Daddy."

So, Jack joined them and enjoyed the film as much as the children and Upala. The song "When You Wish upon a Star" triggered an unease in Jack that took a while for him to figure out. There was a void in his life, and he was ready to fill it. A certain spirited, black-haired woman kept entering his thoughts. He still remembered how relieved he had been to hear she was not Manny's mistress. Sometime soon, he would do something about it, but this leave he wanted to enjoy his children.

Upala had other ideas. She took the children exploring by riding in trams around the city. They visited bazaars, parks and went to the cinema several more times.

"I think everyone loves Shirley Temple," Jack commented one morning on hearing they were off to the cinema that afternoon to see *The Little Princess*. "Upala, I'll be at the races with Mr. and Mrs. Rodwell today. Here is their home phone number should you have a problem."

Jack caught a taxi to the Rodwell's home. They were about twenty years older than he was, yet they had become firm friends. Bill was an administrator in the Burmese government when they met. With Bill married to Rose, an Anglo-Indian, and Jack married to Burmese Su Su Yi, they had a lot in common, especially presenting a united front should they come across any prejudice about their choice of spouses. When Bill's children, Henry and Maureen, were old enough to go to university, their parents had moved to Calcutta to be near their children attending the University there.

Rose was placing a fantastic creation of turquoise organza and ruffles on her head when he arrived. From there, Bill drove them to the Calcutta race course. Rose and Bill were members of the Royal Calcutta Turf Club; as such, they had access to the Reserved Stand, set aside for members and guests. They ordered Pimms and watched the horses being led around the pre-parade ring before being saddled.

"Do you want to place a bet, Jack?" Rose asked.

"Of course, which horse shall I pick?"

"Here's the list of runners, but I'd bet on Starlight."

Jack started. Rose's choice had Jack thinking again of a raven-haired beauty in Rangoon that he hardly knew. Is this an omen? The song "Wish upon a Star and now a horse called Starlight?

Rose handed Bill fifty rupees. "Put a bet on for me please, darling."

Jack went with Bill and put on a large bet.

When they returned to the members' bar, Rose was talking to a middle-aged couple, the Napiers and their daughter Audrey.

Introductions over, they settled down to enjoy the race. Bill had his binoculars around his neck.

"Which one is Starlight?" Jack asked, watching the horses parading.

"Starlight has the big white star on her forehead," Audrey said.

Jack smiled. "Of course, I should have realized. Do you come to the races often?"

"I come regularly, not often."

"Why is that?"

Audrey laughed. "I lead a busy social life." She took Jack's arm. "Come on, the horses are at the starting gate. The race is about to start."

The gates opened. Starlight was away with a head start. Thundering hooves passed the stands and Starlight stayed in the lead. Another horse edged up to Starlight's rump. Starlight's jockey urged his horse on. She surged forward, giving it her all and won by a length.

Jack raised his glass to Rose. "Cheers, Rose, your tip made me a fortune!"

The evening was spent at the Calcutta Club. With Rose being Anglo-Indian, it was the only club Bill and Rose would use because of its non-racial policy. Over dinner, Rose said, "It has been lovely to see you after all these years. You're looking well."

"Thank you, I'm feeling fine. However, I should be honest, if war hadn't broken out in Europe, I would have taken Pamela and David to England to meet their British relatives and show them the small fishing town of Whitby on the Northeast coast of England where I grew up. Unfortunately, and fortunately, the war required a change of plan."

As soon as fresh drinks were served, Rose, not one to mince words, asked Jack, "Have you given any thought to remarrying yet?"

"Not particularly."

"It's about time you did. You're a young, handsome man, too young to be alone. You need a wife. Your children need a mother. Audrey's a very sweet woman."

Jack could see from Bill's flushed face and his looking at the palms behind Rose that he was embarrassed by his wife's forthrightness. Nevertheless, Bill said, "Every man needs a companion. Has there been no one of interest since Su Su Yi died?"

So, Bill's in on this too.

Jack wasn't sure if it was the excellent Scotch that loosened his tongue, but, staring into his cut crystal glass of golden liquid, his voice softened as he began telling them about a woman named Kate, a beautiful woman with long black hair. An English woman, a widow. He barely knew her. Only met her briefly, and he couldn't stop thinking about her. He wanted to know her better, but she lived in Rangoon, more than four hundred miles from his home in Maymyo.

The waiter brought more drinks.

Bill glanced at Rose, who seemed fascinated by Jack's dilemma and said, "How well do you need to know her now? Go exploring after you're married."

Rose sat up straight at her husband's words. "Wait a minute, Bill. Jack needs to be sure she won't hurt his children. That she's kind and warm-hearted. Interesting to talk with. Honest and loyal."

Jack gulped down his drink. "She had a child, a son. He was killed. I don't know the details. All I know is, I would hate to return to Maymyo without her, and if I don't, I could easily lose her to another man."

When it was time to leave, Rose accompanied him into the hallway. While waiting for their car, she touched his arm and said, "You may want to return to Rangoon armed for the hunt."

Jack looked at her, puzzled.

Rose smiled. "If you're sure she's the one for you, best place to buy a ring is the Anglo-Swiss Watch Company. in Dalhousie Square East. There's bound to be a ring there she'll like."

Next day, Jack, Upala and the children went to the newspaper offices of *The Statesman*, where the Rodwell's son, Henry, was an editor. He had offered to show the children how newspapers were made from start to finish. He was young to be an editor, but his flair for the work and the quality of his writing had been recognized and rewarded.

Henry took David's and Pamela's hands and led them down the aisle to a reporter's paper-strewn, battered oak desk. "This is where reporters come back from gathering information and type up their stories Let's start with what people are writing about, shall we?" He introduced bespectacled Edwin Singh, a middle-aged Anglo-Indian with prematurely white hair, who told them he was writing a story about another riot that had happened.

David wrinkled his nose not understanding the word riot. "What's a riot, Mr. Singh?"

Jack smiled at Edwin Singh and turned David away before he could be told about people setting a police station on fire or planting bombs in various offices as part of the Quit India

Campaign to get the British out of India. "It's a fight that develops when people are dissatisfied with the government for some reason," Jack told his son. He sighed, relieved, when David seemed to find that explanation acceptable.

Henry took them to see the printing press. The room was large. Pamela stood close to Upala and pulled on Jack's hand. "The machine is very big and noisy, Daddy."

"Let's see what the print-setter is doing," Henry said, leading them to a room off the large printing room. He took them to where an Indian employee was placing little metal letters in lines to create columns of text for the printing press. Henry explained his intricate job to the children, then returned them to the printing press to watch the newspapers being printed, folded and dispatched onto a conveyor belt.

Pamela clapped her hands. David's eyes shone. "Is this what happens so you can get your newspaper, Daddy?"

"Yes, it is. A lot of work goes on behind the scenes to make everyday items for us to buy."

Henry led the way back to the journalists' office. "Did you find it interesting?"

The children nodded their heads.

"More importantly, did you learn something today?"

Again, the children nodded their heads. "Thank you, Mr. Rodwell."

"Call me Uncle Henry. I'll see you again before you go home."

Jack stood with his family on the platform at Rangoon's large Victorian railway station, saying goodbye to Pamela and David, who were traveling home to Maymyo with Upala. The children were disappointed he was not returning with them.

"Yes, I know it's not the best way to end our trip, but we had a marvelous time in Calcutta, didn't we? It was very different from Maymyo. And then sailing back to Rangoon on a calm sea was pleasant, and so was seeing the flying fish and porpoises alongside the ship."

"I liked seeing the fish, Daddy," Pamela said.

He felt conscience-stricken at leaving them to finish their journey without him, but he had business in Rangoon to attend to and with only two weeks to seal the deal, he needed to focus without distraction.

Once they boarded the train, he placed the two suitcases on the rack and told them to be good for Upala. "I'll be home soon. Upala, Nyan Sein will collect you from the station."

"Don't worry, I'll take care of things, *thakin.*"

Bess slowly improved. With the dog out of danger and on the mend, Kate resumed rehearsal's and caught up with her social life.

Then Jack phoned. Manny took the call.

"Bess has been no trouble. I'm sure you would like to see her as soon as possible. So, you are spending a week or two in Rangoon before returning to Maymyo. That's interesting. Would you like to come to dinner tomorrow? Good. Kate will be here. We'll see you at 6:30."

When Kate returned from her date with Bob Watson, Manny told her, "I invited Jack Bellamy to dinner tomorrow night."

"Oh! I arranged to meet the crowd at the Yacht Club dance. Maybe I should cancel. I'll need to tell Jack that Bess is not one hundred percent yet."

Manny observed Kate over his newspaper. "Yes, good idea. I'm sure Jack will want to thank you personally for taking such good care of Bess."

"Yes. You're right. I'll cancel."

Manny disappeared behind his newspaper.

Kate studied the newspaper Manny was holding up. Did I see the glimmer of a smile before the paper hid his face?

Next evening, Kate kept changing dresses, unable to decide what to wear.

"This one, *thakin-ma?*" Mya Sandi asked. "It goes well with your black hair."

She held up a garnet colored dress with a cowl neckline and swirling taffeta skirt. Kate held it to her and studied herself in the mirror.

She handed it back to Mya Sandi. "Too sophisticated for dinner at home."

"You are taking much trouble for an evening at home, *thakin-ma*," Mya Sandi said, with an impish grin.

Kate tilted up her nose then picked a dress the color of golden sand with a black belt and black piping around the collar, turned up sleeves and pockets.

"Perfect," Kate said. "Smart, understated, elegance."

She caught Mya Sandi looking at her with amusement. "Why are you looking at me like that?" she asked with mock indignation.

"No reason, *thakin-ma*," Mya Sandi replied with a giggle.

"I'm making too much fuss about this, aren't I?" Why? Kate shrugged, shook her head, and went to the living room. Jack had already arrived. With Bess glued to his side, he was sitting in an armchair across from Manny, who was regaling him with his opinions on the progress of the war in Africa. Both men held a glass of Scotch.

"Ah, there you are," Manny said as Kate entered the room. Jack stood.

Kate's cheeks reddened under his appreciative stare.

"Good evening, Kate."

Kate's heart was fluttering. "Hello, Jack."

Manny put his glass down. "I'm afraid I have to disappoint you both. I'm feeling a bit queasy today, so I told the cook not to bother. Sorry to let you down. I didn't want to spoil your evening, so I made reservations for you at The Golden Garden. You two will have to go out to dinner without me. I hope that meets with your approval."

Kate and Jack looked at each other in surprise. Exasperated, Kate raised her eyes to the ceiling then looked at the floor. She turned beetroot red with embarrassment at Manny's maneuverings. Her eyes flashing daggers, she tried to laugh it off, and said, "That was rather sudden, wasn't it?"

Jack looked delighted. He seemed to be taking the change of plan in his stride. "I'm so sorry you're not well, Manny. It was kind of you to make a reservation at The Golden Garden."

"I'll see *you* later," Kate told Manny.

Ignoring her threatening tone, Manny cheerfully responded, "Off you go. Have a good time." He took hold of Bess' collar. "She'll be fine with me until you return."

Jack squatted down and patted Bess. "See you later, girl." He looked at Kate with a grin. "Shall we?" he asked, taking her arm.

As they descended the veranda steps, Kate apologized. "Jack, I'm so embarrassed. Manny's maneuverings were hideously obvious, weren't they? You don't really have to take me out to dinner. You can drop me at the Yacht Club instead."

"It would be a pity to waste reservations for one of the best restaurants in Rangoon. Wouldn't you like to dine with me? I'd like to dine with you."

Kate paused to study Jack as he held the Wolseley's door open for her. "All right," she said, light-heartedly. "Let's not disappoint the old rascal."

8

At the restaurant, they were seated at a table in a cozy corner. Kate looked about her. Golden-fringed Chinese lanterns provided subdued, romantic, lighting. Gold and red candles lit the tables. Mouthwatering culinary aromas wafted by as waiters carried food past their table. The low hum of conversations filled the room. The prohibitive social mores of mixing socially with other races was less prevalent in Burma compared to India, Manny had told her soon after her arrival. Kate could see this as she looked around. Tables were filled with government officials and smartly dressed Chinese and Anglo Indians seated together.

Jack checked out what Kate was looking at. "This is how it should be; people of different races being able to live and dine together without being subject to rancor. I visited my friends in Calcutta and because Rose is Anglo-Indian, Bill is careful about where they choose to dine and which clubs will have them as members. Some clubs don't admit people of mixed race, as if that's of any importance!"

"I've never really understood these dividing lines. I didn't mix with foreigners in England, but that was because there weren't any about." Kate sipped her wine and focused on Jack. "You told me you were from Yorkshire?"

Jack's eyebrows lifted. "You're full of surprises. I didn't think you'd remember."

"It's a long way from Yorkshire to the wilds of Burma."

"My grandfather pushed me to go to Cambridge University. He was disappointed I opted for a degree in Forestry. I think he hoped for something more salubrious. But when I said I wanted to work for one of the timber firms in Burma, he arranged an interview with Foucar Brothers through an acquaintance, and here I am. Been here eleven years, man and boy."

"Do you intend to stay here or will you eventually return to England?"

"At the moment, I've no plans to return to England. I would have gone home this leave to introduce my children to their English relatives, but the war put the kibosh on that. So, I took them to visit my friends, the Rodwells, in Calcutta instead."

Kate was about to ask another question, when Jack asked, "How about you? How long do you intend staying in Burma?"

The waiter arrived with the Chinese egg soup, giving Kate time to think of her reply. "I have no plans. One day, I'll return to England to visit my family, but I have no definite intentions for the future."

As casually as he could, Jack said, "Taking it one day at a time?"

"Yes," Kate said. Her tight shoulders relaxed when she realized he was not going to ask questions she preferred to avoid.

"Manny told me how your nursing skills saved Bess' life. I wasn't aware you were a nurse. I can't thank you enough. Bess means a lot to me."

"I haven't worked as a nurse in years. Anyway, it felt good to be able to help Bess. Besides, you'd entrusted her to our care. You'd never have forgiven us if anything had happened to her."

"It would have been a hard loss to take. She's filled a void in my life since my wife died."

"It's hard to lose someone you love. Was your wife ill?"

Jack drank the last of his whisky. "Snakebite—I was away on tour."

Kate's voice was soft. "So, you never had a chance to say goodbye."

"No, I didn't."

They finished the soup in silence.

"What family do you have at home?" he asked.

"Mum died when I was young. I have my father, and I'm very close to my brother Andy and his wife Evelyn and their children. My father was upset when I left for Burma, but he has a new lease on life since he's taken on two boys, evacuees from the London bombing. They keep him on his toes, and he's busy teaching them about the countryside and how to grow vegetables. Andy has joined up. He's in the army, the Royal Engineers."

She said nothing about her deceased husband, son, or husband's side of the family.

"You said when we met that your husband and son died."

"Yes, an accident. I miss my son very much."

After a silence, Jack changed the subject, filling the remainder of the meal with lighthearted banter. They discussed Kate's involvement in amateur dramatics, life with Manny, Jack's experiences on his jungle tours, and his rescue of Kate and Manny from the angry elephant.

When the meal was over, Kate suggested they go on to the Yacht Club for a nightcap.

When they entered the club, Jack saw it as a good sign that both men and women greeted Kate with an equal amount of warmth. She obviously knew how to mix in, didn't ruffle feathers or cause jealousies with her relationships with the men in the group. Kate confirmed these assumptions by not hesitating to introduce him to her friends, both male and female. He cheered instantly, thinking she could not be so relaxed in her introductions and have a special relationship with any man there.

A man at the bar hailed Jack, who took hold of Kate's hand. "Come meet my friend, Herbert Billings. He works for Steel Brothers."

They arrived by Herbert's side. "I didn't know you were coming here tonight, Herbert. Meet my friend Kate Cavanagh."

"Good evening Kate." Herbert put his hand to his mouth to speak in a stage whisper to Jack. "I've often seen Kate around. She tends to stay close to the fun-loving amateur dramatics crowd, not fuddy-duddy clerks like me."

Kate feigned being slighted. "Herbert! Is that how you see me? I'm about to introduce Jack to my acting friends. Why don't you join us?"

"Thanks for the invite, but," Herbert nodded to the two men sitting beside him, "my friends and I are leaving as soon as we've finished our drinks. Have to be up early for work, you know." Herbert winked at Jack. "Go and have some fun."

Jack and Kate joined her thespian friends at a table— Dudley, Daphne, Vera, Bob and the Winthrops. Introductions were pleasant, but Jack noticed Bob seemed dismayed that Kate was with him. After ordering drinks and some social chitchat, Jack whispered in Kate's ear. He stood and held out his hand for her then addressed the group. "If you'll excuse us, I'm going to show off my dancing skills to this attractive young woman. Come and join us?"

As Jack led Kate in a foxtrot, he asked, "Who's the Bob fellow? Have you been breaking his heart? He looks positively miserable, watching you with me."

"I've been out on a couple of dates with Bob. Nothing serious. He does seem to have fallen hard for me, but you must have noticed, Daphne can't wait to console him, and she's not giving Vera a chance with him either."

Her words were like ambrosia to his soul. Not sure when he stopped breathing, Jack let out his breath and, for the rest of the evening, he whirled Kate around the dance floor to waltzes, foxtrots, and quicksteps.

"You're a man of surprising talents, Jack Bellamy, capable of driving off raging elephants and dancing like Fred Astaire." Kate tilted her head back, revealing her smooth neck and throat as she giggled breathlessly with delight.

Jack struggled to control the urge to cover her neck with sensual kisses. "My mother insisted I learn to dance before going to Cambridge. I tried to get out of it, but she convinced me it would make me popular with the girls."

"Did it?"

Jack grinned. "I had my share of fun."

The small quartet began to play Jerome Kern's "**The Way You Look Tonight**." Jack pulled Kate close. Even when he felt her stiffen, he kept a firm grip while pressing his cheek to her hair. Kate's Jasmine perfume intoxicated him as much her closeness. Gradually, the tightness left her. His joy knew no bounds. She was succumbing to his charms. By the time the song ended, she seemed reluctant to pull away from him when he suggested returning to the table. An hour later, with their companions beginning to head for home, Jack and Kate bade everyone goodnight and took their leave.

Jack drove her home and opened the car door for her.

"I had a wonderful evening, Kate," Jack said, his voice soft.

Kate gave him a peck on the cheek and ran up the veranda steps then turned back. "So did I."

"Would you like to do it again?"

Kate dipped her head, looked from under her long eyelashes. "Yes."

As Jack bounded up the steps, Kate closed her eyes and waited to be kissed.

"Great. Tomorrow at eleven. We'll go to the zoo," he said, going past her to the door. "Mustn't forget Bess," he offered by way of explanation, leaving Kate open-mouthed on the doorstep.

Bess wriggled and wagged her tail, ecstatic to see him. Jack pounded her ribs. "Hello, Bess, old girl."

He turned his attention back to Kate. "Until tomorrow, then."

"At eleven," Kate said, her voice tight. "Goodnight."

She stepped inside and closed the door.

Jack grinned and followed Bess down the steps. "I think she's hooked," he told his tail-wagging dog.

9

Kate was rosy-cheeked from her morning ride with Manny and the effort of choosing an attractive dress to wear when Jack arrived. Her beauty took Jack's breath away. He stood thumb and first finger on his chin, admiring the purple fleur-de-lys patterned dress, which complemented her black hair and pink cheeks. "Madam looks absolutely stunning. Good color for you."

Kate curtsied. "Thank you, kind sir."

Outside, Jack ordered Bess to the rear seat, and wiped down the passenger seat before Kate got in.

"How come you have a car in Rangoon? Did you drive in?" asked Kate.

"No, Herbert, we met him last night, is letting me use it to chauffeur a very special person around town."

It took a moment for his words sink in. "Are you telling me you think I'm special?"

"Very," Jack said, giving her hand a quick squeeze.

He put the Austin into first gear. Her heart was pounding. Kate kept up a cheerful chatter on the way to the zoo, distracting herself from the effect of Jack's obvious interest in her. At least, she believed he was interested in her. Her feelings about him were confusing. Sometimes she felt almost giddy, thinking he was special enough to unlock her heart. Then other times, it was all business. He would be leaving soon. This was just a pleasant interlude, and then it would end.

Inside the zoo, he took her hand. She didn't pull away. "Nice place for a stroll," he said, indicating the attractive landscaping along the paths. Drawn by laughter and shrieks, they wandered towards the playground with Bess at Jack's heels. They stopped to watch exuberant youngsters enjoying a miniature train ride.

"I brought my children here a few days ago, before they returned home," Jack said. "We had a lot of fun. There's something special about miniature steam engines, isn't there?"

"How old are your children?"

"David is six, and Pamela is four."

"Too young to be losing their mother."

"They're bright, happy children. Upala, their *ayah,* who has been with us since David was born, has been a wonderful substitute mother. She loves them as if they were her own."

Jack paused before he spoke again. "How old was your son when he died?"

"Five."

"It must have been devastating."

Kate looked down. "Yes, it was."

Jack could barely hear her words. He squeezed her hand. They continued watching the excited children wave to their parents and *ayahs* from the circling train.

"I loved him so much," Kate said. "Joey was everything to me. My marriage . . . left a lot to be desired."

Kate felt he was absorbing her revelations and seemed to understand she was fragile and fearful of becoming close. He's a sensitive man!

They moved on to look at the lions and tigers in King Edward VII Carnivora House where Jack teased her that one of the lionesses kept eyeing her with an unhealthy interest. At the elephant house, he expressed his dismay at the distressed behavior of the large pachyderms swaying back and forth.

"Shouldn't be cooped up here. They need to be out in the wilds."

They went to look at the great hornbills, leopards, and other animals then headed to a small café by one of the lakes, where they ordered chicken sandwiches and ice cream for themselves and a dish of water for Bess.

"Would you marry again someday, have more children?" Jack asked her.

Kate studiously stirred her melting ice cream with her spoon. "I love children, and yes, I'd like to have another child—someday. She looked at Jack. "But first, I'd have to find a special man. Someone dependable who wouldn't let me down. Someone I can talk to, laugh with, share a life with."

Jack smiled. "I see you set high standards."

"I want only the best; won't settle for less," Kate said lightly.

Jack rubbed the small jeweler's box in his pocket. Plucking up his courage, he began his marriage proposal. "Bess has really taken to you . . ."

A large, noisy family swarmed to the next table. The baby was screaming and the children grouchy. The mother and the children's *ayah* hurriedly organized lemonade and ice cream for all.

Jack cast an irritated glance their way and sighed. He let go of the box and removed his hand from his pocket. "Shall we move?"

"They're probably tired and thirsty," Kate said, as they moved away.

They strolled around the exhibits. Kate enjoyed being with this charming man-about-town, but he seemed edgy and ill-at ease as though the noisy family had upset him.

"When we leave the zoo would you like to have dinner with me and then go to the cinema?" Jack asked.

"I'd like to," Kate said, "but tonight is the final performance of *Lady Windermere,* and I must be there."

"In that case, I must come to the play, and we can dine afterwards—if that's all right with you?"

"I'd like that, very much."

To great applause, the most enthusiastic from Jack, the curtain came down on the final performance of *Lady Windermere*. Kate slowly removed her stage make-up, changed out of her costume, giving herself time to recover from the draining emotions the lines had required of her. She and Jack joined the cast for a meal. Kate could see Daphne was delighted that Jack was Kate's date, which left the way open for Daphne to try and seduce Bob with her charms. Kate smiled at Bob, then caught a glimpse of Daphne's tight face when she noticed Bob sneaking lovesick glances Kate's way. She figured if Daphne was being more successful in her quest to win Bob over, she would look less jealous and a lot happier.

Jack and Kate left early. Pulling up outside Manny's house, he took Kate's chin in his hand and pulled her towards him. She responded to his long, sensual kiss, was elated when she heard him moan in pleasure.

The kiss left Kate breathless. She reluctantly pulled away. "Mmm, I think we'd better stop."

"What a spoil sport," Jack murmured, kissing her hand. "Are you free tomorrow?"

"Yes."

Jack got out of the car and opened the car door for her. "For lunch?"

He pulled her close. Kissed her deeply. "Wonderful. I'll be waiting."

They kissed once more. Feeling as if she was walking on air, Kate entered the house and shut the door. She leaned against the wall, touched her lips. That was some kiss, Jack Bellamy.

Outside, Jack tap-danced down the steps and bowed left and right to the empty street, before jumping into his car and driving away, singing at the top of his voice.

10

Manny spread butter on his crispbread. "How are things between you and Jack?"

"Very civilized and congenial."

"So, you'll be seeing him again?"

"Yes, lunch today and hopefully the rest of the time he's in Rangoon."

"He's a nice chap, good man, stands out in a crowd."

"I know."

"You could do a lot worse in a man. He's a special breed. He spends months in the forest, camping beneath the teak trees. That makes him rugged, practical and able to deal with any situation thrown at him."

Manny opened his mouth to say more, then clamped it shut.

Kate picked up her riding crop and stood up to put an end to Manny's sales pitch. "Ready when you are."

Manny folded his napkin and stood too. "Then let's be off."

At eleven thirty, Jack called for Kate. "How are you this fine morning, my darling Kate?"

"I feel on top of the world, my dearest Jack."

In the car, he asked, "Have you given any thought as to where we'll go? Have you seen the Shwedagon Paya?" referring to the golden domed pagoda, which dominated the city's skyline.

"I've been once before," Kate said. "Manny took me. It was the first thing I noticed when I first arrived in Rangoon."

"How about the reclining Buddha at Chaukhtatgyi? It's huge. Quite a sight."

"I haven't been there."

"Let's go there then," Jack said. "On the way, we'll stop at a tea shop I discovered near Scott market."

Jack found a spot to park near the tea shop where they drank Indian tea and ate vegetable samosas, rice noodles with fish and eggs and sweetened sticky rice. Outside, women shopped for groceries, street vendors sold tasty snacks, passers-by crowded the footpaths. Inside, the atmosphere was more serene, even with waitresses running in and out of the kitchen to bring food to the tables.

Kate was not ruffled by the well-worn décor and basic furniture. She settled at the scrubbed-bare, wooden table as if she ate in such places all the time.

"Good food, isn't it?" Jack said. "I like the way you seem to feel at home here, the club, the jungle, anywhere."

"I guess I'm a versatile woman, and the food *is* delicious. How did you find this place?"

"Herbert brought me here a couple of years ago. I come here every time I'm in Rangoon. When you've finished your sweet rice, we'll set off to see the Buddha."

Respecting Burmese custom, they removed their shoes to enter the Chaukhtatgyi Paya. Inside, they found a colossal figure of a reclining Buddha housed in a metal-roofed shed. The head towered fifty feet above them. The Buddha's robe was covered in gold leaf. On the surrounding platform, they discovered fortune-tellers offering palm and astrological readings. Kate sensed someone's eyes on her. She searched for the culprit and discovered a fortune-teller staring at her. He beckoned her to approach him. He wore an orange silk tunic and white turban and had a white goatee beard and piercing black eyes.

Kate indicated the man to Jack. "I think I'll get my fortune told. Have you ever . . . ?"

"No. I'm not sure I believe in it."

"Would you mind coming with me. I may need an interpreter. My Burmese is only so-so."

Jack followed Kate across the platform.

The palm reader indicated a chair. "Please to sit." He held out his brown, blue-veined hand and took Kate's long fingers. She glanced at Jack.

"You have traveled long way carrying ghosts," he said in clear English. "Now you halt, catch breath, before move on. Ahead, more journeys—some difficult. To come, times of great happiness and times of great despair. New beginnings. Good." The palmist looked at Jack. "This man, tied to you forever. He, man of great courage. Have no fear. This time different. Meant to be."

The reading left Kate confused. The fortune teller's mention of carrying ghosts? True! Despair and danger? I don't want it. And Jack, meant to be? Kate thanked the man and, with a shaky hand, handed over his fee.

As they walked away, Jack asked, "Do you believe what he told you? It seemed to me he made up everything."

Kate laughed. "Even the bit about you being a man of great courage?"

Jack burst into laughter. "Well, I mean, it stands out a mile, doesn't it?".

Kate laughed too. "It was only a bit of fun. However, if he really was a fraud, I'm sure he'd have found more comforting things to tell me than to warn of difficulties and despair. He'd have told me I would have a happy marriage and two or three children, and live happily ever after in a palace."

"Is that what you want?"

"Not the palace part, but children maybe—in time."

Kate sensed she had let Jack down. He quickened their pace to the 197-foot long reclining Buddha and stood in awe studying the statue's massive feet. Gold symbols decorated the soles, and toeprint swirls decorated his toes. Moving on to the Buddha's head, the comings and goings of a sparrow flying in and out of the statue's nostril, where the bird obviously had a nest, captured their attention.

"Well, that makes a change from snot coming out of a nose," Jack said.

Kate chuckled. "Jack, don't. Laughing could be considered disrespectful, even insulting."

"You're right, Kate. Stop it right now."

They both burst into laughter, hiding it behind their hands. They left the Chaukhtatgyi Paya to spend the remainder of the afternoon wandering around Scott market. It was housed in a large white building with mixed colonial and Asian architecture. The long aisles were crowded with end to end stalls offering gems and jewelry, carvings, food, clothing, anything to tempt people to spend their money. Kate and Jack looked at Burmese handicrafts. Kate liked that she was drawn to the same things as Jack. Several times when she picked up an object, such as an inlaid teak box or an ornate statue and drew his attention to it, she found he was holding up the same thing.

With dusk drawing in, Jack suggested going to Royal Lake to watch the sunset. They strolled around the lake until Jack approved the vantage point. They stood, waiting, Jack behind Kate, folding her in his arms. He pressed his lips to her hair. The sky blazed orange with purple streaks. They stood silently, watching the orange-tinged Shwedagon's golden reflection in the mirror-smooth lake.

As the great orb of the sun began to disappear beneath the horizon and with his cheek against her hair, Jack whispered, "Will you marry me?"

Kate froze. The only sound was lake water lapping against a nearby jetty. The sun gave one last effervescent flash before disappearing. Jack remained silent, holding her. Kate stared at the pink glow on the horizon. "I told you, I need a man I can depend on, a man I can trust who will be a true companion, a man who won't let me down."

Jack turned her towards him. "If it's as simple as that, then I'm your man. I'm loyal, hardworking and steadfast . . . and I love you."

"I don't want to be a substitute for your wife."

"You're not a replacement for my late wife. I loved her deeply for all the qualities that were special to her. Now I feel I'm the luckiest man alive to have met another wonderful woman, wonderful in her own unique way. You're strong, beautiful, independent. You've got courage and you've brought happiness back into my life. I ache with desire for you. Please say yes."

Kate stayed quiet. Conflicting feelings were ripping her apart. She had thought marriage to Charles would be warm and affectionate. Instead, she'd married a man who'd turned out to be a homosexual recluse, who'd turned into a monster and murdered her son.

But Jack is different, solid. I feel safe with him. Surely, he would be a real husband. An inexplicable surge of joy and longing flooded her. She looked up and relaxed in his arms.

"Yes," she said, enjoying seeing his eyes light up.

Starbursts, comet flares, and Roman candle fireballs exploded in his heart. "What did you say?"

Kate smiled. "I said yes."

Jack picked her up and whirled her around. "I love you."

Kate looked down into his eyes. "I love you too. I think I began to love you the minute you came out of the jungle and scared the elephant away."

11

At breakfast, Kate held up two letters she had written the previous night. "I've written to both Dad and Andy and Evelyn. At least one of the letters should get through to England safely."

"They should all manage it. At the moment, the war hasn't disrupted the mail too much." Manny observed Kate's radiant expression. "Important news for them?"

"Yes. Jack proposed last night, and I accepted."

Manny shook his newspaper and folded it. "What took him so long?"

"Are you happy for me?"

"Very. He's a real man. One of the best. You couldn't have done better if I'd chosen him for you myself."

Manny smiled to himself.

"Manny, I know why you're smiling. You've been scheming for this to happen, haven't you? And you're smiling because your machinations have worked.".

Manny just smiled more. Kate raised her eyebrows at his unusual silence. "Anyway, we're getting married by special license, so today Jack and I will be dashing around getting things organized."

"Where are you getting married?"

"Jack wants to get married at Holy Trinity Cathedral. He wants to pledge his love for me in God's eyes." Kate drank some tea. "Hopefully, it will be too short notice to marry there, and we'll have a civil wedding."

Hearing the coldness in Kate's voice, Manny asked, "Is something wrong with having a church wedding?"

Kate chewed her lip, wondering if she should reveal how she felt. "I don't believe in God, Manny. After what happened to my son in England, I know it's just a cruel hoax."

She had shocked him; she could tell by his expression. Speechless too, so unlike him.

Manny coughed. "Tell the chaplain to give me a call; I'll vouch for the pair of you." Manny paused as if in thought. "I'll pay for your wedding photos, my treat. Go to Patel's photography studio on Anawrahta Road. He's very good."

"Manny, would you give me away?"

"What! Walk you down the aisle?"

Kate cheerfully cracked her boiled egg with a spoon. "Yes, please."

"What does an old bachelor like me know about giving away the bride?"

"Enough to put one leg in front of the other. Come on, Manny, don't be shy."

A lump formed in Kate's throat seeing Manny struggle through his emotions, seeming proud and full of affection for her because she wanted him to walk her down the aisle and a trace of sadness that she would soon be leaving. The wave of sadness touched her too.

His voice was husky when he spoke. "I'd be honored, old girl. Why don't you invite Jack for dinner tonight?" He stood up to go riding. "Coming?"

Jack arrived later that morning. Kate showed him a list she had scribbled of things they had to do—photographer, flowers, invitations, newspaper announcement, reception, cake.

"I've already arranged with my hotel to have the reception there, so that's taken care of," Jack said.

"We'll have to decide how we're sharing the cost of the wedding. Manny's paying for the photographer. I'm happy to pay for the newspaper announcements, the cake, flowers, and invitations," Kate offered.

"I was thinking I would pay for everything, Kate," Jack said quietly.

"I don't think that would be fair. The bride's parents normally pay for the wedding expenses, but Dad won't know about the wedding until the deal is done. However, I do have a small annual income, courtesy of my previous marriage, so I'll pay my share."

"I didn't know about your income!"

Kate laughed and collected her purse ready to leave the house. "I didn't want you marrying me for my money. Seriously, it's *is* only small."

"Well, if you're sure you want to pay for some things, I'll pay for the reception and honeymoon."

Kate stopped dead in her tracks. "Honeymoon? I thought we'd be going straight to Maymyo."

"No, we need some time alone first. Is it all right if we spend our short honeymoon in Rangoon?" I would have liked to have taken you to Ceylon to show you off to some close friends, but I must return to Maymyo soon. And when we arrive in Maymyo, my children, Pamela and David will be there. Do you think you'll come to care for them, become fond of them, Kate?"

Kate stroked his cheek. "Of course, I will. I love children and because they're your children, I'll love them all the more."

Jack took her face in his hands and kissed her. "I am so happy, Kate."

"Me too."

She lingered in his embrace, then said, "Now, back to business. Tomorrow, I'll take Mya Sandi with me to go shopping for my wedding outfit, so we'd better get a move on if we're to get everything else done today." As they went outside, Kate said, "Talking of Mya Sandi, if she's willing, I'd like to bring her with me to Maymyo. Would you mind?"

"Of course not."

The next few days were a whirlwind of activity. Jack surprised Kate by presenting her with a sapphire engagement ring. On the day of the wedding, Kate was relaxed enough to leave packing her suitcases until she and Manny had their last early morning ride together. After a light lunch, Mya Sandi helped Kate to dress and style her hair in a shoulder-length, turned-under bob. Kate twirled round in her silk, pale-mauve suit with small matching hat and veil.

"Will I do?"

Mya Sandi appraised her mistress. "You are very beautiful, *thakin-ma.*"

"You look radiant," Manny said, when Kate entered the living room.

"And you, kind sir, are looking positively handsome," Kate said, observing his smart suit with its razor-edged creases in the trousers.

Mya Sandi handed Kate her bouquet of cascading lavender roses framed by eucalyptus, then pinned Manny's white rose buttonhole to his lapel. She turned to Kate and announced, "*Thakin-ma,* all the servants wish you a long and happy marriage."

"Thank you, Mya Sandi," Kate said, with tears in her eyes. "I do wish you would come with me. But I understand. You have family commitments . . ." Kate's words dried up. She squeezed her maid's hand in appreciation. "I'm so glad you were here to take care of me when I arrived."

The chauffeur drove Kate and Manny to the cathedral. On the way, Kate told Manny, "Thank you for taking me in and helping me when I needed someone."

Manny waved her thanks away. "It was nothing, my dear. I'm sorry to see you leave. The house will be empty without you. But you couldn't have chosen a better man to leave me for." He patted her hand. "Are you shaking, Kate? Afraid?"

"No! Well, a little. I don't really know what I'm going to. All I know is that Jack is a good man, I have a ready-made family waiting for me, and that my life will change. I'll see you before we leave for Maymyo," Kate said. "We'll have dinner together."

"Good. A small farewell party."

In what seemed no time at all, the car arrived at Holy Trinity. Kate peered through the windscreen at the redbrick, gothic-style church with its rose window and spire.

"Well, we're here. Are you sure about this?" Manny said.

A warm glow enveloped her. This was a very different feeling to when she married Charles to enable him to receive his inheritance and for her to elevate her social standing by becoming Lady of the Manor.

Kate nodded. "I'm sure."

Manny helped Kate from the car. Strains of **"Jesu, Joy of Man's Desiring"** floated from the cathedral entrance. Manny threaded his arm through Kate's. Puffing out his chest, he walked her to the main porch. Kate tugged at her suit jacket, smoothed her skirt and took a deep breath. The music changed to **"Here Comes the Bride.***"* She and Manny exchanged looks.

"Ready?" Manny asked.

"Ready."

Her future husband was standing at the altar with Herbert, his best man. Jack turned to look at her when she started down the aisle. His eyes were puffy from a night on the town with his friends. Seeing his appreciative smile, a wave of reassurance washed over her. Everything will be all right. As she stood by his side, Jack bent his head and whispered, "You look beautiful."

Kate squeezed his hand. "I love you."

The ceremony went without a hitch. The chaplain's voice was clear and cheerful, and his rich baritone carried the hymn singing. Herbert had managed not to lose the ring, and Jack easily slipped it onto Kate's finger.

"I now pronounce you man and wife," the chaplain said. "You may kiss the bride."

Jack lifted Kate's veil and gave her a lingering kiss. The photographer posed them signing the register. Grinning broadly, Jack walked out of the cathedral beside his new wife. The photographer organized the small wedding party for the camera then followed them to the hotel to take more photographs at the reception. With Kate and Jack's twenty exuberant friends making the most of the happy occasion, the task required some patience.

"You've got boisterous friends," Jack said, as the lively thespians and athletic crowd took advantage of the free drinks.

"*My* friends," Kate said, laughing, "I thought they were yours."

In his best man speech, Herbert made witty jokes about Tarzan having found his unsuspecting Jane to carry off to his jungle lair. Toasts to the happy couple were followed by toasts to Kate, brave woman that she was to take on a man such as Jack.

Manny made a humorous speech, insisting Kate's father had been very clever in sending his daughter halfway around the world. After more jokes in such vein, Manny became serious. He turned to Jack.

"Kate came to my house a complete stranger, where I, a confirmed bachelor, had reigned in peace for many years. Kate's arrival brought the utmost disruption. She insisted on conversing at dinner. She played loud modern music on the wireless. She came home late from her nights on the town. Brought home waifs and strays. Caused me no end of trouble." Manny paused and looked around the room for effect, receiving sympathetic "aahs" from his audience. He turned back to Jack. "And now, old boy, she's moving into your house." "Oohs" erupted from the guests. "I hope you enjoy the blessings she brings with as much happiness as I did."

The wedding guests greeted Manny's speech with loud applause. His emotional revelations touched Kate. Her eyes shone with unshed tears. Kate bent close, "I didn't know you cared so much. I'll miss you, my friend." The quartet began to play, and she and Jack moved onto the dance floor to lead the dancing.

"Well, Mrs. Bellamy, have you enjoyed your day?"

"Darling, it has been the most wonderful day of my life."

"I managed to book a berth on an Irrawaddy Flotilla Company ferry going up the river to Mandalay, but not until the day after tomorrow." Jack pulled her close. "That will give us five days to get to know each other better without family and work getting in the way. Is that all right? From Mandalay we'll take a train to Maymyo."

"It sounds absolutely perfect."

Shortly before midnight, weary but glowing with happiness, Jack and Kate made a farewell circuit to the few inebriated stragglers wringing the last drop of pleasure from the celebration. Risqué comments followed the couple as they left for Jack's room. Laughing, they ran hand-in-hand along the hallway to his door. He pulled Kate to him and kissed her passionately.

"I love you, Mrs. Bellamy."

"I love you, husband Jack," Kate said.

Jack held her to him, then pulled the door key from his pocket. "Let's do this right." He scooped Kate up into his arms. She squeaked in fright as she almost slipped from his grasp while he struggled to put the key in the lock. They laughed, kissed again then Jack triumphantly turned the key. "Ready?" he asked. Kate nodded. He pushed the door open and carried her across the threshold.

"Now we truly are man and wife," he said, setting her down.

Kate stroked his cheek, studied his lips then reached up and kissed him tenderly, with longing. They pulled apart, eyes bright with desire.

"I'll just go check on Bess, see they're taking good care of her in the staff quarters, while you, er, get ready for bed," Jack said, giving Kate a lingering kiss before leaving the room to give her privacy to prepare for his return.

Kate took the oyster-colored, satin nightgown with thin straps that she had bought for this night and held it to her, admiring her reflection in the mirror. Eyes closed, she tried to remember when she had ever been so happy. She smiled. *It was holding newborn baby Joey in my arms.*

The smile faded. *Well, at least for a while, before Charles became reclusive and paranoid.*

She took off her mauve wedding outfit and hung it up, rubbing the silk against her face.

But now I've found my prince.

She dabbed Jasmine perfume behind her ears and between her breasts then slipped into the nightgown. She was tense lying in the bed waiting for Jack. She hoped and prayed that this evening would be everything she had dreamed it would be. She blushed, self-conscious of her burning hunger to share her passion with this man.

Jack tapped on the door. "May I come in?"

He entered, smiled at her, and started to remove his clothes. His pants slid to the floor. He folded them neatly over the trouser stand.

Kate flushed hot with anticipation. "Jack, don't take so long. You look like a Greek statue. I want to kiss you all over."

Jack sat on the side of the bed, kissed her long and gently. Slipping into bed, he pulled her close, ran his hand along her thigh and hip. He tugged at her nightgown. "Let's take this off."

They struggled and giggled until bare skin met. He covered her face with kisses, expertly teased her mouth with his tongue. Kate moaned and gasped. Pressing against him, she wrapped a leg over him, opening the way to the pleasure she was offering. Jack gently took the proffered gift, then stopped.

Dread froze her soul. No, not a horror of a wedding night again! Kate almost sobbed. "What's wrong?"

"It's been a while. I want to make it last."

She laughed with relief. "Darling, it's all right. We have a lifetime together, and right now," Kate said, her voice thick with desire, "I need you."

Recovering from the intense waves of pleasure that had spread throughout their bodies, Jack took Kate's face in his hands and kissed her.

"I love you. I love you."

"I love you too."

He lay down beside her. She kissed his sweating face and dabbed his damp chest with the sheet.

Jack wrapped her in his arms. "I can't bear to be apart from you. I want you near all night, every night."

Kate's heart filled with unimagined joy. Her eyes, moist with gratitude, savored Jack's face. His passion, tenderness and the security she felt wrapped in his masculinity made the emptiness of the past melt away replaced by the certainty of a future beside this steadfast man to whom she dared open her heart.

It was almost lunchtime when they emerged from their room. Kate was blushing with embarrassment. Hotel staff and guests must know from their radiance that they were honeymooners.

Kate waited in the lobby while Jack went in search of Bess. He found her sitting outside near the dhobi-wallah who was busy bashing sheets on a large rock by a pool. Bess's tail began wagging as soon as she saw Jack.

Jack tapped the dhobi-wallah's shoulder and slipped him some money. "Thank you." He patted Bess's head. "Come on, girl; we'll eat then go for a walk."

After lunch at the teashop, Jack and Kate strolled in Dalousie Park, laid out around Royal Lake. Halfway across the bridge crossing the lake, they leaned over the rail, searching for shadowy forms of carp swimming below the lake's surface.

Jack reached for Kate's hand. "This park is our special place. It's where I proposed and you ruddy well said yes. I still can't believe it." He reached down to pet his dog. "Can you believe it, Bess?" Bess cocked her ears, head to one side. "No, neither can I," said Jack.

Kate laughed and kissed Jack's cheek. "Everything feels perfect, Jack. Just perfect. I can hardly believe it myself."

Kate suddenly straightened up. "Oh, Jack! We need to buy some books to read. And I want to pop into Rowe and Co. to be sure I have everything I need. We won't be down here again for a long time."

"They *do* have stores in the north. But you're right about the books. I'd like some new murder mysteries."

They rushed from the park and hailed a taxi to Smart and Mookerdum's bookshop, famous for having the latest novels from England. Stepping through the door, their eyes lit up like children's in a toy store.

Limit twelve each," Jack told Kate, leading the way to the shelves, "or we'll have to buy another suitcase."

Sorting through the store's varied selection of books, Kate said, "That might be a problem."

Bess flopped down in front of the philosophy section while Kate and Jack searched shelves, running fingers along book spines, looking for favorite authors. Out came Agatha Christie from the shelves, Graham Greene, Ernest Hemingway, Rex Stout's Nero Wolfe books, and many others. They searched with diligence, only speaking to call out a selection so as not to duplicate their choices. They laughed with delight on discovering they both enjoyed murder-mystery and suspense.

At the end of the search, they counted the books stacked in piles on the floor. Thirty. Jack and Kate stared at one another, jaws set, neither prepared to relinquish a book, not one.

"Thirty it is then," Jack said, picking some from the pile to take to the counter.

Kate touched his arm. "Wait! We need books for the children."

Her heart warmed when she saw Jack's surprise and gratitude at her thinking of the children. He squeezed her hand. His voice was tender when he finally mustered, "Yes, good idea."

With their own books stashed by the register, they went to the children's section.

"You'll have to help me choose, Jack. You know what they like," Kate said.

"Hmm, not really. I'll leave it to you, darling."

Kate pounced on the Ladybird books, Pinocchio, a collection of Grimm's fairy tales, and Enid Blyton's Noddy and Famous Five books. "This should help us get to know one another. I'll enjoy reading to them."

Jack kissed her forehead. "Thank you."

That night they dined early with Manny and a few friends at the Yacht Club one last time before their pre-dawn departure on the ferry. Engrossed with good company, dancing, and laughing with one another, they ignored Bob Watson's dismayed glances and his date, Daphne's, turned down mouth and jealous annoyance that Bob's attention kept drifting to Kate.

Kate was in one of the stalls in the powder room when she heard a group of garrulous women enter. She immediately recognized Daphne's whining voice.

"I don't understand the man. Bob continues to pine over that woman. They hardly dated and he's walking around with lovesick eyes and a pouty mouth. Still, she'll be gone tomorrow. I'd love to be a fly on the wall when she sees what she's walking into."

"What do you mean?" asked another voice.

"Don't you know? A little bird told me that Jack Bellamy, supposedly such a good catch, has a black mark to his name."

Daphne's friends gasped and oohed then one said, "Oh do tell."

"His first wife was *Burmese!* Kate's going to play stepmother to a couple of little half-castes. Poor girl, she must be the only woman who doesn't know and keeping it hush-hush is probably how he caught the poor woman to care for the brats."

Kate covered her gaping mouth with her hands. Why hadn't he told her?

A voice said, "I thought they seemed madly in l . . ."

The voice fell silent as an outwardly composed Kate emerged from the stall and faced Daphne, red-faced and blotchy with embarrassment. Kate smiled sarcastically. "Poor Daphne. In case you hadn't realized it, we *are* in Burma, not Calcutta with its rigid social limitations. You're so narrow-minded you should leave for India at once. You're much better suited to Indian mores. You really don't belong, do you?" Kate said, her tone full of unkind pity. Kate looked every friend of Daphne's in the eye. "For your information, I find Burmese children delightful." Then she left with her head held high.

She was numb as she walked back to the table, the sense of betrayal a stake through her heart. As the night progressed, she was quiet, sad, tried valiantly to put on a good show.

Manny patted her hand. "You all right, old girl?"

"Feeling a bit sad to be leaving. I'll be all right."

Manny gave the couple a ride back to their hotel. Manny engaged Jack in conversation. His responses seemed short, tense and edgy. Kate barely said a word.

"All right, what's wrong?" Jack demanded as soon as the door to their room closed. "You've been stiff and withdrawn most of the evening."

Kate strode to the far side of the bed then turned on him. "You said I could trust you. You deceived me!"

Jack looked taken aback. "What do you mean, I deceived you?"

"Why didn't you tell me your wife was Burmese? Why did I have to find out from that horrible Daphne woman?"

Jack seemed stunned, ran his hand through his hair, walked up and down before he spoke. "I didn't mention it because I never thought of it as something to mention. It wasn't . . . isn't . . . relevant. My wife was loyal, a wonderful woman and a loving mother."

Kate stamped her foot. "Well, I'd liked to have known. Daphne caught me completely by surprise. She was so spiteful, almost gloating, wondering how I'd feel raising another woman's children, half . . . half Burmese children. I didn't let on that I didn't know. Wouldn't give her the satisfaction. But you should have told me."

"Have you told me everything about yourself?" Jack asked his voice low and somber. "I don't know anything about how your husband and son died. You haven't told me a thing. What secrets are you keeping?" he challenged her, his face cold as stone.

Stunned, Kate looked at him, the bed between them, his words a slap in the face. She wrapped her arms protectively around her ribs. Jack crossed his arms, defying her to remain silent. Kate's mouth was suddenly dry. She ran her tongue over her lips. For what seemed an age, she stared at the intricately embroidered peacock displaying his tail in the wall-hanging above the headboard, then she turned to her husband. Fighting her abhorrence at saying the words, her voice so low Jack could barely hear her, she said, "My husband killed my son, Joey."

Jack's arms dropped to his side, his expression of horrified disbelief barely registering with Kate. "What?"

"My husband killed my son . . . then killed himself," she whispered.

Jack tore across the room, wrapped her in his arms, pulled Kate's head to his chest. He stroked and kissed her hair. "Oh God! I'm sorry. I'm so sorry." Kate sobbed against him. They stood melded together, clutching, rocking, Jack holding Kate until her tears stopped. "Why would he do such a thing?"

Kate shrugged. "I don't really know. Charles was a depressed recluse." And I can never tell you the full story.

Jack stroked her hair then held her away from him and lifted her chin to make her look at him. "Kate, you must learn to trust me. I'll never, ever, let you down."

12

Five days on the Irrawaddy River, sailing through the sweltering central plains, brought the ferry to Mandalay. It was mid-afternoon, and the land was as pancake-flat as the central plains. Kate was ready for the hills and the more temperate climate Jack had promised she would find at Maymyo. Even her short-sleeved cotton dress and open-toed shoes failed to keep her cool in the heat and humidity.

On seeing the gangplank that disembarking passengers had to negotiate to cross five feet of river water and a wide swath of mud to reach *terra firma,* Kate's heart sank.

"Jack, isn't there another way off this boat?"

"It's safer than it looks. I'll go first." Bess trotted past him and went down the gangplank. "All right, I'll go second." He balanced along the gangplank to the riverside. "See, you'll be fine."

Kate stepped carefully along what seemed to her to be a very rickety gangplank and on reaching Jack, breathed a sigh of relief. Jack found a driver who managed to squeeze them and their luggage into his horse-drawn *gharri* and take them to the Royal Hotel.

The hotel was popular with big corporations' employees who were passing through to their work areas in timber, oil, cotton, and tea. Jack had arranged to stay in Mandalay for two nights to show Kate some of the sights.

In their room, first order of business was to strip off their sticky clothes. They playfully bathed together in the large cast iron claw-legged tub, washing each other's backs, running hands over chest and breasts, exchanging long, lingering kisses and talking while soaking with legs intertwined until the water became cold.

After one last kiss, Jack jumped out, grabbed a towel for himself and handed one to Kate. "When I get back to work, I'll be away on tour a lot of the time. You'll be a forestry manager's widow, but there are a number of wives in Maymyo in the same situation so you shouldn't feel too lonely once you make friends and become involved with club activities."

"I'm not too worried about that. I'm sure I'll cope. Anyway, there is an upside to your touring."

"Oh, what's that?"

Kate smiled coyly. "Well, after you've had a hot bath on your return, we can make up for lost time. It will be like another honeymoon, won't it?"

She flushed with pleasure when Jack grinned. She relished that her passionate nature had surprised and pleased him. Indeed, it had even surprised her. They lay in companionable silence on the bed. Then, weary from the long trip, they napped until dinner.

Relaxing over an after-dinner brandy, Kate smiled at her husband. "I love you so much. The way you care for me, the way you cherish me, a woman couldn't ask for more. Our days on the ferry were sheer bliss."

She had no words to express the oneness she felt with this man, the keeper of her heart. She had told him what she had been running from when she left England, and he had loved her even more. She had told him all, except for Charles having killed Joey after discovering he was not Joey's father. That would forever be a guilty secret buried in the recesses of her heart like a thorn that would forever hurt and twinge because she could never bury it deep enough to get away from it, only deep enough to keep it at bay.

The next morning, Jack hired a trishaw for the day. First stop was Mandalay Hill's south entrance. Stepping from the trishaw, Kate looked skywards. Her mouth dropped open at the immensity of the two giant *chinthes* towering over her.

"At least forty feet tall, I would guess," said Jack. "You already know they're mythical half-lion, half-dragon creatures that guard the temples, don't you?"

"Of course," Kate said smugly. "We came across them at the temples in Rangoon."

"Ah, but did you know that Mandalay Hill is almost eight hundred feet high and we have over seventeen hundred steps to climb." Jack crossed his arms and grinned.

Refusing to show her shock or dismay, Kate put on her happy face. "Fancy that. So, let's get moving. We've a long climb ahead of us."

Seeing Jack's expression fall, apparently disappointed at his failure to provoke even a small display of horror from her about the long climb to the summit, Kate swatted his back with her sun hat. "You beast," she said, laughing.

The Sutaungpyei Pagoda was situated at the top of the hill. Out of respect for the Buddhist religion, they removed their footwear at the entrance and handed them to the man in charge of shoes. Then they started to climb. Taking their time and with numerous rests, they eventually reached the terrace at the summit. Bess immediately flopped down and slept in the shade of a wall. Kate and Jack gazed out, admiring the panoramic view of the Mandalay Plain dotted with hundreds of stupas, pagodas and temples. It was the dry season and most of the ground was mushroom-colored earth.

Jack pointed east. "See those blue hills. That's where we're going tomorrow. An hour on the train and we'll be home."

Thirty minutes later, they began their descent of the hill. So much easier than the climb. No gasping for breath. Less sweating and being overheated. No calf muscles about to explode. Having missed lunch, they settled for afternoon tea with lots of lemonade to quench their thirst and ice cream for the sheer pleasure of it.

"There's one more place I want to take you," Jack said, "and that's U Bein's Bridge. It's almost a hundred years old, made of teak and is about a mile long. These are my two favorite places in Mandalay. Sunset at the bridge is just incredible, and I want you to see it."

Kate patted her large shoulder bag. "I've still got some film in my camera."

After a leisurely ride in the trishaw, they arrived at the bridge shortly before sunset. Jack took Kate to the best vantage point and told her to get her camera ready. "I'm going up on the bridge with Bess. See if you can get a photo of us," Jack said, calling Bess to heel. Supported by numerous teak poles, the bridge spanned the lake thirty feet above the surface. People were crossing the narrow bridge, cyclists walked beside their bicycles, monks strolled along deep in conversation, being passed by couples enjoying evening constitutionals.

Waiting for Jack and Bess to find a suitable spot on the bridge, Kate gazed at the boats on the lake, filled with people trying to be in the best position to watch the sunset. A commotion in one of the boats caught her attention. The boatman was frantically bailing water out of his sinking boat. Passengers scooped water from the boat with their hands. The boatman tried to maneuver the boat to dry land before it sank, all to no avail. His passengers had to wade ashore through knee-deep water. Excitement over, Kate focused on the sunset, but seeing the sinking boat had left a dark shadow hanging over her, a premonition. You never knew when life would spring a leak like the boat and you would be left to wade through water rather than remain on dry land.

The sky began to change color. Tinges of pink and mauve appeared; clouds turned purple, then an orange radiance infused everything. For a few minutes, the bridge and the people on it became black silhouettes against a vivid orange background and Kate took her pictures, including one of Jack waving and Bess looking through the railings to the dark water below. Then all faded away to greyness, and a cold shiver ran through Kate.

In the train the following day, excitement made Kate's stomach flutter. Her fingers trembled as she followed their journey on the map that Jack had gone out of his way to find for her. She was going to her new home, a home she would share with a man she adored and his two young children. She hoped they would like her. She wanted nothing more than the love and security found in a loving family. She had been ten when her mother died of breast cancer and although her dad and her brother had tried to make up for her loss, she had never really recovered. And then, after her empty marriage to Charles, she thought she would never find the warm glow of love she had experienced in her early childhood.

Jack had been concerned that Kate may not be happy moving into his late wife's home. But Kate had no strong feelings about it. She had moved into Charles' home and not made changes. She had adapted to her sparse bedroom at Manny's. Kate figured if her surroundings were adequate, she would be happy anywhere as long as she was surrounded by love.

The plain with its dusty palms was left behind. The gradient became steeper. The train slowed as they entered an area of rolling hills, covered in oaks and pines.

"Maymyo is 3,500 feet above sea-level," Jack said. "It's like England, cool and fresh, with pine trees. You'll like it."

The train lurched along, stopping occasionally where there were scatterings of bamboo huts. Somewhere along the way, mushroom-colored soil changed to rich red. White egrets stood like statues patiently waiting for lizards to appear while flocks of green parrots flew overhead.

An hour later, the train came to a halt at Maymyo station with squealing of brakes, hissing of steam, and clattering of buffers. Porters deposited the luggage on the footpath outside the station.

Jack looked up and down the road. "My friend, Tom Hubbard, is supposed to be meeting us with his car. I should have asked someone else. Tom has a habit of being late."

"I don't mind. I'm enjoying the cool breeze and my dry skin. It's the first time in weeks that I haven't been hot and sticky," Kate said. "I think I'm going to like living here."

A large black Austin raced up and braked hard. Out jumped a tall, ginger-haired, mustached man with a ruddy face. Jack stepped forward and Bess wagged her tail.

"Tom. Thank you for meeting us." Jack reached back to take Kate's hand. "Tom, this is my wife Kate. Kate this is my friend Tom Hubbard. He's the assistant superintendent of police."

Tom greeted Kate in his usual exuberant manner. "Well, I say!" Tom looked Kate up and down and said, admiringly, "Jack certainly knows how to pick them." Tom clicked his heels, bowed his head, then vigorously shook Kate's hand. Her eyes widened in amazement at such an enthusiastic greeting. She looked over Tom's broad shoulders to Jack, who gave her an apologetic smile. "Delighted to meet you, Kate. Welcome to Maymyo. I do hope you play bridge. We need bridge players at The Club."

"I'm not very good, I'm afraid, but with some practice, I'm sure I'll soon be up to speed."

Tom opened the rear door of the Austin for Kate. "Hop in."

Bess promptly jumped in. Kate pushed the dog to the far side of the seat. "Bess, I think Tom was talking to me."

Kate settled herself in her seat. A Burmese porter emerged from the shadows of the station to load the luggage into the trunk then squeeze some bags onto the floor of the rear seat. He shikoed, joining his hands and bowing to the two men in gratitude for his tip.

Tom drove along Maymyo's wide main street planted with eucalyptus, silver oak, pines, and cherry trees. Burmese open-fronted shops lined the street. Jack pointed out The Motor Association head office next to the Golf Club Repairing Shop and Diamond Confectionary.

Tom gestured down a road on the left. "Two miles back that way is the garrison. There's a Yorkshire regiment there now, the King's Own Yorkshire Light Infantry."

"Look! All the roads have English names! Charing Cross Road!" Kate laughed. "Downing Street! The Mall! Is this what you meant when you said it's like living in England?"

"The town was founded by a British Army officer, Colonel May," Tom said. "Word soon got around about Maymyo's beauty and climate. British company employees, army officers, and civil servants came to visit, fell in love with it, and made it a small corner of England to escape from Burma's scorching heat and monsoon weather."

They left the main street behind to drive along pine-scented lanes. English-style, red-brick houses surrounded by large well-kept gardens nestled in the green hills like flecks in a Harris Tweed.

The car stopped in front of a wooden garage beside a red-brick bungalow. Kate noted the driveway was outside the fenced front garden. Probably to keep the children safe, she thought. The children!

The flurry of two male servants rushing forward to carry bags and suitcases into the house diverted Kate's attention from her somersaulting stomach, as did the yapping of two excited smooth-haired fox terriers that quieted immediately Bess walked over to them. Kate felt more nervous at meeting Jack's children than when she interviewed to be a private nurse for Charles' father.

The two men joined the colorful ensemble of servants waiting on the veranda to greet the returning master and his new wife. Under instructions from his wife Edith to tell her how it went, Tom observed the introductions.

The first man in line was Jack's houseman. "This is Nyan Sein," Jack said. "If you have any problems at the house while I'm away, Nyan Sein will take care of it."

Kate nodded and smiled at the middle-aged Burman, looking proud and smiling slightly as if to say I have taken good care of your home while you have been away *thakin*. He looked smart in his lime green turban, dark green loose shirt and cream *lungyi*. He shikoed to Jack and Kate, as did his serene wife Za Za Lay, who peeked at Kate from beneath lowered eyelashes and said, "Welcome, *thakin-ma*."

"This man here, hiding behind them," Jack said, "is Hasin. He's a wonderful cook." The Indian cook, in white shirt and *lungyi,* reacted to the praise with a large grin that showed his perfect Clorox-white teeth and a large expanse of gums. He wobbled his head from side to side. His young wife Diti quickly glanced up when introduced to Kate, before returning her gaze to the veranda floor.

"And this is Bikram, the *mali*." The crinkled, wiry *mali*, half naked in a *dhoti* loin cloth, stepped forward and saluted. "He's responsible for the eye-catching garden we have here and does odd-jobs around the house."

"Thank you, everyone. It's a pleasure to meet you," Kate said.

Nyan Sein clapped his hands and the servants trailed from the veranda, leaving only the children who were waiting with their *ayah*. Jack bobbed down in front of them and held out his arms. "Come and say hello to your dad."

The children jumped into his arms and hugged him. They were dressed in English clothes, short trousers and white shirt for six-year-old David and a blue dress with puffed, short sleeves for four-year-old Pamela. They had pale bronze complexions, strong, straight black hair and studied Kate with velvet-brown eyes. Behind them stood their kind-eyed, plump *ayah*, whom Jack introduced as Upala. She wore a pretty, coral-colored sari. Her black hair was dressed with coconut oil and fastened in a bun at the nape of her neck. When Jack stood up, the children returned to stand in front of Upala. The *ayah's* hand rested on David's skinny shoulder. To steady him? Was he the one most affected by the loss of his mother compared to his sister who had only been two years old at the time? Both children stared at Kate with curiosity. Their innocence and vulnerability tugged at her heart.

"Kate, this young man is my son David, and this is my daughter Pamela. Children, come and say hello to your new mother."

The unsmiling but polite *ayah*, gently urged the children forward to offer Kate the marigold garlands they held. David looked serious as he handed her his garland. "Hello, welcome to our house."

Kate thanked him and put it around her neck then accepted Pamela's garland, handed to her with a shy smile. Fear gone.

Anxiety gone. It occurred to Kate she and the children were bonded by loss. She knew she would love them and protect them fiercely. Kate knelt, hugged them at the same time, one in each arm, and said, "I hope we can become good friends."

The children looked down, avoiding eye contact. Jack ruffled his son's hair with affection. "We'll soon get used to one another and then maybe we can be a happy family again."

"I am happy, Daddy," Pamela said. "Upala takes care of us."

Jack looked at Kate, rolling his eyes in apology.

Kate placed her hand on his shoulder. "There's no rush. We must go slowly."

Upala looked on, her face inscrutable.

Za Za Lay led the way to the picnic table on the lawn at the side of the house where refreshments awaited them. The table was covered with a white tablecloth. A bowl of scarlet hibiscus decorated the table. Tom pulled Kate's chair out for her. Jack sat the children one on each side of him and put his arms around them. Kate looked tenderly at them. She was glad she had black hair too, like their mother; she would not seem so different from them. She scanned the garden delighted at seeing the English-style plantings of phlox, huge petunias, sweet peas, and hollyhocks skillfully intermingled with tropical hibiscus and frangipani.

Za Za Lay poured lemonade and left. Jack took hold of Kate's hand. "What do you think?"

Her eyes glistened with unshed tears of joy. "I think we'll be very happy." She turned her head away before the tears spilled. She waved her arm to indicate the garden. "Look at how beautiful the garden is. Big enough to play cricket."

"I have a surprise for you when you've finished your lemonade. Tom is eager to see if you like it."

Kate glanced at Tom, surprised. "Tom is?"

"Me, too."

Tom stood. "Come on. I can't stand the suspense."

"David, Pamela, lead the way to you know where," Jack said.

Bess trotted after Spot and Patch, the two terriers jumping and running around the children who raced ahead, laughing and squealing as they approached a building at the rear of the property.

Kate's footsteps faltered when she saw it. From the smell, it was obviously a stable with a pile of manure beside it and lots of buzzing flies. "Jack! Is that what I think it is?"

"What do you think it is?"

Kate laughed and broke into a run to catch up to the children. Tom and Jack overtook her, reaching the door first.

Jack put his hand on the door latch. "Ready, Kate?"

She took hold of the children's hands. "Are we ready?"

"Yes," they shouted, hopping around with excitement.

Jack opened the stable door and led the way inside. Two of the four stalls had occupants. A grey mare in the first stall nickered a greeting. In the next stall stood a chestnut gelding with a white blaze.

Jack stopped at the first stall. "This is my beautiful Princess." Kate stopped to stroke her face. Jack moved on to the second stall. "And this is your horse. I bought him for you so we could go riding together. Tom found him for me."

Kate gasped and rubbed her horse's forehead. "Oh, Jack, he's wonderful. Does he have a name?"

"Do you really like him?" Tom asked. "I was worried you wouldn't like my pick. Terribly difficult choosing a horse for someone I hadn't met. The children have named him Blaze."

"That's perfect. Thank you, children," Kate said. "Jack, it's unbelievable."

Jack squeezed her hand. "Now that the children will have a full-time parent here, I can see about getting them some ponies so you can all go riding together."

David and Pamela jumped up and down. "We're getting ponies, Daddy? Hurray!"

Jack pulled sugar cubes from his pocket and handed them to the children. "Calm down and give Princess and Blaze some sugar cubes."

A tight spasm seized Kate's chest. At first, she couldn't breathe as scenes of Joey and his pony filled her mind. Then memories came of the fun and laughter they had shared while Joey rode his pony in the grounds. The spasm melted away and her breathing returned to normal.

"I say, Jack, lemonade's not really my thing. Do you have any beer?" Tom asked. "My success as a horse-picker requires a splurge."

The adults left David and Pamela petting the horses and returned to the picnic table where Za Za Lay was putting out dishes of fruit.

"Would you bring two beers, please, Za Za Lay?" Jack asked. To Kate he said, "I don't usually drink until evening, but this is a celebration. I had my doubts that I'd be able to entice you to marry me and come here."

Tom raised his glass. "Rubbish! He was irresistible, wasn't he, Kate? I, for one, toast your presence here in Maymyo. You're easy on the eye and your smile is dazzling. Welcome, and I hope you soon feel at home. Cheers."

Tom took a mouthful of beer then, apparently disconcerted and embarrassed by his comments, blushed and looked down, suddenly seeming to find the tablecloth of great interest. Kate and Jack grinned at one another.

Tom lifted his head, a twinkle in his eye. "Better not tell Edith what I said about you being easy on the eye. Edith's my wife, Kate, and she'd have my guts for garters. However, I know she would love to go riding with you, especially when Jack's away. The Forestry Department has made miles and miles of trails through the pine forests around Maymyo. You could go riding every day for a month without riding the same trail twice."

Tom set down his glass and stood to leave. "Oh, I almost forgot. It's the military parade on Saturday. Any excuse for the garrison—King's jubilee, King's birthday, Armistice Day. You name it, they'll march for it. Good spectacle though, isn't it, Jack? Edith and our son Colin will be going. I dare say we'll see you there. Well, pleasure to meet you, Kate." The children came running up. "Cheerio, everyone, cheerio children."

The children looked at Kate. They seemed as self-conscious as she was. "Come and sit down. Would you like more lemonade? Your Uncle Tom is fun, isn't he?"

They nodded.

"Would you like to have ponies someday so we can go riding together?"

They nodded again.

"I want a dapple-grey pony like Daddy's" Pamela said.

David picked at the tablecloth. "I want a friendly one that I can feed carrots to."

Kate looked at Jack. "Then we shall have to see what we can arrange, won't we?"

David and Pamela enthusiastically nodded their heads.

Upala, the *ayah,* approached. "May I take the children to see the baby chicks?"

And off they went to see the new baby chicks near the servants' quarters at the back of the house.

Jack held out his hand. "Ready to see inside?"

Stepping through the door, Kate found her new home to be well-lived in and spotless. She walked on solid teak floors polished until they gleamed. Hunting trophies, sambhur deer antlers, adorned the white walls along with black and white photographs of Jack with a college soccer team and scenes of Whitby, a small fishing town on England's North Yorkshire coast. Kate stopped by the photos of Whitby. "Do they make you feel homesick?"

"Not homesick, no. I feel happy that I grew up in such a lovely place. For me, home is where I am. How about you?"

"I think I'm like you. I miss my close family, but home is where I put my roots." Kate gestured around the room. "I will be very happy here, Jack."

Jack led the way to the dining room dominated by a huge teak table, and the kitchen at the rear of the house in a lean-to where the cook's wife Diti was grinding curry paste. He showed Kate the gunroom and the children's bedrooms before moving onto the master bedroom with its four-poster bed covered by a mosquito net. Jack pointed out an intricately embroidered, framed needlepoint given to him by his mother as a wedding present for him and his first wife. While Kate was distracted examining the workmanship and beautiful colors of the English cottage and garden scene, Jack swept a silver-framed photograph of his first wife into a drawer.

He went to a doorway off the bedroom. "And this is our bathroom." Kate looked in and saw a WC with a wooden seat, a large claw-foot bath tub and a small lavatory in the corner. A washbasin and pitcher, decorated with large pink roses, remnants of a time before running water was available, perched on a small chest of drawers holding towels and soaps. Now hot water was produced by a boiler in a building at the back of the house.

Jack put his arm around Kate's shoulder and drew her into him. "Do you really think you'll be happy here?"

"Of course, I will. I've already had an omen."

"Oh? What's that?"

"The roses on the wash basin and jug. They're the same kind of roses that grow around Dad's cottage door. Every morning they'll make me smile and think of good things."

Jack kissed the top of Kate's head.

"Jack, what did you do at the bureau? I think you hid something."

Jack paused, stared at Kate then went to the bureau and opened the top drawer. He hesitated, reached in and brought out the framed photograph and handed it to Kate. "It's Su Su Yi. I didn't think it was a good idea to leave it where it was."

A jolt of joy swept through Kate at her husband's sensitivity. "You are so thoughtful, darling." Kate studied the photograph. Su Su Yi had been poised and beautiful, her smile mysterious and confident. No wonder Jack had fallen in love with her. Although Su Su Yi was Burmese and Kate English, one thing they had in common was lustrous black hair. Kate felt no jealousy or threat only a sadness that Jack had lost someone he loved, same as she had. "Shall we put it in the living room? I'm sure David and Pamela would enjoy seeing their mother every day. She paused before continuing. "I would like to put out a photograph of Joey too. Would that be all right?"

13

It was a warm sunny day for the parade, a regular spectacle put on by the King's Own Yorkshire Light Infantry Regiment garrisoned at Maymyo. The children were excited to be going to the parade with their father. They wanted to make the most of the time he would be home. He would soon be leaving on his three-month tour beginning in June.

Before leaving the house that morning, under the watchful eye of Upala, who hovered in the background to safeguard her charges, Kate had brought the children to one of the corner tables. She placed their mother's framed photograph on the table. "Children, I thought you would like to have this picture of your mother here. Would you?"

The children nodded. Pamela stroked the picture. "I don't remember my mummy."

"I do," David said, sadly.

"Then you must miss her very much, so seeing her everyday will bring back happy memories."

Alongside Su Su Yi's picture, she placed a framed photograph of Joey. "This was my son Joey riding his pony. He died too."

David touched the photograph. "He has white hair."

Kate stroked Joey's face with her finger. "Not white really. More a light blonde. It looks white because this is a black and white photograph."

"Was he bitten by a snake?" Pamela asked.

Kate's throat tightened, her mind assaulted by nightmare images of Charles suffocating her sleeping child with a pillow then putting a noose around his own neck and jumping over the bannister to hang himself. Eventually she managed to say, "He couldn't breathe and he died."

She put her arms around the children's shoulders. "My son Joey had a pony, as you can see. We had a lot of fun riding around our garden, and we will too as soon as we get some ponies for you." Kate looked up at Upala to include and inform her. "So, this is a special place where we can come at any time to feel close to our loved ones who are no longer with us."

"Can Daddy come too?" David asked as Jack entered the room. Kate looked up at him. "Yes, he can. Sometimes, we all miss the people we love who have gone to heaven."

Jack gave Kate a grateful nod.

Kate straightened up, ready to give her first instructions as lady of the house. "Now, where is Za Za Lay?"

Za Za Lay walked in. "You called me, *thakin-ma.*"

"I did. We have made this our special place, a shrine to our loved ones. I'd like you to put a vase of fresh flowers beside these pictures every day."

Za Za Lay's eyes widened and she pursed her lips on seeing her previous mistress's photograph on display then a slight smile developed. She nodded her approval, picking up Joey's picture. "This boy, *thakin-ma?*"

"My son, who died in England."

Za Za Lay nodded slowly. She reverently replaced the framed photograph. "I will always have beautiful flowers here."

With her first orders as *thakin-ma* under her belt, Kate told Upala to take the morning off. Having sensed Upala's protectiveness, Kate wanted space to relate to the children without hindrance. She hoped the children were happy with her decisions; Upala's tight-lipped, barely veiled disapproval indicated to Kate that she did not like being separated from her charges.

At the parade ground, Pamela and David enjoyed their father's company, hopping and skipping and holding his hands until the need to join their friends lured them away.

Jack waved his hand high above his head. "Here's Tom and Edith."

Edith, energized and full of pep, was ploughing through the crowds, waving and shouting "Yoo-hoo!" as she led her family toward them.

David returned briefly to say hello and collect seven-year-old Colin to take him to join their friends.

It only took Kate an instant to know she and Edith would become good friends. For one thing, they had the same tastes—they wore almost identical hats—but she saw Edith also had a warm, open, attractive disposition with a mischievous sense of humor and sparkling joyous eyes.

Edith took hold of Kate's hands and studied her. "You're even more beautiful than my husband described," she said, glancing back at Tom who was blushing. "We're going to become good friends."

"I hope so. Look at this crowd. It seems as if everyone in Maymyo has turned out."

"The parades are very popular, and we ex-pats are very patriotic," Edith said.

Although hunting was a favorite pastime of residents and visitors, Kate was pleased to discover that Edith, like herself, had little interest in the sport, apart from eating the game killed. However, she would enjoy going with Edith to the polo matches, horse racing, rugby matches and the many other delights Maymyo society had to offer.

In the excited buzz of the occasion, Edith and Jack introduced Kate to numerous people. Kate whispered in Edith's ear. "My head's spinning. I'll never remember all their names."

"Don't worry. You'll soon know who's who."

The regimental band struck up "**The Merry Month of May**." The crowd hushed. Out marched the soldiers in perfect formation. They wore broad-brimmed bush hats sporting the swinging green pompom of the King's Own Yorkshire Light Infantry. One march followed another. It seemed as if everyone had turned out for the spectacle. Spectators' toes tapped to quick and slow marches alike. The troops displayed their drill skills to perfection. Kate looked around at the people. Everyone seemed proud and reassured at this display of British prowess and protection. She observed Jack. He too was completely at ease. She felt so happy, it had to be better than being in Heaven.

With the parade over, Edith suggested they go to the tennis club for lunch. "They make a delicious chicken salad and mango ice cream. It will give you an opportunity to meet people."

They rounded up the children and drove to the tennis club. The children laughed and giggled through lunch and, itching to go off and play, asked to be excused.

"Go on," Edith said, taking control, "have your fun and don't get too dirty." She turned to Kate. "Should have brought our *ayahs* to keep an eye on them, but the children should be safe on the club's premises."

Tom and Jack excused themselves to go talk to other members. Kate noticed Jack kept looking her way. Checking how Edith and I are getting along I shouldn't wonder. She saw his shoulders relax on seeing their happy faces and lots of shared laughter.

By the time the afternoon was over, Kate and Edith were firm friends, with Edith promising to help Kate improve her bridge game. "Don't worry about missing Jack when he's on tour. Maymyo's social calendar will leave you breathless, happy, and in a whirl as if you were on vacation. Our social activities go on around the clock—full-dress balls, sports galore, lots of socializing, lots of gossip, a ton of back-biting. You'll be fine. And I'll introduce you to the most interesting people here. You'll enjoy yourself in Maymyo as much as you ever did in Rangoon's social circles."

Jack and Kate went riding together almost every day he was in town, sometimes accompanied by Edith and Tom. Jack wanted Kate to know her way around the many riding trails so as not to get lost.

They made good use of The Club's facilities, frequently playing tennis and attending the dances. They often went to the racecourse and played golf, too. If they did not go to The Club in the evenings, they went to cocktail parties and sometimes dinner at one of the officials' houses. Edith was right; the social whirl was no less exciting than Rangoon's.

One cloud hanging over Kate's happiness was the difficulty in getting close to the children. Relationships between parents and children were so different from the way she had been brought up in England. Adults here seemed to spend most of their time socializing, leaving the *ayah* to take care of child-caring duties. Kate found a role reading to the children at bedtime, but she wasn't always home at that time of day.

She confided her frustrations to Jack, who put his arm around her shoulders. "I'm sure Upala doesn't intend to cause you problems with the children. She's been with us six years, and I have nothing but gratitude for her presence."

"I think it's the way of life here. No real time to be a parent, and I want to get to know the children better," Kate said.

"I think it's time to buy two ponies, don't you? The children's birthdays are coming up and we can teach them to ride, then you can take them riding with you sometimes."

"Oh, Jack, that's a marvelous solution. I love you so much, and please don't think I want to get rid of Upala. She's a tremendous help. I guess I'm having trouble finding my place with the children. It will be all right."

A week later, learning that a Captain Taylor at the garrison had two ponies to sell, Jack went to see him. Jack thought the ponies would be ideal for David and Pamela and arranged to take the family to see them the following Saturday when they would not be at school.

"David! Pamela! Hurry, we don't want to be late."

"Where are we going, Daddy?" David asked.

"Surprise," Jack answered.

"We're having a surprise?" Pamela asked.

"We're having a wonderful surprise," Kate said. "Let's go." To Upala, Kate said, "We'll be back after lunch, so if you want to take the morning off and go to the bazaar, you can."

Her face expressionless, Upala said, "Thank you, I will visit a friend, *thakin-ma*."

Jack stopped the car at a neat bungalow, larger than the accommodation provided for regular soldiers. Captain Taylor came out to meet them and led them to the rear of the premises. Turning the corner of the house, Pamela squealed with delight. Two ponies were tied to a tree in a small paddock.

"Daddy, Daddy, look!" she called, running to the white Welsh Mountain pony. She hugged the pony around its neck. "It's just what I want. How did you know?"

Jack looked at Kate. "A little birdie told me."

"Mummy you told him what I wanted." Pamela ran to Kate and wrapped her arms around her waist. Kate gasped then grinned with delighted relief. *She called me Mummy. I made her happy.*

Jack put his hand on David's shoulder. "What about you, David? Do you like your pony? He's really handsome."

David grinned and nodded and took his father's hand and pulled him to the pony. He stroked its nose. Jack pulled a piece of carrot from out of his pocket and gave it to David, who gave it to the Palomino. "What is he called, sir?" he asked Captain Taylor.

"This little chap is Prince. The white one is Duchess."

"I think Duchess is a bit too big for Pamela," Jack said. "We'll have to be careful, but she's growing quickly. It should be all right."

The captain's two sons came from the house. They looked subdued as they began to stroke and pat the ponies.

"Are you sad?" Pamela asked.

The taller of the two boys told her, "Yes, but we've outgrown them, and we're leaving for boarding school soon. We want them to go to a good home."

His brother said, "Prince will do anything for a carrot treat."
David laughed. "I said I wanted a pony who liked carrots."

Three weeks later Jack had to leave on a tour. He hoped he
had shown Kate enough so that she could manage alone. He
had asked Edith to take Kate under her wing. His big fear was
that Kate would discover she did not like this life of
honeymoon periods when he was home followed by loneliness
while he was away. Similar to a sailor's wife, he thought. Not
everyone's cut out for it. Other wives had gotten caught up in
Maymyo's hectic social life. The holiday atmosphere and
intemperate use of alcohol often caused usually sensible people
and bored, lonely housewives to indulge in extra-marital affairs
and flirtations with the many lonely bachelors who came to
Maymyo for its recreation facilities. He didn't know why he
was worrying. He trusted Kate and Edith was as steady as they
came. No worries about her leading Kate astray.

Jack hugged and kissed Pamela and David goodbye as they
left for school. It was much harder to leave Kate. She had lit up
his life. Kate tilted her face up for a kiss. Jack kissed her gently
on the lips. "I'm not good at farewells, Kate. Don't like them.
Never have. So, no long goodbyes, darling. Stay safe. I love
you. See you in two months. You'll be all right, won't you?"

"Don't worry. Go on now. Everything will be fine."

Too choked with emotion to speak, Jack jumped in the car
for Nyan Sein to drive him to the station. He waved to Kate,
and the car disappeared down the drive.

Kate had not realized her husband had such a phobia about
goodbyes. Dumbfounded at first by his hasty departure, she
soon broke into laughter, shaking her head at her husband's
peculiarity. Then she fell silent. Goodbyes aren't easy, are they,
my darling? Well, at least she had Edith, Upala and the children
for company. She was fortunate to have such a strong,
forthright friend. Kate's first visit to The Club after Jack's
departure had been marred by a meeting with Mrs. Freemont,

the doctor's aging wife. She was strong woman who, in spite of her years and use of a cane, was a driving force. She seemed full of vigor. Unfortunately, she had a tendency to spitefulness.

Edith had called to suggest going to The Club for lunch and a game of bridge. After lunch, they sat in a quiet corner of the veranda, heads together, drinking mimosas, getting to know one another better, and celebrating winning at cards. Recently returned from visiting her cousin in Ceylon, Mrs. Freemont ignored others on the veranda and joined Kate and Edith. She kept staring at Kate. Edith's face became tight. She smiled and was polite to the intruder, but there was definitely an air of hostility.

Edith saw Colin's teacher, Rajat Singh, enter the lounge. "I'm sorry, Kate. Would you excuse me a minute? I need to talk to Mr. Singh. I'll be back soon."

She stared sternly at Mrs. Freemont before walking away. Kate wondered what that was about. It wasn't long before she found out.

After Edith left, Mrs. Freemont fixed her lizard eyes on Kate. The hair on Kate's arms and neck prickled. She felt like a creature about to become a predator's lunch.

"I have lots of relatives in England with whom I correspond," Mrs. Freemont said. "They send me all the gossip, when someone dies, or gets married or mars their good name. I eventually get to know all the scandal."

A knot formed in the pit of Kate's stomach. This woman is not trying to be friendly.

Mrs. Freemont smoothed her hair and patted it into place. Her dark, beady eyes assessed Kate, piercing her defenses. She smiled malevolently and continued in a low, menacing tone. "A little bird told me you left England and went to live with an unmarried man in Rangoon. Then you managed to nab poor Jack Bellamy to marry you. You must have been escaping some scandal in England to become stepmother to two half-caste children. You can be sure I'll find out."

Kate gasped at the woman's malice. She stood up and bumped into Edith who had returned.

"Sorry, Edith, I have to go," Kate said and fled.

Edith turned on Mrs. Freemont. "What have you been up to, you old witch?"

Mrs. Freemont gave a smug smile and shrugged.

Edith hurried after Kate. They drove to Edith's house. Kate was shaking and crying she was so upset. Edith called her servant to bring a jug of lemonade and some gin.

"Here, sit down, Kate. Tell me what the old bat said."

Kate recounted the events of the past few minutes. Taking Edith into her confidence, Kate told her about Charles and how he murdered her son. "I don't want the world to know about that. I've done nothing wrong, yet it feels like a stigma clinging to me, and now it's followed me half-way around the world. I don't want my past to spoil my happiness with Jack."

"Does Jack know about this?"

"Yes."

"Then no matter what that woman says, whatever scandal she tries to create, Jack knows the truth and will stand with you." Edith took hold of Kate's hand. "The audacity of that woman never fails to surprise me. Leave Mrs. Freemont to me. I'll deal with her. I know a thing or two that would cause her great embarrassment if I opened my mouth. She won't bother you again.

"She tried to hurt Tom one time, spreading rumors about how Tom wasn't much of a man because his father had beaten all his manliness out of him. And it was true, Tom's father was a—a—cruel and sadistic bastard! Excuse me. Edith held her hand over her chest and took deep breaths to calm down. "Tom lost all confidence and belief in himself."

Kate squeezed Edith's hand. The hale and hearty outgoing Tom who welcomed her at the station was, according to Edith, lacking confidence and belief in himself. She would never have suspected it.

Seeing Kate's surprise, Edith said, "Yes, he's a very good actor, isn't he? He's blossomed since he got away from his father, who died a few years ago, thank goodness. Tom gets his strength from me and Colin. He knows we love him, even adore him. We're his anchor, his hold on the good side of life. I tend to take control and be bossy, but in a kind way, and my strength makes Tom feel safe. I told his father where to go and I'll do the same to Mrs. Freemont. Don't you worry anymore."

Three days later at the club, Mrs. Freemont kept her distance. It was her husband, Dr. Freemont, droopy-eyed, turkey-necked, with a bulbous nose prone to dripping, who was holding court. He considered himself an armchair expert tactician, blustering about the war in Europe and Africa, delighted that the Royal Navy had sunk the Bismarck and no one could beat the British navy.

"Do you think the war will come to these parts, Freemont?" the owner of the Golf Club Repair Shop asked.

The question peaked some members interest and had them, waiting for the doctor's words of wisdom.

"Absolutely no chance. It's all Europe and Africa. It will never approach these shores," was his definitive reply.

Members, listening intently, nodded their heads in agreement, others tried to grab an opportunity to contribute. Not wanting to encourage Dr. Freemont's holding court, some members retreated behind magazines and newspapers or played chess in a quiet corner.

Some British clubs did not allow people of mixed race to become members. Maymyo was more open than most. The Anglo-Indian postmaster and the Anglo-Burmese deputy headmaster of the government high school, Mr. Halpin, were considered acceptable. Geoff Bostick, manager of Bombay Burmah Trading Corporation who lived with his family in an imposing home in Maymyo called Woodstock, was a popular member. He often threw well-attended parties in his large house. Gossip had it that many a secret, adulterous tryst took place in Bostick's large garden during these parties with alcohol contributing to reducing attendees' inhibitions. Numerous members of the government administration enjoyed spending time in The Club, their home from home, as did many young men on leave from the teak and trading companies in Burma that employed them. Bored and neglected wives delighted in the opportunity to brighten the leaves of these young men eager to partake of polo matches, tennis, hunting and female company after months of deprivation.

Tired of the struggle with Upala, from whom she felt an underlying suspicion, Kate spent much of her time at The Club with Edith.

"I sat Upala down and reassured her that her job was safe, that I had no plans for her to leave," Kate confided in Edith. "I wouldn't do that. The children love her. She has cared for them since they were born. They have already lost their mother. I won't allow them to lose someone else they love. I'm just not sure where I fit in."

"It's difficult to spend time with your children in this society. You lose the ability to be with your children if they are sent to boarding school. If they stay with you and attend a local school, the *ayah* steals their time and attention. In some ways, it's good and in others bad. Your children can grow up without you really knowing them or becoming close to them."

"Do you plan to send Colin to boarding school?"

"No, Tom would hate it. He needs us both around him."

"Jack and I talked about boarding school in England and ruled it out. We feel the children would be teased, or bullied, or treated badly because of their mixed race."

"It looks as if you and Jack are in agreement as far as the children are concerned. That should reduce the number of arguments you'll have."

"We're still finding out who we are and how best to relate to one another. I'll probably never tell him about Mrs. Freemont's nasty comments. Nothing good would come of it."

"Wise girl. As for the children, have you taught them enough about riding their ponies so they can come riding with us? That would give you time with them without Upala's presence."

"I've been teaching them to ride around the garden. They might be ready for a short outing on a leader rein. That's a good idea, Edith."

14

Christmas was fast approaching. Kate asked Upala about the children's previous Christmases and decided to make this one, her first with the children, as near as possible a typical English Christmas. Upala's reception to the idea was cool. Kate wondered if she was making a mistake by not doing the usual Christmas celebrations for the children. When Jack returned from his tour, she expressed her doubts to him. Jack thought it a great idea. "Could we have Christmas pud and crackers to pull? What about funny hats?" he asked.

Certain of Jack's approval, Kate threw herself into the holiday spirit, dragging Edith around the bazaars, searching for things she needed: paper to make paperchain decorations, plasticine to make glove puppets, dried fruits for puddings, materials to make tree angels and toys.

Out riding one morning, she talked with Jack about Upala. "This looks as if it will be a long talk," Jack said. "Let's dismount and sit on this log and look at the view while you tell me what's on your mind."

Once settled on the log, words spilled from Kate's lips. "I don't want to try and have the usual mistress-servant relationship with Upala any longer. She has been involved with the children since they were born. The last two-and-a-half years, she has been the only mother figure they have had. She is closer to the children than I am, at least at the moment, and I don't want to usurp her from that role. It would be too unsettling for both Pamela and David."

Jack opened his mouth to say something.

"Don't say anything, Jack. Please, let me get this out. I've been thinking about it for a long time. The children feel safe with her, and I believe they are as fond of her as she is of them. I'm the interloper. I'm starting to fit in, somewhat, but the social demands of living here eat up my time. Which brings me to the point I want to make. I want to treat Upala as an aunt to the children. I want your approval to be able to confide in her on more friendly terms, more as an equal when you are away on tour."

"Well, I wasn't expecting that. I could have expected you, or rather a second wife, to force yourself on them as their mother. Or to have ignored them and left their care to their *ayah*. This is a bit different."

"So, what do you say?"

"Kate, I think this is the wisest and kindest thing you can do." Jack put his arm around Kate's shoulder and pulled her to him. "I never told you before, but when Su Su Yi and I asked Upala to be David's *ayah*, she was a widow and in financial difficulties. She is intelligent and educated and could do so much more than be a children's nurse. But she is very happy with us and loves the children. She and her husband were looking forward to starting a family, but he died suddenly while young, and Upala never got the children she wanted." Jack put his finger under Kate's chin and tilted her head to kiss her deeply on the lips. "How could I ever have been so fortunate as to find you?" He kissed her again more deeply. Kate felt as if her heart would burst with joy. "All I want is to have a warm, happy, family life with you, a woman who loves me as much as I love her."

Two days later, Kate and Jack were in the garden about to mount their horses to go riding when Nyan Sein ran onto the veranda. "*Thakin! Thakin!* Mr. Hubbard is on the telephone, sir. You must come to the phone. It is urgent."

Jack hurried indoors and picked up the receiver.

Sounding breathless, his voice urgent, Tom said, "Did you listen to All-India Radio this morning?"

"No."

"Turn on the radio. Japan attacked America yesterday. At Hawaii. Jap planes bombed the American fleet at anchor in Pearl Harbor. Britain and America have declared war against Japan."

"Good God! We're at war with Japan?" He felt unsteady, as if the floor had given way beneath him.

"Yes. Not content with bombing Pearl Harbor, the yellow devils also bombed Singapore, Hong Kong, Malaya, The Philippines—what on earth are they thinking? Are they trying to take over the world?"

Jack looked through the window at Kate stroking Blaze's nose. "Damn! The war has come to The East. Singapore? Malaya? Do you think we can avoid it?"

"Not sure, old chap. I'm going to The Club for lunch. See you there?"

Tom's words had dimmed Jack's bright light of happiness. "Yes." His mind in turmoil, Jack slowly returned the shiny black receiver to its cradle. He looked around his living room, so perfect, peaceful, filled with a wife and children and happiness, all paid for by a job he loved. It was all he had ever wanted. Nothing more. Anxiety gnawed at his stomach. How long will it remain like this? Will it all be lost?

Kate went with Jack to The Club. Edith was there with Tom. Jack looked around.

If news of Japan's attacks on Britain's colonies and America had jarred Club members' self-satisfied smugness, they were keeping it well under control. The British stiff upper lip at its best. Wouldn't do to show weakness in front of the natives, would it?

Nevertheless, Japan's unprovoked attacks were the main topic of conversation.

As usual, Dr. Freemont was controlling the discourse. "Little yellow men will never beat Great Britain's might. We have over a hundred thousand well-trained soldiers in The Far East. They'll rue the day they took us on."

"You don't think they'll reach Burma, Freemont?" Jack asked.

"They'd have to get past all our might first, and I can't see them getting past Singapore. It's an impregnable bastion, standing guard in the right place."

Seated beside her husband, Mrs. Freemont sat upright, like a queen on her throne, hand on her walking-stick, looking defiant and haughty as if daring anyone to disagree with him

Jack lit a cigarette. "I'm not so sure we'll remain untouched. So far, our military might hasn't stopped them attacking our colonies in South East Asia."

Dr. Freemont bristled. "Malaya, Hong Kong, and The Philippines are far away. We'll turn the tide before the Japs can do more harm."

Jack held his tongue, rightfully assessing the general consensus among members being that Burma would be able to remain safe from the warring eddies swirling around Asia. Reassured by Dr. Freemont's word, worry-lines disappeared from members' brows. Those confident in Britain's history as conquerors puffed out their chests and ordered fresh drinks from the Indian servers.

Tom and Jack exchanged looks. "I would say they're being complacent, wouldn't you, Tom?"

"While our government is remaining oddly silent about everything, Freemont and the others can hide from the facts," Tom said. "Stay close to the wireless. I'll do the same."

"Why aren't they more worried?" asked Edith.

"Because it's all so far away right now, like Europe and Africa. We'll just have to watch, wait, and listen for the time to do something," Kate said.

"Do something?" Jack asked.

"Yes, do something. We have children to protect, homes, our lives. At some point, we'll have to do something."

Edith stood close to Kate in a show of unity.

"We'll stay alert. That's all we can do at the moment until we see how things go," Tom said.

The following day, All-India Radio announced two British battleships, HMS *Repulse* and HMS *Prince of Wales,* had been sunk by the Japanese off the coast of Malaya. Kate and Jack sitting at the bar with Tom and Edith looked on as enraged Club members blustered and paraded their bravado.

"Look at them," Tom said, "still convincing themselves their world will not be disturbed by vile, yellow heathens."

"Not everyone feels that way," Edith said, nodding to a group of younger men at a table in the corner. "They're having a heated discussion. I can read some of their lips. Some of them are full of bravado. They feel it's time to leave or go and fight, and others seem to be swaggering, no doubt to hide their fear and to not be considered weak. but not yet prepared to change anything."

Kate smothered any qualms she might have about the war by throwing herself into the Christmas preparations. She steeled herself and invited Upala to help while the children were at school. Upala acquiesced with not much enthusiasm. The plan was to have the children do some small task each evening, such as make paperchains to decorate the living room. She asked Upala to knit two large stockings to hang up at the fireplace and help make glove puppets, same as Kate's mother had taught her to, with plasticine and papier-mâché. Once the papier-mâché was hard and dry, they raked out the plasticine, and the children spent an evening painting faces on the hollowed-out forms. Kate gave Upala some fabric she had bought in the bazaar to sew the glove part of the puppets. Jack helped the children make up a Punch and Judy show with the puppets to entertain the adults. He also showed Bikram, the *mali,* how to build a cabinet that would be a small theater to accommodate three children—Pamela, David and their friend Colin who would be included in the fun.

As preparations progressed, the two women sat making angels to decorate the tree. Kate often caught Upala looking at her with an inscrutable expression devoid of the warmth and ease she had hoped would develop as they worked together. Although never rude, Upala kept her distance. Disappointed that it appeared she and Upala would never become close as joint caregivers to the children, she was nevertheless relieved that Upala so obviously loved David and Pamela.

Thoughtful Hasin deliberately timed his cake-making to give David and Pamela the treat of scraping cake batter residue from the mixing bowls when they returned from school. Jack and Bikram found a suitable tree in the forest and set it up in the living room. The children helped the adults decorate it with the angels Upala had made, all the while singing Christmas carols and songs in front of the log fire that kept December's chilly nights at bay. Kate could not find any Christmas crackers for Jack, but the children made funny hats for everyone, including the staff, from stiff paper decorated with crayoned pictures. Jack had bagged a wild goose for the pot. Edith, Tom and Colin would join them for the Christmas Day feast and Kate's first Christmas as Jack's wife.

Kate was happy. All her planning and work was coming to fruition. She was trying to recreate the happy Christmases she'd spent with her father and brother before she married Charles., She hoped every Christmas with Jack would be as warm and cozy as they had been. Kate's face fell. Andy! Last news she'd received was that he was doing well, so far surviving unscathed in his Majesty's Army.

And Dad. I haven't had a letter from him in a while and Manny hasn't replied to my last one asking about the Japanese threat and what is happening with him in Rangoon. He usually writes once a week.

She hoped their letters, when they eventually arrived would contain good news. She promised herself she would write as soon as Christmas was over.

Christmas morning, David woke early and put on his dressing gown and slippers. He stood and listened. The house was quiet except for Hasin who was in the kitchen lighting the stove. David tip-toed to Pamela's bedroom, shook her awake, held his finger to his lips, then led the way to the veranda. Their eyes lit up at the piles of presents crammed there. Pamela could remain quiet no longer. "David! Look what Father Christmas has brought us!"

"Shh, you'll wake Mum and Dad."

"Oh, will you now?" said a smiling Jack at the doorway, with Kate looking over his shoulder.

Pamela and David giggled.

"Can we open our presents?" David asked.

"Of course, you can," Kate said, settling herself in one of the cane chairs.

"I'll see if Hasin has made any tea," Jack said, returning soon afterwards with two steaming cups. He sat on another cane chair and placed the drinks on a round, cane table. He pulled a small package from his dressing gown pocket and handed it to Kate. "Merry Christmas, darling."

"Oh, Jack!" Kate opened the package and found a jewelry gift box. She glanced at her husband and opened the lid just as dawn's light reached the veranda, making the golden metal sparkle. "Oh, Jack!"

"Do you like it?"

"That's pretty," Pamela said, stroking the medallion.

"Of course, I like it. I *am* puzzled about why you think I need a St. Christopher, such a beautiful one at that," Kate said, gazing at the golden disk engraved with St. Christopher and an inserted small ruby representing the sun.

"I want you to stay safe, always."

"Daddy, look what I've got," David said, lifting up a toy gun to show his father.

"That's great, David. We'll play cowboys and Indians later." Jack turned back to Kate. He flushed and cleared his throat. "I've never been able to forget what that fortune teller told you in Rangoon, about going on journeys and being in danger. And now there's a war that seems to be coming closer. I don't want anything to happen to you, so I turned to St. Christopher to keep you safe." Jack laughed, embarrassed. "I suppose it could be considered a gift to me."

Kate squeezed his hand and shook her head. "I'm amazed you remembered that, but nothing is going to happen to me, darling. St. Christopher will see to that."

She handed the medallion on a chain to Jack and pushed her hair up from her neck. Jack fastened the clasp and lightly kissed Kate's neck. The children saw and giggled.

Kate looked lovingly at Jack. "I'll wear it always."

After admiring the children's presents, Kate went inside and returned with Jack's present.

He stood up and took it from her. "Large parcel, Kate. Long."

Jack shook it. Kate would not give a clue. He grinned and tore open the paper. Inside, he found a Wesley Richards rifle. He gasped in surprise. "Kate, it's beautiful. Exactly what I wanted. And it has a Mauser action." He pulled Kate to him and kissed her. Pamela and David began giggling anew.

"Careful, or I'll start kissing you," Jack said, catching Pamela and kissing her cheek, making her laugh and squeal. Laughing, David tried to make his get away, but Jack lifted him up into the air. Nyan Sein came to the door and coughed politely. "Breakfast will soon be ready, *thakin.*"

Jack lowered David to the floor. "Thank you, Nyan Sein." David again tried to slip away. "Oh no, you don't." Jack hugged his giggling son and kissed his head. "Okay now, ask Upala to dress you. Kate are you taking a bath first?"

"Yes, and Nyan, let's have breakfast out here. Za Za Lay has decorated the veranda steps with all these pots of beautiful flowers and hanging baskets filled with sweet peas. Tell her thank you."

Kate strolled to the bathroom, her heart racing with elation.

All that laughter. All that fun. Oh Joey, you would have had all that if I'd not married Charles. I'm so sorry you missed the joy of Christmas. I tried to make it fun, in spite of everything. This is how it really should have been for you.

That afternoon, Edith, Tom and Colin came. Wisely, Edith had ensured Colin had brought some of his new toys—a truck, a Meccano erector set, Chinese checkers and a pack of Snap cards—to be sure no friction would develop about sharing new toys. And no matter how much the boys and adults tried to avoid it, they would have to christen Pamela's new tea set by taking tea with Pamela and her new doll.

With the meal over and stomachs full of tasty goose and fruit pudding, Za Za Lay placed dishes of candy, fruit and nuts around the living room for people to eat later. Jack and Kate went into the kitchen and handed out presents of cash to the staff. Upala received a mauve sari.

"It's Christmas Day. Work is over for you. Go and spend time with your friends and family. We will see you tomorrow," Jack said, shaking everyone's hand. "Merry Christmas."

Kate brought out packs of playing cards and the adults settled down to play Whist. Colin was going to stay overnight and later Edith and Tom would go to The Club. "Like a date," Edith said, squeezing Tom's arm.

"I've switched to listening to the news broadcasts on Radio Tokyo," Tom said. "They give more information about what's happening than either Rangoon or All-India radio."

Jack poured drinks. "Thanks for the tip. I'll do the same."

Next morning, Boxing Day, Kate and Jack went to The Club to meet Edith and Tom for breakfast. The buzz of voices was louder than usual. Tom and Edith walked over to the fired-up group. They looked to be in shock.

"What's going on? Jack asked. "The place is in an uproar."

Tom looked around. "Not everyone's upset. It's split fifty-fifty. Half the crowd is quiet and stunned; the other half is up in arms about it."

"About what?"

"Didn't you listen to the radio this morning? Not content with bombing Rangoon on the 23rd, the Japs bombed the city again yesterday. Christmas Day! Can you credit it!" Tom said. "The radio said Rangoon is in flames and over 4,000 people have been killed or wounded."

Kate's hand rose to her chest. Manny! Was he all right?

Mr. Halpin, deputy headmaster, joined them. "I love this land. Why does the war have to come here? Why can't it stay in Europe and Africa?"

They joined a group sitting with Dr. Freemont, who was saying, "I hear the Japanese will soon invade. I say sit tight. Our army will hold them back and drive them out of the country."

"The Governor believes the Burmese will rise up against the Japanese," said Tom. "I'm afraid I don't have the same confidence."

The vociferous crowd began quieting down. People gravitated to tables where they could more quietly discuss their concerns in small groups. Occasionally, someone would blurt out some nonsense bravado. Club members seemed to be split between those who were in total denial of any danger from foreign invaders and those who feared their whole world was about to crumble.

15

Six weeks after the New Year celebrations, Kate pored over the map of the four-hundred-square-mile Indaung Forest where Jack had marked the route the tour would take. She was grinning like a Cheshire cat. This time she was going with him. They would travel the twenty miles to the forest on horseback along rutted cart tracks to reach the first base camp. Touring in the forest would be split between hiking on foot or horse riding along elephant trails not marked on any map. It would be quite a tour involving the crossing of numerous creeks and hiking up and down three to four thousand-foot hills. Jack had to inspect ten elephant camps based on each side of the watersheds to make sure the men had all the supplies they needed. The camps were around seven miles and one high hill apart.

Jack organized all the supplies required for the tour. Even though he was taking a radio so they could listen to All-India Radio, Delhi, he made sure they had several books to read, medicines, a first aid kit and enough warm clothing to counteract the bitterly cold nights and early mornings of the winter months.

Kate kept humming and singing, she was so happy to be going. Even though she had an active social life and the children to keep her occupied, she had hated being left behind when Jack went on his previous two tours since their arrival in

Maymyo. She had kept her true feelings hidden, but Jack's farewells didn't help. He hated goodbyes. It was a hurried hug, kiss, and a muttered, "No long goodbyes, darling," and with a quick wave, he was gone. Kate was left bereft with a resurrection of all the sad, lonely feelings of abandonment she had experienced during her first few years with Charles.

But not this time. This time she was going with her husband.

It was dark and cold when they left on their horses followed by Bess and bullock carts loaded with supplies. Goodbyes to the children had been said the previous night after reading their bedtime stories. Kate knew that Upala and Jack's household staff would take good care of them, plus Edith would check up on things.

They passed Burmans going to work, heads muffled, faces puckered with cold, and arms clenched against their chests. Sunrise revealed white mist shrouds hiding valley floors until the sun's warmth liberated them from their nightly cover. The scent and sight of wild honeysuckle and field roses, even orchids and violets in dark corners, delighted Kate's senses. Hornbills in flight against the cool, blue sky caught her attention. She felt whole and at peace sharing her wonder at this world with Jack.

Reaching camp shortly before nightfall, they found Burmans putting the finishing touches to a set of bamboo jungle buildings in a clearing beside a stream.

"We're going to be based mostly here, Kate," Jack said, helping a very stiff Kate from her horse. A bit more rustic than your tours with Manny, but we should be comfortable enough. "What say you, Bess?" Jack addressed his dog, who was lying wearily on the ground.

Belongings were unpacked and a log fire lit near the entrance to their night's shelter, a hut with bamboo roof covered with wide leaves and canvas covered walls. An oozie called Jack over. They had a brief discussion. Jack came back to collect his new Wesley Richards rifle.

"Supper," he said.

The oozie's elephant was kneeling, waiting for his trainer and Jack to scramble up his leg to sit behind his large head. When they were settled, the oozie signaled the elephant to stand and walk off into the long grass at the river's edge. Shortly after, Jack returned with two suckling pigs for the pot.

As on the evening Kate and Manny had first dined in Jack's camp, his cook again provided gourmet jungle dining with rich fungi and vegetable soup and roast suckling pig. Sitting on logs by the warmth of the fire, Jack drank beer as he told Kate about the oozie taking him to a wild pig's nest.

She sipped her whisky. "Please don't take anymore of her babies. I can't bear the thought of a mother, even a wild pig, losing her all babies. We can find other game."

Jack squeezed her hand. "I wasn't planning to and yes, I can. I knew you would feel this way."

Listening to jazz on the radio, they stared at the dancing flames in silence, the servants and oozies squatting quietly at the edge of the circle of light, too shy to intrude on the *thakin* and his wife.

Later, Kate snuggled in the warmth under the three blankets on the bed. She and Jack read by the light of the Petromax lamp. When Kate fell asleep with her book open, Jack gently took it from her fingers, put it on the chair, then adjusted the mosquito nets and turned off the light. The chatting in the servant's camp ceased. He lay listening to the silence then switched his attention to the stream's sleep-inducing murmur and the steady dripping of dew falling from the trees like rain. Reassured, he fell into a sound sleep.

He woke to the sound of elephant bells. The oozies had already searched the jungle for their hobbled elephants and brought them back to camp. Jack washed and shaved while the oozies squatted around silently eating their breakfast of steaming boiled rice off a banana leaf. As Kate and Jack ate a breakfast of scrambled eggs and rice, the oozies harnessed their elephants and disappeared into the jungle to start their working day, clearing paths so they could drag logs to the streams.

Jack persuaded Kate to stay in camp. She was still stiff from the long ride. "I'm going to the nearest camp so I should be home by late afternoon. I'll leave Bess with you. The camp won't be quiet for long. The elephants don't work after ten; they need a lot of time to feed. The oozies will unload them and take them down to the stream to bathe if you want to go and watch. After that, the elephants spend their day grazing."

Kate didn't protest too much. She *was* sore. She read her book and took Bess for a walk along the riverbank. Surrounded by trees and lush greenery, Kate felt serene and safe as if she were in 'The Garden of Eden.' The discovery of a leopard's pugmark in at the edge of the stream jolted her from placid to agitated in two seconds flat, and she hurried back to camp. When the elephants returned to bathe, she took out her sketchbook and pencils and found a place to sit near the stream. She hoped her drawings would be good enough to show the children. The oozies called to their elephants, "*Lah! Lah!*" (Come on! Come on!) or, "*Digo lah! Digo lah!*" (Come here! Come here!) They lathered up suds from tree bark and proceeded to wash the elephants. From the laughter and trumpeting the activity generated, it would seem both men and beasts were having a good time.

When Jack returned, the cook had a curry and a cup of tea ready for him. Jack sat down with Kate. "Hello, darling, how did your day go without me?"

"I'm used to being without you. Remember, you're away on tour a lot. But I'm glad you're back. I saw a leopard's pugmark by the stream this morning."

"How do you know it was a leopard?"

"Manny taught me well when we went on tour."

"I'll warn the boys to watch out for it. I want nothing to happen to you when we're away from camp." Kate showed Jack her sketchbook. "I watched the oozies wash their elephants."

"You have talent!"

"Thank you, darling, but did you notice the suds I sketched? Where do the oozies get soap suds to wash the elephants?"

"Oh, there's a tree bark that lathers up when you rub it in water."

"Really! So, could I wash my hair with it?"

"Yes, you could." Jack called for more tea, then asked, "Ready to join me on a nine-mile march tomorrow?"

Her reply was an eager, "I'm ready."

"It was only routine work today—checking the harnesses, inspecting the elephants, getting to know the oozies. Treated a couple of injuries and not only on the elephants. At the next two camps they're cutting dragging paths through the jungle for elephant haulage to the creeks; my work will be more involved. There'll be a lot of clearance work. Gorges that the logs travel along will have to be blasted clear of boulders that could clog up the riverbeds.

"At the other camps, I'll be deciding which trees to fell. There are usually ten to twelve teak trees in an acre of forest. Each tree has to be mapped, logged, and measured at chest level. I'll choose only one of them to girdle, the largest with a girth over seven-foot six inches, leaving the rest for another felling cycle."

"What happens to the tree you select?"

"Once the tree bark is ringed, we leave it standing. It takes three years to die and become seasoned. That makes it light enough to float. And that's when we fell it. Green teak sinks. By taking good care not to deplete the forests, we'll never run out of teak.

"The elephants drag the felled logs to the waterway that will carry it to the nearest main river. The logs are made into rafts that float downstream to the mills."

"And you're here at the beginning of the process. That's marvelous."

One of the servants staggered past under the weight of the yoke carrying two kerosene cans of hot water to the wash-house so Jack could take a bath in the folding canvas tub.

Later, Jack showed Kate how to check Bess for ticks. They sat on log, combed her coat and felt between her toes, picking out ticks. "It has to be done every evening," Jack said. As they pulled off each fat, grey tick, a servant hired for the tour crushed it under his big toe.

Sitting contentedly around the fire that evening, Jack said, "I hope you're happy in your life with me, darling. I don't want anything to change. Now that you're with me, my happiness is complete. I love Burma. Wouldn't want to take the children anywhere else. I'm well aware that the British tend to regard themselves as superior in every way to any colored race. I don't want my children subjected to that, but I don't see how I can protect them from it."

"What about the Japanese, Jack? People in The Club seem to have blindfolds on."

Jack squeezed Kate's hand. "They're taking comfort in government assurances that the British Army will foil any invasion attempt. I'm not so sure. I think the government might also be blind."

At bedtime, Jack felt unsettled. He reached down to stroke Bess lying by his bed. He listened to the drip, drip, drip of the heavy dew. An owl was hooting nearby. Next thing he knew, Bess was yelping, then silence. He switched on the Petromax. She was gone.

"Leopard!" he called, grabbing his rifle and flashlight. "Leopard!" He ran from the hut, shone his torch around the camp. He found blood. "Oh, Bess, old girl!"

Kate joined him. "What happened?"

"A leopard got Bess."

Tears sprang into Kate's eyes. She wiped them away with her hand. "Any chance she could still be alive?"

Jack shook his head. His voice hoarse with emotion, he said, "I'll see if I can find her in the morning." He turned to the camp staff who had gathered by the fire's dying embers. "It was a leopard. It's gone now. It took the dog. You can go back to bed. It won't be back tonight." With slumped shoulders, Jack returned to his quarters. Nothing Kate could do or say comforted him.

Next morning, the atmosphere was heavy in camp. Jack and a servant went in search of Bess. They found her partially eaten carcass hanging over a tree branch.

"I'm torn between waiting for the leopard to return to its kill tonight or moving on to the next camp to keep my schedule. I'm so damned angry."

Kate touched Jack's arm. "You're also sad, Jack. Bess meant the world to you."

Jack turned away, squeezed his eyes shut and pressed the bridge of his nose hard between finger and thumb to stop his tears. He nodded. "Anyway, I'd better stay and deal with it for the safety of the people who'll remain here until we return from the first half of the tour."

"And you'll feel better for avenging Bess' death."

Too emotional to speak, Jack gave a curt nod.

Later that afternoon, as Jack and Kate were watching the elephants bathe, a runner arrived with a letter from Foucar Brothers, Jack's employers. Jack tore it open.

His face fell; his eyes darkened.

Kate saw his expression change. "What is it?"

"Foucar Brothers is advising officers in the field, accompanied by family, to return them to Maymyo ASAP."

"Has something happened?"

"They only say it's prudent for women and children to return."

"I'm not returning without you."

"Something must have changed in the last few days. We'll return tomorrow."

That night, Jack sat in a tree offering a clear view of Bess' carcass. By the light of the full moon, he saw a nearby shadow move. He heard the big cat's claws rake the bark as it climbed the tree to his dead pet. Jack slowly lifted the rifle to his shoulder and waited, patient and determined. When the leopard began tearing into Bess' flesh, he switched on the flashlight and fired both barrels. The mangled cat fell, lifeless, gushing blood over Jack's once trusted companion.

16

Late the following evening, Jack and Kate arrived home stiff and tired from their long ride. Bikram helped Nyan unload their luggage and supplies from the bullock cart, then took the horses to the stable. Za Za Lay brought tea and refreshments.

Next morning at breakfast, Pamela and David jumped up and down with excitement at their father's early return. Afterwards, Kate and Jack followed the children and terriers outside.

Pamela looked around. "Where's Bess?"

Kate and Jack looked at one another. Jack joined Pamela sitting on the veranda steps with Spot wriggling and squirming in her lap. He waved to David to join them.

"Bess has gone. A leopard killed her."

The children looked silently at their father.

David's eyes glistened with unshed tears. "She's dead? She'll never come home again?"

Jack shook his head. "No, she's in Heaven."

Turning her head from Spot's licking tongue, Pamela said, "Was she bitten by a snake?"

"No, a leopard killed her, so I killed the leopard. I have the skin in our baggage."

David stood up. "I'm glad you killed it, Dad" he said, putting his head down before turning away and walking toward the stable followed by Patch running and jumping around him.

"I'm glad too," Pamela said, lowering Spot to the ground and running after her brother.

Jack joined Kate at the table. She wiped her eyes. Jack noisily blew his nose.

"I'm relieved that's over," he said. "They took it better than I thought they would."

"They're sad. They've gone to the stable to sort out their feelings. Being with their ponies will help."

Jack phoned Foucar Brothers' office to ask why he had been ordered to return from the tour. He learned the Japanese invasion of Burma was underway. They had taken Tavoy, three hundred miles from Rangoon. They advised: 'No need for alarm at the moment.' The company was only being cautious and wanted to be prepared should employees and their families need to evacuate. However, they were releasing employees who wanted to go and do their bit to help stop the invasion.

Jack told Kate the news. "Japan has invaded south Burma. It's still a long way away. We should be all right, at least for a while."

With lunch over, he stood up from the table and kissed the top of Kate's head. "I'm going to see Tom and go to The Club to find out the latest news. Shouldn't be long."

Fifteen minutes after Jack left, Nyan Sein brought her a letter. It was from Manny, dated February 7th, 1942.

Dearest Kate and Jack,

I'm packing up my belongings to leave Rangoon. It doesn't look good here. After the Christmas bombings killed thousands, streams of people began leaving Rangoon on foot, car and bullock cart, heading north with all the worldly possessions they could carry.

Officials try to convince us that all will be well, that our army will protect us and drive out the invaders. Hardly likely. We only have about 800 British soldiers in Burma whose job has been mainly to police the populace. Maybe they can fight, but as I said, there are only 800 of them.

I am saving my horses by taking them with me before Rangoon is decimated. I truly believe the Japs will eventually take Rangoon. I intended booking passage on a steamer for Calcutta, but I hear the Japanese Navy is sinking ships in the Bay of Bengal. So, my plan now is to travel overland with the horses to India.

Mya Sandi and most of the servants are leaving Rangoon to join their families who live in the countryside some distance inland. Officials are dropping their work and scrambling to get away. One of my colleagues has buried his valuables, hoping to come back soon and dig them up.

Not sure if this letter will reach you. I am sending it with a friend who is taking the train to Mandalay. He promises to get it to you. Please watch events. Things don't look good for Burma. Be prepared to leave and don't wait until the last minute.

Who would have thought that Rangoon would fall? But I'm sure it will, and very soon. Please leave Burma as soon as you can.

You can reach me through friends in Calcutta, address included, as I am not sure exactly where, in India, I will end up.

Best regards
Manny.

Kate's legs were unsteady. She quickly sat down, too stunned to think straight. She had not realized it was so bad.

She called Za Za Lay. "Scotch and water please."

Za Za Lay stared at her mistress. "Are you all right, *thakin-ma*?"

Kate held up the letter. "Bad news."

Za Za Lay placed the drink on the side table. "Is there more I can do for you?"

Kate shook her head. She mulled over the information contained in Manny's letter, desperately taking what comfort she could from Maymyo being four hundred miles from Rangoon and seven hundred miles from the start of the invasion. She looked around her home, listened to the children laughing and playing in the garden. Was she going to lose everything—again?

I've got to show Jack!

Jack found Tom Hubbard in his office.

"Good to see you back in Maymyo. This is where you need to be where you can keep up with what's happening," Tom said, grabbing his hat. "Let's go to The Club."

They were going through the doorway when the telephone rang. Tom hesitated, then answered. He held the phone out to Jack. "It's Kate, for you."

"Kate?"

"You need come by the house," Kate said. "I received a letter from Manny. You must read it."

At the house, Jack quickly read the letter, handed it to Tom then looked at Kate. "It doesn't look good, does it?"

In the car heading for The Club after reading Manny's letter, Tom said, "There's no denying the situation's grave. Your friend in Rangoon, is he a realist?"

"Yes, and he's leaving. He's right. We won't turn things around, unless we get more troops to drive back the Japs."

The two men found several newcomers at The Club, Steel Brothers' employees, apparently recovering from a strenuous game of tennis, lying on wicker loungers, surrounded by tennis rackets dumped on the floor. On one wicker lounger lay a pipe-smoking, large man with a receding hairline. His legs like tree trunks protruded from his shorts. The men were reading The Club's usual reading material—*The Tatler, Punch, Vie Parisienne.*

"Trying to make yourselves homesick?" asked Tom, nodding to their magazines.

"Not me," said tree-trunk legs. "I'm Australian. Name's Braund, Harold Braund."

Tom looked around the group. "Tom Hubbard, assistant superintendent of police." He gestured to Jack. "Jack Bellamy, forestry manager for Foucar Brothers."

Jack nodded. "I don't think I've seen you here before."

Braund looked at his colleagues and said, "Steel Brothers asked for volunteers, so we signed up for Major Mike Calvert's Bush Warfare School near here."

"Volunteers for what?" asked Jack.

"Our employers seem to think the British Army may need help to hold back the Japs. They need men with leadership ability, good knowledge of the country, who can speak Burmese. They're encouraging men with these skills to train at the Bush Warfare School. If we can't halt the invasion, we'll be left behind enemy lines to sabotage their advance." Braund looked at the men with him. "That's us."

Jack and Tom looked at one another.

"Who do we talk to about it?" Tom asked.

Jack and Kate played three games of checkers with the children before sending them off with Upala to be readied for bed. "I'll be in to read to you in a minute," Kate said.

Jack poured himself a whiskey and quickly drank it down. "Kate, I have something to tell you."

The somber tone of his voice caught her attention. Her heart immediately tightened. She'd known something was on his mind when he returned from The Club. "What is it?"

"I . . . Tom and I have enrolled in the Bush Warfare School."

"The what?"

"The Bush Warfare School. I phoned Foucar Brothers and Tom spoke with his superiors. They've given us the green light to enroll. They're proud of our patriotism and that we're prepared to fight to keep Burma. I know Foucar Brothers is desperate to keep the Japs out to save their teak plantation businesses. We're going to do our bit to sabotage the Jap invasion and encourage the Burmese to rise up and fight against them. According to Manny's letter, we don't have enough soldiers to stop the Japs."

Kate gasped, looked around the room. She felt panicked like a trapped animal. "You're leaving us? Why? What about us? The children?"

Jack put his arms around her. "Should the need arise, and I'm not sure it will, but if it does, Tom and I will make sure you're evacuated to safety. It's not looking as good as I would like. The Japs are far away. But we need to be prepared. It's something Tom and I have to do to protect our families, our lives here in Burma, to be able to look at ourselves in the mirror. I can't just run away, Kate."

Kate's heart was pounding. She wanted to scream; you *are* running away! You're abandoning us! But all she uttered was a dull, "When do you leave?"

Jack and Tom, along with a handful of men, leapt from the truck at the secret hill station shaded by teak trees. The Bush Warfare School was only a short drive from Maymyo. Maybe the authorities knew things were not going well for Burma, the two men rationalized. All the more reason to do something useful to prevent Burma falling into Japanese hands.

The school's mission supposedly was to teach jungle warfare to the Chinese, but that was a cover for its real purpose, teaching guerrilla warfare tactics.

Volunteers from The King's Own Yorkshire Light Infantry had claimed the best billets. Jack and Tom had been warned that they were going to share the next few weeks with misfits drawn from dozens of regiments from all over southeast Asia.

The men were called together to meet two of their instructors, Lieutenant-Colonel Brocklehurst in charge of Special Services Detachment 2 (S.S.D.2) and legendary Major J. Mike Calvert, better known as "Mad Mike" Calvert.

Jack and Tom learned they had volunteered to be trained in the latest sabotage tactics and demolition and would be blowing up bridges and railway lines.

Prior to leaving, Jack urged Kate to go to The Club regularly to keep up-to-date with what was happening. She and Edith didn't need any encouragement. The uncertainty of the situation sent them there most nights to play bridge, listen to the latest opinions about the war, and anxiously latch onto the words of those who pooh-poohed the idea of a successful Japanese invasion.

Mid-March, blustering, droopy-eyed Dr. Freemont's bald head shone in the light as he moved his head and dabbed his sweaty face with his handkerchief. He was, as usual, holding court with his opinions. "Where's that punkah-wallah? Get this punkah moving. Cool the air." The punkah-wallah drummed up more energy, enough to make the palm-shaped fan squeak as it swayed.

"Do you think we should be evacuating?" asked Edith.

"There's been no evacuation order by officials for this area, and they should have their ear to the ground, eh? Don't worry yet," the doctor said, "our boys will turn the tide. We'll be perfectly safe, you mark my words."

The doctor's words did not reassure Kate. Other club members were preparing to leave Maymyo. Mandalay had been bombed. The Japanese had taken Rangoon, even though the papers were full of Chennault's Flying Tigers' exploits in protecting Burmese towns. Next day, she told the *mali* to dig a zigzag trench in the garden in case Maymyo fell victim to a bombing raid. Bikram looked at her closely, finished his tea and went for a spade. His digging sparked the children's curiosity.

Kate sat on the veranda, drinking tea, watching the *mali* at work.

"Why do we need a trench, Mummy?" David asked, jumping in and out of the deep furrow forming in the lawn.

"It's a safety measure. If a Japanese plane flies over, we have to hide in there, where we'll be safe."

"Safe from what, Mummy?"

"Just safe. It's a game, like hide and seek. When the siren goes off, everyone in the house has to hide in the trench until it's safe to come out."

"Upala as well?"

"Yes, Upala as well."

Nyan and Za Za Lay?"

"Yes, Nyan and Za Za Lay too."

"Hasin?"

"Everyone, David."

Satisfied, David turned away and jumped into Bikram's trench. "Come on, Pamela. Bet you can't jump over it."

For ten minutes, Kate allowed the children to play their trench-jumping game with the dogs, before calling, "Okay, children, let Bikram get on with his work. He has to dig it deep, too deep for you to play jumping in and out games."

As a break from the doom and gloom caused by all the uncertainty, Edith suggested a stroll around the Botanical Gardens. She and Kate were sitting on a bench overlooking the lake with its serene black mute swans, relaxing and enjoying the peaceful respite. In the background, they could hear joyful shouts and laughter from the children who were flying their kites.

"This was a good idea, Edith. The gardens are so beautiful. It's a great way to wind down, and if we evacuate, we may not see them for a long time."

A dull thud, twenty feet away to their right, caught their attention.

"There's a woman lying on the ground!" Kate said, jumping up and running towards the woman, with Edith following. "She's pregnant."

"I think she fainted," Edith said.

"Roll her on her back and you hold her legs up as high as you can," Kate said. The children came running over. "It's all right," Kate reassured the children. "She's fainted." Thinking she may have low blood sugar, Kate asked, "Who has some candy? Someone must have some."

"I've some mints in my purse," Edith said. Kate took over holding the woman's legs. "Stand back, children. Let her breathe. No, tell you what. All stand this side to keep the sun off her."

When Edith returned with the mints, the woman was regaining consciousness.

"Don't move. Rest a minute and suck this mint," said Kate. "You fainted."

"Did I? I remember going light-'eaded an' dizzy, but nothing after that."

Kate and Edith allowed the woman to rest a few minutes, before putting their arms around her and lifting her to her feet. They guided her to the bench.

"I haven't seen you before," said Edith.

"Probably not. Me 'usband's a sergeant in the KOYLI (King's Own Yorkshire Light Infantry). He's delivering supplies to Mandalay at the moment. I came fer a stroll round the park one last time. I don't think we'll be 'ere much longer."

"We've been wondering about that ourselves. The news doesn't seem to be getting any better. Malaya's gone, Singapore has fallen and the Japs are in Rangoon. We're hanging on to hear from our husbands."

"Where are they? What was they thinking, leaving you and the children 'ere alone?"

Yes indeed, where are they? Kate thought.

She could see Edith bristle at the criticism in the woman's voice. "Like your husband, they're away doing their bit for King and country. They'll come for us."

The woman bit her lip. "Sorry, I didn't mean t' be rude."

"Come on," Kate said, "we'll walk you back to the barracks. I'm Kate and this is Edith."

"I'm Ruth," the woman said. "They told us to be packed and ready, that the army'll be evacuating us any time soon."

We should be leaving too, thought Kate. She wanted to bury her head in the sand, make the danger go away, restore normal family life. But leaving Maymyo seemed inevitable. She had children to care for and a husband—a husband nowhere to be found.

That evening, Kate and Edith went to The Club for the whisky ration. The rumors from Toungoo were disturbing.

Club members worried that Maymyo could be cut off, because the R.A.F. had gone to India and the American Flying Tigers had gone to China, leaving Burma with no air cover. The Anglo-Indian postmaster could not hold back his dismay with Governor Dorman-Smith. "I do believe he is not up to the job. He's out picnicking and hunting and having socials, while our army is destroying the oil fields. Would that not indicate they are expecting the enemy to reach them, never mind us as well?"

"I'm sure Dorman-Smith has everything under control. If you're so worried, why don't you go and leave us to it?" Dr. Freemont said.

Kate felt sorry for poor Freemont. He was in denial that inferior little yellow men could rout Britain's rule in Burma, and now, here he was rankled by an Anglo-Indian daring to criticize his betters.

The postmaster shook his head at Dr. Freemont. "My family and I *are* leaving, in the morning. I'm only here tonight to tell all of you, it's time to wake up and leave. You must have heard the latest news on Radio Tokyo. The truth is we are all in danger."

One member lowered his newspaper, "Radio Tokyo is full of Japanese propaganda. You surely can't believe that rubbish!"

"The garrison has made plans to evacuate the troops' families," Mr. Halpin, the deputy headmaster, said, "If the British Army thinks that is prudent, I am following suit. That's good enough for me."

He and the postmaster walked out of The Club together.

"It's very worrying. I don't want to leave my business and life here, but shouldn't we go to India now?" asked the Golf Club Repairing Shop owner.

As usual, Dr. Freemont shot down as spineless cowards those people who wanted to leave. "Dorman-Smith remains here, taking charge. He's facing up to the scoundrels."

Feeling trapped and anxious, Kate's whole being was screaming leave! leave! but she hadn't heard from Jack. "Edith do you think we should pack up and go?"

"I don't know. Tom and Jack said they would come for us when it was time. Tom has never let me down. I'll wait a little longer, but not too long."

"I've got a bad feeling. We need to leave—soon."

17

Next day, April 9th, Kate and Edith were sitting in Kate's garden at the picnic table, sipping lemonade. The children were playing hide-and-seek and tag around them. Kate was struggling with Jack's absence. Logically, she knew he was doing his duty and what he thought was right for his family and Burma's safety, but she couldn't overcome her feelings of being deserted and rejected.

"How can you take Tom's absence so calmly? You seem to be taking it all in your stride. He's gone off to fight, leaving you and Colin to face everything on your own. I'm struggling not to feel angry with Jack."

"It's how it is, Kate, dear. The men must support King and country, and we must support the men."

"Must we? Why? I'm raging inside. Jack left me and the children to fend for ourselves while he does what he feels is right. It's not right to leave us."

"I had no idea you felt that way. You always seemed sure and capable."

"Oh, I can put on a brave face, and I am capable. Are you really fine with Tom volunteering and possibly putting himself in danger?"

"Yes. But it's not his fault the war has arrived in Burma. Neither is it mine. It just is, and whether we like it or not, we have to knuckle down and deal with it. What other choice do we have?"

Before Kate could answer, a distant rumble caught their attention. It was growing louder. Looking upwards they saw silver flashes flying in formation in the clear blue sky. The warning siren began its wailing.

Japanese planes!

Servants poured from the house. Edith and Kate jumped up. "Children! Colin! David! Pamela! In the trench! Quick!"

Kate grabbed Pamela and ran with her to the trench. Colin, David, and Edith dived in after them. In jumped the dogs. Edith, Kate, and Upala used their bodies to shield the children who were squealing in fear as the bombs exploded, launching waves of heaving ripples across the lawn. Crouching low in the trench, everyone united in a chorus of manic screams that faded with the realization the explosions had moved away toward the town.

When the all clear sounded. staff, Edith, Kate, and children climbed warily from the trench. The dogs ran around barking. Kate and Edith hurried to the roadside, looking after the bombers. A line of craters in a nearby field and a few wrecked, burning buildings, marked the path the bombers took to the railway station. Neighbors emerged from their trenches, wailing in despair at the sight of their damaged homes.

Kate and Edith gathered their children to them. Pamela was crying. The children clung tightly to their mothers who soothed them by repeating, "It's all right now. The planes have gone. You're safe. You're safe."

Kate looked over the children's heads to Edith. "Oh, I wish Jack was here," she said, pushing down anger and resentment.

When the children calmed, they were handed into the care of Upala. "Take care of them Upala. Our house is undamaged. We need to check Mrs. Hubbard's home."

Nyan Sein and Bikram stepped forward. "We come too, to help," Nyan Sein said.

They drove to Edith's house. She was visibly relieved to find it undamaged.

"Thank goodness. I'll be able to bring Colin home."

They sent Nyan Sein and Bikram to neighboring houses to see if their help was needed, but this part of town had escaped relatively lightly.

"Have dinner with us first. In fact, why not let Colin sleep over? I think we should go to The Club to find out what is going on," Kate said.

At bedtime, Edith encouraged the children to say prayers of thanks for being kept safe and Kate tucked them in.

That night, The Club was abuzz about why Maymyo was bombed.

"It's all bloody rot." Dr. Freemont was in his element. "I bet the Japanese bombers were targeting Chiang Kai-shek, General Stillwell, General Alexander, and Sir Reginald Dorman-Smith. They're meeting in Maymyo right now to figure out what action is necessary."

"Makes you wonder how the blighters knew about it," said a teacher from St. Joseph's Convent School.

George Morecombe, a minor administrator in Governor Dorman-Smith's government, kept stroking his mustache absent-mindedly. "Don't expect much from Dorman-Smith. He's way out of his depth," Morecombe said, with distain. "He hasn't the initiative to make decisions, and he was completely taken by surprise when he learned the Japanese were moving freely up the eastern side of the country. He should have already left Burma. Instead, he's living it up in luxury at Government House. Loves the high life too much to leave."

"The Japs are moving up the country?" Edith said. "Are they coming here?"

Dr. Freemont banged the floor with his walking stick like a judge using his gavel to bring order to the court, and tutted his impatience at such an idea. "We've ruled this country for a hundred years. The Army will keep those bounders at bay."

"Haven't you heard? The Japs almost obliterated Mandalay six days ago," said the owner of the Golf Club Repairing Shop. "I was leaving Mandalay when the bombers flew over. I stopped the car on the high ground to watch the attack. They never let up. Mandalay has burned to the ground. It's just acres of smoldering ruins and ash. Hundreds must be dead. We got it light here. We all need to be thinking about leaving."

His words stunned Kate. Mandalay's only forty-two miles away, and Rangoon fell in March?

"What's going on? Should we stay or go? What's the Governor doing besides talking rubbish?" Kate demanded.

When the only response was a condescending, "Now, now, Kate, stay calm," from Dr. Freemont, Kate turned on her heels and marched out of The Club.

Next morning, she asked Nyan Sein and Za Za Lay to pull out a large teak chest and gave orders to put all items of value in it. They journeyed back and forth with Su Su Yi's silver candlesticks and bowls and her gold jewelry put away for Pamela. Joey and Su Su Yi's photographs were tucked in the chest. Nyan Sein carefully wrapped them all in Su Su Yi's silk *lungyis* plus whatever else he thought needed to be kept safe. Kate then instructed the *mali* to bury it in the garden behind the grapefruit tree.

She phoned Edith. "I've made up my mind. I'm evacuating within the next two days."

"No, you can't. Tom and Jack said they would come for us. How will they know where we are? Do you know the way? No, I don't want you to do it."

"Edith, it's our duty to protect the children. We must go. We don't know how much danger Tom and Jack are in. What if they don't come for us? I want you to come with me. Think of Colin."

There was a long pause. "All right, I'll prepare for the journey. Maybe someone in The Club knows the best way to get out."

Kate told her Indian staff, her cook Hasin and his wife, the *mali* and Upala they should pack and leave as soon as possible for their own safety. "They're saying at The Club that people are already walking out to India. When the war is over and everything returns to normal, there will be a job for you here."

Upala refused to leave. She was staying with the children, no matter what. Nyan Sein and Za Za Lay would return to their parent's village and take the dogs and horses with them.

Although frightened of the Japanese, they wanted to be with their relatives if the Japanese occupied Burma.

That evening, Kate packed light for traveling; even so, the haversacks, one for her and one for Upala, were heavy. Three blankets, sturdy shoes, change of clothing for herself and the children, mosquito nets, four days food, first aid kit with medicines for diarrhea and malaria, soap and antiseptic for wounds, bandages and safety pins, Burmese cash, silver rupees, soap, towels and a map of Burma.

Next morning, two weeks after the bombing of Maymyo, Upala shook the children awake and helped them dress. "We'll have some breakfast, then we're going on a long trip. We can only pack a few things so choose two things that are most important to you."

"Is Daddy coming for us?" David asked.

Kate came to the bedroom door. "No, he isn't, but we have to leave now."

Pamela and David were close to tears, dazed, afraid, chins trembling.

"It's all right, children. We have to go to India. It's what Daddy wants," Kate said. "Remember a change of clothing for them, please, Upala."

"Come," Upala said to the children. "You can help me."

Soon after, the children entered the living room. David was dressed in his school blazer and shorts. Pamela wore a blue polka dot dress. Kate put her arms around their shoulders and gave them a quick squeeze. "You'll do."

Nyan Sein and Za Za Lay helped carry the haversacks and bundles to the car. Edith and Colin arrived with her houseman. He placed their bags into Kate's car. Edith shook his hand. "Take our car to get to wherever you feel safe," she told him.

Kate took one last look around her home. Most of the furnishings had been gathered by Su Su Yi and Jack, yet she felt sad. This was where she had put down roots. The thought of leaving pulled heavily at her heart. She rallied for the children's sakes. They were weeping at having to leave their dogs and ponies behind. Nyan Sein held the children tight. "I will take good care of your pets and give Prince carrots every day," he reassured David. "Your horses, too," he said, looking at Kate.

The sound of a vehicle pulling onto the drive caught their attention.

"Daddy! Daddy!" shouted David, leaping into his father's arms.

"Hello, son." Jack hugged his son and looked at Kate over David's head. "What's going on? Are you leaving?"

Kate's heart leapt with relief at the sight of her unshaven husband in his rumpled uniform. "Yes, we decided we couldn't wait any longer. We're running out of time."

Jack swallowed hard and nodded. "Good idea."

"Where's Tom?" asked Edith.

"I dropped him at the end of your road. Wait here. I'll go and get him."

Jack drove off in a Jeep and returned with Tom.

Colin clung to his father while Tom patted his back and told the women, "We're on our way to guard the railway line east of Maymyo, but got permission to make sure you got on a train to Myitkyina before we left. We'll get you to the station. The roads are clogged with people leaving. Using the trains will be better than trying to drive to Myitkyina. They're using army transports to fly people out of there."

Kate's joy at seeing Jack dissolved with the realization that he would not be coming with them.

Jack hugged Pamela and David and put them in the Jeep. "Don't cry, little ones. You have to leave home in order to stay safe. Mummy will take care of you, until I come back." He kissed each child on the head then took Kate inside the house. "I love you, my darling. I'm so sorry we couldn't get here earlier." Her chin trembled. She began to weep. He put his hands around her shoulders. "I know it's scary." He scribbled an address on a piece of paper. "Go to the Rodwells, my friends in Calcutta. I'll join you there. Stay strong. It's just for a short while." Jack kissed her lingeringly on the lips. He stepped back, fingered the St Christopher on the chain around her neck. "Keep my wife and family safe." he told the medallion. "Wear it always, Kate."

"Come on, Jack, we have to get moving," Tom called.

Jack shook hands with Nyan Sein and Za Za Lay and the rest of his staff. "Stay safe."

With adults and three children squashed in the rear, Tom took Colin and sat him on his knee in the front passenger seat. "Let's go."

Jack pulled up at Maymyo Railway Station. It was jam-packed with Burmese, Indians, and Chinese weighed down with all the belongings they could carry. The Bellamy and Hubbard families seemed to be the only Europeans there.

Jack and Tom bought tickets for the family. Tom bid farewell to his family with a deep meaningful look for Edith and hugs for his wife and son, with the promise of meeting up in India. "Take good care of your mother, Colin. I'll see you all soon."

Jack squatted down, hugged his children hard and kissed the tops of their heads. He stood up. "Kate, take care. I'll join you as soon as I can. He pulled her to him for a quick hug and kiss. "No long goodbyes, darling. You *must* get on this train. I'll see you in Calcutta as soon as I can." He looked over her head to Edith, Upala and Colin. "Everyone, follow me. Tom you bring up the rear." He picked up Kate's haversack and, stepping into the mêlée, he forged a path to the platform. People were shouting and shoving, struggling to keep loved ones together. Kate, Edith and Upala gathered the children to them and followed close to Jack

He looks so miserable, I want to hug and comfort him, but he'll crumble into tears if I do.

At last, a train arrived. The platform had been damaged in the air raid, but most of it was still useable. No time for further goodbyes. The heaving hordes pushed the two families onto the train. Edith and Kate grabbed seats and managed a glimpse and a quick wave to their husbands before the train departed.

They were stuck in a third-class compartment, a part of the train never used by Europeans, but at least they were aboard. Squeezed onto the five-seater bench made of wooden lathes, it was going to be an uncomfortable journey. They nursed their bundles on their knees. All the seats were full, and people squatted in every inch of floor space. It was dim inside the carriage. People hanging on the outside of the train blocked the windows. Pamela complained she was hot and sweaty.

"Sorry, children, there are no fans in this compartment. And don't even think of going to the bathroom until we reach Mandalay. It's too crowded to move," Kate said.

"Not everyone is so meticulous," said Edith. "I can smell pee already."

Outside the station, Tom and Jack looked grimly at one another. Tense facial lines eased. They had got their families away.

"Close call," Tom said.

Jack climbed into the Jeep and started the engine. "Better get on to the viaduct."

Thirty miles driving brought them to the highest bridge in Burma, where they met up with Major Calvert and twenty of the men from the Bush Warfare School. Also at the viaduct were several hundred soldiers separated from their units during the fighting retreat. Their job was to guard the Gokteik Viaduct, the only rail link joining Mandalay and Lashio. Twice a day steam trains rattled over the impressive two-thousand-foot-long trestle bridge carrying refugees and troops on overpacked trains.

Six days later, the Japanese cut the Burma road at Lashio, eighty miles to the south. Although inclined to demolish the bridge, Calvert heeded the civil government's orders to keep it intact; for many refugees, it was the only route to safety.

The troops retreated from the viaduct. Tom and Jack and six other men from the Bush Warfare School were ordered to drive to the steel bridge crossing the River Tiang, north of Myitkyina, to blow it up. After that, they should make their own way to India.

The train carrying Kate and Edith reached the outskirts of devastated Mandalay. The sight of burning buildings, the smells of smoke from charred ruins, carrion crows tearing rotting corpses, buzzards wheeling overhead, not a living soul to be seen, spooked the refugee passengers into silence. Fear clenched Kate's insides; her chin trembled. *I've left Jack behind, facing this. I might never see him again.*

At bomb-damaged Mandalay Station, Kate's group stepped into pandemonium. The women formed a circle around the children to protect them from passengers charging around in a panic, demanding to know when and from where their trains would be leaving.

First order of business for Kate's party was a rush to find a functioning restroom but none had survived the bombing.

Edith led the way to a bougainvillea bush. "This will have to suffice for privacy."

Colin tugged on his mother's arm. "Mother, what happened to the town?"

Edith looked at Kate with a sad face and then looked down at her son. "It was bombed by Japanese planes. That's why we have to leave for India, where we'll be safe."

"What about Father?"

"He'll be along as soon as he's finished his duties. Don't worry."

Next was to find out at what time and from where the train to Myitkyina would be leaving. With no platforms left to speak of, boarding the train would take place on the edge of the station where there remained one undamaged rail. The only ticket clerk still at his post expected the train in an hour—or not—it all depended on if the train were attacked—or not.

Everyone was hungry and thirsty. Kate searched for a food vendor among the ruins of the station, but not one was to be found. Her heart sank. The journey to Myitkyina would take around twenty-four hours. She had some apples and biscuits. The rest of the food she had in her haversack needed to be cooked and she had nothing to drink. She found a tap protruding from the crumbling waiting room wall and turned it. Water trickled out. *A miracle!* She waved and called to Edith and Upala. "Here! Come here!"

The party drank their fill. The children complained of hunger. Edith patted their shoulders. "When we get on the train, we'll have a little snack. Be patient. There's no food to be had here."

The train arrived. Desperate passengers charged the train, shoving and pushing to get on. Kate, Upala and Edith, just as aggressive, frightened, and desperate, fought to board the train with their children. They ended up in a third-class compartment again.

As the train left the station, Kate commented, "The train seems slightly less crowded than the train from Maymyo."

"*Thakin-ma*, many people said they are going to Shwebo, to catch planes to India," said Upala.

Kate's stomach knotted. Jack said to go to Myitkyina. Why not Shwebo? She searched in her bundle for the map of Burma, handing out apples as she found them. Spreading it out with Edith's help, they pored over it to locate Mandalay, Shwebo, and Myitkyina.

Kate pointed to a dot on the map. "There's Shwebo." She checked the scale. "It's about fifty miles northwest of Mandalay."

Edith tapped another dot on the map. "Myitkyina."

Checking the scale again, Kate calculated. "Three hundred and fifty miles northeast of Mandalay. Why would Jack tell us to go there?"

"Maybe they know things we don't, Kate. We have to trust they know best."

18

The train stopped at Myitkyina station, the most northerly station in Burma. People streamed from the train then, not sure where to go or what to do next, lingered outside.

Kate, Edith and their families stumbled from the train into the milling crowds. They were hot, thirsty, dirty, and their bladders were fit to burst. The bathrooms on the train had become too disgusting to use except in dire straits.

Edith pointed and shouted, "Here! here!"

Kate looked at the sign. "White Gents Only." She looked for a "Ladies" sign. Not one in sight. She pointed David to the gent's toilet. "David, see if anyone is in there."

There wasn't.

They took turns to relieve bladders in privacy before all piled inside to wash and clean up. A British soldier walked in, interrupting the job of removing grime and the bliss that came from being fresh and clean.

He blushed at finding the women in the middle of their clean up and moved to quickly step outside. Kate and Edith grabbed him to stop him from leaving.

"Are we glad to see you! Our husbands told us to get on a train to Myitkyina then get on a flight to India. Now here we are with no clue as to what to do or where to go next," said Edith. "Can you help us?"

"I might be able to help. I've got to take some rations to an evacuee camp twenty minutes from here. I can take you there in my truck, but you've got to hide out of sight in the back. I'm not allowed to carry anything but rations. Stay here. I'll make room in the back of the truck, then I'll come back for you."

It was a crushed uncomfortable drive in the small space the driver had made for them, painful too. The road was bumpy and jolting along on the bare base of the truck made them sore. They quenched their thirst by drinking juice from the provisions found in the truck and shared a packet of cookies. Kate took comfort from the children seemingly treating the ride as a big adventure like something from Enid Blyton's 'Famous Five' books, and for a few moments, Kate and Edith's worries eased.

The soldier stopped his truck outside a disused army camp being used to house refugees. He dropped off his passengers. Amid many thanks and goodbyes, he pointed them in the direction of the camp office.

Kate and Edith gave the RAF volunteer in the office their names, and he handed them six vouchers. "Go and find six beds in the first long building," he said. "Then you can get tea and rice at the kitchen."

The mention of beds made Kate realize how exhausted she was. "How many people are here?"

"Around two hundred."

"What happens now?"

"You wait your turn to fly out. There's a waiting list. I'll put your names on it. You need to check it every day."

They entered the long building and found six beds that seemed to be free. Some people, looking frail and thin, were lying on their beds. Others were sitting around listlessly. Colin and David counted the beds in the room.

David called to Kate, "One hundred beds, Mummy."

"Only one hundred here? There must be another building somewhere else," Kate said.

Kate and Edith opened their bundles. Kate held up two cans of soup. "What shall we take to the kitchen? Tins of soup?"

"Yes," Edith said, sorting through her cans and holding up a tin of corned beef and a tin of peaches.

Upala volunteered to stay behind and guard the bundles.

"Oh, no, Upala," Kate said. "You must come and eat with us. The bundles will be fine."

They left their belongings on their beds and went outside. Kate scanned their surroundings and bit her lip. "We seem to be the only Europeans."

Damn you, Jack, we should have evacuated sooner.

"I wonder how long we'll have to wait for a plane," Edith said.

Seeing the children running around and playing tag as they walked to the camp kitchen was balm to Kate's soul. "The children seem to be all right."

"Of course, they are," Edith said. "Children are very resilient."

At the kitchen, they were each given a plate, mug, knife, fork, and spoon, and when they received their food, Edith led them to one of the tables with benches to be found dotted about the camp.

Upala ate with them, all social barriers gone. These were not normal times and this was not a normal situation. Social barriers were irrelevant. The women seemed to know they would have to depend on one another and pull together. The food disappeared quickly; the children happy to be free of the unfamiliar pangs of hunger.

"Let's get the lay of the land," Kate said.

"*Thakin-ma,* maybe we should get our belongings," Upala said.

Kate patted Upala's arm. "We'll get back to them, Upala. Let's just walk around a while. We've been cooped up in trains for almost two days."

Strolling through the camp, they found a wired off area that seemed to be a dumping ground, mostly full of bedding and clothing. In another area, they found masses of cars, parked in neat rows, stretching for yards and yards.

"Kate? Edith?" a hesitant voice said behind them.

"Ruth!" Kate said, amazed to see the very pregnant soldier's wife. Thinking of their own horrendous journey to get here, Kate blurted out, "How on earth did you get here?"

"There was supposed to be an evacuation plan for us pregnant wives, but something went wrong and suddenly the married quarters was empty. Everyone had gone. One night, I 'eard 'eavy boots outside and someone tried the door. I were terrified. Thought it were the Japs. Then a Yorkshire voice said, 'Is anybody 'ome?' He nearly fell over with shock when I opened the door. 'What the bloody 'ell are you doing 'ere?' I told him nobody told me it was time to leave. 'Everyone's gone. Wait 'ere,' he said, and left.

"He came back with a truck. He'd been to Mandalay to deliver supplies, and when he got back, he thought he'd check that everyone 'ad gone from married quarters. 'I'm so glad you did,' I told him. He *borrowed* the truck and drove me all the way to Mandalay station. I hope he doesn't get inter trouble for it. Then I caught the train to 'ere."

Kate peered at her bulging belly. "Have you been here long?"

"A couple of days," Ruth said.

Kate nodded towards her swollen body. "You need to be leaving and soon. What's with all the cars and blankets over there?"

"Hundreds of people have been leaving south and east Burma for weeks. They pack their cars with all their belongings and drive north. They end up 'ere to get on a plane to India. Then they find out they have to dump most of their stuff if they want to get on a flight."

"It's good to see you made it this far, Ruth. We're in that building there," Kate said.

Ruth pointed to the other building. "I'm in that one."

"We'll see you tomorrow," Edith said, putting her arm around Colin's shoulders. "The children are about to drop. We need to get them to bed. Goodnight."

They returned to their beds and found a Chinese woman lying on what was supposed to be Kate's bed, with Kate's haversack dumped on one of the other beds.

"What are you doing on my bed?" Kate asked.

"This my bed. Three nights I sleep," the woman said and turned her back to Kate.

Kate looked at Edith and shrugged.

Too tired to deal with a stubborn interloper, Edith said, "Let's push the other beds together. I need to lie down before I fall down. We'll all squeeze in somehow and sort things out in the morning."

Checking through their belongings, they found a thief had paid them a visit. Fortunately, Upala had kept all her valuable jewelry hidden on her person. Items of clothing were missing. Kate was left with only the dress she was wearing and Pamela only one spare dress and no underwear. Edith searched her bundles and gave an angry shout. "Can you believe this? Someone's taken most of the food!"

Staring down into her haversack, Edith said "What a mean thing to do! I've been left with some soup and cheese biscuits. That won't feed us for four days!"

Edith addressed the people in the room. "Did you see anyone by our beds?" Edith looked at an Indian lady and her toddler across the aisle. She turned her head away. Edith asked each nearby woman in turn.

No one answered.

"We'll pool what food we have left," Kate said, "tighten our belts, and hope it's sufficient. Hopefully, we won't be here too long,"

There was not much to do as they waited their turn for a flight. They spent nine days asking newcomers what was happening in the rest of Burma. The news was not good. It seemed nobody could stop the Japanese on their northward push.

As the days passed, tempers flared as anxiety increased to unbearable levels for fear the Japanese would arrive before they got away. And dealing with the poor conditions at the camp aggravated everything: lining up to use the awful, smelly toilet which was a tent with trenches inside that you rarely escaped from without gagging, or lining up to wash in the bathroom, a tent with a few pipes coming out of the ground, where it took a boat load of patience waiting for the trickle to provide enough water to wash your hands and face. At least the children, in their make-believe world of Famous Five, could rise above the squalor.

Kate saw Ruth's name on the list to fly out. Thank goodness! She'll have her baby in India. It felt bittersweet, and she hoped Ruth's husband would make it out of Burma as well. She choked up. And who knows if Jack and Tom will make it out?

Over the days, they had had several air raid alarms, but enemy planes had been flying high. Ignoring us for more important targets, Kate thought. Just as well, because there's no shelter or trenches in the camp. Then one day, as they were leaving the kitchen, the alarm sounded.

"Hurry! Run for that clump of trees!" Kate shouted. "Try not to lose your food."

Kate searched the sky and relaxed. The planes were mere silver specks way up high. She waved a fly from her plate of food. A strangled cry from Edith startled her. "Get down!" Edith shrieked, grabbing Colin's arm, pulling him flat and jumping on top of him.

A low-flying plane materialized from out of nowhere and began strafing the camp. Upala covered Pamela and Kate fell on David. The children were screaming and Edith was shouting, "Oh my God! Oh, my God!"

As suddenly as it had appeared, the plane flew off. Kate looked around and got to her knees. An RAF volunteer, lying near them, waved them down, shouting, "Stay put. It'll be back."

Kate lay over David, bending her head back to watch the fighter plane circle in a slow lazy loop. Her stomach clenched as a hail of bullets rat-ta-tatted into the dirt twenty feet away. Then the plane flew off.

She looked to the RAF volunteer. He waved them to get up. "It's all right now. He's gone."

Each day, Kate and Edith checked the notice board for the names of those going to Myitkyina airfield for a flight to India. The women hoped their names would appear soon. They were seriously short of food, and it was painful to hear their children crying and whining because they were hungry.

Their situation would have been worse if they had not discovered an old Kachin native woman who passed the camp every day. Her skin was wrinkled leather, her eyes deep and when she smiled, they could see half her teeth were missing and those that were left were black from chewing betel nuts. Her shabby lungyi and turban and calloused hands showed she was poor but hard-working. They mimed putting food into their mouths to let her know they needed food. The next day, she came with provisions, a few eggs, mangoes, vegetables, to barter. Kate and Edith paid the high prices. They needed the extra rations.

Then came the day, May 6th, their names were on the list. Kate and Edith fell into each other's arms crying and laughing. On hearing the Japanese were only a few days away from Myitkyina, they had been wound tight with fear and the strain of trying to behave normally for the children's sake They packed their haversacks and bundles and went to the pickup point for transport to the airfield.

The truck dropped them at the wire fence enclosing the airfield. Hordes of evacuees besieged the area around a large stretch of grass where the planes landed. With insufficient numbers of police to control the crowds, youths climbed over the fence. Soldiers backed army trucks against the wire and slid over the wounded, lying on stretchers, to comrades on the far side. Kate's face reflected the fear that was almost tangible like static electricity in the air. The evacuees knew the Japanese were almost upon them. Panic was building. It seemed chaotic. There did not seem to be a system in place for getting people organized to board the planes. There were long lines of waiting people and others milling about in confusion. Among it all, Burmese traders had set up stalls selling produce, dresses, and other possessions bartered by refugees for food and drink.

Kate heard the roar of plane engines drawing closer. Other refugees heard the sound too and began closing in on the runway. A Dakota landed. The propellers kept turning. The door opened. Soldiers held back the hordes to allow the wounded to board first. Then a man appeared in the doorway, waving and shouting, "Hurry! Hurry!" Fifty people scrambled inside. The door shut. The plane flew away. The smell of sweat and fear permeated the air from those left waiting for another plane Five more planes landed, one after another, taking hundreds to safety. Passengers were made to throw away everything they didn't need. The stacks of belongings grew.

Kate and Edith didn't look back at their lost possessions. Elation coursed through their veins. The children would soon be safe in India. That was all that mattered.

Early evening, two transport planes landed, wheels kicking up dust, engines roaring. Caught in one of the aggressive crowds surging toward the planes before they had even stopped, Edith and Colin became separated from Kate's family. Jostled and shoved, Edith looked frantically around for Kate. Seeing Edith's anxiety as the throng she and Colin were caught up in rushed toward the plane, Kate yelled and waved her forward. "Go on! Go on! Don't worry! We'll be on the next plane!" Kate wanted to cry. She wanted her children on that plane. She wanted to be wrapped in the safety India offered. The horror at facing the situation in Burma on her own without Edith overwhelmed her with nausea.

Edith and Colin disappeared into the first plane. Kate, Upala and the children fought as best they could to elbow their way through the crowds to board the newly landed second plane. The door closed, leaving them still on the ground. The refugees left behind were shouting to be taken. They fought with people around them The commotion was deafening. Soon, darkness would be upon them. Would they get away tonight? Kate started to tremble. Upala held her arm to calm her.

"Mummy, Mummy, they've gone without us!" Pamela cried, tugging at Kate's dress.

Upala answered for Kate, too overcome to speak. "There will be more planes and tonight we will have supper with Colin in India."

Kate watched the two Dakotas taxiing for takeoff. Amidst the noise and confusion, she heard another sound. A plane?

Thank God! It banked. Came in low. Squinting up at it, Kate saw the red discs of a Japanese fighter. She grabbed David and Pamela's hands. "Run!" They joined the stampede away from the runway. At the edge of the airfield, she and Upala pushed the children down into the bushes and lay on top of them.

Japanese fighter planes dropped bombs and strafed the airfield. The undercarriage of one of the Dakotas gave way. Bullets riddled the fuselages. When the enemy bombers flew away, one Dakota grabbed the opportunity to take off.

Kate left the children with Upala. Cringing with dread, she approached the downed plane riddled with bullet holes, the plane that Edith and Colin had boarded. Soldiers were already bringing bodies and wounded out. Kate's stomach heaved on recognizing Edith's bloodstained, blue-flowered dress. Her carrot-topped dead son was laid next to her. *Oh Colin! Nooo!* A groan-wail-scream escaped Kate's throat. She fell to her knees. Tears streamed down her face. How would she be able to tell Tom his family was dead?

Sobbing, she staggered back to Upala and the children. Upala needed no telling what had happened. The two women and the children moved back to the patch of ground where they had been sitting and waiting most of the day under the glare of the sun. They had had no food or drink since breakfast. Shriveled from hunger and thirst, they sat, a stunned tableau of despair.

Evacuees slowly returned to the airfield to pick up their dead and wounded and search for their belongings.

A man's voice blared through a megaphone. "There will be no more air lifts from Myitkyina. You need to leave the airfield. The Japanese will soon be landing troops here. You will be in great danger. Leave the airfield and head north."

The man's English accent penetrated Kate's stupor. Her eyelids fluttered.

The refugees' panic was palpable; women were sobbing, children wailing. No more help. They were on their own. And the Japanese would arrive in Myitkyina within the next day or two.

19

With Kate in a state of shock, Upala wrapped her arms around the children's shoulders. "Sit with your mother, while I look for our belongings." The children looked worriedly at their unmoving mother. "It will be all right. I won't be long," Upala reassured them.

She joined the refugees scavenging for useful belongings abandoned on the edge of the airfield. Seeing Kate's haversack and her own colorful blanket, she snatched it up, along with some clothes, another haversack, and food.

Upala returned carrying haversacks stuffed with foraged supplies. "What shall we do now, *thakin-ma*?"

Kate's eyes slowly came back into focus. She looked around with dull eyes. Most people were walking off to the north. "We'll go back to camp."

Upala blanched with fear. "Camp, *thakin-ma?* Don't you think we should go with everyone else and head north?"

"No, we'll be better off going to the camp. We can get a car there." Kate stood. She gave Pamela and David a hug. "Come on, children, let's go."

Pamela started crying. "I'm tired and thirsty, Mummy."

"I'm hungry," David whined.

"I know, darlings, I know. We'll get food in the camp. Let's go."

A passing army truck gave them a ride to the camp. Kate led the way to the lined-up cars where she found one of the RAF volunteers loading provisions into a car, preparing it for escape. He looked surprised to see the bedraggled group arrive.

"I had the same idea," Kate said. "We need a car to take us farther north."

The man spoke with a Scottish brogue. "We're lucky these have nae been commandeered. Hungry?"

"Yes, we are."

The man pointed to the kitchen. "Go and get some food while there still is some left. The staff will soon be leaving. Then come back."

When Kate returned, he had chosen a car for her and found some jerry cans. He handed her a rubber tube. "Ye'll need tae siphon as much petrol as ye can from the other cars tae fill the tank and cans. *Ayah,* children, ye come with me tae get some provisions and a map for the journey."

"I have a map. How far is it to India?" Kate asked the man.

"If ye're lucky, ye'll be able tae drive about a hundred miles before ye run out of paved road. Then it's another hundred and sixty miles of rough track tae Shingbwiyang. After that, it's a very long hike through mountains and jungle to reach India. The monsoon will be upon us anytime. That will be tough going. The Hukawng Valley and beyond gets over a hundred and fifty inches of rain a year. But no matter how tough it will be, it's better than being captured by the Japs, eh?"

The color drained from Kate's face, and she fell to the ground.

"Mummy!" the children cried.

A small, wiry man, the RAF technician reached down to pick her up. "It's all right. She's only fainted. It's the heat, and she looks as if she could do with a good meal. I'll put her in the back seat. She'll be all right."

Helped by Upala, they laid Kate down in the back of the car.

He led Upala and the children to the kitchen, handed them bags of rice, two pans, utensils, cans of fruit, meat, condensed milk, tea, tins of cheese and sardines, packets of biscuits, jerrycans of water, medicines and salt tablets, carbolic soap and matches. On returning to the car, they found Kate sitting up.

"Did I faint?"

"Yes, *thakin-ma*," Upala said, above the clamor of the children demanding to know if she was all right.

Kate addressed the man, "You were telling me to siphon petrol for the car, weren't you?"

"Aye. We need tae get moving. Let me help ye do that so ye'll be ready to leave first thing."

"I'm tired, but I want to get away tonight. I'll drive until I drop."

"I'd rather ye got a good night's sleep here. That's what I'm doing. My friends and I are leaving first thing in the morning. When our units left, we volunteered to stay behind to help the Baptists run the camps. Now they're closing the camps, and we need to be away, like the tens of thousands who are already ahead of us. The Japs will not be kind to British servicemen. Ye can follow us if you like. We'll drive as fast as we can as far as we can. If the monsoon hits before we reach the far side of the Hukawng Valley . . . well, let's just say it could be difficult."

Kate took the Scotsman by his arm and led him aside. "Don't be coy with me. I've got children. Tell me what we'll be up against."

He wiped the sweat from his brow with his sleeve. "Right now, the valley is fine, but as soon as the rains start it becomes a disease infested swamp. What I'm telling ye is we're not going on a picnic. The place will be swarming with jungle diseases, and ye chances of survival, especially with children, go right down. I would rather ye started off wi' me, all right? I've got tae pick up some friends and bring them here. I'll fill yea car when we get back."

Kate touched his arm as he turned away. "Just a minute. What's your name?"

"Duncan MacCallister, but I only answer to Scotty."

Kate held out her hand. "Kate Bellamy. Thank you."

Next morning, Kate and family ate a large breakfast and were at the car before dawn. They put their provisions and blankets in the trunk. Upala had stitched hidden pockets in all their clothing to hold jewelry and silver rupees they would probably need on their journey. Kate felt nauseous and moved to the back of the car to vomit. She was wiping her mouth when Scotty arrived with three soldiers in tow. Scotty took a long, steady look at Kate. "Are ye all right?"

"Yes, I'm fine. I think the strain and the heat got to my stomach."

"Okeydokey. Change of plan," Scotty announced. The Japs are on the outskirts of Mogaung, so we cannae go the way we originally planned." Scotty spread the map on the hood of Kate's car and shone his flashlight on it. The adults, except for Upala, crowded around. "According to the map, we can take a different route, north, towards Sumprabum. We'll be able to cross the Kumon Range at the Dura Pass then head down in tae the Hukawng Valley. However, we have tae travel fast. There's a steel bridge where the Tiang River joins the Mali. We have tae cross it before it's blown. I can't see them demolishing

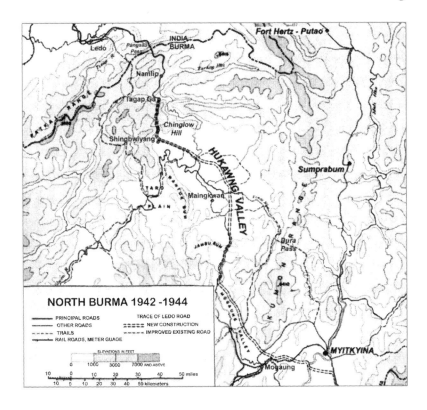

NORTH BURMA 1942 -1944

it until after Brigade HQ and the last British soldiers escaping north are over it. In any event, we need to drive as fast as we can for the next fifty miles."

Kate opened the rear door of the car. "David, Pamela, get in. Upala you ride up front with me."

The two cars left camp as dawn was brightening the sky. Even so, evacuees, mainly Indian, were already on the move, walking in slow-moving processions of rickety bullock carts piled high with all manner of possessions—clothes, books, cooking pots, suitcases, elderly parents. Mules and an occasional elephant carrying provisions accompanied others. Kate followed Scotty kicking up clouds of dust from the dirt road and weaving in and out of the straggling crowds. The pre-dawn sky glowed over Myitkyina and smoke plumes hung in the air where parts of the town were on fire from Japanese bombing raids. Wrecked and abandoned vehicles and scattered possessions cluttered fields and roadsides. Upala looked back at the town. "We left just in time, *thakin-ma*."

It was a bright day with few clouds as they drove across the Myitkyina Plain. The straight road climbed a gentle uphill gradient. To the right, the swiftly moving Mali River flowed south. Soon, the road became nothing more than a wide cart track hemmed in on both sides by dense, tall jungle that blocked out the light. In this murky corridor, Kate and Scotty had to concentrate to maneuver around animals, other private cars, and the hundreds of refugees, mainly Indians, British and Chinese troops, civilians, officials, families—straggling along the track. Kate and Scotty often had to slow down then, once through the jam, drive as quickly as possible the short distance to the next crush.

Late morning, two Jeeps each containing four British soldiers, sped past.

Are they the men who are going to blow up the bridge? Anxiety knotted Kate's insides.

David shook his mother's shoulder. "Mummy! Mummy! I saw Daddy in one of those cars."

"I don't think so, David. Daddy is somewhere else. You must be mistaken," Kate said, her mind on getting to the bridge before it was too late.

When Scotty picked up speed to follow the Jeeps, Kate figured she was right, these were the men sent to destroy the Japanese force's access to the north. She pressed on the accelerator. Three hours later, they were crossing the bridge with the river far below. Scotty waved at the soldiers preparing the bridge for demolition as he drove across. The horrendous strain of worrying about the Japanese capturing the children fell away. That danger was behind them. They were on the safe side of the bridge. Kate's stomach relaxed. She breathed more easily and parked behind Scotty who had stopped a mile along the far side of the river

Scotty and the men got out of the car. He opened her car door. "Come on, Kate, time to eat and have a cup of tea and introduce ourselves better."

Kate brought Pamela and David in front of her and introduced them and Upala to the men. Scotty introduced himself and reeled off the names of his three companions—soldiers from the 1st Gloucestershire Regiment—Bob, a stocky muscular fellow, who had been a cook at the camp. Bruce, tall, quiet and shy, had been helping at a nearby refugee camp alongside Fred, edgy and impatient, who after staring at the children, turned abruptly away.

Pamela tugged at Kate's dress and gestured for Kate to bend down. After Pamela whispered in her ear, Kate straightened and gave a dazzling smile. "Well, gentlemen, modesty insists we must go and hide behind a bush. I'll make tea when I return."

As if on cue, the men moved to the opposite side of the road. Bruce returned with twigs and made a fire. Upala brewed black tea and went around with the pan filling the men's quickly produced cups. The children drank water from the water bottles. They ate crackers and some cans of bully beef, and fresh fruit they had brought.

"When can we go home, Mummy?" David asked.

"Not for a while, David. We must wait until the Japanese leave Burma," Kate said. "Until then we must live in India."

"With Daddy and Colin?"

Kate's eyes filled with tears. "Maybe."

Kate moved away to compose herself. Scotty followed. "Ye all right?'

Kate dabbed her eyes with her handkerchief. "Colin and his mother, my friend . . . Edith . . ." Kate covered her mouth to silence a sob and swallowed hard. "They were killed yesterday at Myitkyina airfield."

"Oh, I'm so sorry. And David doesn't know?"

Kate shook her head.

"Scotty, about Fred . . ."

"What about Fred?"

"He seems hostile towards us."

"He's afraid ye'll slow us down. He'll get over it."

Scotty returned with Kate to the group. "Time to drive on. Want to reach mile marker 102 by nightfall. Kate, the road will get steeper and ye'll need to take more care with the driving. We're entering the foothills of the Kumon Range."

"Show me on the map. It helps me to know what we're doing. I can't just blindly follow you without a sense of where I am."

Scotty pulled out his map and went over their position and the distance they needed to travel to mile marker 102. "To get to India, we have to cross these mountains. They're high, around seven and a half thousand feet." He tapped the map. "But the Dura Pass is only about four thousand feet."

Kate gasped. Her innards began squirming. "It's showing the Kumon is full of ridges and steep valleys! Look at the contour lines! Precipices! Everywhere! How will we ever cross them?"

"With fortitude and determination, Kate, fortitude and determination."

Kate's heart was a lead weight. How can I inflict that on the children? They're not used to a hard, physical existence. Come to think of it, neither am I. She wanted to wail, lose control. Instead, she swallowed the lump in her throat and nodded.

Fred impatiently finished his cigarette and threw it away. "Are you going to take all day or what?"

Bruce and Bob stopped chasing the children around the car and made for their own vehicle.

Kate smiled thankfully at the two men for taking the children's minds off their situation even if only for a little while. "Jump in children, Upala."

After a brief word with Scotty, Bruce walked over to Kate's car and insisted on driving to give her a rest on the next leg of the journey. Kate looked at Scotty and saw he was going to the passenger door on his vehicle.

Catching her glance, Scotty smiled and said, "Got to make these fellows do their fair share, don't ye think, Kate?"

Kate responded with a smile, grateful for Scotty's empathy.

Bruce replaced Kate as driver. Upala joined the children in the back seat. The two cars climbed steep inclines, maneuvered around stomach-churning hairpin bends, and struggled over mounds of earth and rock, the remains of landslides covering the track. Fear of slipping over the road's edge and tumbling down the steep cliffs made Kate's stomach somersault. Wreckage of vehicles at the bottom of the precipices was a constant reminder to take care.

Bruce drove with a fierce concentration. Although reticent, he responded to Kate's questions. Bruce, along with Fred and Bob, had been based at Mingalodon at the airfield outside Rangoon. Bruce had been in Burma seven years. He had been all set to marry a Burmese widow, before the Japanese invaded. "I have no idea where she and her children are. I don't know if they're safe or not. When the Japs started bombing Rangoon, I told her to return to her family's village near Shwebo. I was fighting—Taukyan, then Paungde. We fought hard, but we didn't have the heavy weapons and mechanical transport to defeat them."

He lit up another Woodbine cigarette. Kate studied Bruce's face. She had originally thought him to be young, but noticing the skin pulled tight over his cheeks and the fine lines around his eyes and mouth, she thought he could be in his mid-thirties. One thing for sure, deep down, he was probably feeling as fraught as she was.

"Do you think we have any chance of holding back the Japanese?" Kate asked.

"Look at us. We're fleeing for our lives. I would say we've lost Burma. I've lost my fiancée and the boys I wanted to be a father to. You've lost your home. For all I know, the regiment could still be fighting, but we don't have the fire power or man power to win. We're beat.

"I'd probably be fighting, except I became ill with dysentery along with Bob and Fred. We lost contact with our unit when we were hospitalized. We were put on a train to go to some hospital in Mandalay and then be flown out, only the Japs destroyed Mandalay with bombing raids, so our train was diverted, and somehow, we ended up in Myitkyina to fly out. I didn't want to leave Burma, had dreams of going to find my girlfriend, Ma Hla May. The three of us, me, Bob and Fred were given permission to volunteer at the camp. That's where we met Scotty. So, here we are."

He drew deeply on his cigarette, glanced at Kate and smiled shyly. "You certainly know how to get someone talking."

20

Darkness was closing in when they arrived at mile marker 102. Two hours back, a convoy of army trucks, full of allied soldiers, had passed them at breakneck speed, forcing the cars dangerously close to the road's edge above a precipice. The bridge would be gone by now. Whatever lay ahead, there could be no going back.

They stopped in a small clearing outside the tiny settlement of Mattaing and exited the cars. Cooped up in their vehicles during the long journey, with jungle pressing in on them, they suddenly felt free in the space. The cool night air was refreshing after the day's intense heat inside the cars. It was quiet except for the occasional animal cry coming from deep in the foliage.

Scotty stretched and pointed. "There're some huts over there, probably from the forestry station. Don't look in good shape but let's check them out any—"

The roar of low-flying aircraft overhead stopped them in their tracks.

"Run!" he shouted. "Into the trees."

The group sprinted to the edge of the clearing. Bob and Bruce grabbed the children, tucked them under their arms, and ran. They crouched among the trees, hearts pounding, fearfully watching the sky. The planes flew away without dropping bombs or strafing. Several minutes of eerie silence followed, then they stepped from the tree-line into the clearing, heaving sighs of relief and laughing nervously.

The group walked to the first hut. Scotty opened the door and peered inside. Dark shadows lay on the floor. Someone was propped against a wall. The foul smell of decaying flesh assailed his nostrils. "Aw, God!" he cried, reeling away. "Stay back! It stinks in there. Full o' dead people."

"I'll check the other huts," Fred said.

They watched as he stuck his head inside the other two huts then quickly ducked back, his hand covering his nose and mouth.

Taking deep breaths of fresh air, he hurried back to the group. "Can't sleep in those."

Bob and Bruce drove the vehicles from the clearing, away from the huts. Half a mile along the road, they reached a crowded refugee camp. Government officials and army officers were crammed into the public works division bungalow. Everywhere outside the enclosure, thousands of refugees in family groups sat around blazing fires. The smell of cooking filled the air. So, food is being provided for the refugees from somewhere, Kate thought. Bullock carts, private cars, army lorries and commercial buses cluttered the reception area.

"Let's go back to the clearing," Bruce suggested. "We can have a quick snack and an early night. It's been a long day. The ground is dry. There's space away from the huts. We can spread our blankets under the moonlight."

The nighttime chattering of monkeys and other animal screams made David and Pamela snuggle close to Upala and Kate for comfort. Upala stroked their hair. "Let's say our prayers, children." Following Upala's words, Pamela and David joined in. "Gentle Jesus meek and mild, hold us safe within your arms. Watch over us and protect us from all things bad. Daddy is waiting to see us again. Amen."

Kate squeezed Upala's hand. "Thank you," she whispered.

"Amen," muttered one of the men.

Kate felt utterly forlorn and weary. Noises coming from the jungle were unsettling, especially sudden shrieks as predators killed their prey. Her hand rested on her stomach, protective and comforting. Eventually, she fell asleep and dreamt of mosquitoes sucking her dry of blood.

She awakened next morning to the men stirring. Fred was gathering wood for a fire. He helped Upala make tea and cook rice with canned peas. Twenty-five miles to the west, the Kumon Range's blue mountain peaks pierced the clouds like teeth on a handsaw.

Scotty drank his tea and studied the map.

"Up ahead, about forty miles north is Sumprabum. It's only a small settlement on the way to the outpost of Fort Hertz. I'm proposing we don't go that way. If ye look at the map, ye can see Fort Hertz is surrounded by impassable mountains on three sides. Too easy to be trapped by the Japs there."

Scotty turned to face the Kumon Range and nodded towards the mountains. "I believe that's the only way to escape."

Kate and Upala looked at the steep mountain ridges in dismay. Kate rubbed her forehead. "That's the only way?"

"Yes. I'll show ye on the map."

Kate and the others acquiesced to Scotty's judgment.

In daylight, they saw the jungle was rapidly reclaiming abandoned vehicles. Personal belongings were strewn everywhere. The clearing was not only a graveyard for cars but for people too.

"We may be able to get provisions in Maittang," said Bruce.

He, Bob, Fred and the children walked the half-mile to the hamlet, leaving Kate, Upala and Scotty to pack the food and belongings, dividing them into equal loads for the adults and small loads for the children to carry.

"Upala!" Scotty called, holding up a man's shirt and shorts, "Would ye rather wear these than ye sari? It will be easier for ye to walk."

Unsure what to do, Upala turned to Kate. "That's a good idea. It *will* be a lot easier for you."

Upala disappeared into the trees and returned looking shy and uncertain in the baggy shirt and shorts that came well below her knees.

Scotty gave her the thumbs up sign to show his approval. She folded her sari and added it to her load.

"Do you need to take that?" Kate asked.

"Yes, you will see."

The narrow trail squeezing upwards through the jungle to the pass was suitable only for foot traffic. Scotty studied the spoor. "Looking at the footprints, it's clear some people have been fortunate enough to have bullocks or elephants to carry their loads."

"I envy them," Kate said, looking at the tracks Scotty indicated, "but as we don't have any animals, it's shank's pony for us."

Bob, Bruce and the children returned from Mattaing with rice and canned food. "It's only a small place," Bruce said. "Couple of Kachin bamboo huts and the Public Works Department Inspector's bungalow. There are a lot of people camped there. Kachin tribesmen are sitting on the hillside watching the goings-on. Probably waiting to see what treasures they can scoop up from the refugees lightening their loads before setting out to tackle the mountains. We bought some tinned food that was going to be left behind. We don't speak enough Burmese but David did a good job talking to them for us, didn't you, David?" He patted David's head. "The refugees we spoke to said they'd been walking for weeks, some for hundreds of miles from south Burma. They're resting for a few days to gather their strength before going on. Scotty was right. They said the only way to India from here is over the Dura Pass."

Stepping into the dense jungle, Kate's party began its trek along the trail and up the slope, following the groups of refugees—families, soldiers, the old and weak that had already set out that morning. Kate's group, like the other refugees, was weighed down with as much as they could carry. Unaccustomed to strenuous physical exertion, the two women were soon gasping for breath and the children who had started out gamboling like lambs soon began whining at having to carry their loads. The men stoically plodded on, heads down, one foot in front of the other. Occasionally, Bruce or Scotty or Bob called back to cheer on the children.

During a rest period, Kate squatted in front of the children. "I know this isn't easy for you. It's hard for all of us." David hung his head and glanced from under his eyelashes at Bruce and Bob who both smiled grimly at him and nodded. "We have a long, long way to walk," Kate continued. "This is the easy part. I need you to be brave so when we do see Daddy, I can tell him how well you did, and he will be proud of you. Can you do that for me?"

Pamela and David nodded.

Kate patted their shoulders. "I'm counting on you."

Scotty took a long drink of water. "Where *is* David's daddy?"

Kate ruffled David's hair. "His daddy, my husband Jack and his friend, Tom Hubbard, volunteered for the Bush Warfare School to sabotage the Jap advance. At the moment we're not sure where he is. We're going to meet up in Calcutta."

Later that afternoon, gentle rain began to fall. Progress slowed. They were expending a lot of energy trying to make headway on the slippery the slope. With dark, angry-looking clouds rolling in from the east, the weary party set up camp for the night near a creek, having hiked only twelve miles. They managed to find twigs dry enough to light a fire and cook some rice to eat with canned sardines and fruit.

Kate remembered from her nurse's training that cholera developed from food and drink being contaminated with feces, of which there was an abundance along this trail. She and the children had been vaccinated. She asked Scotty, "Have you been vaccinated against cholera and typhoid?"

"Can't avoid that kind of thing when you're in the forces, Kate. Lined us up and stuck us good."

Kate looked at her *ayah*. "Upala?"

Upala shook her head.

"Then we're going to have to make doubly sure you don't get sick. Listen everyone. This is important. If we're going to make it to India, top priority is to stay healthy."

Fred was sarcastic. "As if we didn't know that."

"I trained as a nurse, Fred, and prevention of disease is mainly commonsense. But I want to lay down some rules because Upala has not been vaccinated."

Fred grunted and muttered, "More trouble."

Ignoring him, Kate said, "We have few medicines, only Betadine antiseptic, some Acriflavine, quinine and some vitamin tablets. Every night, we must wash the mud off and check for cuts and scratches so I can treat them with antiseptic so they don't get infected. I don't want anyone to eat or drink anything that has not been cooked or boiled. So, in the evenings, no matter how thirsty you are, you cannot drink water until it has been boiled. And we need to boil all the water we can for the morning meal and to fill the water bottles."

Scotty looked around all the men, his eyes resting for a long time on Fred. "Ye right, Kate. Good common sense."

Their shelter that night was a waterproof tarpaulin fastened over low boughs. Not perfect, but it was enough to keep off the worst of the rain that by nightfall began sheeting down on them. It didn't, however, keep the ground dry where they were sitting. First, it was trickles of water, then gushing mud flowing down the slope into their shelter. They perched their loads and provisions firmly in the branches to try to keep them dry. However, the adults could not get to a high enough place to keep their bottoms dry, and they stoically prepared for a wet, uncomfortable night.

Kate laughed. "If I'd known it was going to rain this much, I wouldn't have been so insistent on boiling the water. We could have just let the containers fill with rain."

Noticing five-year-old Pamela sitting with her head in her hands, sniffling, Kate asked, "What's wrong, darling?"

"She wants to go home and so do I," David said sadly, his chin quivering.

Bruce stretched his arms around the children. "It's going to be all right. You'll see."

Kate almost cried at the comfort Bruce's brotherly actions brought her. *He's doing exactly what Andy would have done. Oh God, I miss my brother! Jack too.*

Kate's yearning to be with her loved ones was interrupted by Fred, who looked down at his cup of tea and scowled. "We need to make good speed, Scotty, so we can get back to our units."

"Aye, we do need to get back tae them. Don't want them thinking we're deserters in these circumstances, dae we?"

He laughed sardonically at the ridiculousness of the idea and everyone joined in.

The group spent the night sitting propped up against branches and companions. The exhausted children slept with their heads in Kate and Upala's laps. Ferocious displays of jagged lightning lit up the night skies, followed by thunderclaps explosive enough to make the ground tremble, but not savage enough to disturb their deep exhausted sleep. The monsoon had arrived.

By morning the rain had stopped. Mist rose from the ground. Small bands of Gurkha soldiers and a few occasional families, groups of Indians traveling together for safety against predatory Burmese dacoit gangs, passed by as Kate's party ate breakfast. Kate noted that most travelers were in reasonably good physical shape. Except for the elderly. They're showing such determination. Surely that will get them through as long as they have sustenance to keep up their strength and they avoid disease.

Scotty announced they would take ten minutes' rest every hour. Rubbing his brow as if to ward off a headache and sighing with exaggeration, Fred took Scotty to one side. Although he spoke quietly, everyone could hear.

"Scotty, it's about two hundred and fifty miles to India through the worst possible terrain. We don't have enough food. How are we going to make it with women and children holding us back?"

Kate's stomach turned over. The nausea took her by surprise. Is it fear of being abandoned to fend for myself and the children or . . . am I . . .? She swallowed down the sudden rush of saliva to her mouth. Should I say something or stay quiet? She looked at Upala's face and saw her own fear reflected there and found her courage.

"Fred, all of you, I need to say this. I don't want you to leave us. Having said that, it was pure chance that brought us together. There is no obligation, only survival. You are servicemen, and you need to avoid capture by the Japanese. We will understand if you leave us to travel at a faster pace."

Bruce and Scotty spewed heated words at Fred.

"Don't!" Kate shouted. "Don't. As long as we're a group let's stay as a group. There'll be no hard feelings when you leave."

They washed at the stream and rinsed as much mud off their clothes as they could. Their clothes would dry quickly before being soaked again with sweat. The mercury was rising fast. It was going to be a hot, humid day for walking.

Scotty adjusted his haversack. "I hope the rain holds off until this afternoon. It's going tae make things bloody awful for us, but ye know what? It will make things worse for the Japs. I cannae see them coming after soldiers and refugees escaping this way."

"That's good news. I think we should have a singsong, don't you, David?" Bruce said.

David, lost in his misery as he plodded along, did not respond.

"How about you, Pamela? Are you going to sing with me?"

When she nodded, Bruce started a hearty rendition of "This Old Man." By the time he reached the chorus, the children were singing too. **Knick Knack Paddywhack, Give a dog a bone** . . .

He was so lively and comical, the children were laughing, the adults too, even Fred managed a smile. Such sweet sounds, Kate thought, relishing her children's joy. Moments like these would be few and far between during the next few weeks, maybe even months. Bruce belted out his repertoire for several hours until his voice ran out of steam. The group fell silent as they gasped for breath, their bodies clammy in the heat and humidity and eyes stinging from dripping perspiration. They had energy only to force their legs to keep moving.

The trail, already gloomy from the tall, jungle trees and thick vines on either side, suddenly became dark. A roll of thunder shook the ground. Sodden clouds enveloped them. The children clutched at Kate and Upala's legs, watching the men hastily erect a shelter. As if a sluice gate had opened, heavy raindrops pelted down, soaking them before they could rush under cover. The storm came with strong gusts of wind, causing them to hold on tight to the tarpaulin for fear it would blow away. They shivered in wet clothes from the drop in temperature. Dazzling thunderbolts slashed through the clouds.

Hopes for a short, sharp squall faded as hours passed with no letup in the weather. Rain drenched the jungle foliage. Water poured as if from a jug down the steep slopes turning the trail into slurry. Despite the downpour, some refugees kept walking in the ankle-deep mud. The few elephants and buffaloes traveling the path with refugees churned the sopping earth into brown sludge.

Fred, sour-faced, muttered, "We should have kept going. Look at that lot! It's going to be hell when we get moving again."

"It doesn't rain every single day in the monsoon," Bob said. "It only feels like it. The sun could shine all day tomorrow and dry it out."

Fred scowled at him.

"Stop moaning," Scotty said. "Set ye cups and cans out to catch the rain. With all the sweating we did this morning walking in the heat, we have to replenish our fluids."

Cascades of muddy water flowed into the shelter, wetting everyone's bottom to add to the misery. In fun, Pamela and David began plastering one another with mud, until Pamela became a weepy loser and David became too rough.

Upala intervened. "Stop, children. It is better to get some rest. We have a long walk tomorrow."

David's eyes filled with tears. "I don't want to walk anymore."

Pamela chimed in, her lips pouting. "I don't want to walk either."

Kate stopped searching the bundles for food to speak to the children, but Bruce spoke first.

"Do you want to hear a story about a giant whose legs grew small and fell off because he wouldn't walk?"

David, sulking, laughed in spite of himself.

Pamela forgot her woes and cried, "Yes!"

The children snuggled close to Bruce and the tale began.

Kate filled with gratitude for Bruce's wonderful disposition towards her children. She handed out crackers and canned cheese then opened some cans of fruit.

She leaned towards Scotty. "We have a long way to go. Eventually, our food supplies will run out. What will we do then?"

"We have to eke out our rations. Eat just enough to keep walking. Make them last as long as possible. Hopefully, we'll find some natives who will sell us food."

21

The heat was stifling. Sweat stung their eyes as they staggered on. Everyone was covered with mosquito bites, and Kate had to keep admonishing the children not to scratch them for fear they would develop jungle sores. She was glad she had the foresight to pack medications for the journey. It looked as if they were going to need them.

However, Kate had nothing to relieve the exhaustion she and the children were experiencing. The men were walking ahead of them and had not thought to wait by the almost perpendicular, slippery slope to help the family when they reached it. Probably too tired to think of it. An elderly Indian couple were sitting, dejected, at the bottom of the slope, he in a mud-stained suit and she in a soiled pink sari. Kate's gaze moved from the couple to the slope. She and Upala stared at the obstacle in despair, then Kate straightened her shoulders.

"Right, children, we have to climb this slope, on all fours if need be. Scotty and Bruce did it, so we have to do it. What do you think, David? Can you do it?"

"I'll try," he said, and started to climb on all fours.

"Pretend you're climbing a tree," Kate encouraged him. "Upala, you go next. Be careful. Take it steady."

Kate watched Upala struggle after David. "Okay, Pamela, our turn."

Pamela began to cry. "I can't do it. Don't want to. I might fall."

"You have to do it. You have no choice. Let's go."

Kate pushed and shoved Pamela each time she lost heart, faltered or stopped. In the end, Kate resorted to tapping Pamela's bottom and shouting at her to get up. At the top, Pamela sniveled, and David sulked. They squirmed away when Kate tried to comfort them.

"I want my daddy," Pamela cried.

Upala looked at Kate reproachfully.

"Don't look at me like that," Kate said, smearing her cheeks with mud as she wiped tears from her face with her dirty hands. "I had to get them to the top. I'm so afraid of giving Fred or any of the men an excuse to leave us behind."

Kate squatted beside Pamela and David. "I wish Daddy were here as well, but he isn't. He's waiting for us in India and we have to hurry to meet him."

Upala nodded. She hugged the children briefly. "The climb was difficult. You did very well. Your mother is proud of you." With a twinkle in her eye, Upala added, "And now we must catch up with Bruce. Who knows? He might sing to you."

David covered his ears with his hands and laughed. Even Kate laughed. She immediately regretted that she had not spoken as nicely to the children as Upala had. I mustn't let my fear of losing the men become all consuming.

They caught up with the men resting beside a stream.

"Have a good long drink," said Scotty, "then we'll go on until it looks like rain."

The men went on ahead to prepare a camp for the night. Kate, Upala and the children were passed by other families plodding upwards along the trail and sometimes Kate's group passed slower groups. Mid-afternoon, they reached the men sitting around a fire, cooking rice. Fred was cursing that they probably had only covered ten miles at the most. Kate, afraid to look at him, busied herself searching for betadine antiseptic to treat the mosquito and painful sand-fly bites.

The group was subdued that evening and the rain, when it came, was relatively light, unlike their deep, restorative sleep.

They woke feeling rested and refreshed. Upala was straining water through her folded sari. "To filter out bad things in the water," she said. "Keep us safe."

Three hours trekking that morning brought the group to the crest of this first range. They studied the descending trail. It looked steep and difficult.

"Let's rest a while," Scotty said. "Drink plenty of water. We'll have tae take care. The rain has made the trail slick."

A band of Indian soldiers came along the trail. Their *havaldar* (sergeant) seemed agitated. He kept looking back the way they had come. He approached Scotty. "People dying. Many dead. Cholera. Too much shit and dead bodies foul the water. Make sick. You must keep moving." He urged his men on. "We go, stay ahead of it all. Good day," he said, and scrambled down the trail with his unit.

Fred, who had been listening intently, got up and put on his haversack. "I said we needed to hurry. Let's go."

"There's already thousands ahead of us," Scotty said. "We're walking in their slurry. But, you're right, we should go. Don't want more ahead of us than we have tae."

The added threat of disease spurred them on. This time Bruce helped Pamela over the most treacherous parts, hanging onto roots and branches to stop from losing his footing and slithering down the slick path. David watched how Bruce made his descent and followed suit. His arms and legs were soon aching from the strenuous task of remaining upright.

The path turned to sharp, slate gravel with rocky outposts as it neared a creek at the valley bottom. As Kate's spirits lifted at the thought of splashing cold water on herself, her foot caught on a root, and she tumbled twelve feet down the slope. She was unconscious when Bruce caught up to her.

She lay limp in his arms. A bump on her head was already turning blue. Scotty climbed back up the path to help Bruce get her down to the creek's bank. A quick check revealed no broken bones. Her ankle was swelling and turning purple.

Bob brought a cup of cold water and splashed her face. Regaining consciousness, Kate found Upala and Scotty looking down at her with concern.

"I fell."

"Aye, ye did, lass," Scotty said.

Bruce handed her some drinking water. "You gave us a scare."

"I hurt . . . all over." Kate put a shaking hand over her lips. "I think I've hurt my ankle."

A pain in her stomach made her curl up. Oh, no! Please, no!

Scotty stood up. "We'll make camp here tonight."

A stab of fear went through Kate on seeing Fred, Bob and Bruce huddled in a group, talking. They'll be leaving us soon.

Kate groaned with pain. "Upala."

Upala knelt over her.

Kate whispered, "I think I'm losing my baby."

"Baby?" Upala rolled Kate onto her side and checked the back of her dress. "I see blood, *thakin-ma*. I'll get some water."

Scotty approached. "The boys want tae go on without ye, Kate."

"I know. And now I've hurt my ankle, I would slow them down even more. Send Fred to me, will you, Scotty?"

Fred walked over and looked down at Kate. His expression was stubborn and defiant.

Ignoring her stomach cramps, Kate patted the ground beside her. "Fred, sit down a minute. I can see that you want to go on without us burdening you. I want you to tell you, it's all right. We're all terrified the Japs will catch us."

Fred scrambled to his feet. "I'm not scared. We need to be off. We need to regroup in India and get back to fighting."

"Fred, we're all scared. We're either running toward something or running away from something. I've spent most of my adult life running away. I give you my blessing. I don't want you to feel bad, Fred."

Fred nodded curtly and left.

Upala returned with her sari and water, soap and towel to clean Kate, who was now weeping. Whether it was from losing her baby or losing the men, Kate didn't know. It was all loss anyway, and loss hurt. She gave herself up to it. Upala shielded Kate from the men by hanging her sari over a branch. She helped Kate remove her bloodied clothes, wash herself, and then covered Kate with the sari before going to the creek to wash the clothes.

Bruce brought Kate some tea. "You look like you need this. Has Scotty spoken to you?"

"Yes."

"So, you know he and the others are leaving tomorrow morning."

Kate's heart sank at the thought of losing Scotty too. He was so dependable and level-headed. "What about you?"

"Me? Couldn't leave a damsel in distress now, could I?"

"I don't want you to leave us, but have you really thought this through? If you stay with us, you'll reduce your chances of getting to India. I would hate to feel responsible for that."

"That's a shame, that is, 'cos I can't in good conscience walk away from you and the kids. So that's the end of it," Bruce said, lightheartedly. "We'll share out the supplies tonight. Half for them, half for us. Hopefully, it will be enough."

"Not if we have many more mountain ranges and valleys to cross before we even get to the Hukawng Valley."

"Are you injured? I ask because Upala is washing blood from your clothes."

"Because I fell, I . . . I lost the baby I was carrying."

"Oh, that's a bugger. I'm sorry about that." Bruce patted her shoulder and left.

Kate saw him speaking to Scotty. Upala returned and hung Kate's wet clothes over the branches for privacy.

"Are the children all right, Upala?"

"Yes, they help *Thakin* Bob. He makes a game."

Ten minutes later, Kate expelled the fetus and soon after that the placenta. Upala gathered the tiny form in a towel to take it away. Kate grabbed Upala's wrist. "Was it a boy?"

Upala unwrapped the towel then looked sadly at Kate. "I can't tell, *thakin-ma.*"

Tears welled up in Kate, and she lay back. She had felt the excitement and hope that comes from life fluttering inside her and now it was gone, snuffed out like a candle.

Upala went to the fast running creek, opened the towel, and allowed the dead fetus and placenta to fall into the creek. The silt-filled water swallowed it up and carried it away.

Inconsolable, Kate cried. She had lost another child, hers and Jack's. Am I cursed? Will I lose Pamela and David too? Jack would never forgive me. Where is he? He should be here to protect us . . . We've only been traveling a few days and already I am weary. Kate turned on her side and curled up. Her stomach hurt. I don't think we can make it.

Kate woke the next morning as the men were leaving. Their departure jolted her into an internal panic. Inside she was drowning. She wanted to whimper. She wanted to scream, express her terror. But from the outside, she seemed composed, resigned to the inevitable.

"Fred! Scotty! Bob!" she called and waved farewell. "Good luck."

She would not let them see how despaired she felt.

The men trotted over and knelt beside her. "May God be with you, Kate," said Fred. Scotty patted Kate's shoulder. "Bruce will get you through."

Bob, looking grim, waved at Kate and Upala over the heads of Pamela and David who were clinging to him and crying, "Don't leave us! Don't go!" He patted their backs then squatted down and handed David a carving of a small dog and a carving of a cat to Pamela. Trying to stand again, he had to take their arms from around his neck. "When you join me in India, you must show me how well you took care of your pets. You'll do that, won't you?"

The children nodded, tears running down their faces. "We don't want you to go," David said, sobbing.

"I know. I don't want to go, but I have to. The army needs me, and that's my job as a soldier."

Watching their departing backs, tears welled up in Kate. Her feeling of safety was leaving with the men.

At the creek, all three men saluted goodbye then waded across in thigh-high water.

David and Pamela watched, wailing loudly that their friends were leaving without them. The children ran to Kate. "Why are they leaving us, Mummy?"

"I've hurt my ankle, so I can't keep up with them, and they have to get back to their companies." Kate looked at Bruce, gratitude welled up bringing her close to tears again. Choking with emotion, she continued, "Bruce is staying to help us. I want *you* to help him as much as you can."

Bruce brought Kate some tea and biscuits. "Kate, we have to get across the creek before it rises again. As soon as you've eaten, I'll carry you across on my back. I'm taking Upala and the children first, then I'll come back for you."

Kate squeezed his hand and burst into tears. Not sure what to do to comfort her, his eyes appealed to Upala for assistance. She came and sat with Kate and stroked her brow.

As the tears waxed and waned Kate clutched Upala's shirt. Anguished, Kate cried, "Upala, I lost my baby, and now the men have gone. I've signed my children's death certificates." She burst into tears again and sobbed as Bruce kept glancing over, waiting anxiously to cross the river.

Upala patted Kate's hand. "*Thakin-ma,* all will be well. We have Bruce. He will be all we need to get through to India."

Bruce crisscrossed the stream seven times, ferrying everyone and the supplies across. They languished and fretted on the other side of the creek for three days until Kate could walk on her tightly bandaged foot. They rationed the food, so they were never fully free of hunger. Bruce's hopes of supplementing their diet with fish were dashed; the stream flowed too fast for him to catch any. He needed a quiet spot tucked into the river bank to use his fish-catching skills.

One good thing cheered Kate as her ankle healed. The elderly Indian couple they had passed at the bottom of the precipitous slope came through with a group of other Indians who were taking care of them. Among the streams of refugees that trekked past, there was even an English family led by a middle-aged, bossy uncle in a straw hat. Kate figured he needed to be bossy because the rest of his party, middle-aged women, a young married couple and school-age nieces and nephews were acting as if it was all a big adventure. Maybe they had the right attitude. Maybe they could view matters lightly because they had employed Kachin porters to carry their supplies. However, looking at bossy uncle's feet, Kate saw they were wrapped in rags. *Will he ever be able to complete the walk to India? Can we? Our food supplies are dwindling while we stay by the stream instead of making progress.*

While Kate gathered her strength, she used her anger at Jack to rebuild her resolve. *She would show him. She would get the children to India in one piece no matter what it took. It didn't matter whether or not he was with her, so stick that in your pipe and smoke it, Jack Bellamy.* Kate groaned. *I'm being childish.*

When the morning came for them to start walking again, Kate's blood flow had eased, as had her tears. This was not the time to put effort into grieving; everything she had within her had to be used for surviving. She limped only a little. She was still sore and covered in bruises from her fall. The children were awestruck by the big purple bruise on her forehead.

David gently touched Kate's forehead. "I've never had a bruise that big, Mummy."

"Does it hurt?" Pamela asked.

"Only when I press it."

Crossing the valley, Bruce began grinning widely. Then he was hollering and pointing. "Look! Sugar cane. Are you in for a treat!"

He hurried across to the patch and cut some down then scored the hard, outer layer of the stems with his machete so they could suck out the juices. Sucking, slurping and smacking lips, they gorged themselves on the unexpected treat until they could eat no more. Bruce then cut down more stems to carry with them to eat later. "High energy food," he said, taking one final serious suck from his last piece of cane.

Having crossed their first valley, they faced climbing the next mountain range.

"We'll take it slow and steady like the tortoise," Bruce said. "You all know Aesop's story of how the tortoise beat the hare, don't you?"

"We do," Kate said, adjusting the children's bundles. "Let's go. Slow and steady."

They trudged and dragged themselves uphill for hours, crossed several streams by tottering across logs over fast-flowing currents, until the children could go no farther. Bruce and Upala had a shelter erected and gathered enough dry twigs before a squall came. It was fierce but short-lived and they soon had a fire to cook a small portion of rice and tinned peas with a shared tin of sardines.

A chilly night replaced the heat of the day. They spent the night huddled together for warmth and being tortured by the vicious biting of sand-flies.

The next day, it rained and rained. Drenched clothes dripped and stuck to their bodies. In those conditions, Upala saved their sanity, by repeatedly reminding everyone, "Calmly accept the rain and that you will be wet, otherwise you will become angry and tired from fighting it."

Bruce had cut bamboo for use as staffs. The group trudged and slipped and staggered up a ridge in cascades of ankle-deep silt, even mid-calf deep mud in some places. In others, they struggled to cross sections of the trail that had been washed away. Bruce led the way, stabbing the unstable ground, testing with each step to check if it could take his weight before lifting the other foot.

In the deluge, Kate's bandage slipped away. She shrugged. Nothing she could do about it. No energy anyway. Everything she had was going towards staying upright and moving along the trail. They gained a few feet then lost a few feet, slithering down until the staff caught and held them. The children stopped whining, silently plodding on with intense concentration and determination, clutching adult arms that reached out to grab them. Bruce's praise and encouragement kept them going. It was a brutal battle to reach the top. At one point, when they rested to catch their breath, Kate looked back to see a long line of people struggling up the treacherous slope.

The group had passed numerous refugees. Those who were not yet lying dead on the ground, huddled under trees and gazed at them with vacuous eyes, refugees who had given up.

Kate held tight to her children's hands to pull them quickly past. These refugees, having reached the limits of their endurance, would not be setting foot on Indian soil. Kate's group stared back, powerless to help. Such sights reminded Kate, Bruce and Upala that they too could be lying by the wayside in the same dire straits in a few weeks' time.

Descents were even more difficult. Standing at the top of a ridge and looking down at the almost vertical slope, the women's stomachs heaved and twisted with fear. Tension made them forget to breathe. David and Pamela whimpered with fright until Bruce held out his hand to invite them to follow him. Uneasy with their plight, but trusting Bruce implicitly, they stepped into the void. Bruce again reminded them, "Use your staffs, lean back, place one foot so it is secure, bend your knee, then very carefully slide the other foot forward and make sure it is on firm ground. Keep doing this and we'll get down without mishaps." He began to sing "**The Grand Old Duke of York.**" The words came in fits and starts as he concentrated on finding his footing. **He led them up to the top of the hill,** "Hold tight, David." **And he marched them down again.** "Slide down, Pamela. I won't let you fall." **And when they were up, they were up,** "Ladies, how are you doing? Lean back. Concentrate." **And when they were down, they were down, and when they were only half way up, they were neither up nor down.** "Good boy, David. You're doing well, Pamela."

More ranges, more valleys. Streams in violent torrent blocked their way, forcing them to wait and rest, delaying their progress as food supplies dwindled and leeches and mosquitoes tormented them.

With great relief, a few days later, they stepped exhausted from the steamy, hemmed-in jungle path into the fresh air of the Dura Pass, the last mountain crest of the Kumon Range. The rocky path was so narrow, they had to climb the steep trail in single file. Stepping into the clearing at the top of the pass, the sweet fragrance of lantana and rhododendrons filled the air, greeting them as a blessing for successfully making it through the Kumon Range. From here they caught a glimpse of the green jungle canopy covering the Hukawng Valley below, a flat plain spread out, blue and hazy in the distance.

Excited, Kate said, "We made it, Bruce. We made it."

"This far, Kate. Still got a long way to go."

His words were a knife in her heart.

Bruce ruffled David's hair. "Don't be disheartened. We've made it through forty miles of some of the toughest terrain in Burma. We can do the rest."

He didn't tell them that Scotty had warned him the Kumon Range was probably a gentle introduction to what lay ahead.

22

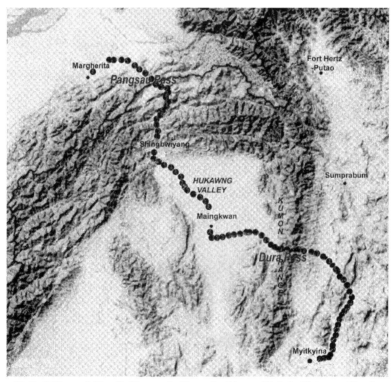

Relief Map of North Burma's Terrain Along Kate's Escape Route

Bruce shed his haversack. "This is a pleasant spot. Let's rest and check your map. It will be nice to enjoy the openness of the clearing before we step back into the jungle."

Kate slipped off her haversack and stretched her tight muscles. Giving voice to the anxiety she always carried with her that their survival depended on wise rationing of their food, Kate said, "We need to take stock of our food supplies too."

Upala and the children dropped their loads, glad to be free of the restriction. They gulped down water. The strenuous efforts required to travel the trail in the horrendous heat and humidity was dehydrating. Bruce spread the map on top of a large rock to show Kate how far they had come. He tapped the map. "Here we are at the Dura Pass, ninety miles from Myitkyina. We still have a long way to go. What do you reckon, Kate? A hundred and fifty miles to the Indian border?"

"At least. Maybe a hundred and eighty."

"Apart from a few small ridges, it looks like it's mainly one long continuous slope down to reach the Hukawng Valley," Bruce said.

Listening to Bruce, Upala noticed Kate's despairing expression. *Thakin-ma*'s sharply defined cheekbones and the gauntness of the children made Upala protective of *her* family. It was easier than allowing the quivering fear in the pit of her stomach to raise its terrifying head.

"How many miles to cross the valley?" she demanded.

Bruce studied the map again. "I would say forty and that will be on level but swampy ground once we get through the ranges. It will probably take us a week to ten days, depending on conditions."

Upala eyes bored into Bruce, trying to detect if he felt any concern even though his voice seemed matter of fact. Not finding any, she opened the flap to her haversack and began checking the food supplies. Her life had been wrapped up with the Bellamy family since David's birth. Like Kate, her sole purpose on this journey was to make sure the children, who had filled her life with happiness, reached India safely. Unlike Kate, she had no hopes of reuniting with her husband there.

A doctor's daughter, Upala had married Darshan as soon as he finished college and qualified to be a teacher like his father. They were born to Indian and Anglo-Indian parents, yet their marriage was a love match, not an arrangement, and when Darshan was offered a position in Maymyo, they left Rangoon to start a new life there.

Bent over her haversack, sorting and repacking the food supplies, Upala's emotions ranged high and low, bringing joy and grief as she recalled how blissfully happy she and Darshan had been for five years. All that time, they hoped for a child, but sadly, no child was born to them. Then Darshan became ill with kidney disease. He struggled to carry on teaching, until he died, suddenly, in his classroom, doing the work he loved. The doctors said it was a brain aneurysm, brought on by his kidney condition.

For a moment, Upala crumbled. Tears dripped on her haversack as she relived the loss of the man she loved. Alone, with no income, Upala began to sell her possessions to survive. She couldn't, wouldn't, return to her parents' protection. Her life and friends were in Maymyo, a town and climate she had grown to love. Then one day, Mr. Bellamy's houseman knocked on her door.

Upala wiped her eyes and nose. She clearly remembered Nyan Sein's words. "*Thakin* wishes that you come to his house. Meet family. Offer job."

The next day Upala arrived at the Bellamy family's home.

Bruce eyed Upala. She seemed too withdrawn. "How long have you looked after Pamela and David, Upala?"

"Almost eight years. Mr. and Mrs. Bellamy, the first Mrs. Bellamy, kindly gave me a job after my husband died. David had just been born."

Upala recalled how her heart leapt at this life-line. She liked the Bellamys. They appeared respectful, generous and kind, and she could stay in Maymyo with her memories of Darshan. It hadn't worried her that her new position would be considered lowly. She would have a child to love and care for, not hers and Darshan's, but a child, nonetheless.

"I will take the job," she had said.

Watching her children, Kate's shoulders sagged in dismay. She was concerned for Pamela and David's mental states. She studied them, at this moment too quiet and withdrawn, engrossed in pulling petals off the colorful wild flowers adorning the place. Finally, Kate turned to Bruce and whispered, "Do you think we'll make it?"

"We'll make it. You and the children have more gumption than most soldiers I know. You give me the strength to keep going. We'll make it."

"No regrets about staying with us?"

"None."

Kate consulted her faithful servant. "What food supplies do we have left, Upala?"

"Enough rice for two weeks if we dole it out carefully and a few cans of protein—sardines, cheese and corned beef. We must look for bamboo shoots and anything else we can find to stretch the rations."

Kate stood up. "On that note let's take a moment to enjoy the view and the beauty of this place. Then we move on and get as far as we can before it starts raining."

Pamela and David dragged themselves to their feet. They had stopped crying and protesting days ago and now remained silent most of the time. Kate and Upala tied the children's bundles to their bodies then began the descent from the pass.

The trail zigzagged down the final mountain, until the ground became more level, an area where large boulders lay among less dense, smaller trees. The relatively gentle descent through pleasant woodland reduced the risk of a steep tumble and made it easier to cope with the ankle-deep mud that kept threatening to suck off their shoes. Taking a rest on a low outcrop, the disconcerting view of the vast stretch of greenery of the Hukawng Valley momentarily struck them dumb. "It looks very wide, more foreboding than it did from the summit." Kate said, cuddling Pamela.

Bruce looked drawn as he stared at the emerald expanse. "Crossing the valley might be as taxing." He patted David's shoulder and smiled at Upala. "But we can do it."

They stirred themselves, and having walked longer and later than planned, were not looking forward to setting up camp in twilight. Turning a bend in the trail, they found three Gurkha soldiers in their late twenties, two Burmese women, possibly their wives, and an older woman. They had already established a camp. They also had a buffalo to carry their supplies.

Bruce shook hands with the men.

"This is a stroke of luck," he said to Kate. "The Gurkhas are highly regarded by British soldiers who have served and fought alongside them. They come from Nepal, so they know the mountains and how to survive in the jungle."

Seeing that they did not understand what Bruce was telling her in English, Kate asked Upala to translate in Burmese.

"I can do it, Mummy," David said.

Kate smiled at him, pleased to see he had some life in his eyes. "So, you can. Tell them what Bruce said."

The Gurkhas were short and stocky with ready smiles. They responded to Bruce's praise with laughter, slapping their thighs with delight then bringing out their large kukri knives and waving them about, pretending to cut enemy throats, which, momentarily, created a flurry of anxiety in the new arrivals, until Bruce burst out laughing.

The Gurkhas were about to eat and willingly shared their camp and meal of rice and lentil curry with the family. The aroma coming from the aluminum cooking pots made the hungry travelers' mouths water. One Gurkha cut banana leaves to use as plates.

A curve in the stream created a place where the current was slow, and they could have some privacy. With the parasitic leeches picked off their bodies, Kate and Upala took the opportunity to bathe away the mud and sweat on the children and themselves, using the carbolic soap as sparingly as they could. Kate felt clean and almost normal for the first time in days. She dabbed Betadine antiseptic onto everyone's leech bites to, hopefully, prevent sores from forming or maggots from entering.

The Gurkhas made short work of helping Bruce erect a framework shelter and covering it with his tarpaulin, then gestured Kate's party to join them around the campfire. The Gurkhas agreed to allow Bruce and Kate's party to accompany them as far as Maingkwan, forty miles ahead as the crow flies where, the Gurkhas had heard, the Burmese government had left a large store of rice in the rest house for refugees. Kate agreed to pay them in silver rupees for sharing their food and getting them safely to Maingkwan. Feeling happier than she had for some time, she hugged David, who was so sleepy he was struggling to keep his eyes open. "Thank you, David. You've been a big help by interpreting. You should join Pamela in the shelter and get some sleep."

Throughout the night, thunder rumbled and lightning flashed, but no rain fell. Kate awoke relieved, knowing the nearby stream would be crossable.

Breakfasting on black tea, warm cans of liquefied corned beef, with crackers to soak up the fatty juices, the group broke camp. At the stream, the buffalo suddenly developed a mind of its own, turning away and stubbornly refusing to enter the water. With the heat and humidity, it took only a few minutes for everyone to be sweaty and soaking wet as they tried to convince the buffalo to see sense. A few extra whacks of a cane brought the buffalo to its senses, and it crossed without further difficulties.

For most of the day, Kate's party, sapped of energy in the sweltering humidity, trailed along behind the Gurkhas. They halted at the edge of the valley, where the path disappeared under swaths of water as far as they could see. The mud they tramped through was ankle deep and churned up by the thousands of trekkers who had preceded them. It was a few hours to nightfall, but with the only light on the forest floor coming from the few shafts of light that penetrated the jungle canopy sixty feet above them, they decided to wait until morning to cross the swamp.

One Gurkha pointed upwards to the dark clouds approaching from the west and, taking out his kukri, mimed cutting down wood for shelters. Bruce worked with the Gurkhas, while Kate and Upala worked with the two Burmese women to light a fire. Kate and Upala exchanged worried glances at Pamela quietly, sucking her thumb. David returned with the men, arms filled with branches and leaves. The Gurkhas built a wooden framework of roof and floor on small stilts to keep them off the soggy ground. Bruce pulled the tarpaulin from his pack to spread over the wooden framework the men erected, and everyone seemed pleased they would remain dry and protected from the rains when the heavens opened.

Next morning, as soon as it was light enough, the Gurkhas cut strong sticks from the jungle to use as staffs for group members to steady themselves and test the ground when walking through the flooded valley. In the dim light, swarms of mosquitoes made life miserable. The next attack would come from tiger leeches as the group waded through the swamp.

Heads down, the two groups waded through water and calf-deep mud. A thrashing noise distracted them from their misery. Looking up, torment turned to admiration at the wondrous sight of five flying Great Hornbills over four feet in length, beating a flight path through the teak trees like flying galleons in full sail. As the birds disappeared from view, a lone monkey's *wa-wa-hu* triggered a cacophony of raucous calls from the hundreds of other jungle animals. The whole forest was awake. Thinking the animal noises were a warning of danger, Kate grabbed Upala's arm and looked fearfully around. "Is there a tiger nearby? Bruce?"

One of the Gurkhas, understanding the word tiger, grinned and shook his head. They relaxed once more into the peacefulness of the forest, and started their trek again.

Despite widespread water covering their path, the first day's hike on the level ground of the Hukawng Valley was relatively easy apart from having to rescue Pamela and David who fell into deep potholes hidden by the water. One of the Gurkhas took pity on them, lifting them onto the bullock's back to ride.

During the morning, they saw a deserted Kachin village a short distance from the track. Rotting bodies fouled the huts and littered the surrounding jungle. The air was so noxious, the group hurried past, holding their breath. In some places, bodies blocked the path. Having no choice but to step on them was a nightmare that brought bile to the back of Kate's throat. Notwithstanding the horrors of the day, they hiked eight miles and found a corpse-free abandoned hut on a small hillock near a stream where they made camp.

Once everyone had bathed away the mud, Kate lined them up, including the Gurkhas, and checked them for cuts and bites. Any bites she found, she dabbed with antiseptic. She smiled as she worked, enjoying the Gurkhas delight at being cared for by her. She also took comfort from the cheerfulness of the Gurkha's domesticity, cooking rice and curry and including her party in their group.

Yet she was concerned about the way the children casually reacted to the dead. Having strolled past so many corpses, they barely noticed them, or they giggled at some contorted position a person had died in, usually trousers off and knees pulled up to bellies, a sign of agonizing dysentery or pain from eating uncooked rice.

She took Bruce to one side. "I'm worried. I think the humidity and heat will be too much for us, especially the children. And did you notice, the corpses we passed appeared to be free of injury, which probably means people are dying from sickness, starvation and exhaustion, not from accidents or being attacked.

"Stay calm. If we follow basic hygiene and first aid, we should be all right and the Gurkhas know how to survive in a place like this."

To keep Pamela and David occupied, Bruce played games about food with the children and Upala, imagining eating chocolate, cream cakes and ice cream. "I never thought I would be raving about eating a cream bun," he said, laughing, "or finding boiled rice so delicious. What do you say, Kate?"

Lost in her thoughts, Kate did not respond.

It hadn't rained heavily during the night, but nevertheless the track was slushy with churned up mud. The path led along the banks of the Tanai River. Everyone had awakened covered in welts from the bites of insects that had crawled from the hut walls during the night in search of a feast, and now the travelers were under daytime attack as well. Kate swatted at the clouds of midges flying into hair, ears and noses. "As if last night wasn't bad enough, now we've got this to contend with. Upala, I don't know how to protect the children from this."

"There is nothing we can do, *thakin-ma*. It's miserable for the children, but since we can't stop the attacks, we shall just have to put up with it."

Kate pressed her lips together and held her tongue. Irritated and worn down by the myriads of midges, she was in no mood for Upala's stoicism.

The group marched longer than planned, a tiring fifteen miles that day in order to get away from the annoying insects. They also saw more dead than live refugees. Coming across a deserted Kachin village, hearts lifted, until the smell of rotting flesh drove them to make camp outside the area. Kate urged everyone to wash, applied betadine to bites and scratches. They searched each other for leeches and disposed of them with the Gurkhas' salt. With darkness quickly falling, Upala and the Gurkha women boiled water. Kate opened cans of cheese and corned beef for supper before they fell sound asleep on the bare earth covered only with damp blankets.

With a breakfast of rice and tea under their belts, Kate's group trailed after the Gurkhas. Pamela and David, had not recovered from the previous day's long ride and were weary from the effort they made to stay on the bullock's back. They opted to walk but traveling through the swamp with thick glutinous mud up to their thighs was particularly tedious and tiring. The mud sucked at their shoes and socks. After repeatedly reaching into the mud to replace shoes on feet, brother and sister looked at one another conspiratorially, stepped out of their shoes, and left them in the mire. Freed of the impediment of trying to keep their footwear on, their spirits immediately lifted. David whispered to Pamela, "I've had enough of this. Tomorrow I'm going to ride on the buffalo."

The gagging smell of putrefaction assaulted the group from deep within the foliage on both sides of the trail. Masses of orange butterflies delighted Kate's party when first spotted, until they discovered the insects were feasting on the juices of rotting bodies on the jungle trail. The Gurkhas called back to Kate's group and began walking faster. Fearful of being left behind, Kate's group hurried on.

"David, what did he say?" Bruce asked.

"We need to get away from this death place, and they hope to buy food and shelter from a village up ahead."

But as they drew close to the small hamlet, they could see it was overrun with Chinese troops, fortunately too busy preparing shelters to notice them. The Gurkhas signaled to Kate and Bruce that they would detour around the huts to avoid being seen. They had all heard tales from various refugees, of rampaging, starving Chinese soldiers robbing and even killing villagers and travelers alike.

Further on, the Gurkhas spotted two huts in a clearing a little way off the trail. Up close, the travelers found the huts had been abandoned and the roofs were falling in, but the bamboo floors remained intact. The men set-to making the roofs waterproof, using the tarpaulin for Kate's hut and broad-leaved bushes for the Gurkhas' hut.

While the men prepared their accommodations, Kate, accompanied by Pamela and Upala with David, went in different directions as the Burmese women showed them how to find edible jungle plants and vegetables. Moving through the undergrowth, Kate and Pamela became aware of an unpleasant smell. With Kate in the lead and Pamela close behind, they inched forward. Brushing aside some dense foliage, a monstrous cloud of buzzing black flies rose up in front of her.

Kate hurriedly covered her mouth and nose and pulled her daughter to her, hiding Pamela's face in her dress so she would not see the brown rotting mass heaving with hordes of wriggling maggots. Kate gagged at the foul fumes. A jolt of adrenaline had her tense and shaking almost running away in panic from the disgusting sight of what had once been a human being. Will we end up like this? No! Not my children! Not me! Not Bruce! Not Upala!

"Oh, God!"

Pamela looked up at her mother. Kate patted Pamela's head reassuringly. Did I speak aloud? She took a deep breath and looked again at the bloated body. Defiance and determination flooded her being. The feeling brought a soothing calm, and she knew, with absolute certainty that this would not be their death. She would not allow it.

Returning to the huts, Kate found the shriveled old woman boiling water and cooking vegetables, made especially tasty by the addition of spices and a few lentils and grains of rice, with enough left over for breakfast.

That night a series of squalls pounded on and tugged at the roof. Kate listened to Upala and the children breathing. The squalls weren't disturbing them; they were sleeping too deeply. She couldn't hear Bruce's light snoring.

"Are you awake?" Kate whispered.

"Yes."

"I can't sleep for fear the tarpaulin will blow away."

"Don't worry, it's well fastened down."

"I'm losing heart about ever returning to Burma. After the last few horrible days, seeing all the death and destruction, it doesn't feel like the Burma I knew and loved anymore."

"I want to come back. I want to find Ma Hla May, my fiancée. To be truthful, I think I'm fooling myself. The army discourages soldiers from marrying local girls. But I've never met anyone like her. Only woman I've ever loved."

Bruce's voice faded away in sadness.

"If it's meant to be, Bruce, it will happen for you. But you can't focus on your fiancée now. Your only thought must be survival. If you survive, you can come back and find her. Stay strong and give everything you've got to surviving."

The wind and impenetrable curtain of rain continued the next day, forcing the travelers to lose a day's walking, a hardship they could ill afford with their supplies barely enough to reach Maingkwan. The Gurkhas braved the deluge to forage for edible plants and Kate opened her last tin of corned beef. That was when Kate noticed the children were without shoes.

"What happened to your shoes?"

Kate's sharp tone stunned her children.

Waving her arms and raising her voice, Kate continued, "How could you lose your shoes?"

Pamela and David giggled nervously.

"This is serious! We have a long way to go. If you get cut on sharp stones or stuck with thorns, you could develop a Naga sore. You've seen people with Naga sores, haven't you? They're nasty and dangerous things. They eat away your flesh, get filled with maggots. It's not a pretty sight, is it? And we've already used up half our antiseptic."

Seeing the children's fearful faces, Upala patted Kate's arm as if to warn she had said too much, and that she was scaring the children.

Bruce smiled, held up one of his feet. "My boots will soon fall apart. Yours too, Kate. We'll all be walking into India in our bare feet. We will have to be extra careful where we step."

Kate shook her head. "Sorry, I'm just so worried about this."

Next morning, attempts to reinforce the disintegrating roofs on the huts were unsuccessful. Over a meagre breakfast and with supplies running low, they decided they had better hurry on down the track, despite the heavy rain, to avoid being cut off by rising rivers.

The Gurkhas loaded the buffalo. Kate and Upala stood in their hut doorway and peered at the flooded landscape that looked like a vast lake.

"Walking in that with the children will not be easy, *thakin-ma*," Upala said.

"You're right, but I don't know what else to do," Kate said, "I want to stay with the Gurkhas. At the moment, they're our lifeline."

Upala nodded. They plunged into the water and began wading. All day they waded through two feet of water and even when it became time to set up camp, they were still not free of it. Bruce and the Gurkhas built a high, platform well above the water level. They hastily constructed walls and a roof to keep off the rain. Kate found a few crackers and two tins of sardines to share with the Gurkhas. Then she gathered her children to her. "I'm so proud of you. It is harder for you because you are small, but you kept on going and even sang with Bruce." She looked at Bruce with a grin. "Today was a big challenge and you won through. We will have to get you a medal each when we get to India."

The discomfort of wet clothes, hunger and exhaustion were inconsequential in their exhaustion. After sleeping soundly, the pre-dawn light found the two parties already wending their way through water above their knees. Progress was slow. They spent as much time helping one another up after stumbling into the water as they did wading through it.

To Kate's relief, by mid-morning, they had walked out of the flood. She was worried about the skin on their feet and toes, which had become soft and wrinkled by being in water for so long. She would have to be extra vigilant about cuts to their feet.

Less than a mile further on they reached a surging stream they could cross by jumping onto the large boulders not covered by the torrent. The Gurkhas took rope from their supplies on the buffalo's back. They would tie themselves together in a line and, this way, if one of the children slipped, he or she would not be washed away. Engrossed in the task, the group did not notice the buffalo move off the trail to graze. Its distressed bleating caught their attention. Dashing to the animal, they found it trapped in quicksand. No amount of pulling and tugging could free it. A Gurkha jumped on its back. Taking out his kukri, he fired off what sounded like rapid expletives to his companions. He cut free their belongings and what little food supplies they had left, throwing them to the other Gurkhas, before leaping to safety. Kate pulled the children away from the scene, so they would not see the animal perish beneath the sludge. Everyone's grim expression showed the seriousness of losing the animal. It was a huge blow. Having to carry their supplies would make the trek so much harder.

Stunned, they stood staring at the ground and one another, absorbing how the loss of the buffalo had drastically changed things for the worse. Then attention turned to crossing the stream. With much encouragement to the children and Upala, all crossed safely with no scary incidents. On dry land on the far bank, they made a meal of boiled rice and green plants from the forest. Then they divided up the loads to carry and started walking.

The trees thinned out. They came across slash and burn clearings and paddy fields with increasing frequency.

"Can't be far to Maingkwan," Bruce said.

"And we are seeing more people," Kate said.

Five minutes later, they rounded a curve on the track. Kate cheered at seeing hundreds of people trailing along, well spread out. "I feel safer being among so many people."

"I think you spoke too soon, Kate. Look at them. They're in poor shape."

It was then Kate noticed how gaunt and haggard and slow-moving they were. Children were being carried on shoulders. Women were weighed down with belongings and food. People were rushing to the side of the road with uncontrollable dysentery.

The Gurkhas called to Kate's party, waving at them to hurry past the crowds and the increasing number of bodies they were seeing by the roadside.

Kate immediately understood their concern. Most of these people were at the end of their tether and struggling along at a snail's pace. The Gurkhas did not want to get stuck in the same slow pace behind them.

"Come on, children, our Gurkha friends want us to move quickly and follow them," Kate said. People were stepping off the trail to collapse at the roadside, people who would probably never get to their feet again. To Bruce and Upala she said, "Let's get the hell away from here. It's like Dante's Inferno."

Following the Gurkhas' lead, Bruce and Kate rallied the children and the group marched hard, breathing heavily. It was only their determination to reach Maingkwan and stock up on food that gave them the strength to hurry. They passed rifle-carrying, scowling Indian and Chinese soldiers trudging along with an air of defeat and anger.

With numerous hungry and undisciplined soldiers around, Bruce thought it was time to have a weapon. Coming across a British soldier who had recently died with his trousers down, probably because of dysentery, Bruce took the rifle, ammunition and cleaning oils from his corpse.

More clearings appeared. The trees became smaller. Upala sniffed the air. They all began sniffing the air. They could smell food. Someone was cooking food. Soon they were passing Indians cooking by the roadside. Kate pulled out some rupees and found a few Indians who were willing to sell cooked food to them.

Other people, without the will to continue the walk, without food or the means to buy it, sat stupefied and lethargic, staring at them passing by.

23

Catching sight of Maingkwan on a low hill, they walked through hordes of refugees, Europeans, Chinese, Indians, and Burmese, huddled in groups beside the broad dry weather cart and motor vehicle track that connected Maingkwan to Mogaung and the railway line one hundred miles to the south. At the now deserted Kachin village that was Maingkwan, a small colonial outpost with a mission house, hundreds of emaciated, inadequately clothed people were roaming around, seeking the food stores that had kept hope of survival alive, food stores that were supposed to be there. Puzzlement, concern and anger surged in the new arrivals.

Bruce told his companions, "Sit and rest. I'll go and check out the food situation."

He walked through the village and found Reverend Darlington, standing in front of the Baptist Church, telling the crowds, "There is no food in Maingkwan. Soldiers looted the supplies. There is nothing left, not even for the villagers. The Kachins have gone to relatives, deep into the mountains. You must go too, on to Shingbwiyang, where the Frontier Service can give you food. Planes are dropping supplies there."

"How far to Shingbwiyang?" Bruce called.

"About fifty to sixty miles. Travel as fast as you can before the monsoon washes the track away. There are rumors that the Japanese have not only taken Mogaung but are advancing up the road and could soon arrive here at Maingkwan. You must go on."

The grumbling crowd turned away. Some clearly did not believe him, accusing him of keeping rice for himself.

Bruce returned to the group. "There's no rice here. We need to move on to Shingbwiyang, fifty to sixty miles up the road. The Reverend says the RAF is dropping supplies there, and the Frontier Service is in control of the rations."

Unshed tears filled Kate's eyes. No food. Kate observed the emaciated people gathered at Maingkwan. She looked at her skinny wrists, felt her protruding collar bone, saw the lack of flesh on the children and Upala. A chill of doubt about her party's survival froze her insides. Almost as thin and ragged as the people around us. And now Bruce says there's no food here. Can I impose on the Gurkhas to help us? Will they?

Kate took a deep breath, gathered herself. "Upala, will you interpret for me, please." She looked deep into the eyes of each Gurkha and each woman in their group as she spoke. "Will you help us reach Shingbwiyang?"

The Gurkhas fidgeted uncomfortably at the question. Kate's spirits sank. It's not looking hopeful. They're itching to get moving. They talked briefly among themselves, and one Gurkha looked Kate in the eye and nodded.

Too choked to speak, chin trembling with relief and eyes damp with gratitude, Kate nodded in return. She held out her hand, and the Gurkha shook it.

With Upala interpreting, the Gurkha said they were soldiers from the Burma Rifles, who had left their unit to collect their wives. They needed to report to the military as soon as they reached India.

"Tell them I am doubly grateful for their help," Kate said.

They moved away to find a place as best they could from the crowds and corpses and set up camp. With the children asking for food and only an hour of daylight left, Bruce called to David and signaled to a Gurkha to go with him. They wandered along the bank of the rushing stream until Bruce found a curve in the bank that created a quiet pool. Signaling the Gurkha and David to lie down on the grass beside him and putting his finger to his lips to tell them to be silent, Bruce slowly lowered his hands into the water up to his elbow. Ten minutes later, he pulled out a fish and threw it on the grass for the Gurkha to kill. He tried again, and this time found a whopper. Forty minutes later, he had five fish.

With Bruce more of a hero to him than ever, David raced ahead of them back to camp. "Mummy! Mummy! We have fish to eat! Bruce caught some fish with his bare hands!"

That night the glow of the camp fire lit up smiling faces. Carefree laughter and banter filled the air. The cheerful feast of fish and rice lifted their spirits and energized their bodies for the grueling day that lay ahead.

"How did you manage to catch fish without a fishing rod?" Kate asked.

Bruce shrugged, seemingly embarrassed. "I have an uncle who does a bit of poaching. It's one of the things he taught me. Said it might come in useful one day."

Kate laughed. "How right he was. You must teach me and David."

"He taught me how to bet on the horses too, but that's no help here," Bruce said, with a chuckle.

The next day, with only a breakfast of crackers and black tea to sustain them, they set off walking. The morning mists gave way to a dry day filled with glorious sunshine. The good weather lasted two days which somewhat eased the difficulties of trekking on the track that had been trashed by elephants, ponies, bullock carts and thousands of feet. Yet it was still not easy. Too many potholes, caused by elephants' legs, to fall into; too many bodies to step over or avoid, and knee-deep mud too widespread to by-pass.

Unruly troops in tattered uniforms fired their rifles into the air to intimidate the crowds pouring from Maingkwan, forcing them to make way. Fearful heads of families herded loved ones to the roadside, out of the soldiers' path. Like other adults protecting families, Kate, Bruce and Upala placed themselves as a barricade between the children and the soldiers. Younger members of Indian families grabbed belongings and food and scattered into hiding places in the undergrowth. The soldiers pushed past. A collective sigh of relief filled the air at having safely weathered yet another danger.

The Gurkhas stepped into the dense trees on either side of the road, returning with staffs for everyone. The sunshine had turned the sloppy mud into a glutenous mess. Constantly having to pull legs free of the sucking, glue-like clay made for heavy going. Soon, all of Kate's group were without shoes, and she worried that they were less than halfway to their destination.

When the children became exhausted, the men took turns to carry them on their backs. They managed to walk five miles the first day out of Maingkwan, same on the second. Then the heavens opened, and rain squalls came finding every gap and opening in their shelters to pour through, leaving the travelers soaking wet.

Unable to find dry wood and hampered by deep mud, the group chewed the last of the biscuits and drank cold tea before packing their haversacks and setting off.

"Isn't it strange?" Kate said. "No birdsong anymore. They've deserted the forest. Only pesky mosquitoes, leeches, carnivorous flies and butterflies exist in this sweaty hell-hole." No one answered. All were concentrating on keeping from falling in the slippery mud. She looked at her wet, thin friends and children. Lack of food had almost brought them to their knees, but they were not done yet. She dug her staff into the mud to struggle up the slope, up two steps and a slide back, hopefully, without pitching face first into the mire. They trailed numbly behind the agile Gurkhas climbing nimbly through the mud and descending like sure-footed goats down the slopes.

At the foot of the hills, they waded through swampy waters attracting black, six-inch tiger leeches which had to be removed from their bodies by using the dwindling salt supplies or a burning twig. Kate treated the wounds with betadine to prevent infection. Everyone was so malnourished and exhausted Kate worried it would be too easy for someone to fall ill.

With only jungle plants and watery rice soup to eat for two days, they arrived weary and hungry at the Tanai River. The sight of hundreds of exhausted refugees, sitting listlessly among the dead and dying, while they waited to be ferried across, brought Kate close to tears. I don't want my children to see all this. They're too young for it, and there's nothing I can do about it.

Kachin natives pulled rafts to and fro, by rope and pulley, across the 250-yard wide tumultuous river. The group watched as men with weapons forced back those who were about to take a place on a raft. One Anglo-Indian man, whose bearing seemed to indicate he was some high-ranking official, started shouting and resisting. A bullet to the head shut him up and anyone else who thought they might intervene.

The Tanai's riverbank was littered with the corpses of those whose time had run out and people lying on the ground soon to join them. Another group of Gurkhas and their families drove their six bullocks carrying their possessions into the river; half made it to the far side, the current swept away the other three animals.

Kate and her companions waited almost two hours for their turn to bargain with the Kachin tribesmen to be ferried cross. Listless and hungry, Pamela and David stood close to Kate and Upala, waiting quietly, watching the violence and suffering that surrounded them. Without speaking one another's language, Bruce and the Gurkhas negotiated an acceptable price with the ferryman.

Kate stood seemingly calm, but the continual tucking of hair behind her ear and wringing of hands revealed her dread. "Bruce, this looks so dangerous. I'm worried we'll be swept away like the buffaloes."

He patted her shoulder. "Lots of people have crossed safely and besides, this is the only way forward. We need to get moving. Come on. Get on the raft."

Bruce's reassurances didn't register with Kate. Her heart raced as she helped Upala and the children onto the rickety bamboo raft. She hoped their own deaths were not imminent. But risking a watery death was better than sleeping among the hordes of dead and dying who seemed to be infected with disease—cholera, typhus, typhoid or dysentery, take your pick, all deadly without medical help.

They completed the perilous crossing without mishap. Her hands were trembling as she rushed Upala and the children off the raft to the safety of firm ground.

The buzzing clouds of biting insects that infested the riverbank forced them all to drive their exhausted bodies a half-mile farther along the track, away from the river, before setting up camp for the night.

They rose at dawn. Everyone in Kate's group was bone-deep weak. Breakfast consisted of tea and heated up jungle vegetables left from the previous night. The children complained of hunger. Who can blame them? Kate thought, her heart constricting from guilt, failure, inadequacy, and panic. But they *had* to keep up with the Gurkhas who were able to travel at a faster pace. She knew they were traveling more slowly than they would be if free of the hindrance of Kate's party. The thought of them leaving terrified her. They depended so much on the Gurkhas' knowledge of the forest to get them through.

Drenched by pouring rain, they slipped and fell and battled mud that felt to Kate like a huge octopus wrapping them in cloying tentacles trying to suck them down into a muddy ocean floor.

With her head down, Kate was so focused on making headway through the muck, she was surprised to hear a Chinese officer speaking English to Bruce who was in the lead. She saw Bruce was edgy, ready to raise his rifle the instant he felt danger. They had already learned that most refugees' encounters with Chinese troops ended badly.

The Chinese captain, accompanied by eight soldiers, had recognized Bruce's uniform.

"British Army?"

Regardless of looking like a tramp with his mud-stained clothes and unkempt bushy beard, Bruce pulled himself tall and straight. Kate realized he was hoping to appear strong and resistant should trouble erupt. "Yes, British officer, 1st Gloucestershire Regiment."

"You surprised I speak good English?"

"Yes, sir."

"I went to Sandhurst Military Academy. I learned to be officer in England. Do you have matches?" the Chinese officer asked.

The question caught Bruce off guard. He stood speechless.

"I will give you a leg of ham in exchange for good matches," the Captain said, waving a man forward and speaking to him in Chinese. The man removed a ham from his haversack.

Kate's and Bruce's mouth suddenly filled with saliva. He looked at Kate, who was busy mentally calculating how many matches they had and how many they would need to use before reaching India.

"If you give us some rice as well, we can give you twenty good matches, not the ones that fail to light," Kate said.

The Chinese captain's face was stubbornly set. "We need the rice to get us to China."

"You need matches to cook it," Kate said.

He stared at her, looking for weakness. Finding none, he nodded. "You are right. Rice and ham for matches."

Bruce kept close watch on the Chinese soldiers as Kate felt in her haversack for the precious matches wrapped in an oil-cloth and kept in a tin.

The exchange was made. The captain saluted. "Good luck, people," he said and set off down the trail followed by his men.

"Why are they going the wrong way?" David asked.

"They're going home to China, which is over there." Bruce pointed to the east. "We're going to India," he said, pointing in the opposite direction, "over there, where the sun sets."

Having meat and rice to look forward to for their evening meal cheered everyone. Even trudging another mile in heavy rain to reach the Gurkhas did not dampen their spirits.

The Gurkhas laughed with delight when they saw the food, and the women quickly set about its preparation. The going had been slow today, less than four exhausting miles. The Gurkha men built a platform above ground for Kate's group to sleep on. A creek near the path provided water. Upala strained it through her sari and then boiled it to make it safe to drink.

Upala spoke to Kate in a low voice. "Why did the Gurkhas stop here? There are dead bodies everywhere." She pointed to several bushes from where limbs and bodies protruded. "Who knows what diseases they died from, and the air stinks from those we cannot see."

Kate nodded. "You saw what we passed today. There was not one place where people had not fallen and died beside the path. We need to make sure we don't join them. Let's get the children bathed to remove what mud we can."

Upala joined Kate in taking the children to the creek.

It was only six miles from the Tanai River to the Tarung. Next day, feeling a little stronger from the food they had eaten, they reached the river crossing around midday. It was a depressing sight. The crossing was a bottleneck. Hundreds of refugees filled the area. The wait to cross was long, as long as several days. With the river swollen by monsoon rains, the heaving waters made the flimsy raft operations slow and dangerous. Naga and Kachin tribesmen worked all hours ferrying people across to the far side until, exhausted, they could work no more.

Fighting kept breaking out for places on the rafts. Armed soldiers threatened ferrymen and refugees alike to seize the rafts and be taken to the far side. Anyone who got in their way was shot. Thugs preyed upon the weak. All around people were arguing and suffering. Refugees, verging on craziness, looked blankly at the chaos, or sat and mumbled, or screamed and wailed over the dying.

Kate and Upala flanked the children and kept them close. Bruce took David to help him confer with the Gurkhas. Kate and Upala looked on, wondering what the plan would be.

Bruce and David returned. "We could be here some time. We're going to build a shelter and watch for our chance to cross."

The two groups pooled their money, enough they hoped to tempt a ferryman to help them. Late in the afternoon, the Gurkha leader stood and looked around. Not an armed soldier in sight. He urged his companions to hurry. They picked up their haversacks and belongings, Bruce kept his rifle handy and followed him to where a tough, sinewy Naga with a well-lined face was returning to the south side of the river. The Gurkha showed him their money. The Naga nodded and put it in his pouch. As soon as they were aboard, he began hauling the raft across the river by pulling the rope through the pulleys. Muscles and tendons strained as he battled against the force of the torrent. The two groups balanced on the raft a mere couple of inches above the raging waterline. The rapid beating of Kate's fearful heart pounded in her ears. The raft was only made from logs with bamboo poles on top fastened together with rope. What if a large piece of debris such as a tree trunk should crash into the raft? What if the children fell into the water? She held Pamela tightly. Bruce held David's hand.

Looking back, Bruce saw a group of armed soldiers emerge from the gloom to stand on the riverbank. "We nabbed the raft just in time."

Kate saw where Bruce was pointing. "We'll need to make camp hidden from the track to stay safe, in case they cross tonight."

In the last bleak remains of daylight, they trudged a short distance from the Tarung, stepped into the jungle out of sight of the track, found a brook and washed at Kate's insistence. With only a slice of ham each, they lay on the wet ground and, with stomachs still rumbling with hunger, they slept.

24

With a dry start to the day and a breakfast of rice with the leftover ham before it turned rancid, the group was energized and eager to get on. By mid-morning, drenching squalls returned them to misery as they doggedly plodded on in the deep mud.

In the afternoon, Kate was horrified to notice Bruce was experiencing bouts of shivering. She had been making sure everyone took their daily quinine tablets, but it had failed to protect Bruce. Who else would fall? She felt his forehead. Hot.

Bruce struggled on as best he could, but it became impossible to sustain the effort required to lift his legs up out of the cloying mud. Knee deep in mud, he froze unable to summon the energy to move then fell face down in the mud and did not get up.

Kate yelled and yelled to the Gurkhas, who were ahead, out of sight. No one came.

She scrambled to Bruce, lifted his head and felt his pulse. "David, I want you to sit down here and rest Bruce's face on your thigh, out of the mud."

"Will Bruce be all right?"

"I think so. He has malaria. He won't be able to walk for a day or two, until his fever subsides. We'll have to take care of him, like he has taken care of us. Upala will stay with you to keep you safe. I have to make a shelter. Pamela, you come with me. I'll need your help."

She took a deep breath, a moment to gather herself, before relieving Bruce of his machete, hiding his supplies behind some shrubs and stepping into the brush. She had watched the Gurkhas build shelters. She knew how it was done. The question was, did she have the strength?

Kate started hacking a small clearing out of the jungle. She could do it as long as she kept stopping to rest and garner her energy. Pamela helped carry and stack the trimmed branches in the clearing. Kate was thinking the lack of a stream or river could be a problem, but for now they would fill all their containers with rainwater.

She assembled the platform, sides and roof support.

"Pamela ask Upala to come and help me throw the tarpaulin over the frame."

Together they fought against the wind and succeeded in tying the tarpaulin into place. Kate patted Pamela's head. "This should keep us dry. We'll have to stay here until Bruce recovers, which could take a few . . ."

The thought stopped her mid-sentence. They had all seen whole families at the side of the track, lying side by side dead together, often beneath a blanket. She, Upala and Bruce had frequently noted that if refugees stopped traveling because one family member became ill, it seemed to result in the death of them all.

And here we are in the same situation. Can we walk on and leave Bruce? No. It would be the sensible thing to do to survive. Kate looked at her feverish friend, shaking, sitting on the ground. But I couldn't live with myself if we did that.

The children helped Kate and Upala drag Bruce toward the shelter. Fortunately, he had lost a lot of weight, the extra notches in his belt testimony to that. Still, it took a long time. The deep mud, their exhaustion and weakness hindered their ability to pull him. Bruce tried to help, shoving with his feet when he could. The effort required frequent rests, but eventually they were all in the shelter and out of the rain.

Kate searched Bruce's haversack for his blanket. "Children, I want you to run around outside to let the rain wash the mud off you. And put out some containers to catch the rain. Upala help me undress Bruce. We'll hang his clothes outside on branches to get clean in the rain." Kate almost cried on seeing Bruce's bony rib cage. They had depended on him so much and he had responded without complaint. Now he was wasting away and sick too. The surge of protective emotions that flooded through her awakened a fierce determination in Kate. She would get him through. She would get them all through. Nothing would stop her.

Kate felt his forehead. Hotter. He was burning up, mumbling feverishly.

"Would you bring me some water, Upala? I'll rinse the mud off, treat his leech bites then we'll tuck him up in his blanket to keep him warm. Tonight, we'll sleep on both sides of him to give him some warmth."

Upala hung up Bruce's clothes in the rain. She undressed the children and sent them into the shelter to put on some dry clothes from their haversacks. With Bruce settled, the children dry, Upala and Kate stripped to their underwear, hung their clothes outside to be cleaned by the rain then stood in the downpour to clean their mud-covered bodies. Both noted with sadness and concern how bony the other's body had become. They were slowly starving. Kate found two dry, frayed shirts for them and the second blanket for the children. She hoped they would be warm during the night. Now they were trudging at higher altitudes, it was becoming progressively colder when the sun went down. Unable to get a fire going with the saturated twigs, Kate gave up. She brought twigs into the shelter hoping they would dry enough to make a fire the next day.

Upala handed out small balls of cold rice.

Pamela looked at the small offering in her hand. "Is there any more?"

"No, it is the last of our cooked food until we can make a fire to cook some more. Eat up, it's the best we can do."

"When Bruce is better, he can catch some more fish," David said, gobbling down his morsel and licking his fingers.

"Yes, he can," Kate said abstractedly. She leaned closer to Upala and said in a low voice, so the children would not hear, "We seem to have lost the Gurkhas. I hope we can manage on our own."

"They helped us a lot, but we learned from them, how to find jungle vegetables to eat, how to make a shelter. As long as we are not robbed of our money and can find or buy food to stay strong enough to travel, we will be all right. We are more than halfway along our journey."

Hearing Upala's support, Kate nodded and squeezed Upala's hand, too overcome with a flood of emotions to speak.

Hungry and depressed, they sat, morose, under the tarpaulin, being pelted by hailstones. A fitting end to a bloody awful day.

During the night, violent shivering bouts wracked Bruce's body interspersed with bouts of mumbled gibberish. He sweated profusely and the women took turns to wipe his face with wet cloths and snuggle next to him to keep him warm. Kate was grateful the children slept deeply, oblivious to the drama.

Black clouds sodden with rain blanketed the hilltops. Thunder rumbled and rolled all around. The group huddled in the camp for two days of intermittent rain, waiting for Bruce to improve. At first, he was unconscious most of the time. Then he occasionally surfaced to weakly ask for food and water. Upala had put out small twigs to dry whenever the sun shone and eventually had enough dry twigs to light a fire. The children crowded around her, mouths watering as she made a thin soup of rice and boiled greens, while Kate enviously caught glimpses of the few desperate refugees struggling past, making progress.

The morning of the third day, they opened their eyes to clear skies and sunshine. Even better, Bruce's fever had subsided. He was weak and pale, with dark smudges under his eyes, but he insisted he was well enough to walk. "You should have gone on without me. You know the rules of survival here.

You could have signed your death warrants by staying with me."

"Couldn't do it. It would be like cutting off my arm. Now shut up. I want to hear no more about it. It's done."

It took longer than usual to pack up camp and return to the task of placing one foot in front of the other, but Kate's spirits lifted. They were making headway again.

The narrow track was cut into the side of a ridge. In places it had deteriorated into a series of deep mud-holes filled with sticky, wet clay. The group climbed upwards, moving slowly to accommodate Bruce's frailty. Kate rationalized, even if we only walk two miles today, it will bring us two miles nearer to Shingbwiyang, where there is food.

A party of ten ravenous, emaciated Chinese soldiers, armed with Lewis rifles, suddenly appeared from around a sharp bend. Seeing Kate's party, they strode down the track towards them, their demeanor aggressive and hostile, a wolf pack in hunting mode.

"Upala! Kate! Take the rifle. Act as if you are holding me up," Bruce said under his breath. "David, Pamela, get behind us and stay there."

Kate felt the wave of aggression surging ahead of the soldiers intent on razing the group. She almost froze in fear then quickly reacted, thrusting the rifle to David. "David, Pamela, lay it on the ground and sit on it. Don't let the soldiers see it."

David quickly sat pulling his sister with him.

The soldiers barged into the adults, trying to pull off their haversacks. They pushed Upala, pulled on her clothes. She let go of Bruce and fell to her knees as if to vomit. Bruce dropped to the ground pretending to be ill. He reached up as if trying to protect the women. One soldier unnerved Kate by poking her in the chest with a rifle. The Chinese officer pushed to the front of this melee, pulled out his pistol and pointed it at the group. "Him, on ground. Why?"

Kate suddenly understood Bruce's ruse. "Sick. Very sick. Cholera. Maybe typhoid." Bruce rolled on his back, hiding his haversack and machete. He groaned and held his belly, pulled his legs up.

The Chinese officer covered his mouth, shouted at his men and signaled them to quickly move past. The men rushed off down the trail, scowling and shouting what seemed like threats.

Having escaped serious harm, Kate pulled her ashen-faced children to her. Pamela was fearful and whimpering; David's expression was one of hate.

Bruce stood up and raged. "May they rot in hell!"

Kate hugged the children. "We got off lightly thanks to your quick thinking, Bruce. Otherwise, they would have taken the last of our food."

"And they didn't get our money," Upala said. "Thank God, I removed my earrings and jewelry after I saw an Indian woman earlier on the track whose ears were bloody and ripped because someone had robbed her."

Kate could not stop hugging her children, wishing she could have protected them from this experience of mankind's inhumanity to man.

Feeling Kate trembling, David asked, "Did they hurt you, Mummy?"

"No, I'm shaken more than anything. Let's find a place to rest and have a cup of tea."

A trail of people passed silently, taking in the scene like a herd of wildebeest aware that one of their own has fallen afoul of lions and tomorrow it could be their turn.

They moved off the trail for a cup of very weak tea and a small portion of rice. "I think we should set up camp here," Bruce said. "A longer rest will help us recover our strength for tomorrow, me especially. We may not have been robbed of our physical belongings by the Chinese soldiers but speaking for myself, the encounter has sapped my confidence and left me questioning that I can get us all through to India. I need to get my mind sorted."

"I think I can speak for Upala on this as well as myself," said Kate, looking questioningly at Upala, "I feel pretty shook up. I'm scared for my children. I'm scared for us. This is a dangerous undertaking. But I have never let fear control my life. What are our options?"

"We can keep going or we can give up and die by the wayside," Upala said.

Kate held out her hand. "I say, never say die."

Bruce covered her hand and with a serious expression said, "Never say die."

Upala placed her hand on top of Bruce's hand. "No dying."

Pamela and David added their small hands. "No dying," they said.

Satisfied at their commitment to plod on, their strained expressions relaxed. They cuddled the children and recited poems.

Only Bruce continued fuming that he had failed to protect the women and children as he felt he should. Fury stiffened his back and shoulders and made him clench his teeth as he cleaned his rifle by the campfire. Next time, he would be better prepared.

A noise in the trees caught his attention as he put away the oil and cloth. He searched the trees for a bird, hoping to shoot it. Instead, a flying squirrel launched itself into space. Bruce fired, and it fell to earth. Kate and Upala, filled with delight at this deliverance from hunger, searched for the animal in the undergrowth. The mood in camp that night was joyful. Bruce was feeling better. They had escaped unscathed from the attack by Chinese soldiers, and they were eating a tasty squirrel stew.

In the early dawn light, they slogged along the path enveloped in fog and mist. They were cold, damp and shivering. With the ground slick underfoot, they traveled in silence, concentrating their energy on staying upright. Mid-morning, the drizzle stopped, but no sunshine emerged from the clouds. Too weak to do anything but stumble along slowly and steadily, they focused on extricating their feet from ankle-deep mud.

They staggered past two skinny Indian boys about four and five-years old sitting beside a body, possibly their father. Kate's party gazed numbly at the boys as they passed. Kate took six more steps and stopped. Swaying, she looked back.

Upala touched her arm. "*Thakin-ma,* we have no strength, no food. We cannot take them."

Feeling drained, Bruce took the opportunity to sit and rest. The children sat with him.

Her need to survive and save her own children battled with her need to save the boys who would definitely die without someone's help. Feeling torn in two, she screamed with frustration. With tears streaming down her face, Kate turned to Upala. "I can't walk away."

"*Thakin-ma,* we have passed hundreds of bodies and dying people along the trail. We cannot help them. Your children, we, will die if you try. We must use our pitiful strength to save ourselves."

"I've lost two children, Upala. I can save someone else's."

Exhausted, Kate stumbled back to the boys. They were in a bad way. Dressed in fraying shirts, they had distended bellies and stick-like limbs. Maybe her help would be too late. Impassively, the boys watched her stagger toward them. Glimpsing a flash of white-blond hair among the trees behind the boys, she halted suddenly, reached out her arm. "Joey?" A giggle. *His* giggle. "Joey! Joey!" The giggling receded. The blond hair of her dead son bobbed behind the bushes and disappeared, swallowed up by the jungle. Kate's chest heaved with sobs; tears flowed like waterfalls. The young boys looked at her dully. Collecting herself, she held out her hands. "Come. Come," she gently coaxed. She felt revitalized. Joey had shown her. He had giggled. All would be well. "Come." The starving boys got to their feet and tottered alongside Kate.

Kate saw the anger in Upala with her tight lips, paled face and flashing eyes. "Upala, all will be well. I promise. David, Pamela, welcome these boys." David managed a small wave of his hand. Pamela remained mute and stupefied.

Kate's glowing expression, like one filled with religious fervor, left Upala rooted to the spot. A look of concern flashed between Upala and Bruce. They had seen these symptoms in too many people driven crazy by the horrors of the journey.

Kate scraped around in her haversack and found her portion of cold rice to share between the two boys. She hugged them to her. "It's going to be all right."

Upala stared warily at Kate. Her mistress was becoming unbalanced and the stench of death surrounded them.

Moving on, they passed bodies on the trail, even the bodies of starved Chinese soldiers. Too weary to walk around the dead, the children stepped on corpses littering the trail. The numbers of people sitting by the wayside, weeping in defeat, were increasing. Two hours later, they came upon the body of a Gurkha man. The man's shirt caught Bruce's eye. He bent over the corpse to look more closely.

"What is it?" Kate asked.

"It's one of the Gurkhas we traveled with. He's been shot twice in the chest. Probably had a confrontation with those Chinese soldiers."

David stared, his nostrils flaring like a raging bull. He had liked this man who always seemed to be laughing. "The soldiers killed him, didn't they?"

Kate squeezed his shoulder. "I think they did, dear."

They stood for a moment of respect before stumbling up the trail.

Two more days of travel in pouring rain, torrents of water flowing down the path, aggravated the struggle of moving through molasses-like mud. Suffocating heat and humidity drained them and increased their thirst. Floundering knee-deep in glutinous mud had Kate weeping with frustration. She tried to be strong so as not to upset the children. She was even wondering if it was worth it. It all seemed so pointless, so much effort, so much trouble and adversity day after day. Bruce was lurching all over the path. Kate prayed to a God she did not believe in, asking for Bruce not to collapse. A few minutes of hard slog required a halt to regroup, to tap into their courage and determination in order to continue on. Kate pictured Joey hiding in the jungle behind the two Indian boys. Her belief that he was with her, guiding her to safety, helped her muster her strength. But they were all so hungry and weak. The children trailed along like silent robots, unless they became stuck too deeply in the mud to move. Then they wailed for help.

In the afternoon of the thirteenth day out from Maingkwan, the trees thinned out, the path became wider. They were leaving dense jungle behind. Through the trees they saw a dilapidated Naga settlement, a few scattered huts beside a field. Behind it a river. On the far side of the river, to the west, ridge after ridge of blue-green mountains soared into roiling clouds.

The exhausted party turned off the track and trudged to the huts hoping to shelter there. They didn't need to look inside. The odor of rotting flesh deterred entry. They moved nearer the river and settled by a clump of bamboo with lots of new shoots to cook and stems to make a framework for the tarpaulin. Hordes of attacking insects feasted on their flesh, resulting in welts and swollen bites. Tonight, it was not a concern. They would be dealt with in the morning. For now, they were sleeping the sleep of the dead.

The group was drinking their morning tea in the thick damp mist, when some Naga men approached. They had wooden dug-out canoes. With gestures they asked if the group needed to cross the river. The cheery disposition of the Nagas lifted the group's spirits despondent from the weeks of dismay and misery they had experienced.

They packed their belongings, relieved not to be doing it in the rain, and plodded to the river. A canoe containing three Europeans in pith helmets and Frontier Service khaki uniforms landed.

"Good morning," one of the men said. He pointed to the collection of half a dozen Naga long houses halfway up the hill on the far side. "You've reached Shingbwiyang. Go and get some breakfast." And off they marched past the group.

The river water, flowing from the lower regions of the Himalayas, was cold and clear, the current not too wild, and the price to cross reasonable.

"Look!" David said, pointing behind them.

They all turned. The Frontier Service officers had set fire to the corpse-filled huts beside the field. Soaring orange flames sent sparks into the air, a cheerful dance macabre. Smoke spiraled upwards, signaling the fire's success in devouring bodies, cleansing buildings, and destroying disease. In a moment of clarity, Kate knew she would never return to this land. *My future will be elsewhere. Where will that elsewhere be? And who will it be with?* She stroked the Indian boys' heads and cheeks and smiled. *We need to discover your names.*

25

The bedraggled group, clothed in rags, walked into the village. The smell of death assailed them. Filled with misgivings, they passed huts containing bloated bodies.

Any hope Kate had turned to despair. "We've walked into hell." She looked at her companions, saw her own desperation reflected in their faces. With a straightening of her shoulders, dejection turned into a stubborn resolve. Like a thirsty woman at a well, Kate pulled a bucket of strength from the reservoir deep inside her. Her voice strong, she said, "We're staying here only long enough to build our strength for the next leg of the journey, then we'll be on our way. If we stay here, we'll die here."

"I am filthy. I want to wash, and the children need to eat," Upala said. "Is there anyone to tell us where to go?"

Bruce pointed west to some steep towering ridges. "To get to India, we have to go over those hills to reach the Pangsau Pass. We'll need to be strong. I had a quick check of the map this morning. Th . . .th . . .ere's n . . not much detail." Bruce's teeth were chattering. He suddenly became sweaty and flushed. "Steep ri . . .ridges shown, but the . . .the map is mainly bl . . .bl . . .ank." Bruce was staggering. Kate and Upala grabbed his arms to hold him up. "Unadministered a . . . area." Bruce fought to finish what he had to say. "W . . .we'll be at m . . . mercy of tribesmen and r . . .robbers."

He groaned, fell to his knees, mumbling.

An Indian man came and looked at Bruce. He pointed to a hut. "Hospital there." He pointed to another hut. "Breakfast there." They half carried Bruce to the hospital. When they arrived, nobody seemed to be in charge. Upala and Kate sat Bruce on a bench on the veranda.

Pamela stroked Bruce's hand. "Is Bruce poorly, Mummy?"

"Yes, he is. We must get him well. Stay with Upala."

Kate entered the hut. It only took a moment to realize that half the patients were dead, and nobody seemed to be in charge. She searched in cupboards for medicine. Nothing, only clean drinking water available. She turned on her heels and left.

They went to get breakfast, a meal of rice, dahl, bamboo shoots and tea. They sat on logs among dozens of other refugees, propping up Bruce, coaxing him to drink tea and eat a little dahl. Then a man came and told them, "Everyone must leave. Go to next camp, not far, along track."

Anger gave her strength. She stood up, hailed the Indian man. "Wait a minute. We're too weak from lack of food to walk and our companion has malaria. He needs medical care, and we need to stay."

Black clouds sodden with rain blanketed the hilltops. thunder rumbled and rolled all around.

"No one can stay who can make the next camp before dark. You must go."

Fear jerked Kate's stomach. "We're too weak!"

She had expected Shingbwiyang to be their salvation. A place that would nourish them, build up their physical health to continue their journey. Already there were signs of some B vitamin deficiency in herself and the children, sore red tongue, burning sensation in the hands. The Indian boys needed warm clothes. Hot tears of anger and frustration rolled down her cheeks.

"We cannot carry our companion to the next camp. Show us where we can stay for the night."

The Indian man wobbled his head yes and pointed them in the direction of a Naga long house, one of a cluster of four fifty-foot-long buildings made of wood, bamboo and thatch.

Jungle surrounded them on three sides and a meadow with a stream running through it on the fourth. The houses stood on stilts, five feet above the ground.

Kate's heart sank. How would they ever get Bruce up that log ladder?

They pushed and pulled, and Bruce tried to help until they tumbled inside. It was clear from the smell the place was full of death. They found the first corpse lying in the central corridor near the entrance. She wanted to cry at their impotence. Will we never be free of the dead?

Kate looked back to help the children and was relieved to see more than a dozen Indians with torches setting fire to the houses they had passed, containing the putrefying dead.

"Come inside," she called to the children. Supporting Bruce, she and Upala shuffled past the body. Behind her the children giggled at the dead man's happy, wide-eyed expression as if he had died laughing at a good joke. They amused themselves by waving their hands to make the flies crawling on him buzz loudly and fly up in a cloud.

"Get away from that man!" Kate called. "You'll get sick."

It took a moment for Kate's eyes to adjust to the windowless, dim interior. In a room at the end of the corridor, they found scores of people lying on hessian sacking that had once held rice. Some fires were burning on hearth stones. With no chimneys for the smoke to escape, the air was hazy.

Upala spotted a space at the end of the room, where they laid Bruce. They knelt beside him, looking at one another. Their eyes said it all. Hopeless despair. The search for safety had brought them to a hell-hole. Voices called and rambled and mumbled and no one came to help. Flies swarmed everywhere, settling on the dead. The smell of excrement made Kate and Upala want to gag. People were lying and dying in their own mess.

"Upala, get some soap and take the children to the stream to wash. And bring some water back for Bruce. I'll start a fire soon. We must be able to get food to cook somewhere here."

Left alone with Bruce, now semi-conscious and mumbling, Kate used the machete to cut holes in the woven bamboo walls to let in light and fresh air. She sat and breathed in deeply, hoping the overhanging roof would hold off the worst of the rain during downpours. She wanted to cry. She, the young woman who thought herself invincible when she married Charles. Still, she had had the fortitude to make a reasonably happy life for herself with him. It hadn't destroyed her. But this! At times she had braced herself against the hardship and knew she would make sure she got them all to India. Then at other times, she crumbled, didn't think she could make it, screamed silently to be rescued by a knight in shining armor. Of course, no one came. A warmth filled her, made her smile. That last thought—not true. Joey came. He was there, telling me to rescue the boys. He's journeying with us. Surely a sign we'll make it. The thought soothed her, offered some hope. With Bruce sleeping, Kate sat and stared through one of the holes she had made, blotting out the dramas taking place in the shelter and in her head.

Agonized squealing brought her attention back to the room. She found a mature, white man in an Indian Army uniform, attending to a wound in a young boy's head. He was sitting behind the boy, pulling maggots from the wound with tweezers then dabbing the wound with a kerosene-soaked swab. Unable to help herself, Kate approached to watch.

"I have a little antiseptic with me."

"Nice of you to offer, but kerosene is better at killing the maggots." the man replied in an impeccable British accent.

"Will you get them all out?"

"I work on him for about an hour a day. It's all the poor chap can take. Tomorrow may be the last time he'll need my help."

The soldier introduced himself as Major Brookes, Medical Officer. Kate thought he looked ill. "Are you all right? You look ill."

"Touch of malaria."

"My friend has it too," said Kate, indicating Bruce. "If you need my help, I'm a trained nurse."

"That's good to know. Unless people are too ill to travel, the political agents normally chase them on to the next camp.

Want to move them out of Burma and into India where they can get proper care. Those that are ill, well . . . they shouldn't coop us up in these germ-infested places," he said impatiently. "People are dropping like flies. This boy has lost his father and four sisters in only a couple of days, and because the camp administration is overwhelmed, he and his mother were left sitting with the bodies for two days."

The story only confirmed Kate's worst nightmare. They would die if they didn't get out of there.

"Major Brookes, where can I get some food?"

There's a godown (storage place) where they store supplies dropped by the RAF. You can go and get your rations—three mugs of rice and three-quarters of dahl for men. Women and children receive smaller amounts. Make sure to get marmite if you can, for the B vitamins. Most of us are malnourished. If you have the strength, help collect the dropped supplies. The camp administrators give you extra food. But it's dangerous. The Chinese troops often fire on you, so they can snatch up most of the supply drop."

"Thank you for the heads up," Kate said and returned to Bruce. Upala came in with water and clean children.

"*Thakin-ma,* this is an awful place. Pray Mr. Bruce soon is well so that we can leave."

Kate noticed Upala had lost the stiff face of disapproval towards the young Indian boys. "How are the boys doing?"

"They are no real trouble, *thakin-ma* and, no matter what they have been through, seem to be sweet natured. They don't speak English, only Burmese and Hindi. David has discovered their names. The five-year-old is Varun and his younger brother is Dilip. More than that they could not tell him except that their family is gone, and they are very hungry."

Kate looked around their squalid accommodation, at Pamela, David, Bruce, Upala and the two small newcomers. Fear squeezed her heart, hard, almost to the point it stopped beating. She leaned against the bamboo wall and closed her eyes. A picture flashed to mind of the first time she laid eyes on Jack. She smiled, a flicker of joy lifting her spirit. He had appeared from the jungle, firing his rifle into the air to scare away a raging elephant that had her and Manny trapped up a tree for hours, while it vented its temper below. The smile faded, replaced by tears wetting her cheeks. Oh, Jack, where are you? Please come and rescue us. We're going deeper and deeper into hell.

26

Jack crawled from the grass and tarpaulin shelter into the rain and morning mist. The handsome man Kate had fallen in love with was hidden beneath a bushy black beard, curly black locks, and lice-infected, ragged clothes. Jack scratched his beard and his head. The lice infestation was their latest torment. He and Tom spent a good deal of time in fierce scratching. He looked down at his boots and wondered how much longer they would last. They had been trapped on this island for a week, in the middle of the raging Dapha River, swollen by monsoon rains and melting snow water from the Himalayas. The deluge was so noisy, they had to shout to hear one another. Sixty-eight other soldiers, Gurkhas from the Burma Rifles and Garhwalis who had been involved in the fighting retreat, began emerging from their shelters. Like Jack, they were skinny and starving.

Tom came and stood with Jack as he stared at the far bank and cursed. "The water's way too violent to attempt to cross. Even if we had some strength left, we'd never reach the far side."

They had only just made it from the riverbank to the island by forming a chain with the Gurkhas to withstand the current. Except for the last few in the chain, who were swept away when the water suddenly surged, seventy men successfully set foot on the island, situated in the middle of the river. And now they waited for water levels to go down so they could complete the crossing.

Tom nodded. "It's a bad do, Jack. We made it across some of the most hostile terrain in the world in some of the worst weather in the world and if help doesn't come soon, we're going to die of starvation in this God forsaken place."

"We've got to figure something out. Let's do it over a spoonful of rice. Our brains will work better after a good meal."

Tom grimaced at Jack's sardonic humor.

They returned to their shelter and ate two spoonfuls of cold rice put aside from the previous night, then sat in silence. The water's roaring prevented casual conversation, and Jack's thoughts drifted to the start of his nightmare journey.

The Japanese had overrun the Allied armies much faster than their officers could ever have imagined. He, Tom and six other commandos who had been guarding the Gokteik Viaduct were sent to blow up the steel bridge over the Tiang River once Brigade HQ and the last escaping British soldiers had crossed. Orders were that once the bridge was blown, it was every man for himself. Get out of Burma and make for India as fast as you can. The road crossing the Tiang River bridge led to Sumprabum and Fort Hertz in northeast Burma. The men planned to escape by going east to China and then fly from China to Assam.

Driving past Myitkyina, Jack and Tom saw smoke billowing up from a town in flames.

"Good job we got our families on the train to Myitkyina in plenty of time. At least we know they're well out of this and safe in India," Jack said.

Tom and Jack and the two soldiers with them turned away from the sight of the burning town.

"Time to take our leave. The Japs are hot on our trail and Myitkyina will be in their hands in a day or two," Tom said.

From the rear of the Jeep, one of the commandos said, "Let's blow that bridge, and get the hell out of Burma."

The hordes of refugees walking along the track leading from the town slowed them down to ten miles an hour. It took five hours to reach the bridge. They prepared the bridge alongside some Royal Engineers who had also been told to blow the bridge. With explosives in place, the Bush Warfare commandos left the bridge in the capable hands of the Engineers and traveled on. The bridge could not be blown until HQ Brigade passed through. The journey to Sumprabum that should have taken three hours from Myitkyina took thirteen, plus time setting explosives at the bridge.

Next day, they pushed the Jeeps over the edge of a ravine, making them useless for the Japanese. The men arranged for two muleteers with their mules to get them and their food supplies to Fort Hertz. They talked over their plans to cross into China with Mr. Molloy, Burma Frontier Services, who was in charge of the British government's administration of the area, telling him they thought it was the best way to reach India. He gave them a map. "I couldn't interest you in going to India via the Chaukkan Pass instead, could I? You'd be taking on an almost impossible task when the monsoon breaks, but then, my good fellow, I think a few hundred administrators and others, myself included, will be behind you. The Japanese are racing up the eastern edge of Burma to cut off the China escape route. Therefore, for us, there soon will be no other way to get out except by going through the Chaukkan Pass to India, and so the impossible must be achieved.

"Of course, if you decided to go to China, the journey would be shorter but not much better. Lots of Chinese troops are escaping that way. I think many will starve to death before reaching safety. The thing is, I need fit men to take the Chaukkan Pass route to help refugees that get into difficulty. No need to go into Fort Hertz at Putao, bear west and head for Hkam Ho. There are Frontier Service *daks* to stay in all along the way."

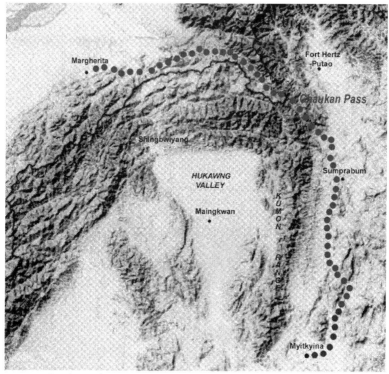

Jack and Tom's Escape Route in North Burma

Responding to Mr. Molloy's request for help, Jack and Tom agreed to go the Chaukkan Pass route. They parted ways with their six comrades who decided to continue to China.

The *daks* were welcome places to stay each night following a vile day of slogging along in pouring rain. Despite the bad weather, in the early days of the trek Tom and Jack managed almost ten miles a day, but then, after nine days and seventy-two miles traveled, the muleteers refused to go any further along the horrendous track, claiming there was no fodder for the mules. Jack paid them off and the two men trekked on, carrying their own supplies.

The camp at Hpaungmaka was host to myriads of winged pests of every kind—sand flies, blister flies, anything-that-would-make-their-lives-a-misery flies. From Hpaungmaka onwards everything went downhill. Loathsome marches in disgusting weather conditions, struggling up and down slopes, some of them almost vertical. The track was a stream of mud inches thick. They saw not one village or villager after leaving Hpaungmaka, the jungle and terrain being too inhospitable for humans to endure. This area was one of the wettest places on earth. Some days Jack and Tom were so exhausted from the struggle, they had to stay put and rest, protecting themselves as best they could from the constant downpours by making crude shelters.

They reached and followed the Paungma River, which had numerous ox-bow bends. Using the track shown on the map required that they cross the river thirty-six times, twenty-six by perilous tree bridges. Other crossings required wading through swift currents knee deep or waist deep and sometimes chest deep. The dangerous track included walking on slanted slopes for long distances.

Another difficult trek over a 2000-foot mountain range and the same drop down on the other side brought them to the Nam Yak River. It was in heavy flood and could not be crossed. Jack and Tom waited there two days to see if the water would subside. It didn't. They set off along the east bank, cutting a path through the jungle to reach the Chaukkan Pass almost 8,000 feet above sea level. They were finally blessed with fine weather on arrival at the pass. Looking down on India, they could see that even in India, the going would not be any better; it was going to be more of the same for almost another two hundred miles.

Jack and Tom camped at a place where they found a tree carved with the message: A. B. Waltz 1st Gurkha Rifles, Shillong, arrived here January 29, 1942 with a party of 92 Gurkhas, also J. Kennewel I.O.G.R. (Intelligence Officer, Gurkha Rifles). This confirmed they were on the right track.

Moving on, travel was vile and treacherous most days—pouring rain, liquid mud, slippy mud, steep hillside mud, leeches that they had to stop and remove from one another at regular intervals. Freezing cold nights spent in wet clothes sapped their strength. Hills of terrifying steepness filled their days and their dreams, on those rare occasions when they weren't too wiped out to dream. Jack recalled a saying he had come across years earlier: "Suffering ceases to be suffering once you accept the way things are." To stay stoical, he repeated it multiple times a day, especially on the most damnable days.

The worst day was when the two men were leaping from boulder to boulder to cross the Dehing River. Tom slipped and fell into the water. The fierce current swept him away.

"Christ! Don't drown! Tom, don't drown!" Jack screamed, throwing off his haversack and racing down the riverbank like a gazelle escaping a lion. Tom was swept against a large rock and managed to hold on until Jack jumped onto the rock and grabbed Tom's arm then his haversack. He pulled him far enough onto the rock so he could grab his belt to haul him to safety. Jack fell backwards, gasping for breath. Tom, exhausted, lay on his belly, coughing up water. Recovering from the effort, Jack hooked Tom under his arm and hoisted him to his feet.

"That was a close call," Tom said.

Jack landed a playful punch on Tom's arm. "Don't do that again. I'd hate to lose a good friend."

Jack held Tom at arms' length. They looked one another in the eye and laughed with relief, before Jack pulled Tom close and they slapped one another on the back.

Tom stepped back, patted Jack's shoulder, cleared his throat. "Glad you caught me, Jack. Edith and Colin would never forgive me if I didn't meet up with them in India."

Having had all the excitement they wanted for one day, they made camp early to recover from the fright and to dry Tom's clothes and kit.

Finally, after more wretched days walking, they arrived at the Dapha River only to end up trapped on the island.

Jack tapped Tom's knee to get his attention. "I'm going to shave this bloody thing off," he shouted, tugging at his beard. "If I'm going to die of starvation, I'm going to die clean-shaven."

He filled his mug with water, rubbed soap in his beard, and began shaving. His beard was half-way off when he became aware of a commotion on the island. Standing up, he and Tom found most of the soldiers on the edge of the island facing the far bank sixty yards away.

Tom whooped. "Jack! Jack! Someone's here with elephants!"

Jack and Tom shared a slow, cautious smile. Could this be really happening? They could see a white man on the far bank among the elephants and mahouts. The Gurkhas on the island were frantically putting fingers to their mouths to show they were starving. The man acknowledged their gestures with a wave. The thunderous roar of fierce flood waters made all voice communication impossible.

The mahouts valiantly tried and tried to get their elephants across the torrents to the island. The elephants flailed against the power of the river. With water up to their eyes, they struggled to move forward, eyes filled with terror as downed tree trunks and deer carcasses swept by, any of which could have easily collided with the animals, sending elephants and mahouts to their deaths. Several hours later, night fell. The white man called off the rescue attempt.

Relief and hope lost, lines of disheartened men, shoulders slumped, heads hanging down, stumbled back to their grass shelters. Overwhelmed by powerlessness, loss of hope and despondency, Tom and Jack ducked into their shelter as well.

"How much longer do you think we can hold on? The torrent's eating away at the island. Have you noticed? The edges are eroding more and more each day," Tom said.

Jack scraped at his beard with the razor. "Help is here. I hope they're in time to save us. But just in case, I'm preparing to die clean-shaven."

"This is a stupid way to die! If I'm going to die, I want to die a hero, not trapped like a rat on a bit of land about to be washed away. I want Edith and Colin to be proud of me." Tom shouted above the noise.

Jack finished his shave and felt his chin. Smooth as Kate liked it. A wave of sadness swept over him. Unless a miracle happens, I'll never see Kate and the children again.

"Edith and Colin should be safe in India with her cousin. She's my rock, Jack. Everyone thinks I'm the strong one, but I'm not. It's Edith. She's like a sturdy oak tree in the forest where everything spreads out from. I can't wait to see her and feel safe in her arms."

Jack lay down to sleep. "We can only hope we're in God's good books and that he'll deliver us to our families."

In the middle of the night, a change in river noise woke the men both on the island and in the rescuers' camp. The volume had decreased, accompanied by a four-foot drop in water level. The mahouts rounded up their elephants. Trapped soldiers watched as the elephants, a few at a time, crossed to the island to ferry three men per elephant to safety. By midday all the men were on the far bank. Cooks were struggling to turn out food faster than seventy starving men could eat it. The no-longer-trapped soldiers laughed and talked energetically now they were safe. Two hours later, snow water surged down again. The roaring torrent swept over the whole island. The voices fell silent. If the men had still been on there, none would have survived.

When Jack and Tom landed on the riverbank, they ecstatically thanked the mahouts. Then, vigorously shook the European man's hand. Jack introduced himself. "Captain Jack Bellamy. Are we glad to see you! Thank you for saving our lives."

Tom shook the rescuer's hand. "Captain Tom Hubbard. I thought we'd had our chips on that bloody island. It was starve to death or try and swim for it and drown. Thanks to you, we didn't have to make that choice."

"Gyles Mackrell, tea planter. Glad to be of service. An advance party of soldiers warned that refugees fleeing Burma were trapped and starving, held up by the flooded Dapha. Through my work, I had access to elephants, so I gathered twenty of them and came here as fast as I could to help."

"Just in time, sir," Jack said. "I really can't thank you enough. And there're more people coming after us who will need help too."

"Go and eat. I know you're both very hungry. If you need medical treatment, come and see me."

At the sight and smell of the food, Jack rubbed his hands together. His mouth was watering prolifically.

Tom licked his lips. "This has to be the best chicken I've ever tasted."

There was no shortage of food. An Indian kept coming by with more rice, more chicken, some dahl, a pot of jam and biscuits.

"I'll never take food for granted again," Jack said, wiping crumbs from his clean-shaven face. He looked at Tom's feet. "Your feet are swollen. You need to see a doctor."

"We were saved just in time, Jack. I was beginning to get worried about a sore place under my arm where my wet clothes have been rubbing. I was afraid it would turn into a Naga sore."

Mackrell came by with a jar of Marmite for Tom. "I saw your feet were swollen. It's a sign of B vitamin deficiency. Here, eat this. it will help. Tomorrow, you will rest and eat to build your strength. The following day you'll be taken out on elephants. It's a three-day trek to Miao where two tea planters have a base camp."

Miao was also the headquarters of a company of Assam Rifles, with a havildar in charge of forty-eight men. The camp doctor attended to the worst of the ailing rescued Gurkhas. He treated Tom's sore spot and gave him B vitamins. Jack and Tom stayed in Miao for one day, enjoying the warm, sea-level climate, relieved to be walking on level ground, free of mountains and cold nights. They ate heartily and were treated with DDT to kill the lice. They bought new clothes and burned their lice-ridden rags.

Seven hours travel by elephant next day brought them to Simon Camp where Captain Lancaster and Lieutenant Smith extended a warm welcome. More medical attention was provided and heaps of food to build them up for the three-day journey in large dug-out country boats to Margherita. The warm sunny weather contributed as much to everyone's recuperation as the food and medical care.

Margherita had a railway station and a small European community. The Gurkha soldiers were cared for in the Margherita Evacuee Camp. Tom and Jack were put up by a tea planter, Mr. Thomson, in his bungalow. After the ordeal of their journey, Jack and Tom basked in the warm hospitality offered them. Sinking into a tub of hot water was a luxury marking their absolute return to the comforts of civilization, and the joy of eating delicious bread pudding topped it all.

After dinner, they sat contentedly with Mr. Thomson on the veranda, drinking beer, sharing how relieved they were to be over their ordeal in the mountains.

Jack stretched out his legs. "We can't wait to get a flight to India to see our wives and families to let them know we're safe."

27

With the promise of an RAF flight to Calcutta in two days, Jack and Tom spent their time doing necessary shopping and building their strength. On the day of their flight, a corporal drove them the thirty miles to Dinjan airfield where they boarded a Douglas C-47 plane for the six-hundred-mile flight to Dum-Dum airfield, Calcutta. Tom had planned to stay at the great Western Hotel, but that was overcrowded. Instead, he went to the Grand Hotel. Tomorrow, he would see about traveling to Ranchi where Edith had arranged to stay with her cousin.

Riding in the taxi to the Rodwells, the anticipation of taking Kate in his arms and hugging his children, electrified Jack. His heart was light and joyful. He wanted to gambol like a spring lamb in the fields. He impatiently tapped his fingers on his knee.

A servant ushered him into the dining room where the Rodwell's were having afternoon tea. Bill Rodwell stood and shook hands with Jack. "Nandin, whiskies all round. Bring the bottle."

Rose Rodwell, looking ill at ease, began wringing her hands. "Would you like a sandwich and a cup of tea?

Not seeing Kate and the children, Jack asked, "Where's Kate? Has she taken the children to the park?"

Rose stood and gently touched Jack's arm. "Kate and the children didn't arrive, Jack. We've no idea where they are." Her eyes appealed to her husband.

Bill cleared his throat. "Hearing about the evacuation and the terrible conditions the refugees have endured, we've been so worried. We tried to make inquiries, but had no success."

Jack felt as if he had been cut in two by a Japanese sword and that he would topple to the floor. Bill steadied him as he swayed and put a whisky in his hand. "Sit. Drink the whisky, for the shock."

"They didn't arrive in Calcutta?" Jack felt empty, abandoned by God's goodness. Surely, they aren't dead. Not my sweetness. Not my children. "What could have happened.?" His face filled with anguish. A whimper escaped his lips. Bill refilled his glass. A fearful chill enveloped Jack. He gulped the second large whisky, savoring the burning of his throat, but it was no antidote to the numbness and fear he felt. Jack put down his glass. "I have to go find out where they are."

"I'll drive you. Where do you want to go?"

"The Grand Hotel."

Bill dropped Jack off at the hotel entrance. "Keep us informed, and if there's anything we can do . . ."

Jack threw his haversack on his bed and went in search of Tom. He found him in the hotel dining room, looking morose, sitting with some other officers.

Tom leapt to his feet. "Jack!" He wrapped his arms around Jack and banged his back then stood back, sniffing hard. "Am I glad to see you! What are you doing here?"

"Kate and the children aren't with my friends. Never arrived from Burma. Where's Edith and Colin?"

"I don't know. Nobody knows. They're not in Ranchi with her cousin."

"So, they didn't arrive either?" Jack rubbed the back of his neck. "Where the hell can they be? Surely, they left Burma!"

Tom could hardly breathe. "Where do we go to find out what happened?"

"We'll find Major Calvert," Jack said.

Next day, they discovered Major Calvert was seven hundred miles away in Jhansi, central India, training troops in jungle warfare. Tom and Jack sat in the hotel lounge trying to figure things out. Tom leaned forward in his seat. "We got them tickets to Myitkyina to get on a flight to India. It's just too improbable that they didn't manage it."

Unable to sit still, Jack jumped up and paced back and forth. "If they *had* flown back to India, they would be here, now, safe—and they're not. It may be unlikely, but what if they had had to walk out of Burma?"

The two men looked at one another in horror.

Tom rubbed his forehead. "How will we find out about that?"

"Do you remember? The Indian Tea Association turned Margherita golf course and polo ground into a reception camp for refugees. Surely, they'll have made records of refugees emerging from Burma."

Jack sent off an air gram to both Major Calvert and the Indian Tea Association administrators asking for information. Next, the men went to the Royal Air Force headquarters to inquire if their families had been on any flights from Myitkyina. There was no record of Kate and the children having flown out of Burma.

A young wing commander strode down the hall towards them and stopped in front of Tom. "Would you come into my office, Captain Hubbard?".

A few minutes later, Jack heard Tom shouting. "No! no! I don't believe it. You're lying, dammit. It's not true!" More time passed and Tom emerged with wet cheeks and buckling knees.

Alarmed, Jack hurried to him. "Tom, what is it?"

Tom shook his head unable to speak. Jack helped Tom to a chair and turned to the wing commander. "What happened?"

"Are you a friend of Captain Hubbard?"

"Yes. Captain Bellamy."

"Captain Hubbard has received bad news. His wife and child were killed May 6th at Myitkyina in a Japanese bombing raid of the airfield.

Jack gasped. "My wife and children were with Captain Hubbard's family!"

"Their names? I'll check again."

The wing commander returned holding a piece of paper with a list of names on it. "They're not listed here as deceased."

"How do you know Captain Hubbard's family was killed in the attack?" Jack demanded.

The wing commander scanned papers attached to the list of the deceased. "Apparently, we found proof of their identity in Mrs. Hubbard's handbag."

Stunned, Jack sat next to Tom, who was staring blankly at the far wall, and weeping silently. Eventually, they stirred themselves. Tom wiped his wet cheeks with the palms of his hands. Returning to the Grand Hotel, they found an air gram had arrived in response to their query to the Indian Tea Association, which stated they had no record of their families having come through Margherita as refugees.

Tom barely said a word and didn't want a drink. Jack went to the desk for Tom's key. Handing Tom his key, Jack noted the deep pain in his friend's eyes. "Don't go off by yourself, Tom. Stay. Let's have a drink in the bar."

Tom shook his head. "Can't bear it. Edith was everything to me."

Jack patted Tom's shoulder. "Take care. I'll see you at breakfast."

He watched Tom drag himself upstairs to his room. *Should I go after him? I don't know how to comfort him. How can a man who has lost his family, the most precious thing in his life, be comforted?* Then, remembering he had no idea where his own family was, Jack headed for the bar, ordered a whisky and despaired. *Have I lost my family too?* His eyelashes suddenly felt wet.

At breakfast, Jack didn't see Tom in the dining room. He bounded up the stairs and knocked on Tom's door. No response. He banged louder. Nothing. Anxiety struck the pit of his stomach. Something wasn't right. He hurried downstairs and went to the reception desk. Tom hadn't checked out. He found the manager and asked him to check Tom's room. Jack raced back up the stairs, followed by the manager. The manager's knocking and calling brought no response. He dug into his pocket for a key. "Did Captain Hubbard have a lot to drink last night, Captain. He could be sleeping it off."

Jack impatiently shook his head. "Open the door."

The manager unlocked the door and went in followed by Jack. The form in the bed was totally covered by the bedcovers. The manager pulled them back. "Oh no!"

He rushed out ashen faced, bumping into Jack behind him.

"What is it?" Jack demanded, grabbing the manager as he tried to race past. The manager could only gasp with shock and point behind him. Jack pushed past him into the room. Tom lay cold on the bed. Dead. A bloody mess on the pillow and a bullet wound in his head.

"You stupid bugger!" Jack cried and reeled out of the room, gasping for air, leaning back against the hallway wall for support.

He answered questions from the Calcutta Police and Military Police as best he could. Tom had left a short note for Jack that said, "Sorry, Jack. Can't go on. Forgive me."

Jack sent an air gram to Major Calvert in Jhansi, seeking permission to return to Burma to search for his family. At this point, no matter what the dangers in North Burma from the Japanese, he was going, permission granted or not. He pinned his hopes on assessments he'd heard that the monsoon had stopped the Japanese advancing so far north.

First, he attended Tom's funeral. The padre had been kind enough to find other soldiers, who had escaped Burma, to attend the funeral service, otherwise Jack would have been the sole mourner. As the burial service droned on and hymns were sung, Jack's thoughts were of Tom. How he had confided that Edith and his son were his strength. She had been his anchor, his compass, ever since he met her, he'd said. Why didn't you try to build your own strength? Build up your own mental state so you didn't need a prop? I'm sure Edith would have wanted that for you to be an example for Colin. Yet you didn't. Now look at you. He squeezed the bridge of his nose in a vain attempt to stop his tears.

The following day, he received a letter granting permission to return to Burma, with chits provided for travel warrants.

Jack arrived in Margherita July 5th. With a growing sense of urgency gnawing at his guts and a feeling that time was running out, Jack was impatient to be off. He asked around about expeditions going into Burma. He learned a group of Assam Rifles were returning to Burma to relieve Political Officer, Mr. North, who was still at his post helping refugees at Shingbwiyang. They were willing to allow Jack to go with them.

He borrowed a mule from Captain England, in charge of the Mule Company, bought a month's provisions for himself and extra supplies for his family, who he was sure would be extremely hungry when he found them. He paused outside the store, arms full of supplies, and made himself face the possibility—if I find them. A lead weight settled on his chest. He took deep breaths, forced himself to focus on hope rather than fear. He had been told the route to Shingbwiyang was the best bet for finding them. It was the escape route traveled by most refugees coming out of north Burma. He would find them. He thought of his friend Tom. We couldn't both lose our families, could we?

Filled with trepidation, Jack set off with the mule-train party two days later in pouring rain.

28

Major Brookes stormed into the hut. "How dare he?" Kate overheard him say to his wife. "North's banned everyone from traveling forward from Shingbwiyang! Says it's too dangerous to survive in the monsoon and there'll be no services available for refugees further on."

Kate went over to the Brookes family. "I couldn't help overhearing. Who is this North?"

"He's the officer in the Burma Frontier Force, who is in charge of Shingbwiyang. The civil and military authorities closed the route to India June 15th, so he has ordered that no one can leave Shingbwiyang until the end of the rains or until further orders are issued. That probably won't be until October."

Kate covered her mouth with her shaking hands. "We can't stay here. People are dying all over the place. We've got to go on."

"I don't see how he could stop you if you sneak away well before dawn. But if that is what you are thinking, I would stay here a week to build up your strength. It will take about a month to reach the railhead in India with no help available to you along the way, so you will need a month's supply of food and the stamina to do it. It seems the Frontier Service and tea planters' organization are pulling their men out for their own safety. They don't want them falling foul to diseases that develop too easily during the monsoon."

Major Brookes sat down, suddenly weak. He had chills and a fever and when Kate took his pulse, it was rapid. He looked steadily at Kate. "Blackwater fever. It's treatable but no medicines here. I'm going to die." He looked over to the Indian boy with the head wound. "Help me up, will you? Would you assist me with the boy's maggots?"

They worked together to remove the last maggots from the whimpering boy's head. They were almost finished when Major Brookes moved closer to Kate and said, quietly, "If you defy the ban and leave, take my family with you. Get them to India. I'll give you a map that shows the route and villages along the way."

Kate blinked in surprise. She was torn between hope and fear. The idea of adding more people to her small group made her stomach turn anxious somersaults, but having the map would be so useful. "Of course, I will. They'll be welcome in our group."

As Major Brookes weakened, Bruce recovered from his bout of malaria. He found a quiet pool a short walk along the stream, around a bend, and was soon providing his group as well as Major Brookes' family with hand caught fish, a skill he taught David. Soon, Bruce was strong enough to join Major Brookes' twelve-year-old son, Stephen chasing down canisters and bales of supplies dropped by the RAF, which they took to the godown to earn extra supplies for their families. Bruce carried his rifle slung over his back to deal with Chinese troops trying to steal the food. He had even seen Chinese officers shooting their own men and still, it did not stop the starving soldiers from using brute force to steal supplies that were meant for the whole camp.

One day, Bruce discovered David about to enter a dense forested area. "David don't go in there! Stay where I can see you. We don't want Chinese soldiers following you into the trees."

"It's all right, Bruce. Joey has something to show me."

"Who's Joey?"

"My friend. Come on. He knows the way."

Bruce followed David into the trees. They were so dense in places, he had to use his machete. David led the way to a supply-drop canister.

"How did you know it was here?"

"Joey said we needed it and we should hide it."

Puzzled, Bruce opened the canister. It was full of tinned food. "We should take it to the godown."

"Joey said *we* need it—to get to India."

Bruce hesitated. David's insistence had him flummoxed. "All right. We'll leave it here, for now. We'll mark a trail to it like Hansel and Gretel."

That evening when the children were asleep, Bruce told Kate about David and his imaginary friend finding the supplies and the need to hide them for their walk-out to India.

Kate covered her mouth with her hand to hide her quivering chin. "Did he say his friend's name?"

"Joey. David called him Joey."

Kate gasped, looked down until she stilled her heaving breast. Then she beckoned Upala and Bruce to come closer. "I need to tell you something, but I daren't in case you think I'm mad." She paused and looked around. No one seemed to be listening. Major Brookes' Burmese wife, Ma Sein, was focused on holding her comatose husband's hand. Kate lowered her voice. It shook when she spoke. "I've seen Joey too. He is my son. He died in England when he was five. I saw him when I took in Dilip and Varun. I feel he's watching over us." She sat up straight. The relief of sharing had lifted the burden from her shoulders. "Because he is with us, I know with absolute certainty that we're going reach India safely."

Both Upala and Bruce sat back and stared incredulously at Kate.

"There, you think I'm crazy, don't you?"

After a silence, Upala said, "No, you are not crazy. I have seen my husband many times since he died."

Bruce and Kate stared at Upala in surprise.

Kate squeezed her hand. "Then you understand."

Upala looked into Kate's eyes and nodded. Like an arrow piercing a bullseye, an intense, powerful and lasting connection was made.

Bruce observed the women. Something momentous and unfathomable had just happened between them. He scratched his beard. "Well, that's it then. I'll go into the forest and inventory what's in the canister and then hide it so we can collect it easily when we leave. When do we go?"

"I have something to tell you." Kate shifted uneasily. "I promised Major Brookes I would take his wife and two children with us when he died, so we'll have to wait. It won't be long now."

Bruce cracked his knuckles. "Have they prepared for the trip? Have they enough supplies to make it to India?"

Kate glanced at Mrs. Brookes, sitting by her husband and lowered her voice. "I don't know, Bruce. We'll have to cross that bridge when we come to it."

During the night, somewhere in the camp, a distressed woman began wailing. It went on and on, hour after hour with a ferocity that pained all who heard the grieving cries. Kate clenched her fists trying desperately to blot out the picture of another woman, another time, wailing with grief over the loss of a blond-haired, five-year-old child. She brushed back damp hair sticking to her sleeping children's foreheads then lifted her head and determinedly set her jaw. Her heart flooded with a mother's protective instincts. Her eyes became moist. Show me the way, Joey. Let me not lose these children."

Then a softer sound. Major Brookes wife was crying, smothering her sobs beneath her hands. Kate scooted over to newly-widowed Mrs. Brookes and put her arms around the weeping woman's shoulders until her tears dried.

Together they wrapped the Major's body in a blanket, constantly checking the Brookes children were still asleep. A cold shudder ran down Kate's back. She hoped that no one in her own group would ever require this of her. When the children awoke, Stephen looked at his father's wrapped body and began to shake. His sister Maisie cried and held on to her mother. Ma Sein knelt and wrapped her arm around her weeping child.

"I want to see my father," Stephen said. "Please, Mother, please. I want to see him."

Ma Sein Brookes turned the blanket back from her husband's peaceful face and Stephen kissed him. "Goodbye, Father," he said, then he collapsed weeping on his father's chest.

Too weak to bury him herself, Ma Sein and the children waited all day by her husband's body for someone to come and bury him. In the evening, two British soldiers, a major and a sergeant and two Kachins, came to the longhouse. The Kachins carefully placed Major Brookes on a stretcher. The two soldiers stood to attention and saluted before he was taken away.

"I'm so sorry, Mrs. Brookes," the Major said. "I'll arrange for a British soldier from the Burma Auxiliary to stay with your family in the longhouse to fend for you."

The oppressive heat and humidity sapped everyone's energy. Most families slept in the heat of the afternoon after cooking and eating lunch, usually rice with bully beef or dal and any bamboo shoots they could find. The tops of the hills were usually covered in roiling black clouds and most days heavy rain fell in torrents. This day, the sun was shining. A sudden rumbling roar shook the longhouse. "Plane!" Bruce yelled, on his feet in seconds. He called to David and Stephen, "Come on! There's work to be done." And he was off.

The Dakota turned and roared past again, so low Bruce ducked. The ground shook. Several thousand Chinese soldiers poured from their huts as did all people able enough to snatch sacks and canisters raining to the ground as lethal as bombs if you failed to dodge them. The sky was filled with hurtling supplies, swishing and thudding onto the meadow at high speed, splashing up water from the soggy ground. Then they bounced, one, two, three times before rolling to a stop. People jumped on them as quickly as they could. Bruce grabbed one.

Stephen and David grabbed one between them working as a well-trained team and off they staggered to the godown. Bruce saw them stop to gather up some contents from a burst sack, stuffing their pockets with stolen bits and pieces. Later that day, David shared his spoils, hard biscuits and a squashed tin of bully beef, with Pamela, Dilip and Varun. Upala almost stopped David sharing the bully beef with the Indian boys because it was taboo for Hindus to eat beef, but she turned her gaze away. They needed to build their strength and they would never know about it when they were older.

That night, Kate told Mrs. Brookes of her husband's wishes that she and the family should leave for India with her.

"No, I'm not doing that. I can't risk losing any more of my family. He can't have been in his right mind to have said that—traveling in the monsoon? It's crazy!"

"Mrs. Brookes, disease is rampant here. They're constantly having to burn huts full of corpses and there's too many dead to be buried for the administration to keep up with the work of collecting bodies. Please, your husband knew what he was asking me."

"I said no! We are getting food drops here. We will remain here, safe, until the rains end. Thank you, but no."

Kate paused and took stock of Ma Sein's determination. Her refusal made Kate exhale with relief. "I'm sorry to hear that. I'm breaking a promise I made to your husband, but I respect your wishes and wish you well."

Kate returned to Bruce and Upala. "She's won't come with us. I'm feeling guilty that I didn't try harder, but Bruce is right, they haven't planned and are not prepared for the journey."

Upala sat up straight like a school teacher scolding her class. "Like Mrs. Brookes, I, too, think it is foolish to go in the bad weather, but I am not staying here alone. And I cannot be separated from Pamela and David."

Kate took hold of Upala's hand. "I'm glad, Upala. We've all come a long way together. Now we need to go over our plan."

"We have almost all the food we need except for more rice. We use the tinned food when we cannot light a fire," Bruce said, checking off each point he was making by touching his fingertips in turn. "The canister David found is aluminum and its domed nose can be used to cook rice. We can use the canister itself to boil water and make tea. The parachute can be used as bedding, clothing for Dilip and Varun and even for us if our clothes disintegrate further. It can be used as a tent, although I've still got the tarpaulin, and the cords can be used for belts."

"Major Brookes told me that officials have cleared a trail from here to the Pangsau Pass, which should make the going easier," Kate said. "We have to be careful. Our bodies have been weakened by malnutrition. We must try and get some Marmite for B vitamins. Unfortunately, our medicines will be sorely stretched to get us through to India and there are none available here."

Bruce went to the godown to talk to Corporal Katz, one of two British RAMC privates who had volunteered to stay in Shingbwiyang and take charge of the godown. He asked Katz for some Marmite to treat a member of his party with swollen legs and feet. Katz gave him a jar of the rich-in-B-vitamins spread.

"Would you like to help out here, stacking supplies for us?" Katz asked. "You'll get extra rice rations."

Bruce wasn't going to let an opportunity like that get away. "Set me to work," he said.

As he worked, Bruce casually plied Katz with questions. He found out that Tagap Ga, the next village along the track, was twenty-five miles away. Then Shingbwiyang's headman came by and stood talking to Katz. Bruce overheard Katz ask him, "When are we going to get a break from the rain, chief?"

"You do not like the rain?" The headman laughed at the miserable face Katz made. "Rain for two days then sunshine for three," he said, laughing as he walked away.

When Bruce returned to the longhouse, he found David, Pamela and the young Indian boys sitting outside on a log by the stream, a habit they had developed, weather permitting, while in Shingbwiyang. Upala had worried for their safety at being alone in such a place, but Kate had calmed her fears. "They need to be surrounded by butterflies, flowers and trees. They have seen more death and horror than any child should. Soon we will be on the road again walking through death and destruction. Let nature do its healing work."

That night, when the children were asleep, Kate, Bruce and Upala huddled around the fire. Bruce told them of the headman's weather forecast. "I say we leave in three days. It will allow one dry day to give the track a chance to dry out a little."

Kate stared at an elderly man lying nearby. He had been delirious and mumbling for two days. He was fading fast and smelling of excrement. He continued soiling himself even though he could no longer keep food down. A lethargic family across the room had recently lost three members.

"I don't see how staying here is helping us," Upala said. Twenty people die every day and are left to rot in the longhouses because there is no one to bury them. The place is swarming with flies."

"Major Brookes told me there are camps every three to ten miles all one hundred and thirty miles to the railhead at Tipong," Kate said. "But when North banned travel, the Major wasn't sure if help would continue to be available in the camps. Let's hope it is."

The corners of Bruce's mouth turned down as he thought. "Maybe we should only try and make contact with villagers and avoid the camps in case any officials there try to stop us from traveling on."

"Are you well enough to make it?" Kate asked.

"Yes."

"Oh!" Kate exclaimed. "You know what I forgot!"

Concerned, Bruce and Upala looked at her.

"I forgot Pamela and David's birthdays. They were two weeks ago, June 6th and June 8th. We must have a party."

Next day, Kate produced a tin of peaches, a special treat for David and Pamela, and extra rice. They sang happy birthday to them. David's face crumpled, and he cried hard and openly without trying to be strong or hide his feelings. Bruce put his arm around him.

David looked guardedly at Kate. "When are we going to India, Mummy? Daddy's waiting for us."

"Soon, David. Very soon."

The tone of her voice made David stop crying and study his step-mother. Then hope showed in his eyes.

"Very soon?"

Kate nodded. "Promise."

David broke into a broad grin, the happiest Kate had seen him in weeks.

"Mummy, that is the best birthday present ever."

29

In their corner of the long house, to the accompaniment of mumbled deliria of a dying man, the peaceful breathing of young children and the stench of excrement, Kate, Upala and Bruce tallied up their food supplies. They had stashed away enough, they hoped, to reach help in India, with enough canned food for meals when rain made lighting a fire impossible.

"As the strongest," Bruce said, "I'll carry the bags of rice and dal, the tarpaulin, my blanket and whatever canned food I can carry in the canister that David found."

"The children can each carry half a blanket," Kate said. "We'll share out packets of dried figs, dried apricots and cans of condensed milk for the children to carry."

Upala and Kate would carry their blankets and as many canned foods as they could. "I'll carry the medicines, as well," Kate said. She counted out the matches and the silver rupees they had left and shared them equally between the adults. "In case anything happens to any one of us, the others will still have money and matches."

Ignoring Kate's suggestion that anything bad might happen to them, Upala said, "I'll carry the soap and towels."

Kate smiled at Bruce. "Hopefully, we will come across an occasional small river not in full flood where Bruce can catch some fish."

"Maybe we could buy some eggs from natives, too," Bruce said.

With heavy loads, the going would be slow and tiring, but hope and determination gleamed in their eyes as they planned to leave in the early hours of the morning before anyone would be awake to stop them. Bruce had already moved the canister to another hiding place more convenient to collect as they left Shingbwiyang.

The last week in June, they woke the children, putting fingers to their lips to warn them to be silent. Sneaking from the longhouse was difficult in the dark. They moved slowly, feeling their way with their feet to avoid tripping over corpses or sleeping people. Once outside, they took deep gulps of the fresh air and set out for India. Kate took it as a good omen that there was little cloud cover, allowing the full moon to light the way. The children were sleepy and staggered along holding the adults' hands. The ground was glutinous and slippery, but fortunately level. The biggest danger would be passing the Chinese camp. If discovered, the Chinese soldiers would rob them of their food.

By the time daylight arrived, the group had passed the Chinese without incident and were well on their way. With no certainty that the tea planters' support system was still operating, they had no one to depend on but themselves. Leaving cultivated fields behind, the path began to climb where the jungle began. Haversack straps cut into shoulders, their loads agonizing. Everyone was wet with perspiration even though tall trees shaded and gloomed the trail. They struggled and groaned up seven miles of steep grades and curves. Half way to the top of Chinglow Hill. they had to rest, eat and drink to prepare themselves for the final push to the top. Bruce led the way, reaching back, offering his hand to David, behind him. All did the same and, in this way, the group climbed, pulled and dragged one another to the summit.

A stream flowed alongside the narrow path most of the way. There would be plenty of water for cooking and bathing. They had only come across an occasional body in an advanced state of decomposition. Kate wondered if the Frontier Service had cleared the path by throwing bodies over the edge of the precipice to lessen the risk of spreading disease. Although exhausted by the ascent, she was looking forward to thoroughly washing herself and the children to remove Shingbwiyang's filth.

Kate washed the children, Upala cooked rice and dal and made tea. Bruce built a shelter. The meal was small, barely satisfying their hunger, but food had to be conserved; who knew what obstacles lay ahead to delay them? Weary from the climb, they settled under the tarpaulin, hopes high because they had made good progress that day, walking between seven and nine miles and tomorrow they could expect one more sunny day for easier travel.

Kate kissed David and Pamela's heads and put her arms around Varun and Dilip's shoulders. "You did really well today. I'm very proud of you."

Upala smiled at the children and nodded agreement. The adult's praise managed to returned some sparkle to their eyes.

Bruce proceeded to tell them a fantastical tale about leprechauns, rainbows and pots of gold. The children laughed and giggled at his funny facial expressions. Ten minutes into the story, they were struggling to keep their heavy eyes open, but one by one their eyes closed. They were fast asleep before the story ended. Upala tucked the children's blankets in around them to keep them warm in the chilly night air.

Kate pulled out Major Brookes' map. "I think we still have about one hundred miles to go and food for close to a month."

Upala brightened. "Unless something bad happens, we can take it steady, three to five miles a day, for the children."

"You're right, Upala," Bruce said, poking the fire with a stick, "but if we get bogged down in serious mud, we'll be lucky to travel three miles a day. We have to push on as fast as we can while the weather holds."

"Of course, *thakin*."

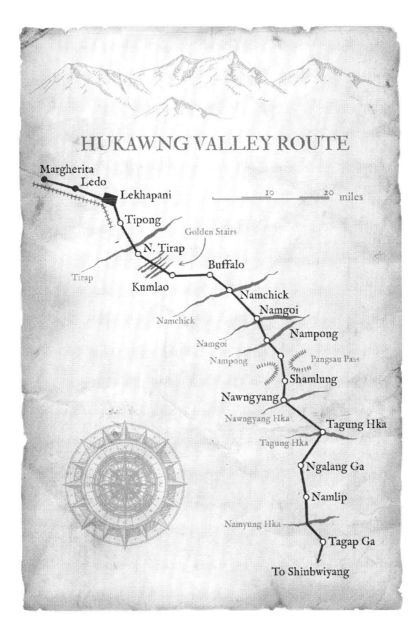

Studying the map, Kate said, "We should reach the village of Tagap Ga the day after tomorrow, if we keep up today's pace. We may be able to buy food there."

"There were not many people on the road today," Upala said.

"Could be the travel ban or maybe most people trying to get out have reached India already," Bruce said.

The group slept deeply that night, breathing the sweet-smelling highland air. A breakfast of cold rice and sardines prepared them for the day's trek. They broke camp and a few miles on reached a steep, twisting trail.

Bruce made everyone halt while he searched in his haversack for the parachute cord. "I'm tying us all together," he told Kate and Upala. If one of the children slips, it should stop them falling off the path."

Then it was upwards along a narrow path on a cliff face. Sweat heavy with fear oozed from the adults' foreheads and armpits, forming wet patches on their clothes. Kate was jittery. She couldn't stop imagining one of the children slipping off the path and pulling the others down the precipice with him. They moved carefully, relieved when the path leveled into open ground, only to be dismayed to discover the trail then became a narrow path atop a knife ridge above terrifying, steep walls that fell away on both sides to gullies far below.

Departing the knife ridge brought no respite from the tension. It was arduous to try and stay upright on the steep descent. The heavy haversacks affected their balance. Much of the time the children skated down on their backsides looking anxious and biting their lips in concentration. They laughed with relief on reaching Bruce, who caught them, stopping their wild slide down.

The rain started late next morning. Rumbling black clouds rolled in, blotting out nearby hills. Grey mist surrounded the group with a cold dampness; then heavy drops splattered the ground.

"We're in for a soaking," Bruce said, starting an ascent that brought them to another knife ridge trail. Kate's heart pounded with fear. Terrified for the children's safety, she struggled to breathe.

"Let's hurry off this ridge so we can find shelter," Kate said, her voice cracking. Upala looked at Kate and nodded, her face reflecting Kate's dread.

The camp that night was wet and miserable. They had no dry clothes to change into and it was hard to sleep in wet, freezing cold clothing. They spent an hour using salt to remove leeches, treating the bites with antiseptic. Kate inspected the children's feet for cuts and wounds. In a day or two she knew her shoes would be worn out and she too would be barefoot. Hope the skin on my feet is tough enough for the walk. At least with plenty of tinned food we don't have to go without a meal.

Rain fell throughout the night, stopping with the arrival of dawn's light. A short trek brought them to Tagap Ga. They stood and observed, wondering how wise it would be to approach the settlement. The village was positioned on a jungle-free, wide, grass-covered spur, surrounded by green hills. White mist still veiled the valleys. One hut claimed the top of the spur; the other huts were lower down, dotted about the spur like mushrooms. The village seemed well-populated by the numbers of people moving about.

Bruce slipped off his haversack. "Stay here, out of sight. I'll go in and see what's what."

Kate grabbed his arm to stop him leaving. "It could be dangerous. Why don't we just go past?"

"I'll be all right. We need to get an idea of what's ahead. Don't worry," Bruce said cheerfully and walked off.

But Upala and Kate did worry. To take their minds off Bruce's scouting mission, they made Pamela and David practice their times tables and played pat-a-cake with Dilip and Varun.

Two hours later, Bruce returned. "The villagers seem to have run away except for the headman. There are several hundred refugees there for the duration of the monsoon and the RAF is making food drops. It's a more pleasant place than Shingbwiyang, but the headman and some Sikh soldiers are looting the food drops and selling it to the refugees for high prices." Bruce pulled some bars of chocolate from his pocket.

"I bought a treat for us." He handed half a bar to everyone. Kate and Upala gasped and laughed, close to tears, almost overcome by the normalcy of eating chocolate.

Kate gave Bruce a quick hug. "You really know how to cheer people up."

She popped some chocolate into her mouth and made it last as long as she could and wasn't the least bit upset when the children wiped their sticky hands on their clothes. As if it matters now, she thought.

Licking melted chocolate off his fingers, Bruce said, "I don't think we should go into the village. The refugees seem to be covered in scabs with some kind of skin disease. It must be contagious because so many have it."

"Did they say what lies ahead?" Kate asked.

"Some refugees are camping on the banks of the Namyung River hoping for the water to subside. It's a few miles up the road. The headman said many people had drowned or lost their food supplies while trying to cross and we shouldn't try it. He could, of course, be wanting us to stay in the village to help fund his money-making scheme."

"I think we should go to the river and not Tagap Ga," Upala said.

"Me too," Kate said.

"Oh, they told me that all the government camps on the way to India have closed down," Bruce said, "which may or may not be true."

Kate nodded. "We'll be all right. We prepared for that eventuality. Children pick up your packs. Let's go."

The mud was sticky but nowhere was it more than ankle deep. The group reached the river two hours later and set up camp away from the several hundred people already camping there. Bruce collected silt-filled water from the heaving river and filtered it through Upala's sari. Upala went to talk to people in the camp.

She returned to inform Kate and Bruce that some had been there more than a week, waiting for the waters to recede.

At least we have plenty of food thought Kate. We'll have to figure out how to keep it safe and dry. Our lives depend on it.

After setting up camp and eating rice and dal, Bruce and Kate left Upala with the children and went to the roaring river. Large trees carried along in the fierce current bucked like broncos in the churning waters. The force of the water, speeding along like a dozen semi-trucks whose brakes have failed going downhill, tumbled large boulders along the riverbed. Kate could have sworn she felt the riverbank tremble.

"We could have quite a wait," Kate said.

"Let's pray for fine weather so the water will go down," Bruce said.

On the way back to their camp, Kate's spirits lifted as she took pleasure in clumps of bright incandescent color, thinking they were patches of flowers. But as she drew near, the bright petals flew into the air and her joy drained away. She knew at once what she was witnessing. Butterflies, multitudes of them, feasting on a decomposing corpse's juices. "Oh, hell! Will we ever escape this horror?" Kate suddenly felt sluggish. Almost comatose with fatigue, she stumbled back to their shelter and at once fell into her blanket.

During the five days they were held up by the rushing river, Kate made sure everyone washed with carbolic soap and treated all bites with antiseptic. They ate three small meals a day, told stories to the children, sang songs and gave Pamela and David mental arithmetic problems to solve. Bruce checked the river twice a day. At the end of the fourth day, he returned to their camp looking brighter. "I think the water may be about to drop. It seems to have eased slightly. We'll watch for people moving to the river tomorrow."

After breakfast the following day, Bruce returned from a check of the river. "Time to pack. We might be able to cross today."

Along with numerous other refugees, the group waited on the river bank. Some refugees were too exhausted, too emaciated to stir themselves. For them this was the end of the road.

Late morning, two Gurkha men of typical short stature, waded chin deep across the river. They took a rope and tied it to the far side as a guide line to help people cross. Wanting to keep the rice and dal dry, Bruce tightened his haversack straps as tight as he could to lift it and the canister above the water. He found another stretch of rope near the first and tied it off with help from some Indian refugees and waded into the water. Being tall, the water only reached his chest. He used the first guide rope to keep him on his feet as he battled the current and reached the far side. The two Gurkhas helped him up the bank.

Using signs, he indicated to the men to protect his haversack. He was going back across the river. One of the Gurkhas went with him. Wasting no time, refugees were already using both ropes to cross. Bruce and the Gurkha had to carefully make their way around them without losing their grip on the rope. A couple of elderly Indian refugees, being too weak to hold on as they fought the current, were swept away. Reaching Kate and the children, Bruce fastened everyone in his group to the guide rope with parachute cord, along with the Gurkha who accompanied him. Then they each picked up a child to carry to safety. Eyes big and skin pale with terror, they clung to the adults like monkeys.

"Go slow. Slow! The current is strong." Bruce shouted over the loud rush of the river. Pausing every so often to gather strength, Bruce reached the far shore. He dumped David onto firm land. Leaning back, he grabbed Kate's arm and pulled her and Pamela onto the rocks. He pushed Kate further onto the bank, where she lay on the ground panting from her exertions. Bruce dragged Upala and Dilip out of the river. Gasping for breath, Upala began to laugh in hysterical exuberance. Alarmed at this outburst, Kate put her arms around her, recognizing a weakening of Upala's mind. The Gurkha arrived safely with Varun.

Following a round of shaking of hands, the two Gurkhas took their leave as rain began to fall.

30

Kate looked at Bruce and Upala. "I know we ought to put up camp soon, but I think we should go on another mile? The rain will provide water to cook with, and we'll get ahead of the crowds."

Resigned, Upala nodded and helped the children put on their packs.

Bruce patted Kate's shoulder. "Good thinking." He hoisted his haversack and canister onto his back then led the way along the trail towards Namlip camp. "It's a pity we won't arrive at Namlip before nightfall. There may be huts there for shelter," he called back.

Leaving level ground behind, they entered the forest and began to climb. Having expended what little energy they had crossing the river, it was all they could do to put one foot in front of the other. The grey weather and steady, drenching rain made them lethargic and depressed.

Bruce suddenly halted and waited for the rest of the group to join him. He nodded to a young Indian girl, about two years old, caked in mud, sitting at the side of the road. Kate cast about for nearby bodies and saw nothing.

Bruce whispered in Kate's ear. "I saw him, Kate, your little boy. Couldn't miss his shock of blond hair."

Kate's eyes suddenly became moist. "We'll take her with us."

He scooped up the child, held her to his chest, and placed her skinny arms around his neck. She acquiesced without protest. Upala tutted. Her mouth tightened and she mumbled her disapproval under her breath.

"We'd better make camp at the first suitable place," Kate said. To Upala she said, "At least we have food. We can help her, Upala."

"And if we come across more children, *thakin-ma,* what then?"

"We'll do what we can. I know we can't save everyone."

Kate helped Bruce make camp close to a stream that flowed down the hillside. It would be a good place to wash the sticky clay from their legs. Upala sat drenched, on a stump, staring into space. Just as wet, the children sat around her. Having finished helping Bruce make the shelter, Kate saw Upala doing nothing. She had not put out containers to catch rainwater, had not brought out canned food to eat. Kate was about to say something sharp when she noticed Upala was not her usual self. She was closed off, seemed far away. Her lips were moving, but she was not making a sound.

Kate put her arms around her, lifted her up and guided her under the tarpaulin. "Come into the shelter. I'll get you some food." Kate turned to Bruce. "Would you find some canned food while I wash the children?"

Kate found the carbolic soap and the thin towel. She washed the little girl, who was wearing a tattered dress of good quality. She gave the emaciated child a warm hug. "I wonder what happened to your parents, little one." The child remained mute and unresponsive. But when she saw food, interest flared in her eyes and she eagerly ate her cold rice, canned cheese and dried figs.

It rained all night, a steady gentle rain not a blustery storm.

Kate sat near Bruce, their heads close together. "Upala doesn't seem well. She didn't eat her food," Kate whispered.

"We'll be at the railhead in India in about three weeks. She'll make it, won't she?"

"I'll do my damnedest to see she does."

Bruce squeezed Kate's shoulders. He was about to say more but the children pestered him for a story. He smiled at Kate, shrugged his shoulders in submission, and began. "Once upon a time . . ."

Kate gave the girl more food then put her to sleep in her blanket, so she could keep the child warm during the night. In sleep, the child snuggled into Kate. The feel of her triggered tears Kate desperately tried to hold back. She, too, so wanted to feel safe snuggling against Jack's broad chest. Will it ever happen again, my darling?

Over breakfast, a breakfast Upala did not eat, Kate said, "We must choose a name for our new companion. We can't keep calling her little girl. What do you suggest?" she asked Pamela and David.

David looked serious as he thought of a name, then his face brightened. "Betty Boop."

Pamela giggled at his joke.

"Mmmm, do we like that name?" Kate asked looking around.

"She needs a prettier name than that. She's a pretty girl," Bruce said.

"Shirley," Pamela said firmly, "after Shirley Temple. *She's* a pretty girl."

"Good choice," Bruce said.

With that they packed up and set off. Upala remained enveloped in her mental collapse. The rain had almost stopped. Hopefully, the sun would come out so their clothes would dry as they walked.

They found Namlip to be a place they did not want to stay. The few huts in the settlement stood in a soggy black mire surrounded by slimy pools of stagnant water. Moving past what had once been a camp for refugees, Kate pulled out her map.

"Major Brookes said something about this place. What was it?" She saw two trails leaving Namlip, one going west towards India and one going north straight up a steep ridge to Ngalang Ga. "Oh, yes! I remember! He said you will think you have to go west to Assam, but it's only a fair-weather road and you won't reach India that way in the monsoon." She looked up from the map, her face crestfallen. She pointed to a steep path winding through the trees. "We have to go up there."

All eyes followed her finger. Necks tilted back as far as they could go. The silence was deafening.

"Come on," Bruce encouraged. "It's not so bad for intrepid adventurers like us."

Still nobody moved.

Kate broke the silence with a laugh. "The thought of making the climb floored me for a moment. All right, everyone, we'll take it slow and steady. Besides, it will be slick from the rain. And we don't have to do it all in one go."

"Staffs at the ready, children," Bruce said, taking Shirley's hand.

"I'll help Upala," Kate said, pulling Upala's arm.

Legs ached and calf muscles trembled by the time the trees thinned out. They stepped from the trees onto grassy slopes where a few gaunt refugees were camping. Bruce moved across the clearing to an area away from the other refugees. The next leg of their journey came into view.

Kate gasped and her heart sank. Several miles further on, the summit of a large domed mountain loomed against the grey sky.

Bruce shook his head. "Oh, brother! That's going to be some steep climb tomorrow."

David picked up a stick and poked the ground. "I'm sick of it, Mummy."

Kate stroked his hair. "I know. Only a few more days."

Bruce looked around their surroundings and warned, "We'll have to be secretive about our food. If these people find out how much we have, they may try to take it from us. Don't bring anything out until I have the tarpaulin up."

"There's no water here," Kate said, "only what's in our canteens. We'll have to ration it until we find a river or stream."

They drank condensed milk and ate dried fruit. Kate managed to persuade Upala to drink a whole can of condensed milk. The night turned bitterly cold, which was not helped by their damp clothes. Bruce and the boys curled up together to share body heat and the girls pressed close to the women for warmth.

Next morning, they tackled the steep climb. Bruce tried singing some songs for the children, but they, along with everyone else, were focusing too hard on putting one foot in front of the other in an almost vertical situation to consider singing. They were thirsty and soaked in sweat by the time they reached the summit.

Checking the map, Kate said, "There seems to be a river at Tagung Hka, but it's eight miles away. We'll not get there today."

Bruce touched Kate's shoulder and pointed. "Look, through the trees. The sun is glinting on something down there. Water I think."

"Well spotted. And it's on our way. We'll camp there tonight."

When they caught glimpses of the view, they discovered they were surrounded by jungle-covered mountain chains as far as they could see, and they were descending into a steep valley. Bones and skulls, animal and human, littered the sides of the path. The trail was dangerous and uneven where elephants had previously sunk into the mud. The group traveled slowly so no one would be careless enough to break a leg.

The water they found was from a spring and pure. It took a long time to drink enough to quench their thirsts.

They awoke to a sunny day. It didn't help much to alleviate the red clay quagmire they had to travel through. The children mostly slid down the trail on their bottoms, a better mode of travel when carrying loads. Then it was up the next ridge. The wide path made for easier traveling through the dense, tall, trees. At the top, it looked as if there had been a refugee encampment judging by the amount of bones they found. The sight of children's skulls particularly saddened Kate. She turned and smiled at Shirley and the Indian boys, glad to have rescued them from a similar fate. She caught Upala looking at the skulls and mumbling. If Kate had been looking at a stranger, she would have said Upala's expression was almost demented. But this was Upala. Kate's stomach tightened in fear. She needed Upala's solidness and here she was cracking under the strain of the walk-out

On the far side of the ridge, they came upon woodland with large trees, four feet in diameter, their crowns blotting out the sun. They struggled down the dizzying two-mile descent to arrive on the valley floor, where they found a small river with a clear pool full of small fish.

Bruce quickly erected a lean-to shelter with a bamboo floor then went to the pool to fish. He returned with a dozen. Before cooking them, everyone jumped in the pool and swam and laughed and splashed and washed away clinging dirt on bodies and clothes.

"Who could have thought that getting clean could be such fun, Pamela," David said, splashing his sister.

She splashed him back, as did Varun and Dilip laughing and squealing.

In the valley, it was warm enough to strip off their clothes to dry by draping them over branches near the fire and cover themselves up with blankets. The spot seemed idyllic. Then the sandflies started biting, too many to be ignored. The only way to escape attack was to go to bed early First thing next morning, Kate was dabbing antiseptic on the bites to deter the children from scratching. They were too close to India to be starting with Naga sores.

They crossed the valley, heading towards the Tagung River, passing a few skeletal refugee stragglers tottering along. The sun was shining, and spirits lifted despite finding numerous animal and human bones that sparked David's curiosity.

"Is this a buffalo?" he asked Bruce. "Is this a horse? Oh, these are a baby's bones! There's bones everywhere!"

Bruce looked around. "The animals probably died or were killed for food because it was impossible for them to cross the river when it was in full flood."

The thought that they may face a hold up at the river made Kate's stomach lurch.

She let out a huge breath on finding that the fifty-foot wide river had a narrow stepping-stone crossing protruding four inches above the fast-flowing water. "No wet feet this time, eh, children." Relief was replaced by consternation. She frowned, pursed her lips. How do we cross it safely with our heavy loads and five young children in tow?

Seeing Kate's expression, Bruce touched her arm. "It's all right, I'll take our haversacks across one at a time then come back, tie us together with the parachute cord and we'll cross all at once. If anyone slips, they won't get swept away."

Kate nodded. "Thank goodness for the parachute cord." She sank to the ground to rest while they waited for Bruce to return. From the corner of her eye, she watched Upala who was mumbling again. Kate caught only a few words—jungle, leeches, dead, hell. Kate gripped her haversack so tightly her knuckles turned white. Her *ayah*, a woman she respected for her common sense and stoicism, seemed to be heading for a breakdown.

When Bruce returned, he fastened them together with the cord, quipping they were like the three musketeers, all for one and one for all.

Pamela wrinkled her nose. "What are musketeers?"

"Tell you later," Bruce said, leading the way onto the bridge, a series of close stepping stones. Bruce carried both Indian boys, one clinging to his back and the other to his chest. David took Upala's hand and led her to the crossing. He whispered in her ear, "Hold me tight, Upala. I'm scared."

The lack of a response from Upala made Kate nervous. She watched them closely as they started to cross. Kate took hold of Pamela's hand and held Shirley close to her chest. Her heart fluttering with anxiety and her stomach churning, Kate called to David. "Are you all right?"

"Yes."

Pride at David's care of Upala warmed Kate's soul. He's concentrating too hard to lead Upala safely across to say more.

They reached the far side without incident.

"There, that wasn't so bad, was it?" Bruce said.

Upala stared up at the mountains ahead of them, muttering to herself and rocking. Bruce looked at Upala then quizzically at Kate. She moved close to whisper in his ear. "I'm worried, Bruce. We need to watch her. I think she is about to crack."

Bruce nodded to indicate he understood. He pointed east to some thatched huts on stilts. "There's a Naga village over there. Should we stay there tonight?"

"I'd rather move on. The sun's very hot, and it looks marshy ahead, so it won't be pleasant with leeches and flies. Let's have a quick meal of dried fruit and cheese, then we'll walk as fast as we can to higher ground and the shade of the forest," Kate said, opening the children's back packs to search for the fruit. "Let's fill our canteens to capacity here and drink our fill. We may not find water in the hills."

"How far to the next river?" Bruce asked.

"The map shows nine miles. We won't get there tonight, but we could get a good way up that ridge," Kate said pointing to the 4,000-foot obstacle in front of them.

Hot and wet with perspiration they arrived at the base of the cliff, where they spent some time resting and picking off leeches. The ascent was difficult. They had to keep stopping to adjust their haversacks that were agonizingly heavy and causing pins and needles in their arms. The first 2,000 feet they struggled and gasped their way along a narrow trail through thick bamboo jungle, after which they entered a gloomy forest filled with huge trees that blotted out the sky.

Pamela was trailing behind when she yelled, "Mummy, I've found water."

Bruce walked back to where Pamela was pointing. "Well spotted. Hey, Kate! Pamela's found a spring, beautiful, clear water trickling from between two rocks. Let's make camp."

Kate needed no prodding. She was exhausted and ready for a rest. Bruce searched for wood to build the frame and floor of the shelter; David and Pamela scavenged for wood for the fire.

"Lots of it, please," Kate said. "It will be cold up here tonight."

She saw David beckon the two Indian boys to go with him and her heart melted. I guess I have two more sons, not to mention another daughter.

While Upala withdrew into herself, Kate prepared a corned beef curry and rice supper, followed by stewed dried fruit. Feeling light-headed and fall-down-weary, she noticed Upala was not eating her food. Kate tottered next to her and coaxed her to eat as if she were feeding a baby.

David sat next to Bruce. "Will you tell the story about the three . . . the three . . . musk—"

"Musketeers?" Bruce asked.

"Yes," Pamela said, moving close.

The little ones curled up in their blankets and Bruce began Dumas' famous tale. One by one the children's eyes closed.

31

They spent a bitterly cold night shivering beneath their blankets despite Bruce's efforts to keep the fire going and all snuggling close together. Teeth chattered as they ate a breakfast of rice and sardines followed by hot tea. Legs aching, they resumed the climb to the razor-edged summit.

Descending the ridge, they found land cleared for agriculture called *jhums*. A hut stood in each *jhum* that a Naga farmer would have used while he tended his fields. Looking for a place to make camp, Bruce and Kate hurried to the huts they came across, but both huts and *jhums* were filled with bones where refugees had taken refuge and died. Ever the optimist, Bruce checked each hut as a place to shelter, then would say, "You would think we'd know better by now, wouldn't you?"

Further along the trail, they encountered additional bones, revealing more of the refugees' tribulations. They came across a huge tree that had fallen across a part of the trail that was so narrow it was barely passable. Beside it was the skeleton of a horse, still wearing its saddle. Bruce took out his machete and cut foliage and branches from the tree, made toe and hand holds to create a path over the obstacle rather than attempt the dangerous way of squeezing past along the edge of the precipice.

The trail swept down through huge stands of bamboo to the Nawngyang River where they rested, ate cold rice and condensed milk.

Kate checked the map. "I would say it's fifty miles to the rail head in India. And guess what? Only about seven miles to the Indian border."

"Even if we only walk four or five miles a day, we'll reach the railway at Tipong in about ten to fourteen days," Bruce said. "That requires a celebration. Let's open a tin of peaches."

Her spirits lifted by Bruce's cheer, Kate said, "Let's make it two."

For a fleeting moment, Kate felt contentment, listening to the children's laughter as they slurped and sucked on the syrup-coated fruit. Then she looked at Upala's solemn face and felt sad, but at least she was eating the peach slices.

Bruce took David and Pamela for a stroll along the reed-lined riverbank under the heavy shade of tall trees. They loudly sang **"Knick Knack Paddy Whack."** He found a Naga tribesman, with a raft, ferrying people across the river. Bruce walked back to Kate. There was no desperate rush anymore with India so close. There were no hordes, only a handful of refugees waiting to cross.

The current was swift, but the strong, sinewy Naga with his ready smile and a cheroot held between his teeth instilled confidence in his passengers with the expert manner he pulled on the rattan cane spanning the river to deliver them to the north side.

A short distance beyond the river, the group set up camp. Upala waved her arm around the continuous, steep, 5,000-foot high mountain chain surrounding the valley and started to cry. "How are we supposed to climb these?"

Kate put her arms around her. "We put our heads down and concentrate on taking one step at a time. Before you know it, we'll be over the top."

David took Upala's hand. "If I can do it, you can do it Upala. And we'll help if you get tired."

Kate studied her son, who was staring at Upala seemingly trying to figure out what was wrong. Kate choked. *He's going to grow up to be a good, caring man.*

"We'll get a good night's rest, have a hearty breakfast and we'll be fine, Upala," Bruce encouraged.

Upala did not respond. She had gone, disappeared deep inside herself. Kate rubbed Upala's shoulders. *I hope we can get her out without mishap.*

Most of the next day was spent stumbling through thick bamboo and evergreen forest along the steep path winding up the ridge. The trail was in good condition except for a few places where passing elephants had destroyed the path. It was in these locations that Kate's group found numerous bodies of animals and people, testament to the difficulties caused to the travelers. The soft parts of the corpses were long gone, eaten by ants and beetles, but tendons and sinewy tissue remained clinging to the bones. David poked the bodies with sticks. Laughing and giggling, Dilip and Varun followed suit.

"Stop that! They could be diseased," Kate cried.

The children tried to obey her. Then the temptation became too much to resist. It was easier for exhausted Kate to give in. "All right. Make sure you don't touch the bodies."

"What's this, Mummy?" asked David, poking tendons around a knee bone.

"That is strong, tough tissue to fasten the muscles to the knee bones. Bones can't move until a muscle tightens or relaxes," Kate said as their exploration turned into anatomy lessons. Whenever they found a body, new questions were asked, and the lessons resumed.

Shamlung was near, on the far side of the ridge. There had once been a refugee camp there run by officers from the Indian Tea Association. The group stopped for tea and rice and a rest.

"Do you think we should we go into Shamlung?" Kate asked. "I'm worried the administration might still be there and try to prevent us from going on to India."

"Let's see what's what when we get there," Bruce said. "Right now, I'm too tired to think straight."

"Me too. Scrambling up on all fours in places is tiring. Let's call it a day."

They set up camp just below the summit and suffered through a freezing night, awakening to heavy rain. Thick clouds engulfed them, obscuring their surroundings. Kate, wrapped in her blanket, failed to find wood dry enough to make a fire. Instead, she pulled canned sardines and crackers from her haversack. Shivering and muted, they sat on wet logs to eat the cold food. Bruce took down the tarpaulin. Kate packed haversacks and bundles, while Upala sat with as much life as a mannequin. David urged Upala to her feet and pulling her hand made her start walking. Slipping and sliding in the wet earth turning into mud, the joy of reaching the border faded in the effort required to keep moving forward. They were filthy, hands, knees, clothes, haversacks covered in mud. The children's faces wore smears of mud from trying to keep flies off.

The jungle thinned. A steep three-hundred-foot climb on open ground brought them staggering to a large, red, sandstone boulder on the summit. On it were scratched the words ASSAM, with an arrow pointing north, and BURMA, with an arrow pointing the way they had come.

"We've done it! We've reached the Pangsau Pass!" Kate pointed north. "David, we've reached India!"

David stared. His face crumpled. Soon he was sobbing uncontrollably. His distress made Pamela cry. Kate bobbed down next to him. "David, what is it?"

He pointed to the trail ahead. "You said we would be safe in India."

Kate looked to where David was pointing. The rain was easing. Cloud cover had fallen away to reveal a jungle track descending into a valley, still hidden by white rolling mist. And jungle-covered hills stretched away to the horizon.

She held David tightly, put her arm around Pamela, her poor traumatized, brave children, and let them cry. When the sobbing stopped, she said, "Let's rest a while."

Bruce ruffled David's hair and pulled him close to shelter him from the cold wind. "I know it looks like more of the same, but it isn't, not really. Look back at where we came, all those mountain ridges. We had to climb them. It was hard, wasn't it? Now look ahead. The track is going mainly downhill. We're going into a valley. No more mountains to climb. The worst is over. A few more days and we'll be sleeping in real beds and getting real baths."

David sat unmoving. Silent and morose.

Kate's throat was tight with emotion. They had been through hell and come out the other side. She looked at her clothes, ripped and ragged, her legs, knees bony, her feet bare, muddy and scratched; she felt her hair, all silkiness gone. It was now coarse and clogged with dirt. So different to the woman who set out on this journey. She looked at the children, Upala, Bruce. I guess we all are.

They could see Shamlung camp on a hill a short distance away. There seemed to be several hundred refugees there.

"What do you think? Should we go into Shamlung?" Kate asked.

Bruce studied the camp. "We don't know if there's still any administration there. It's hard to tell from here. All those people must be getting food from somewhere. Do you think the RAF is making food drops?"

Turning to look at Kate, he saw Upala sitting behind her, staring with blank eyes.

Bruce glanced at Kate and nodded toward Upala with a questioning expression. Kate shook her head. She, too, was worried about Upala. She pulled her blanket tighter around her. "I think the cold wind is freezing our brains. The children's teeth are chattering. We should walk on. It will get warmer as we descend into the valley. We have plenty of food, though we need to find water soon."

"Then let's go," Bruce said, standing up.

The path sloped downwards leading out of the Patkai Range toward the Assam Valley. In dry weather, it would have been a pleasure to walk, but in the rain, keeping upright in the slippery mud strained leg muscles. Kate observed David staying close to Upala. He knew something was not right with her. She was almost in a stupor, had closed out the world.

Kate didn't blame her. They had been through hell, and right now, it was still a miserable world. They were walking in the rain, along a road carved out of a dark, gloomy forest for Jeep traffic. No sunshine to lift their spirits. No sunshine to celebrate their accomplishment of reaching India.

They passed a village, deserted except for a couple of Nagas by the roadside selling rice, corn on the cob and fresh vegetables to the trickle of refugees passing by. Kate bought some corn and vegetables. They would eat them tonight for a celebration. In fact, tonight, they would have a feast.

A mile further on they came to a stream. A good place to camp just off the trail. Bruce slumped down. He shivered uncontrollably. Kate felt his forehead. He was burning up. His malaria was back.

Groaning with fatigue, she took the machete from his belt. "Upala, if you can find any dry wood, would you make some tea, please and bathe Bruce's head with cold water?"

Upala sat mumbling.

"Upala! Wake up! I need you to help me."

David jumped up. "I'll help Upala, Mummy."

"Thank you. I'm going to cut some branches to make the shelter."

Kate stepped into the forest and slashed at long, thin branches to make a framework. She was so tired and weak, she had to stop frequently to rest. Satisfied she had enough, she returned to camp. Upala, David and Pamela were nowhere to be seen. Varun, Dilip and Shirley sat quietly in the rain. Upala and the children must be washing at the stream, she thought.

Kate began to erect the lean-to framework and install the floor. She was pulling the tarpaulin from Bruce's pack when she suddenly stood upright. Something's wrong!

Kate stepped onto the track. "Upala! David! Pamela!"

No response.

A passing couple stared at her.

She cupped her hands around her mouth. "Upalaaa! Daviiid! Pamelaaa!"

Nothing. Kate screamed. Panic suffocated her. She clutched her chest gasping for breath. Oh, God! It will be dark soon.

She looked back at the camp then stumbled half-a-mile down the muddy path calling and calling.

Nothing.

Sobbing, she climbed back to the camp, not sure what to do. Perhaps Upala walked off and David and Pamela decided to follow to make sure she would be all right. Yes, that must be it. They'll have to stop traveling when it gets dark. They have no blankets or food! They'll be so cold. Don't cry my darlings. I'll find you in the morning. If you're there, God, please keep them safe.

Kate finished covering the shelter with the tarpaulin and used the last of her strength to drag Bruce inside. She plopped down on the floor, held her head in her hands. Her tears would not stop flowing. Fresh vegetables lying forgotten on the ground, she opened a can of corned beef, brought out a packet of dried dates and fed the three children still with her. She filled a canteen at the stream and bathed Bruce's face. With some effort, she managed to force some quinine between his lips before he lost consciousness.

She couldn't sleep. Her imagination was running riot as to what was happening to her children and Upala. Next morning, as darkness faded to dawn, Bruce was semi-conscious and delirious. Kate forced more quinine into his mouth. She knew what she had to do. It was breaking her heart, but she had no choice. Crying, she knelt beside Bruce lying inert, his face burning up.

Kate wiped her nose and face dry with her skirt. She cleared her croaky throat with a cough. Her voice sounded like a small, sad child's. "Bruce, dear friend, I have to leave you. I have to find Pamela and David. I am so sorry. I'll come back for you." Kate kissed her finger and put it to his lips. Her voice thick with pain, she said, "Stay safe. I've left you some food and the rifle."

She repacked the haversack with items for her and the children's needs and hoisted the haversack onto her back, the machete handle protruding from the top. She wiped her face dry with the palms of her hand then reached for Shirley's hand.

32

Between bouts of hard sobbing, Kate called Pamela and David's name every few minutes. She hoped, even believed, that despite her unbalanced state, Upala would never allow anything bad to happen to the children. She had to believe this, or she would have gone mad herself.

The deep mud slowed the four of them. The cold mist made them shiver. The children gamely struggled on. Kate admired their focus on the task. These skinny, young children had to walk, and no matter what the difficulty, they walked. Whereas all she wanted to do was catch up with her family. Filled with desperation, she was on the point of jettisoning the heavy haversack that her plunged her deep into the mud with each step when she saw Gurkha soldiers with a mule-train coming towards her.

She stumbled to the lead soldier. "Have you seen a little boy and girl with their Indian *ayah*?"

He and the soldiers close behind him shook their heads to show they did not understand English.

Kate wanted to scream. She took deep breaths and tried again in Burmese.

"Ah, yes, I understand," the Gurkha said. He pointed behind him.

Kate looked further along the mule-train and saw a man she recognized. Her knees buckled. "Jack!" she cried and crumpled to the ground. Jack ran to her, wrapped his arms around her, felt her bony ribs. Tears stung his eyes. His voice was filled with deep sorrow. "Oh, my, darling." He removed the heavy haversack from her shoulders and hugged her close.

Kate, sobbing, pressed her face to his chest. "You have no idea how many times I've dreamed of being this close to you." When she pulled away, she saw tears of sadness and pity in his eyes.

He stroked her hair, once glossy and thick, now matted and grey. "I was so afraid I'd wouldn't find you."

He pulled her to him again and held her tight. When Kate had calmed, Jack lifted her to her feet.

She immediately became agitated, gripped his shirt. "I can't find Pamela and David!"

Jack pulled her to him again and stroked her hair. "Ssh, it's all right. They found me at Nampong. They led Upala into the village last night in the dark. David is here, with me, hoping to remember where he left you."

David stumbled up behind his father and fell into her arms. "Mummy!"

She knelt down and pulled him close. "Thank goodness you're safe. I was so afraid for you." Kate looked up at Jack. "What happened to Upala? Where is she?"

"Upala is lying down. She is . . . under the weather. And Pamela is being looked after by Dr. Robertson's aides."

Distressed, Kate pressed her hand to her quivering lips. "Oh, Jack."

"Where's Bruce?" David asked, looking past Varun, Dilip and Shirley.

"Bruce!" Kate clutched at Jack's shirt. "Jack! We have to get Bruce! I had to leave him a couple of miles back. He's ill with malaria."

Jack called to the Gurkha sergeant and explained they were looking for a sick man a few miles ahead. The Gurkha *havildar* went off calling orders to his men and the mule train set off.

Jack picked up her haversack and felt its weight. "Oh, Kate. You poor thing."

Jack sat Shirley on his mule and relieved Kate of the haversack. Kate walked beside Jack. Varun and Dilip followed with David. Jack looked back. His eyebrows lifted. "Who are these youngsters?"

"I rescued them along the trail. They're orphans. I . . . I think they're ours now."

Jack stopped suddenly and studied Kate. "Ours?"

"Yes. If we can't find any family for them, we must take them in."

"We must, must we? Well, let's find this Bruce first and bring him to Dr. Robertson, then we'll talk. Tell me about Bruce."

"I hope you're not just changing the subject, Jack. I'm adamant. I want to raise those children."

"Don't be upset. I'm not changing the subject, just dealing with first things first. "

Satisfied, Kate said, "He's a British soldier who traveled with us all the way from Myitkyina. When his army friends left us to travel on, he stayed to keep us safe. We wouldn't have made it without him. We owe him our lives. We must hurry back to him."

Kate stopped suddenly. "You're here! You found us. How?"

"Come on," Jack said. "I'll tell you as we walk. I walked out too, with Tom, over the Chaukkan Pass. When I arrived in Calcutta and went to the Rodwell's and found you hadn't arrived, it scared the living daylights out of me. I made inquiries. No one had a clue where you were. You seemed to have vanished from the face of the earth. We, Tom and I, found out that Edith and Colin were killed during a bombing raid on Myitkyina airfield. He was devastated. Fell to pieces." Jack's voice went soft. "He killed himself."

"Oh, God!"

Jack nodded, unable to speak.

Kate touched Jack's arm. "I was on the airfield with Edith when they were killed. It could so easily have been us. After that, there were no more refugee flights to India. We drove as far as we could and then started walking. I'm not sure what the date is now, but we've been walking since May 7th."

"I had no idea that you hadn't made it out. When Tom and I drove past Myitkyina, it was on fire from Japanese bombing. We congratulated ourselves for making sure you all got away in time." Pain dulled Jack's voice. "Only you hadn't."

Kate's mind was spinning. "Did you blow up the bridge on the Sumprabum road?"

Jack looked at her, sharply. "We laid the explosives."

Kate gasped. A rush of tears wet her eyes. "David said he saw you there as we crossed. I thought he was imagining it."

Jack fell silent. A cold shiver went down his spine at what might have been. "I was frantic when you weren't in Calcutta. My CO gave me permission to come looking for you. Fortunately, these men," Jack indicated the Gurkhas, "were planning to come this way, and I joined them, hoping to find you." Jack squeezed Kate's hand. "And I did. St. Christopher kept you safe."

Kate's hand touched the gold chain and medallion Jack had given her for Christmas. She had been hiding the medallion by moving it to the back of her neck, out of sight of possible thieves. Today it gleamed at her throat.

"But why were the children alone with Upala? How did you get separated?"

"Bruce went down with malaria, and I had to cut branches to make a shelter. When I returned to camp, Upala, David and Pamela had gone. I ran down the track and called and called, but I couldn't find them. It was getting dark. All I could do was hope they would be safe, and I returned to Bruce and the younger children."

One of the Gurkha soldiers walking ahead shouted that he had found Bruce. Kate struggled forward as fast as she could then, suddenly afraid Bruce might be dead, she hesitated, stopped and listened. No buzz of flies. Her heart soared with joy. He's alive! She pushed through the foliage, knelt beside Bruce and felt for a pulse. Bruce's eyes flickered beneath closed eyelids. His cracked lips moved. "Hello, Kate."

"Thank God you're alive. I'm with my husband and some soldiers to take you to a doctor."

She tenderly lifted his head, gave him a drink, then felt his forehead

"Do you think he can make it to the hospital?" Jack asked.

"I don't know, but we have to try."

Jack and the Gurkhas lifted Bruce onto the mule. Jack shook hands with the Gurkha *havildar*. "Thank you, *Havildar*. Safe journey to Shingbwiyang."

Jack was pensive as they returned to Nampong. He saw how tender Kate had been with Bruce. *What's her relationship with him? She was so desperate to return to save this Bruce fellow.* Jack's thoughts were in turmoil. He didn't want to think badly of Kate. His jaw hurt from clenching his teeth. *I trust her, but in adversity people can become very chummy. They've been together night and day in dire circumstances for over ten weeks! He and Tom's relationship had changed, grown closer as they sabotaged alongside one another. How close had Bruce and Kate become?* Jack took deep breaths to calm himself. *It would be too easy to lose control and say something that could destroy his and Kate's relationship. Does it matter how close they were? Does it matter now Kate is back with me? Do I really want to risk losing her by making accusations?* The answer was a simple no. He was just glad to be with her again.

"Penny for them," Kate said.

"Um?"

"You're deep in thought."

"Just thinking of all you've been through."

"None of it matters now. We're together again. The children are safe."

Jack squeezed her hand. "With some to spare."

"Yes. About that. I really do want to take care of these orphans and make them part of our family."

"You do, do you?"

"One day, I'll tell you the story about rescuing them, but for now, it's enough to know they are meant to be with us."

"Then when we reach the railhead, I'll do what's necessary to make it happen. I want to you to be happy, darling."

Kate bit her lip and watched Bruce. He was managing to stay on the mule, with an occasional shove from Jack when he started slipping as the animal lurched along the muddy trail. That was a good sign, wasn't it?

At Nampong, they took Bruce straight to the hut with a red cross. Pamela came running out and hugged Kate. "We're all right now. We found Daddy."

Aides helped Jack carry Bruce inside then went to fetch Dr. Robertson, a tea planters' doctor who had volunteered to care for the refugees. He was the Medical Officer in charge of Nampong camp.

David was worried and kept peeping inside. "Mummy, is Bruce going to be all right?"

"I don't know. He's very sick."

"I didn't want to leave you last night, Mummy, but Upala needed—"

"You did the right thing, son," Jack said. "You made the right choice. We're just very glad everyone is safe."

David's face was downcast. "Except Bruce."

Jack patted David's shoulder. "You like Bruce?"

"Oh, yes. He showed me how to catch fish using my hands. He knows all the children's songs like "**Knick Knack Paddy Whack.**" He tells funny stories. He made me laugh when I wanted to cry."

"I like Bruce too," Pamela said, wanting to be included.

Kate put her hand on Jack's arm. "We all love Bruce. He could not have been more of a brother to me or a better uncle to the children. Bruce held us all together. Like I said, we owe him our lives."

Jack visibly relaxed; the tightness in his shoulders melted at hearing Bruce was like a brother to Kate.

After examining Bruce, Dr. Robertson came outside. "He should pull through. He's young but very underweight and malnourished. With large doses of quinine and good food to build him up, we should have him on his feet soon."

David tugged his father's hand. "I want to see Bruce, Daddy."

"Let's wait until the morning. Give him a chance to rest," the doctor said.

"We'll call in before we leave," Jack said.

"Leave?" Kate's head swiveled from Jack to Dr. Robertson. "Will Bruce be fit to travel tomorrow? What about Upala? Is she fit to travel with us?"

"I would prefer Bruce stay a few more days. Same goes for you all. You need building up. As for Upala, her mind is dulled and confused from the stress of the journey. She has some small Naga sores too. With treatment they'll heal. As to her mind, it's hard to say. Now her ordeal is over, recovery could come quickly or it may take time. I'll organize accommodation for you all and would appreciate it if you would dine with me tonight," the Medical Officer said.

"Is there a place we can wash away the mud and clean our clothes?" Kate asked. "I'd like to see Upala and I'd like to be clean first."

"Jack knows a place, don't you Jack? See you tonight."

Kate looked expectantly at Jack.

"It's a small pool in the stream. Let's grab some soap and towels. Coming David, Pamela, children?"

He ushered the children ahead of him and borrowed some shirts from Dr. Robertson's aides, so his family could wash their tattered clothes and hang them up to dry in front of a fire.

Kate's dress was still damp when she put it on to visit Upala in the hospital. She had left Jack putting the children to sleep. Kate slipped into the hut. Upala was lying on a blanket on the floor, mumbling and staring at the ceiling. Kate sat beside her and stroked her hair. Upala did not acknowledge her.

"Upala, we're leaving tomorrow. Jack must return to his army duties. I want you to come with us, if you can. Because of everything we have been through together, you are now my sister, my friend, my mother. I can't leave you behind. You are family. Together we will make a new life in India until this war is over. Sleep well, sister. We'll come for you in the morning."

33

Next morning, the stress of their impending departure almost erased the romantic glow of the previous night's reunion. Kate paced the floor, repeatedly sliding her St. Christopher medallion up and down the chain around her neck. She was partially packed, preparing to continue her journey to the railhead. She should be happy. This time her husband would be with her. But Dr. Robertson did not think Upala was well enough to travel, and the thought of leaving Bruce behind, still weak from malaria, distressed not only Kate but Pamela and David, who were sulking and having tantrums and crying that they were not going without Upala and Bruce.

Jack entered the hut and drew Kate to one side. "Kate, my leave to come and find you will soon be up, but I can't bear to see you all so upset. I've spoken with Dr. Robertson. He thinks Bruce and Upala may be able to travel in a couple of days. I have to get back to my unit soon. There's sure to be an offensive in the works once the monsoon ends in September, and they'll be training for it now. But we can stay here a few more days to build up your strength and, hopefully, the others will be fit enough to travel. I have a mule, so anyone who's too weak to walk can ride. It's about thirty miles to the railhead. The track is mainly good, only a few rough patches."

Kate flung her arms around Jack's neck. "This is why I love you, darling. The children, me, Bruce, and Upala, we've been through so much together. I want us all to leave this jungle nightmare together."

Pamela and David jumped around cheering. Even Varun and Dilip joined in. "Thank you, Daddy. All for one and one for all, Daddy," David said.

Kate laughed at Jack's surprised expression. David and Pamela giggled too.

"Where did that come from?" Jack asked.

"Bruce said it when he tied us all together to cross the river."

"Then later, he told you the story of the three musketeers, didn't he?" Kate said.

"Yes."

Jack lifted Pamela into the air. "Then it will be all for one and one for all."

For Kate and Jack those two days in Nampong were like a second honeymoon, but for Kate, it was a honeymoon tinged with desperation. Once they returned to civilization, duty would take her husband away and, as Edith had shown her, she must let him go. Jack woke early one morning and propped himself up on his elbow in bed. "Kate, are you awake? I need to talk to you about India. It may not be pleasant for you. The British there tend to be more prejudiced against other races than the British in Burma—and sometimes they could be bad enough."

Kate snuggled close to Jack. "What are you trying to tell me?"

"Because the children are Anglo-Burmese and Indian, the ex-pat contingent will mostly be pleasant to your face and disparage you behind your back—that is if they deign to meet you socially at all. And I won't be around much to help you."

"Then who needs them. Before I came to Burma, I was an outcast in my husband's upper-class social circles. Disparaged behind my back would be a polite way of saying how I was treated for not belonging to the right social class. I made my happiness with Joey. I'll make my happiness with people I like and who like me *and* our children."

"The Rodwell's are good people, they'll support you and help you."

"Then let's not worry about it."

Jack visited Bruce later that morning, taking the children with him, allowing them to stay for only a few minutes. Their boisterous hugging and energetic delight at being with him tired Bruce. Once when they were alone, Jack said, "My children obviously adore you. They and Kate told me how good you were to them, telling them stories and singing songs to keep their spirits up."

"We all kept each other's spirits up. It was because I was so determined to get them out alive that I saved myself as well."

"I want to thank you. I'm in your debt for saving the people most important to me."

"Kate is amazing. There were times I was depressed and felt I couldn't go on. I had to leave my fiancée and her son behind in Burma. Kate really chewed me out. If she'd been kind, I would have given up. She kicked my backside instead."

Jack laughed. "This is a Kate I don't know. I do know you were her support and strength. She was so afraid you would leave her when she hurt her ankle—and yet, you didn't."

Bruce was struggling to keep his eyes open. "Couldn't."

He fell asleep and Jack tiptoed from the room.

On the third day, against Dr. Robertson's advice to wait a few more days, and, even though he was weak, Bruce insisted he leave with Kate, Jack and the children. He looked young and gaunt after-shaving off his beard. Upala was still in a state of near-apathy, but physically able to travel. The next village was Namgoi, only three miles away. If Bruce and Upala seemed to be weakening, the plan was to stay there for the night. If the two were able, and the road in good condition, they would press on to Namchick, eight miles past Namgoi.

With Jack's mule carrying the supplies, walking in ankle-deep mud was less of a trial. Jack put Shirley on the mule and walked beside her to make sure she didn't fall. "I don't know why I'm concerned she might fall," he said to Kate, "she's riding as if she was born on a horse."

Kate saw the way her husband had begun interacting with the new children. He was so much at ease with them. Without warning, she was blinking back tears triggered by the thought that Jack would never play with the child she had miscarried. Then she looked at Varun, Dilip and Shirley. She was fiercely attached to these three children. She imagined watching them grow up, a constant reminder of Joey's gift to her and the strength and resilience she had developed on this trek out of Burma.

Kate gasped in delight as they approached an open-sided hut beside the track just before the suspension bridge over the Namgoi River. "Jack, am I hallucinating?"

"No, we've reached the first signs of civilization. Ye Olde Teashop."

Two Naga women, possibly mother and daughter, manned the tea shop. They wore traditional red, black and white stripe patterned lungyis and baggy men's shirts. They called out a cheerful Naga greeting as the group approached. Kate's group sat on low, wooden stools at two low, rough-hewn tables. The women poured boiling water into a pot, and, while the tea brewed, brought boiled rice on banana leaves and fresh plums and bananas. The children stuffed their faces, and Jack called for more. Kate was clutching her stomach. Jack squeezed her hand. Her voice was shaky. "Sorry I'm being so emotional. There were times I thought I'd never experience such a pleasant, normal activity as drinking tea in a teashop again, even a ramshackle one like this."

Bruce bit into a juicy plum. "Me too. I'm having trouble making the adjustment to being safe instead of scrambling to be safe."

"Can you go on?" Jack asked Bruce.

"Yes, as long as it's not a forced march."

"Can you, Upala?"

Upala looked toward the road and lowered her head.

Jack took that as consent.

The road descending to Namchick valley was in good condition. It was easy to walk along the ruts in the mud. It was hot and humid at these lower altitudes. Kate was cheered that freezing nights in the mountains were a thing of the past.

They came to a cane and bamboo suspension bridge. The mule refused to cross. Jack pushed and shoved and still the animal would not budge. "There's nothing as stubborn as a mule that won't do as it's told," he muttered stripping off his clothes and handing them to Kate. "You cross. I'll take the mule into the river." At the steep bank, the mule dug in its hooves. Jack shoved and pulled at the mule. "Get moving you bag of bones before I send you to the glue factory!" Jack slapped its rump. The mule jumped in, taking Jack with him. Kate covered her mouth so Jack would not see she was trying not to laugh on hearing him cursing the mule and the chest-high cold water. She hurried across the bridge and pulled out a towel on the other side. As soon as he emerged from the water, she rubbed his pink, shivering back dry then handed him his shirt. "You'll soon warm up in this heat."

"Thank God!"

Late that afternoon, they arrived at Namchick camp, run by the Indian Tea Planters Association. Few refugees were in the camp. As the group had its own food supplies to cook, Jack refused to take the camp's supplies. Nevertheless, when an orderly made Ovaltine malty drinks for the children, they eagerly gulped down the treats. The group was directed to a clean *basha* to stay in. Jack and Bruce collected firewood. They washed muddy feet and legs in a bucket of water. Kate treated Upala's sores and checked the children's feet for cuts.

Once the children were asleep, the adults sat around the crackling fire, watching the flames and sparks.

"What are your plans when we arrive at the railhead?" Jack asked Bruce.

"I'll have to report to my regiment, the 1st Gloucesters, ASAP. I don't even know if they're still in India. And I'd like to find out if Scotty, Bob and Fred made it out OK. What about you? Burma was your home."

Jack took hold of Kate's hand. "Yes, it was. I guess we'll have to live in India until the war ends and then, hopefully, return to Maymyo. Fortunately, I have friends in Calcutta, so

Kate and the children will have someone to watch out for them while I'm away fighting."

Kate suddenly felt sad. She would soon be alone again. Damn this war! She hated being apart from Jack. Still, she had the children, and she would throw all she could into their care until life returned to normal, but she much preferred to be able to snuggle with Jack every night and see his smiling face over breakfast each morning.

"Upala," Kate said, trying to draw her into the conversation, "you may be wondering what will happen to you now we have lost our home."

Kate waited for a response. None was forthcoming.

"I want you to know that your home is with us, always. You are family, and once we're settled, we'll see about finding out if your parents got out safely."

"I'm done for. Got to go to bed," Bruce said. He smiled apologetically. "Still a bit weak." He patted Upala's hand and left.

Next morning, they set out for Buffalo camp. The march, though short in distance, took four hours through cloying mud that would not dry in the shady jungle. They spent the night at Buffalo in an empty hut near a stream. The next part of the path to Kumlao would be up and down hills, and they did not want Bruce to push himself too hard.

They sat and drank tea and admired the beautiful view of the Patkai Range, an ever-changing spectrum of golds and oranges, ending in deep plum as the sun disappeared behind the horizon.

Leaving Buffalo next morning, the ground was level, at first, running through a tunnel of overhanging trees and bamboos that shaded them from the sun's heat. Then came a long, hot, sticky climb out of the valley to Kumlao, two thousand feet above sea-level, according to Kate's map.

After numerous rests, they stepped from the edge of the forest. Kumlao turned out to be a pleasant village of twenty to thirty Naga houses, built above ground on poles, and situated in the middle of a large meadow. On one side of the village was a fruit plantation with pomelos and pomegranates. A nearby slope was stepped with rice fields. The villagers raised pigs, extremely fat pigs from feasting on the waste created by the thousands of the refugees who had passed through the area in the past few months.

The children ran to explore the ten-foot long ceremonial drum, made from a hollowed-out tree, standing in the village center. A middle-aged Naga man came. Kate assumed he was the headman because he wore both a Christian cross and a headhunters' necklace, which was a silver three-inch-high miniature face mask on a string of beads. He was bare from the waist up and wore British army shorts, possibly taken from a dead soldier. Unable to speak English, he invited the group to stay in his house using gestures. The front of his house opened to a platform where women tended a fire. The bedrooms in the back had no windows.

Kate and Jack shared their rations with the headman's family, who provided pork, rice, dahl and a bitter, dark green vegetable. Kate's opened their last two cans of peaches and some dried figs. They were a big hit with the Naga family. The headman's wife poured rice beer from a gourd container into bamboo cups. Unable to speak one another's language, they sat contentedly, sipping the *zu* rice beer and watched another striking sunset.

Kate could feel herself beginning to heal. She hoped the children and Upala too were allowing normalcy to flush out and replace the horrors of the journey. She looked at Upala, her eyes were closed, face lifted to the sun's setting rays. A warmth spread through Kate as if her mother were wrapping little girl Kate in her arms. She gave Jack's hand a squeeze. He squeezed back.

All would be well in time.

34

The next day, the headman led them along a track, cut out of the side of the hill, to a trail at the edge of the forest.

"Don't lose heart," Jack said, before the steep descent came into view. "We're coming to a place known as 'the golden staircase.'"

Before Kate could say anything, the headman stopped at the top of a steep descent. He was smiling, nodding, encouraging them on with his gestures saying this is the way. The group stood speechless.

Bruce looked crestfallen. "We've got to navigate that?"

Jack said, "Yes, all eight hundred steps of it."

The headman shook hands, waved, and left. The group resumed gaping at the daunting task that lay ahead. The steps were cut into the steep clay slope. The forest walled in both sides of the steps, preventing sunlight from drying out the clay after heavy rain.

"We must be very careful going down these stairs," Jack said, "and I won't be able to help much because I've got to get the mule down. The steps are treacherous. You can see stakes have been driven in and bamboo poles laid across to secure each step, but the rains have liquified the clay. In some steps, it's deep enough to cover a man. You'll find the bodies of people who've fallen in and who've been too weak to get themselves out. It may look firm on the surface, but it's only a crust, and you could fall through into deep, liquid mud."

"Do you think the best way down is for us to slide down the sides, holding onto branches and foliage?" Kate asked. "Do you think Pamela and David could manage that?" She looked at Upala and wondered if she could do it with her mind so dull.

"What do you think, children?" Jack addressed his children. "If I go first with the mule, sliding down the edge, do you think you could follow?"

Pamela and David nodded.

He turned to Kate and Bruce. "Will you be able to help the little ones?"

"Yes," said Bruce.

Kate nodded. "I think Upala should go down after you, Jack. Do you think you can do that Upala? Then David can encourage you if you find it difficult, can't you, David?"

David placed Upala behind Jack, and he and Pamela stood behind Upala.

Brow creased with worry, Jack said, "Let's go."

He pushed the mule forward. The animal soon sat on its haunches. Bracing itself with its front legs, it began sliding downwards on the muddy earth. Upala sat down and followed the mule, grasping at branches, occasionally bracing herself by placing her foot on the end of a stair's bamboo pole. Pamela and David followed.

Bruce sat down, put Dilip and Varun between his legs, he pushed himself forward using the foliage to sometimes slow him down and other times pull him forward. Kate sat down with Shirley between her legs, following Bruce's example. On the way down, they passed several decomposing bodies trapped in the steps. Kate saw David push a corpse's head with his foot. She was heartbroken to think the events of the journey had made him so callous about people dying. From the stripes on the corpse's khaki sleeve, the body appeared to be a British Army corporal. Kate felt sad. So close to the railhead and still some people did not make it.

Shaking off the sadness, Kate kept watching everyone's progress, looking out for problems, wanting everyone to reach the bottom and escape the smell of this death trap. Then Varun, copying David, wriggled free of the restrictions of Bruce's legs to push the dead corporal's head with his hand. He lost his balance and fell into the mud-filled step. Bruce caught Varun's arm and quickly pulled him back, but not before Varun had cried and filled his mouth with the foul mud. Bruce pulled off his shirt and wiped the mud from crying Varun's face as best he could. Kate threw him her water canteen and Bruce washed the mud remaining in Varun's eyes.

With Jack too far away, he called to David. "David, I'm giving Varun some water! Tell him not to swallow. Only rinse his mouth and spit it out!" Bruce lost his foothold. For a few yards, it was all he could do to keep the children between his legs as he slid down on his back until he managed to grab a strong root. It jerked his shoulder, pulling a muscle. He pulled himself back into a sitting position. His concern that the boys could be scared, dissipated when he found them laughing and giggling at the short, wild ride.

David shouted Bruce's instructions back to Varun.

"Good. Varun, keep spitting out the mud."

Having reached the bottom of the stairs, Pamela and David were jumping and laughing. "We did it! We did it!"

"You did well, the pair of you. How about you, Bruce? Doing all right?" Jack asked.

"Yes. I pulled a muscle in my shoulder, but I need more water to wash the mud out of Varun's eyes and mouth."

Jack took a water bottle from the mule, and Kate took over the job of caring for Varun.

Bruce ruffled Dilip's hair. "We're fine, aren't we, Dilip? Sliding down hills is a lot less tiring than climbing them."

Jack went to Kate. "Are you OK?"

She nodded and looked towards Upala. "I am so relieved Upala managed to do it."

"I remember the next bit of road as being really swampy. It will be tiring. When I came through before, the mud was up to my knees. I'll put the three youngest children onto the mule." He spoke to Pamela and David nearby. Sorry, but you'll have to walk. Try and walk in our footsteps and you're less likely to get stuck."

It took over two long, exhausting hours of hard slog to reach a part of the road that was firm, level and followed the river.

Jack looked around the group. Everyone appeared washed out by the past two hours' effort. "It's only a short distance to North Tirap, but I say we stop and have a cup of tea and wash off the mud and sweat in the river."

No one argued.

They quenched their thirst, bathed in the river and ate some dried fruit to restore their energy. The hoot of a locomotive had Kate lifting her head in surprise.

"There's a coal colliery at Tipong. The railway, too," Jack offered by way of explanation.

Kate slumped with relief. "It's almost over."

Part of her was relieved; part of her was sad. Together she, Upala, Bruce and the children had conquered the world, and in a short time, there would be a parting of the ways. Bruce would have to leave. She blinked back tears, tried to swallow down the lump in her throat. She felt as if her leg was going to be amputated. She didn't want to lose him, not after everything they had shared. She sat quietly, staring at her tea, waves of sadness emanating from her.

"We should pack up and get on," Jack said. 'There's an Assam Rifles outpost in North Tirap. It's a muddy hole. Maybe we should have waited to wash until after we'd been there. Anyway, I must call in and return the mule to Captain England, in charge of the Mule Company, who kindly loaned him to me."

Kate pulled out her map. "From North Tirap, it's four miles to Tipong. Should we try and reach there today or wait until tomorrow?" She turned to Bruce. "Would that be too much for you, in this heat?"

Before Bruce could answer, Jack said, "I'm sure Captain England would provide mules to take us to Tipong. We could be there in an hour, and then catch a rail car to Lekhapani."

Captain England offered more hot tea, sandwiches, and four mules to take them to Tipong. Upala, Bruce and Kate each rode one with one of the younger children. Pamela and David shared one. Jack and four Gurkhas walked alongside. The road improved as they neared Tipong. In parts they walked on bare rock where the monsoon had washed the mud away. Forest edged the road. Perched on a high cliff, a Naga village's thatched roofs peeped out above the trees.

The mules passed a bungalow with a verandah where a gardener was tending plants. "That's the colliery manager's place," Jack said. "We'll be at the station in a few minutes."

Soon after arriving at the station, a rail car pulled in and Kate's party settled into some seats. Half a dozen refugees joined them, having been released that morning from the small hospital at North Tirap.

Pamela and David and the Indian children sat quietly during the three-mile ride to Lekhapani, watching tea gardens and a small bazaar flash by. Purple-grey clouds darkened the sky. It was going to rain.

"How are you, David?" Jack asked, noticing how unusually quiet his children were.

A sob caught in David's throat; his chin quivered. "I'm glad I'm out of it, Daddy."

Jack squeezed his son's shoulder.

Pamela swung her legs. "We've left the mud behind. Can we have some new shoes now?"

Kate looked at herself and her companions and caught Jack's attention. "We look like a bunch of dirty ragamuffins. I'd like to buy some clothes as soon as possible."

"We'll do it at Margherita, once we get the administrative stuff out of the way."

At Lekhapani, they changed trains for Margherita. Kate and Bruce fell silent, each lost in their own thoughts during the six-mile journey. At Margherita station, they were met by refugee administrators, reception camp officers and women volunteer helpers. A white, male official from the Indian Tea Planters Association approached Jack. "Do you want a ride to Margherita golf course? It's being used as the evacuee reception center. Refugees are sorted there and sent to various camps according to their race and classification."

Jack stood as tall as he could, a hand each on Pamela's and David's shoulder. "No, thanks. Yes, these children are Anglo-Burmese. They're my children and they are coming with me. The English woman is my wife. The Indian woman is my servant. The Indian children are mine. They're all coming with me."

"Sir, it's against regulations to—" the official began to say.

"Stick your regulations."

Jack gathered his family and, turning his back on the blustering official, set off to leave the station. Bruce stood still. Kate turned back. "Bruce?"

"I should leave you now and register at the reception center so I can get back to my unit and see if Scotty and the lads have passed through."

Kate ran to him crying and pressed her face against his chest. "I can't bear to say goodbye after what we've been through together."

Bruce glanced at Jack and cautiously patted Kate's shoulder. Pamela and David ran over. Each grabbed a leg. "Don't go, Bruce! Don't leave us!"

Bruce squatted down. "Come here," he said, wrapping the children to him. "Hey, we made it. We've come to India and joined up with your dad. That was the plan, and we did it. Pats on the back all around. I helped you and you helped me. And now that job is done." Bruce stood the children in front of him and wiped their cheeks with his hands. "I have to get on with my next job now, which is to fight the Japanese. You, young man and you, young lady must spend some time playing with your dad." Bruce looked up at Jack and grinned. "I'm sure he knows the words to "Knick-Knack-Paddy-Whack.""

Jack came over. He held out his hand and affectionately squeezed Bruce's shoulder with the other. "I owe you a great debt."

Bruce shook Jack's offered hand. He nodded, struggled to find his voice. "I must go now." He raised a hand in farewell to

Upala who was standing close by. "Upala, I hope you enjoyed wearing my lucky shorts and shirt for the trip."

She looked up, smiled slightly, wobbled her head then looked at the ground.

They watched Bruce walk away. He appeared to be wiping tears from his face. He turned and waved before disappearing into the crowd.

Jack pulled his family to him offering comfort and acknowledging their heartache at parting from Bruce. In a way, it was Jack's salute to Tom and the void Tom's suicide had left behind.

Turning to the opposite direction, Jack led the way through Margherita for his family of malnourished skeletons, dressed in rags and covered in mud. Nobody gave a second glance. The place was full of skinny refugees just like them.

Not far from the station, two volunteers were serving meals of oatmeal and sago. Kate heard one man talking with a Scottish accent, telling the refugees such whoppers of tales. She went over to him. "Excuse me, can you remember a Scottish RAF technician coming through from Burma several weeks ago. His name was Scotty, and he may have been with two soldiers."

The man scratched his thick head of ginger hair. "Well, we're all called Scotty, ye nae, but yes, I do. I remember because we were from the same town, even went to the same school. Yes, there were three of them."

Kate's face lit up. "They made it! Thank you."

Jack looked at her, quizzically.

"Oh, Jack, I would so like to tell them we all made it out, so they never feel any guilt about leaving us behind."

He gave Kate a quick hug. "Come on. It's getting late, and we need to find a hotel."

"Just a minute," Kate said. She ran back to the Scotsman. "Do you know anywhere we can stay with our large family?"

The Scotsman studied the family, pulled out a notebook and scribbled something. He tore out the page and gave it to Kate. "This lady is an Indian widow. She has a bungalow. Sometimes, she invites soldiers to come and have a cup of tea and cake. I think she will help you."

"Thank you, again."

Kate handed the paper to Jack. "Scotty thinks this lady would put us up for the night in her house."

"You clever girl. Let's find the house."

The widow lived in a western style bungalow and yes, she could provide accommodation for the night. She looked at their physical state, and yes, she would also give them a good meal and here was the bathroom with hot water and soap. Jack looked in the bathroom.

Kate saw his face. "You look envious."

"I am. What I wouldn't give for a soak in the tub, but I've got to report to the Golf course, obtain travel vouchers to Calcutta, change our Burmese money into rupees and see to the matter of the children. The luxury of cleanliness can wait until I get back."

At the Golf Club, once the officer in charge had dealt with Jack's administrative issues, he sent Jack to a magistrate who, after hearing the story of the children's rescue, made him legal guardian of Shirley, Varun and Dilip, legal names unknown.

Jack returned to the widow's bungalow and slipped into a soothing tub of clean water and luxuriated in Kate washing his back. "I have some papers in my shirt pocket, Kate. You should look at them."

Kate's stomach knotted at his serious tone. She left him and went to their bedroom to search his shirt. She began pulling out the papers. Puzzled, she frowned on seeing an official legal stamp. Then a smile lit up her face. She ran to the bathroom. "Jack, you did it! They're ours!" She took his face in her hands and kissed him hard. "I love you. You're the kindest man on earth."

"I love you, Kate. I just want you to be happy." He dipped under the water and when he surfaced, he stretched out his arm. "Is there a towel around?"

Clean and dressed, Jack rounded everyone up and led the way to the bazaar. "New clothes for everyone. Let's start with the children."

Kate found a stall filled with girls' dresses, next to a stall selling boys' wear. Pamela touched a blue dress, with a white collar and smocking across the chest. "I like this, Mummy."

Kate held the dress against her daughter. "What do you think, Jack?", she called to her husband choosing clothes for the boys at the next stall.

"Beautiful and nearly as pretty as you, Pamela. What do you think of these shirts?"

Kate watched the boys, happy and smiling. Varun and Dilip grinned, showing dazzling white teeth against their dark skin. Apart from being so skinny and needing a haircut, no one would ever guess at the hardships they had been through. "Smart and just right," she answered.

Kate turned her attention to Shirley, who could not take her eyes off a pink dress. Kate added it to her purchases.

As the stall keeper wrapped the clothing and underwear Jack had purchased for the boys, Jack's attention was drawn to a nearby stall. He took Upala's arm and walked her to the stall.

"Upala, would you like to have this sari? From what you told me about your wedding day, I believe you wore a sari this color and—

Upala stroked the fabric, held it to her cheek. "Ruby and gold." She looked up at Jack. "*Thakin!*" Her chin trembled. Tears flowed. Jack put his arm around her. "Upala, it's all right." She cried even harder. The crying became a wail, a painful wail.

Kate saw Jack looking at her, his eyes appealing for help.

"You finish the shopping, Jack. Make sure everyone has underwear and sandals; I'll take Upala to the bungalow."

"No more walking barefoot," Jack declared as they returned to the Indian widow's house, his arms full of parcels.

David sought out his mother. "Is Upala all right, Mummy?"

"Yes, Upala's fine. She's lying down." Kate bobbed down to David's height. "Do you remember how you cried when we reached the Pangsau Pass, and you saw that there was still more jungle to travel through even though we were in India?

Upala should have cried with you, but she didn't, and because she didn't, she is doing it now. When she has cried everything away, she'll be all right." Kate stood and began tearing open the parcels. "Now, let's get you out of those dirty rags."

David snatched up his blue shirt and brown shorts and put them on. Kate tilted up his chin. "As handsome as the day I first saw you."

"Daddy, don't I look pretty in this dress?" Pamela said, as Jack fastened the button on the back.

"Yes, you do, sweetheart."

Varun and Dilip stripped off their ragged clothes and picked up their new shirts. Jack, about to throw their rags in the corner, stopped. His mouth fell open. Upala stood in the doorway, wearing her ruby colored sari. She was smiling. Kate froze as she buttoned up Shirley's dress. She looked in awe at her husband, delighted that his buying a ruby-colored sari had had such a dramatic effect.

"You look wonderful," Jack said.

Upala blushed. She had stopped crying.

"Don't move." Jack went to a parcel on the bed. "I bought a box Brownie camera," he said putting the film in the camera. "This occasion requires a photo."

The Indian widow came to the bedroom door. "Here, I will take your photograph so everyone can be in it."

She took several of Kate and Jack, of the children together, of Upala in her sari, and of the whole group.

Having used all the film, she handed the camera to Jack. "It is time to eat. Come to the table."

She led the way to the large veranda where the mouth-watering aroma of a vegetable and dahl curry, rice and fruit reminded them of how hungry they were. They sat around the oil-cloth covered table.

Kate watched the children stuff their faces with the delicious food, as much as they wanted until as full as they wanted. Had only been three years since Manny met her dockside and her new life in Burma began? A lot had happened in those three years. She had arrived a sad wounded woman; now she was sitting around the table with a wonderful husband who loved her deeply. She had five beautiful children to love and care for, and a new friend, Upala, who in different circumstances would probably never have become a friend. They had been to hell and back together and survived, an experience that would bind them together forever.

What would the future hold? Their home and life in Burma? Gone. They were at war, for how long? Everything's uncertain except what we have here. Kate said a silent prayer of thanks to a God she was not sure existed. Then she heard the giggle and opened her eyes.

Joey, you're still with us.

She smiled.

All would be well.

About the Author

Pauline Hayton hails from the northeast of England. She left her probation officer job in her hometown of Middlesbrough to emigrate to the United States in 1991 with her husband Peter. They live in Naples, Florida, willing slaves to four abandoned cats that adopted the couple.

Hayton never wanted to be a writer, but after listening to her father's war stories and reading his tattered wartime diaries, she felt compelled to write down his tales for her grandchildren. The project turned into her first book, *A Corporal's War: the WWII Adventures of a Royal Engineer,* first published in 2003.

While researching *A Corporal's War,* she stumbled upon Ursula Graham Bower's WWII story and knew instantly she would write a book about this extraordinary woman. *Naga Queen* was the result, a true story based on eight years in Ursula Graham Bower's life. She received a medal for her wartime activities in NE India.

During her research for *Naga Queen,* the author became friends with Ursula's daughter, Trina. This led the author and her husband into sponsoring Mount Kisha English School in the remote Naga village of Magulong, NE India. *Grandma Rambo,* a comedy/adventure is based on a 2011 visit the author made to Magulong. Royalties from Hayton's books go toward educating the more than one hundred children in the village.

Other books by Hayton are: her memoir *Still Pedaling;* an anthology *Extreme Delight; If You Love Me, Kill Me,* a story based on her care of her elderly parents; *Myanmar: In My Father's Footsteps. A Journey of Rebirth and Remembrance,* a travelogue of a trip to Myanmar to celebrate twice overcoming cancer; and Hayton's first children's book *The Unfriendly Bee.*

No Long Goodbyes is the third book in the series Hayton has written about WWII in the China/Burma/India theater of war. She is committed to informing people about this little-known part of WWII history and to giving recognition to the people who fought and made tremendous sacrifices in deplorable conditions.

Websites: 1. Amazon.com/author/paulinehayton,
2. http://bit.ly/2WQdlfN

Sample pages from Pauline Hayton's other China/Burma/India theater of war books:

A Corporal's War: The WWII Adventures of a Royal Engineer

PROLOGUE

The force of the bullet snapped my head back and knocked me from the motorcycle. I crashed to the ground with an agonizing thud.

Only minutes before, I'd been riding through the verdant French countryside, as yet unspoiled by the ugliness of war. Rushing to deliver dispatches, I had slowed, allowing myself a moment's pleasure. With the wind on my face and the warmth of the morning sun on my back, I almost forgot the dire circumstances requiring this ride.

I was also unaware I was being tracked in the rifle-sight of a German sniper hiding in the shadows of the Forêt de Nieppe. Crack! The high velocity bullet gouged a deep furrow across my forehead, narrowly missing my eye before striking my shoulder. There was a savage stinging in my eyebrow. Lying dazed and shaken, blood trickled from my left temple into the hairline. My sense of invincibility in tatters, I was incredulous then indignant. *Oh God, I've been shot! They got me! They bloody well GOT me!* I didn't seem to be in much pain, thought it must be shock. I prayed to make it back to camp. I didn't want to die there on that road.

I lay motionless while my mind raced. *What did they instil in us in training? The sniper could still be watching, waiting to finish you off. If you move, you're dead. If you move, you're dead. You'd be proud if you could see me, Sarge; I'm not moving, just like you taught me.*

When I set out with the dispatches, I hadn't planned to play dead for thirty minutes in the middle of a French country lane. I closed my eyes against the bright sunshine. Brief, violent outburst over, I could hear one of the motorcycle wheels spinning close by, clicking with each rotation as if something was catching the spokes. Beyond the motorcycle, I listened to birds singing, insects droning, life in the country going on as if nothing had happened.

How the hell did I get into this mess?

My mind wandered to that fateful day, less than a year earlier, when I decided to enlist in the army.

JULY 1939—APRIL 1940

How it all Began

With a shriek of tortured metal, the heavy, cast iron doors of the coke oven opened, releasing a monstrous cloud of superheated, fume-filled smoke. It mingled with discharges, spewing from neighbouring steelworks, chemical plants, and domestic chimneys to create the lingering pall of pollution, which covered the lower Tees river basin, besmirching every home and inhabitant in the area.

White-hot walls of coke surged from the oven's innards, cascading into the batteries below. As the coke cooled, I set to work moving railway wagons along the track. I used a long bar and sheer muscle power to lever the wheels, forcing the wagons along, until they were in position beneath the chutes leading from each battery. A hard tug on a heel bar released the coke, which tumbled into the containers with a dusty, deafening roar. Then the wagons moved on, carrying the piled-high coke away for use in the steel foundry.

The day was exceptionally hot and sticky for June. I was ready for a rest when break-time arrived, and I joined the other men on the shift.

"Hiya, Ernie." I greeted Ernie Miller, a solid, fatherly figure I'd taken a liking to.

"'ello, son. Come and sit wi' me," said Ernie in his strong, Yorkshire accent.

Sitting next to Ernie, I wolfed down beef sandwiches and quenched my thirst with tea from a chipped enamel mug, all the while listening as the men discussed the economic situation. The world was slowly coming out of the Great Depression of the 1930's. In Britain, industry was starting to re-employ some of the country's millions of desperate, unemployed men, many of whom had been out of work and struggling to survive for years. I felt fortunate at having secured a job at the coke ovens even though the work was dirty and tiring. Nevertheless, my ears pricked up as Ernie told the group about his son Stan, who, like me, was twenty years old and married with a wife and young child to support.

"As soon as the government came out wi' military conscription a few months ago, our Stan decided to join the army," Ernie told the group.

"Conscription? Isn't that when men are called up at twenty-one years of age to go and do six months military service?" I'd asked.

"Aye, that's right. Our Stan went down to the army recruiting office as soon as 'e found out that 'im and 'is missus would be a bit better off living on Stan's army pay than on the thirty-five shillings a week 'e was getting in the steelworks."

George, who had fought in the First World War, tutted in disgust.

"Silly bugger! Doesn't 'e know we'll be at war soon?"

"Nay, that can't be right. The Prime Minister signed a peace treaty wi' them Germans," Sid interrupted.

"You mark my words," George persisted. "That 'itler's got too big for 'is boots. 'e's going to cause us a lot of trouble, just you wait and see."

"Well, I can't see us being at war anytime soon," said Ernie. He got to his feet to return to work. "But if it does come to that, then all our young lads are going to be called up, and there's nowt we can do about it."

Walking back to the coke ovens, I pumped Ernie for more information. The more I learned, the more I liked the idea of following in Stan's footsteps. During the rest of the shift, I worked on automatic pilot, my mind preoccupied with the idea of enlisting in the army. I argued with myself. *If I go in the army, the extra money will come in useful. It's not much more, but every bit helps. I'll be twenty-one when I get out, and my wages will be higher then. But that means leaving Ivy on her own for six months, looking after Joan. That's not much of a life for her. She'll be lonely. Yes, but sooner or later*

I'll have to go anyway, and her mother and sisters live just round the corner, so she won't be all by herself. How can I tell Ivy that I want to go in the army now? What will she say? I've just got to pluck up the courage somehow if I'm going to do it.

I was filled with dread as I turned the corner into Thorrold Terrace. It was a grand sounding name for the row of tiny, terraced cottages. The boomtown of Middlesbrough consisted of hundreds of similar houses thrown together to accommodate the influx of people seeking work in the heavy industries that mushroomed after the discovery of iron ore in the nearby Cleveland Hills. I walked past the weathered brick walls stained black from years of attack by polluted air. No gardens or flowers here. My living room window looked out onto a cobbled road. On the far side, a mere twenty-five feet away, was an eight-foot-high fence of corrugated metal sheeting topped with barbed wire, all that separated the residents of Thorrold Terrace from Cleveland Bridge Engineering works. My humble home was far from perfect, but it was our first home, mine and Ivy's, and I loved it. Usually, I was eager to step through the front door to be with my wife and daughter. But that day, there was a reluctance. I had made a decision, and I worried about Ivy's reaction to it.

Naga Queen: She Was Awarded a Medal for Her Wartime Activities

"Manipur Road Station next stop, miss-sahib," the Indian conductor announced in his singsong accent.

Ursula inserted her bookmark and closed *The Count of Monte Cristo.* Her stomach fluttered. She had sat by herself for hours while the train rattled along in dim light, the track hemmed in by dark jungle, all made murkier by grimy windows. The train clattered into a clearing. The long, dreary journey was ending, and in celebration, a burst of sunlight flooded the compartment, cheering her.

She stretched her long legs and gazed through the window with interest, eager to leave the train and hoping Lexie would be there to meet her.

Ursula rummaged in her handbag, found her diary and on a fresh page scribbled, October 28th, 1938, 7:30 a.m. Hurrah! After all the commotion and confusion of the four-day journey from Calcutta, I'm finally to escape the confines of this blasted train!

In the gold powder-compact's mirror, she touched up her lipstick, and studied her tawny hair, which she'd had cropped for the trip. The short style made her look younger than her twenty-three years, she thought, almost girlish. She wasn't sure she liked it but was grateful for the ease it gave her in managing her hair. She snapped the compact shut. It had been two years since she'd seen her friend Alexa, and she wanted to look good.

The train screeched to a jerking halt in a hissing gasp of steam. Ursula stood up, and staggered, feeling wobbly, a ghost of the train's motion still in her body. She brushed her blue linen skirt in a vain attempt to remove the creases then moved along the corridor to an open door. Shading her grey eyes from the sun's glare, she looked around for Lexie and caught sight of a conspicuous halo of red hair. Ursula watched Alexa's excited, freckled face, as she bobbed along the platform, peering into carriages, deftly dodging porters and the few travelers descending from the train. She and Lexie seemed to be the only Europeans at the station.

"Lexie!" Ursula called, waving her white handkerchief. "Lexie!"

Lexie broke into a run and Ursula jumped from the train to hug her tightly.

"It's so good to see you."

"At last," Lexie said. "I've missed you."

"Thank goodness you're here. I've been in India only four days, and I feel as if I've been wrung out and hung up to dry."

Ursula had thought she knew what she was coming to, but the reality was so different—the masses of people, jostling bodies, the pungent smells.

"It's all been so strange and nerve-wracking," she continued. "I didn't realize it would be such a long, difficult journey from Calcutta, and it didn't help that I don't speak one word of the language. But, Lexie, it's all been so . . ."

"What?"

". . . fascinating!"

Lexie laughed at her friend's spirit. "You'll be all right now. I'll take care of you, and we'll soon have you speaking some Hindustani."

Lexie bustled about, organizing the porters loading Ursula's luggage into her little Austin car then took Ursula to the tin-roofed travelers' bungalow.

"This is where I stayed last night," she said. While Ursula looked on with interest, her friend reeled off some Hindustani to the caretaker. Two minutes later, he brought a pitcher of water for Ursula to refresh herself followed by a welcome cup of tea.

Ursula poured more tea. "I'm looking forward to making up for lost time. It's been far too long. Have you made any friends in Imphal?"

"Not close friends, more social acquaintances. They're very proper. We ladies lead a leisurely life out here. But oh, Ursula, we're going to have a marvelous time." Lexie settled her cup on its saucer. "We've a long drive ahead of us. Won't arrive in Imphal till evening. Are you up for it?"

Ursula laughed. "Wouldn't miss it for the world, if it means spending the next few months with you."

They set off along a straight road, a gash in the thick jungle covering the foothills. The car trundled along the bumpy tarmac pressed on both sides by tall spindly trees reaching for daylight. Rising from the congested undergrowth, vines and choking creepers ran riot, clinging to trunks and wrapping round branches. A steep escarpment of blue-black hills covered in rainforest towered on the horizon.

"I've been so looking forward to this," Ursula said, "but when I arrived in Calcutta, well, nothing prepares you for the smells, and the crippled children begging—and the hordes! It's so different from my travels on the Continent with Grandmama. I used to think I was worldly but . . ." Lost for words Ursula shook her head.

Lexie glanced at her passenger. "It *is* a shock to the system, isn't it? Thank goodness Richard took some leave and met me in Calcutta, otherwise I'm sure I'd have been overcome by it all."

"Ah, Richard. How is that brother of yours?"

"He's doing as well as can be expected, working in the Indian Civil Service. In fact, we have him to thank for this whole adventure. It was his idea to invite you."

"Do you remember the last time we were in a car together?"

"When we were on holiday in Scotland, the Oban rally," cried Lexie in glee.

They smiled at memories of Ursula veering round tight corners in her MG, spraying mud on the luckless spectators. They had needed woolen jumpers on that windswept day.

"A little different from riding in my Austin, wasn't it?"

"A wee bit. Have you adjusted to your new life as your brother's hostess?"

Lexie pursed her lips in thought before replying. "I enjoy being with Richard. He encourages my independent nature. Only about a dozen Europeans live in Imphal, mostly administrators, and most of them are older. Some of them seem to have been in India forever. In fact," said Lexie, laughing, "they're positively fossilized. Did your parents put up much opposition to your coming?"

"Surprisingly, no. When your letter arrived, the prospect really ruffled poor Grandmama. 'You can't possibly go gallivanting off to India unchaperoned,' she said. But I insisted she write to Mummy about it. Mummy was obviously keen for me to come because she replied that I was to be given 'all help and encouragement to book passage on the next available ship to India.'"

"Gosh, I wouldn't have expected that. Any idea why she was so in favor of it?"

"No. It was amazing! In no time at all, I was on my way, and after several weeks at sea, I was being ferried up the Hooghley River to Calcutta. That part was much easier than I expected."

Eight miles later, Lexie stopped at a sentry post to show their papers. As the car accelerated, she told Ursula, "We've just entered the Naga Hills."

The landscape changed. First, the road took them into a high, narrow gorge then climbed a steep incline beside a turbulent stream. The road twisted and turned, squeezing along the bases of rugged cliffs, passing large boulders, stands of giant fern, tall slender bamboo, and trees that blotted out the sky.

"Lexie," Ursula said, a tinge of reverence in her voice, "the scenery's heavenly!"

Lexie grinned. "I did it all for you. A bit different from the English countryside, isn't it?"

Ursula could not stop looking about her. "It's so wild and awesome."

The car bowled along, climbing and curling round tight bends. Turning a sharp corner, they startled a small group of hillmen who darted to safety at the side of the road and stared in surprise at the two women in the Austin.

Ursula returned the stare, twisting round in her seat to watch as long as she could. Unlike the slim Assamese of the valley, these men were stocky, with slashing cheekbones and Mongoloid features. Hard muscles rippled under coppery skin, and they were, somehow, beautiful. They were naked except for small black kilts round their hips and plaid blankets covering broad shoulders. Strands of brightly colored beads adorned their necks.

A fleeting recognition startled Ursula, a memory piercing the deepest recesses of her mind—and then it was gone.

"Lexie! Who are those people?" she asked, in a voice filled with awe.

"Those? Why, they're Nagas, of course."

"Of course," Ursula murmured. She felt vaguely unsettled and rummaged through her mind for some touchstone. Why had these men stirred her so?

They stopped for lunch in Kohima, a mountain village 4,800 feet above sea level where the Deputy Commissioner had his headquarters. The village perched on a saddle between two mountain ranges, overlooked from the south by Japvo, a 9,000-foot mountain. The hot sun beat down on the handful of red-roofed bungalows spread out along spurs.

Ursula and Lexie left the restaurant they had found in the one-street bazaar, which catered to the needs of the few government workers and the small garrison of Assam Rifles.

"Take a good look, Ursula, this land is going to be your home for the next five months."

"Do we have time for some snaps?" Ursula reached into the car for her new, precision-made, technically advanced Leica camera in its leather fitted case. It had been an extravagant purchase, but she was glad of it now to record this enchanting place.

Lexie smiled at her friend's excitement. "When you've finished here, we'll drive to a better viewpoint."

Stopping outside the town, they found a clear view of the hills. Ursula climbed from the car, pressed the Leica to her face and sighted through the viewfinder. To the east lay wave after wave of mountain ranges, blue fading to violet and gray in the hazy distance. The only way to reach them was along trails winding tortuously round spurs and chiseled precipices, up jungle-clad hills and down deep, steep slopes. Native villages with dingy smoke-stained thatched roofs sat on top of every ridge in sight. The ridge slopes had sharp inclines and thick woods except for the hillsides in the town. These were cleared for cultivation and covered in terraced paddy fields, which, at this time of year, were filled with parched stubble.

She paused, lowered her camera, heart beating fast as she gazed upon the panorama before her. *I belong here!* The thought startled Ursula. Her pulse throbbed; a surge of joy had her grinning

"Ready, Ursula?" Lexie called. "Still another ninety miles to go."

Made in the USA
Columbia, SC
25 June 2019